The Biblioteca Italiana
The First Bilingual Editions

GIAMBATTISTA DELLA PORTA
Gli Duoi Fratelli Rivali

The Two Rival Brothers
Edited and translated
by Louise George Clubb
1980

★

TOMMASO CAMPANELLA
La Città del Sole:
Dialogo Poetico

The City of the Sun:
A Poetical Dialogue
Translated by Daniel J. Donno
1981

★

TORQUATO TASSO
Dialogues

Dialogues: A Selection
with the Discourse on
the Art of the Dialogue
Translated by Carnes Lord
and Dain A. Trafton
1982

★

GIACOMO LEOPARDI
Operette Morali

Essays and Dialogues
Translated by Giovanni Cecchetti
1983

Le Avventure di Pinocchio

The Adventures of Pinocchio

C. COLLODI

LE
AVVENTURE DI PINOCCHIO

STORIA DI UN BURATTINO

ILLUSTRATA DA E. MAZZANTI

FIRENZE

FELICE PAGGI LIBRAIO-EDITORE

Via del Proconsolo.

NAPOLI — FRATELLI RISPOLI

—

1883

Prezzo: L. **2,50.**

The Adventures of Pinocchio
Story of a Puppet

Carlo Collodi
(Carlo Lorenzini)

TRANSLATED WITH
AN INTRODUCTORY ESSAY
AND NOTES BY

NICOLAS J. PERELLA

UNIVERSITY
OF CALIFORNIA
PRESS

BERKELEY
LOS ANGELES
LONDON

University of California Press
Berkeley and Los Angeles, California

University of California Press, Ltd.
London, England

First Paperback Printing 1991

Library of Congress Cataloging-in-Publication Data

Collodi, Carlo, 1826–1890.
    The adventures of Pinocchio.

    Italian text originally published: Le avventure di
Pinocchio. Ed. critica / a cura di Ornella Castellani
Pollidori. Pescia : Fondazione nazionale Carlo
Collodi, 1983.
    Bibliography: p.
    I. Perella, Nicolas J. (Nicolas James),
1927–   . II. Title.
PQ4712.L4A713   1986   853'.8   85–2604
ISBN 0-520-07782-2 (alk. paper)

Printed in the United States of America

08   07   06   05   04   03   02
9   8   7   6

Contents

Acknowledgments

Of the many books and persons I have consulted in preparing this volume, my chief debt is to my ultra-Tuscan colleague and glossologist, Ruggero Stefanini. His own great love for Collodi's text—which he knows by heart—allowed him to endure, nay, welcome my daily queries over a period of months, and his scrupulous surveillance of the translation, in particular, could justify my considering him its co-author. Special thanks are due also to Louise George Clubb for her comments on the first draft of my translation and for her valuable suggestions concerning the organization of the introductory essay. The late Arnolfo B. Ferruolo and Caterina Feucht were generous in helping me search out the most satisfactory English rendering for numerous phrases of the original. I am also indebted to Daniel J. Donno and Amy Einsohn, both of whom painstakingly combed through the typescript making many suggestions that I have been glad to adopt, and to the publisher's third sensitive reader, Glauco Cambon, for his encouraging remarks. Jolynn Milardovich and Leon D. Megrian of the Interlibrary Loan Department at the University of California, Berkeley, were, as always, of great help to me. Narriman Casati Shahrokh, who succeeded in deciphering my handwriting and thereby was able to prepare the typescript, deserves my praise. A sabbatical leave and a Humanities Research Fellowship from my institution enabled me to carry out much of the research.

Publisher and author are grateful to Felice Del Beccaro, president of the Fondazione Nazionale Carlo Collodi, and to Ornella Castellani Pollidori for their kind permission to reprint the critical edition of *Pinocchio* in the present bilingual volume. I recall with pleasure the

warm welcome and assistance given to me by the Fondazione's staff in Pescia. Finally, I wish to pay homage to the memory of Rolando Anzilotti, the founder of the Fondazione and its president until his untimely death in 1982. His advice and encouragement were instrumental to my perseverance in carrying out the research that went into this book.

Pescia, 1983/Berkeley, 1984

An Essay on *Pinocchio*

I

When I was a child, I spoke like a child,
I thought like a child, I reasoned like a child:
when I became a man, I gave up childish ways
[1 Corinthians 13.11].

"Oh, I'm sick and tired of always being a puppet!"
cried Pinocchio, rapping himself on the head.
"It's about time that I too became a man"
[chapter 25].

Astoundingly, psychology turns to the child
in order to understand the adult, blaming adults
for not enough of the child or for too many remnants
of the child still left in adulthood
[James Hillman, "Abandoning the Child"].

THE BRIEF TALE that has made Carlo Lorenzini's pseudonym and the name of his puppet household words was written between July 1881 and January 1883, during which time it appeared serially and sporadically in the *Giornale per i bambini*—one of Italy's first periodicals for children.[1] While it did not create a great critical stir among the literati in the first forty or fifty years following its publication as a volume in 1883, it did enjoy ever-increasing popularity as a book for children. The appeal of Collodi's puppet has proven to be universal,

1. Carlo Lorenzini was born in Florence on November 24, 1826. Between 1856 and 1859 he began to use the pen name Collodi, after his mother's place of birth, a village just outside the town of Pescia in Tuscany. *Le Avventure di Pinocchio* started to appear under the title *Storia d'un burattino* with the first issue of the *Giornale per i bambini*. Although the weekly *Giornale* was published in Rome, the enterprise was in the hands of fellow Tuscans who had migrated after the capital of the newly unified country was transferred from Florence to Rome.

but of especial interest is Giuseppe Prezzolini's remark, in 1923, that "*Pinocchio* is the testing ground for foreigners; whoever understands the beauty of *Pinocchio*, understands Italy."[2] That *Pinocchio* is the literary text that more than any other has been read by Italians in the twentieth century must make one wary about dismissing Prezzolini's judgment as a mere *boutade*. It is also true, however, that no other work of Italian literature can be said to approach the popularity *Pinocchio* enjoys beyond Italy's linguistic frontiers, where its only rivals—but only among cultivated readers and scholars— are *The Divine Comedy* and *The Prince*.

Despite its popularity, *Pinocchio* is not understood as well as it deserves to be, at least in Prezzolini's sense— that is, as an expression of the Italian character. For outside Italy Collodi's tale is still taken almost exclusively as a story for children, who, though unlikely to miss the didactic message the author meant for them, are hardly capable of fully appreciating the tale's underlying linguistic sophistication and narrative strategy, its various levels of irony and sociocultural innuendo, or its satirical thrusts against adult society. Nor do the numerous translations or *rifacimenti* indicate much awareness of these nonchildish features; such versions are so monolithically reductive that most non-Italian adults are unlikely to suspect the book's subtleties and multifaceted context.

But Prezzolini's early remark is clearly intended to call our attention to the virtues of *Pinocchio* as a book for adults, a point upon which he expands fifty years later in an aphoristic pocket history of Italian literature. There, in an appended paragraph, Prezzolini singles out two works that, although outside Italy's primary and

2. *La coltura italiana* (Florence, 1923), p. 185; my translation, as are the translations of all Italian texts cited in this essay, unless otherwise noted.

almost exclusively elitist literary tradition, seem to him so representative of the spirit of the Italian "people" as to merit special attention:

> There are two books that I would say have neither a date nor an author, although both the one and the other are known. *Pinocchio* is a book given to children to read, but it is full of a citified wisdom, worldly and adult, that shows the world as it is—led not by virtue but by fortune guided by astuteness. *Bertoldo* is a triumph of pessimistic rustic wisdom sharpened on the whetstone of experience and on the diffidence of the poor vis-à-vis the rich, and of the ignorant vis-à-vis the pompousness of the so-called cultivated classes. Whoever would understand Italy should read these two books—the one a key of gold, the other a key of iron—that permit entry into the spirit of Italians.[3]

It is clear from this that Prezzolini not only sees *Pinocchio* as a book for adults, but that he also sees in it a Machiavellian vision of the world. The question remains whether that is enough to make it a key to understanding the national Italian character, a concept no less elusive and multiform than the Italian national language.

3. *Storia tascabile della letteratura italiana* (Milan, 1976, 5th ed. 1977), pp. 169–70. *Bertoldo*, written by Giulio Cesare Croce, is an early seventeenth-century seriocomic story, laden with maxims and proverbs reflecting the folk wisdom of a clever rustic who rises to power and subsequently pines away and dies because he can no longer eat his former staple food of beans. Prezzolini (1882–1982) was an influential force in shaping the direction of Italian culture in the first fifteen years of the twentieth century; from 1920 until his death, he assumed the dual role of an indefatigable divulgater of Italian culture to Americans and of American culture to Italians. In 1930 he came to the United States and taught at Columbia University for twenty years. Throughout his long life he harbored a love-hate attitude toward his native land, but his affective nationalism, which led him to accept Fascism, remained constant.

Independently of Prezzolini, and in a quite different way, *Pinocchio* has in recent years been appropriated by the Italian intelligentsia, a radical reversal of the more common circumstance in which a book originally intended for adults becomes a favorite of children or juvenile readers. And without any mention of Prezzolini, the question that arises from his statement concerning *Pinocchio* and the national character has recently been addressed by a panel of more than sixty contemporary writers, who were asked whether they agreed that this "'puppet-people-Italy,' matured through grief and misfortune, represents one of the truest searches into the national identity."[4]

In response to the recent flood of comparisons between Collodi's puppet and heroes or antiheroes—including Ulysses, Aeneas, Christ, and Dante the wayfarer to Don Quijote, Candide, Renzo (of Manzoni's *Promessi sposi*)—and the scores of interpretations and claims made by specialists whose interests range from the sociopolitical, the psychoanalytical, and the mythopoetic to the philosophical, the theological, and the generically allegorical, one is tempted to cry out a recurrent phrase from Collodi's little book—"Poor Pinocchio!" And yet, if it is hard not to sympathize with

---

4. *Le "Avventure" ritrovate: Pinocchio e gli scrittori italiani del Novecento*, ed. Renato Bertacchini (Pescia, 1983). Predictably, not even the Tuscans among those replying are in agreement among themselves; and for some writers from southern Italy, where Collodi's tale was late in having any impact and where more local literary or theatrical personages were taken as representative of the national or regional character, the suggestion seems an odd one.

For a sensible discussion of the arbitrary distinctions that critics are wont to make between children's literature and adult literature, see Glauco Cambon's "Pinocchio and the Problem of Children's Literature," *The Great Excluded* (Journal of the Modern Language Association Seminar on Children's Literature) 2 (1973): 50–60.

a recent editor of Collodi's tale who complains that *Pinocchio* has been so "institutionalized" that one can say anything one wishes about it, the fact remains that there is in the story and its telling something that allows for seeing so much in it. Consequently, one can rightfully be attracted to the view of yet another recent editor of the story who observes that anyone undertaking to write a fable for children cannot be sure of where he may be led. While the author may consciously be engaged only in the invention of witty sayings or amusing adventures, the ancient, mysterious spirit of Fable takes possession of him and involves him with the spirits of air and wood, with the images of the Father and the Mother, with adventures of death and rebirth, with the problematics of sin and redemption.[5]

It is not necessary to think that Collodi was consciously writing a fable or an allegory in the manner of Kafka's stories or Bunyan's *Pilgrim's Progress* in order to feel that his tale reveals something more than first meets the eye. Though the imagery and narrative pattern of *Pinocchio* are suggestive enough to make the tale immediately appealing to children and adults, even those who read it in naïve translations, its telling, despite its apparent simplicity, is at the farthest remove from naïve or primitive art. Collodi frequently and deliberately echoes a wide range of literary and cultural traditions: from the classics of antiquity to fairy tales and romantic operatic libretti, from the most popular forms of folk

5. The two editors referred to are Giovanni Jervis and Pietro Citati; see Jervis's preface to *Le Avventure di Pinocchio* (Turin, 1968), p. xix; and Citati's introductory note to *Le Avventure di Pinocchio* (Milan, 1976), p. vi. Two of the more curious "interpretations" of Collodi's tale include a theological exegesis by the auxiliary bishop of Milan, Giacomo Biffi, *Contro Maestro Ciliegia* (Milan, 1977), and a Steinerian anthroposophical commentary by a physician of Rome, Marcello Carosi, *Pinocchio, un messaggio* (Rome, 1983).

5

and popular art and literature, including the Aesopian apologue, to the Bible, Dante, Voltaire, and Manzoni. Critics are not mistaken in finding parallels between this most fortunate of Italy's minor classics and works of vaster critical fame and scope. Along with the many literary and cultural allusions, the text also offers a rich catalogue of archetypal patterns and images.[6] For this reason, I have in the present essay cast my critical net wide, even at the risk of catching in it some things that may not seem at one with what appears in other parts of it. This will put the reader in mind of the Green Fisherman, who draws up his net and is elated to find a bounty of various fish; but the net also contains Pinocchio, whom he takes to be a crab. In Italian this suggests an irony depending on a play on words, for "to catch a crab" (*prendere un granchio*) means to make a blunder. With some help from a dog he has befriended, Pinocchio will manage to escape, just in the nick of time, the fate of the fish. So too will Collodi's work continue to defy and elude any single or reductive interpretation. Though this marionette is hewn out of a single piece of wood, he and Collodi's tale are not all of a piece. The fault is in great part Collodi's, but in great part it is a fortunate fault.

Like Charles Perrault, whose sophisticated fairy tales he had translated in a colorful Tuscan-flavored prose that anticipates the style of *Pinocchio*, Collodi frequently

6. The exploration of the archetypal imagery and the symbology in *Pinocchio* has been particularly intense in recent years, although much of it is scattered in the myriad articles dealing with the tale from different perspectives. For example, see Elémire Zolla, "Miti arcaici e mondo domestico nelle *Avventure di Pinocchio*," in *Studi Collodiani*, Fondazione Nazionale Carlo Collodi (Pescia, 1976), pp. 625–29; the volume of essays: *C'era una volta un pezzo di legno: la simbologia di 'Pinocchio'*, Fondazione Nazionale Carlo Collodi (Milan, 1981); Antonio Gagliardi, *Il burattino e il laberinto* (Turin, 1980).

winks at his adult readers, the parents, counting on them as accomplices in a pedagogic strategy aimed at inculcating in children a particular behavior. Whatever else may be said of it, *The Adventures of Pinocchio* is an exemplary family drama that, though told with unique verve and inventiveness, follows the nineteenth-century pattern of children's stories in serving as a vehicle of social instruction and, it would seem, of character building in the name of a productive, middle-class ethic. Indeed, the particular relevance of nineteenth-century children's literature to Collodi's Italy compels us to situate *Pinocchio* in its historical and cultural context.

When Collodi was writing his masterpiece, Italy was in the precarious childhood of its modern existence as a unified country under a single monarch. But far from being the *Italia felix* of the nostalgic mythmakers, its problems were immense and, in the final analysis, beyond the solutions of its ruling classes. Chief among the problems was the need to provide education for the children of both the bourgeoisie and the appallingly poor masses. Of course, even before actual unification in 1860 (1870 if one waits for Venice and Rome to become part of Italy), during the years known as the Risorgimento, when Italians struggled for freedom from the governments of the several independently ruled states of the peninsula, signs of social awareness were evident in periodicals and novels.

At the beginning of this period of heightened social and political consciousness stands Alessandro Manzoni's new kind of historical novel, grounded in a profound ethical realism, *I promessi sposi* (*The Betrothed*, 1827–1840). In choosing a humble working-class couple as his protagonists and in setting them against and within the grave historical events of seventeenth-century Lombardy, Manzoni swept away the elitist preju-

7

dice of both high literature and history, which had traditionally concentrated attention on the "important" figures. Literary elitism was further jarred by his use of a nonaristocratic lexicon and a nonclassicizing syntax appropriate to his protagonists and to everyday contemporary reality. Moreover, Manzoni, a Lombard, deliberately chose as the language for his novel a Tuscan-based colloquial idiom—that of Florence—a choice predicated on two beliefs. First, Manzoni thought that the Florentine tongue purged of its most extreme dialectal elements was the language most readily accessible to literate Italians in all regions of the peninsula; second, he felt that linguistic unity could be a cohesive force in the cause of national unity, and he hoped his work would give "Italy" a model of a national language.

At the close of this period, during the 1880s and the uncertain aftermath of unification, stand the stark narrative masterpieces of Giovanni Verga, in particular the novel *I Malavoglia* (1881), which depicts the bitter and desperate struggle for survival of a family of fishing folk in a remote Sicilian village. In turning to a reality and to protagonists even humbler than Manzoni's, Verga, a Sicilian, wrote his experimental novel using the lexicon of the "national" language within the syntactical modes of a "dialect" of his native island. Besides being an obligatory touchstone in any discussion of modern Italian narrative, *I Malavoglia*, like *I promessi sposi*, shares important thematic elements with Collodi's tale.

Meanwhile, during the decades spanned by the two novels, educators and writers of children's literature were concerned with creating a unifying social and national consciousness in the young, as reflected in the ever-increasing number of journals for parents and educators and a plethora of books for children. But this aim required them to face the problem of the poor,

which, as Dina Bertoni-Jovine notes, so troubled the conscience of the liberals that it was present in their every act and statement. To find a compensatory comfort for the poor and to instill a sense of social responsibility in the poor and the middle class alike by appealing to the values inherent in moral principles, religion, and civic concern was the basic purpose, even when not overtly stated, of children's literature.[7]

During the heroic years of the Risorgimento, Collodi had fought in the field as a volunteer with republican principles. His checkered literary career throughout those years and until 1875 included work as a journalist, a theater and opera critic, and a writer of literary caricatures, sketches, and some not very successful comedies. Only after the unification did he try his hand at children's literature, first by translating the fairy tales of Charles Perrault and a selection of those of Mme D'Aulnoy and Mme Leprince de Beaumont, then in a series of books of scholastic intent and use that won him a sizable reputation. Of these, *Giannettino* and *Minuzzolo* were written shortly before *Pinocchio*, while others were written during the almost fortuitous and drawn-out writing of his masterpiece. Although they have a story line of sorts and include the figures of live children, these are unequivocally "schoolbooks," with child protagonists who ask questions for the purpose of being instructed. Narrative line is also subordinate to cultural and educational content in the sequels to *Giannettino*, although the narration is not without its lively moments. Surely, these child protagonists, Giannettino above all, have enough of the scamp about them to be precursors of Pinocchio, but so different is *Pinocchio* that it can almost be mistaken for a polemical anti-

7. Bertoni-Jovine, *Storia dell'educazione popolare in Italia* (Bari, 1965), p. 93.

schoolbook, though it was certainly written, primarily, for schoolchildren.

Perhaps Collodi's scholastic books are best exemplified by Edmondo De Amicis's *Cuore*, which appeared in 1886, just three years after *Pinocchio* was completed, and was soon translated into English as *A Boy's Heart*. *Cuore* and *Pinocchio* remain the most popular books that Italy has produced for children. Indeed, although *Cuore* has gone into eclipse in recent decades, for the first fifty years after its publication it enjoyed a success far greater than that of Collodi's little classic. While this programmatically scholastic, character-building text seems nothing other than a book for children, its stunning international editorial success suggests that adult readers found in it a gratifying presentation of those middle-class values and ideals that transcend nationalistic antagonisms.

Cuore itself is not an instructional text of the traditional kind, yet it is so much a schoolbook that its main setting is an elementary school classroom and its main character a third-grader whose diary records the events of the school year, including the monthly edifying stories dictated by a schoolteacher who is a champion of interclass harmony. Intended to illustrate the idea that heroism, patriotism, sacrifice, and love of family know neither age nor social barriers, the stories take for their protagonists children from Italy's various regions and classes. In this way, the privileged child of the bourgeoisie can learn from the child belonging to the less-fortunate economic strata. De Amicis would like the middle class to be "better," but he is careful not to discredit it. *Cuore*'s ultimate purpose is to invite the inhabitants of Italy's distinctly different regions to a national and fraternal solidarity.

Moreover, the prevailing spirit in *Cuore* is not idyllic; rather, like *Pinocchio*, it depicts an encounter with con-

temporary reality that is dramatic and even traumatic, a feature that sets both books apart from most of the preceding tradition of Italian children's literature, in which painful encounters with reality tended to be underplayed or avoided. In making this important point, Alberto Asor Rosa notes that such traumatic encounters are inherent in any true story of initiation and character development.[8] But for all that, the enormous misery of so much of Italy's population is portrayed sentimentally by De Amicis. Poverty never appears as an unmitigable condition in his pages, where the middle-class gentry stands ready to assist the needy by way of charity and good works. The farthest De Amicis goes is to try to awaken in middle-class children an awareness of the unhappy condition in which the poor live. To see how limited his vision is, one need only read the page on which Enrico's mother explains to him that starving beggars prefer to receive alms from children rather than from grown-ups because then they do not feel humiliated. Besides, she says, it is good to give the destitute something, because then they bless us, which is bound to stir in us a feeling of meltingly sweet gratitude.

Although not all the boys in *Cuore*'s classroom are Good Good Boys, only one, Franti, represents a serious threat and offense to their fierce virtue. Franti, who derides all that is good, noble, and pathetic, shoots paper arrows at the timid substitute teacher, bullies his smaller classmates, steals when he can, lies with a bold face, laughs at disabled soldiers or at the motionless form of a worker who has fallen from the fifth floor, and is even able, alas, to smirk at the schoolmaster's moving account of the funeral of Vittorio Emanuele II, the first monarch of a unified Italy. As the type of the Bad Bad Boy who will be the death, quite literally, of his mother,

8. Asor Rosa, "La Cultura," in *Storia d'Italia* (Turin, 1975), 4:926.

he is appropriately labeled *infame* (infamous) and *malvagio* (wicked), a foil to the chorus of Good Good Boys and a reminder to them of the sort of wicked person who is best dealt with by being detested and removed from society. *Pinocchio* has its own type of Bad Bad Boy in the figure of Lampwick; and Pinocchio himself—a scamp but not a reprobate—could be dubbed a Good Bad Boy.[9] But how much more true to life they both are drawn. And although both didactic tales advocate post-Risorgimento ideals of honesty, family, and the work ethic, all under a paternalistic cloak, in *Pinocchio*, unlike *Cuore*, these values are not connected with God and fervent patriotism; nor does Collodi make any appeal, sentimental or otherwise, to a solidarity of the classes. And although he will bring his willful puppet to heel, he does not spare adult society. Thus, while *Cuore* now strikes us as outdated, *Pinocchio* has never seemed more vital.

The irony of Collodi's Good Bad Boy is that even from the author's somewhat ambiguous point of view, Pinocchio's serious shortcoming is his effort to run away from adulthood, a social and psychological status that his apparently prepubescent age alone in no way barred him from attaining. The lateness in general of the concept of "childhood" in the European consciousness has been asserted by Philippe Ariès: "In the Middle Ages, at the beginning of modern times, *and for a long time after that in the lower class*, children were mixed with adults as soon as they were considered capable of doing without their mothers or nannies, not long after a tardy weaning (in other words, at about the age of seven). They immediately went straight into the great community of man, sharing in the work and play of their

9. I borrow the two expressions from Leslie Fiedler's 1955 essay "An Eye to Innocence: Some Notes on the Role of the Child in Literature," in *The Collected Essays of Leslie Fiedler* (New York, 1971), 1:471–511.

companions, old and young alike." One of the earliest
critics to appreciate the importance of *Pinocchio* was
Paul Hazard, who noted that the superiority of writers
from the North in children's literature results from their
having what Latins lack—"a certain feeling for childhood, for childhood understood as a fortunate island
where happiness must be protected, like an independent
republic living according to its own laws, like a caste
with glorious privileges. The Latins begin to relax, to
breathe, really to live only when they have reached
man's estate. Before that they are merely growing, a
process that the Latin children themselves finish
gladly. . . . For the Latins, children have never been
anything but future men."[10]

In nineteenth-century Italy, thus, the child—the
child of the poor, at any rate—was not perceived as belonging to a world inviolably apart from the world of
grown-ups. Collodi, while not himself a member of the
most destitute classes, chose a child of poverty as his
protagonist, and he would have the child be a diminutive adult or an adult-in-the-making. Though born of a
poor family, Collodi had the rare advantage of an education, supported first by the Marquis Lorenzo Ginori,
in whose employ his father was a hard-working cook,
and later by a maternal uncle. He seems to have chafed
considerably throughout his school years, revealing a
desire for freedom and an independence of spirit that

10. The Ariès quote is from *Centuries of Childhood: A Social History
of Family Life*, trans. Robert Baldick (New York, 1962), p. 411
(my emphasis). Hazard is quoted from *Books, Children, and Men*,
trans. Marguerite Mitchell (Boston, 1960), pp. 109–10; *Les
Livres, les enfants et les hommes* (Paris, 1932). Luigi Volpicelli qual-
ifies Hazard's statement by noting that the precocious candidacy
for adulthood of children from the southern European lands derives from a profoundly realistic and dolorous sense of life and
that misery and poverty dictate the earliest possible emergence
from the dangerous inferiority of childhood; see *La verità su Pinocchio* (Rome, 1954), p. 54.

marked his character ever after. This may explain some of the nostalgia for childhood that the adult reader senses in *Pinocchio*, despite the impression the story often gives that there is no such thing as the innocence of childhood, that children have no rights, only duties summed up under the word *obedience*.[11]

The child protagonists of Collodi's other books—the scholastic texts—are close cousins of the virtuous schoolchildren of De Amicis's *Cuore*, distinguished mostly by the unruliness they share with Pinocchio, although Collodi's treatment of their misbehavior is somewhat forced or mechanical. The puppet's unruliness, in contrast, seems so natural and so pronounced a trait that it serves as the basis for a much more dramatic encounter with the real world—an uncompromisingly egotistical world in which kindness is the exception, not to be banked on outside the formulaic "One good turn deserves another." But this world's essential motto, which Collodi seeks to inculcate in his protagonist and little readers through an ambiguously sadistic admixture of ironic indulgence and severe pedagogical moralism, is the unblushingly un-Christian piece of wisdom: "God helps those who help themselves."

Seen in its historical context, the latter proverb is not merely a cynical slogan justifying the consciences of the greedy and the successful, be they bourgeois or peasant. Rather it is the root exhortation found in popular educational literature of the time—an urgent call to all Ital-

11. As a pedagogue, Collodi is not among the "tenderminded," in the phrase of James Hillman, that is, those "who take their lead from Rousseau, Froebel and the Romantics and their vision from 'childlikeness.'" Rather Collodi is among the toughminded, those "who follow a pattern more Classical, more Medieval, seeing in the child a miniature adult whose waxlike impressionable 'childishness' requires moulding by *Bildung*." See Hillman's absorbing study "Abandoning the Child," *Eranos-Jahrbuch* (1971), p. 397.

ians to better themselves and, thereby, their "nation." In keeping with this hortative proverb, the same literature is replete with appeals to all classes to send their children to school. In this sense above all *Cuore* was so suited to its times. De Amicis propagandized the idea of school as having a great threefold mission—social, political, affective—and therefore as being the place, along with the home, where Italians were to be formed. His optimistic representation of school, complemented by the interwoven story of an equally idealized bourgeois family home, made for his book's huge success. Whatever minor dramas may occur in either setting, the reassuring presence of a benevolent schoolmaster or father, neither of whom has any doubts about what is right and both of whom are always ready with inspiring words, makes both institutions—school and home—secure and sheltered sanctuaries. Surely, one of the most remarkable pages of European nineteenth-century oratory is the letter Enrico's father writes to him, encouraging him to overcome any resistance he might feel about going to school. De Amicis evokes awesome images of the masses of humanity in all stations of life from Italy to the farthest recesses of the world as single individuals and as armies marching to the same goal—the schoolhouse, hailed as the bulwark of civilization, the hope and the glory of the world. Enrico is "a little soldier of the immense army"; his weapons are his books, his squadron is his class, and his battlefield is the whole world.[12]

The vision inspiring De Amicis's purple passage is alien to *Pinocchio*, whose protagonist acquires the most important part of his education "on the road," or so it seems. *Pinocchio*, at any rate, is neither a school story

12. *Cuore* should be read in Luciano Tamburini's excellently annotated edition (Turin, 1974). For the exhortation letter, see pp. 27–29.

nor a scholastic reader, though frequently used as one. But neither is it an anti-schoolbook, though a peculiar incident in chapter 27 might mislead a reader into taking it as one. During the fight at the seashore between Pinocchio and the seven school companions who have tricked him into playing hooky, the latter turn their textbooks into weapons (though hardly in De Amicis's sense) and hurl them all at the puppet who is getting the better of them. Pinocchio, however, is deft at ducking them, and the books end up in the sea. The strewn texts include primers, grammars, and a number of readers much in vogue in the schools of the time, among them Collodi's own highly popular *Giannettino* and *Minuzzolo*.

Then, as the author, interrupting the description of the fight, notes: "Just imagine the fish! Thinking that those books were something good to eat, the fish hurried in shoals to the surface of the water; but after nibbling at a few pages or at a frontispiece, they spat them out, making the sort of face that seemed to say: 'That's not for us: we're used to feeding on much better fare.'" In this piece of self-irony Collodi may be winking at his audience of children as much as at his adult readers. For as the digression points up, *Pinocchio*, though written for children of the earliest school age, is a different kind of children's story. Yet one notes that the fight results from a trick played on the puppet by his seven companions, the real bad boys whom Pinocchio tauntingly calls the seven deadly sins. After a long period of waywardness he had finally settled down with his fairy godmother and had entered school, quickly becoming a model pupil. Pinocchio as an odious head-of-the-class type may at first strike us as incongruous, but the puppet, like his story, is not all of a piece; and school and home are values no less primary in Collodi's tale than they are in *Cuore*.

There are three great periods in the story of the puppet's misadventures, always presented as punitive examples, that can be measured by three different betrayals to school and home. On the first such occasion, Pinocchio is supplied with the necessary spelling-book by penniless Geppetto, who has sold his only coat in order to procure it. Geppetto's sacrifice suggests that he places the highest possible value on education. It is as though this man who is poorer than a churchmouse were responding to the appeals of the educators, a response one can hardly expect the poor to have taken to heart, given the economic sacrifices it entailed. Moreover, Pinocchio, who enthusiastically promised that he would indeed go to school and "do himself proud," understands the extraordinary nature of Geppetto's sacrifice and is sincerely moved by it. As he starts out, he daydreams of quickly learning how to read and write and of putting his education to use, of becoming rich and, since Pinocchio for all his willfulness does have a good heart, of buying his father a luxurious coat. But poor Pinocchio does not even make it to school on this first occasion. Atavistically attracted to a puppet show by the sound of fifes and drums, he sells his spelling-book to a ragman for the four pennies that will purchase his ticket of admission. Subsequent events lead him inexorably to his hanging and apparent death in chapter 15.

The second period of misadventures follows upon the fight at the seashore. Even more than the first case, this truancy is fraught with ambiguity, for it is and is not a betrayal. In a major turning point in his story, Pinocchio told his fairy godmother that he was tired of being a puppet and wanted to become a man (chapter 25). Not merely a real or proper boy, but a man: a distinction suggesting the full acceptance of maturity and responsibilities. To this end, after some residual grum-

bling, he went to school and became a star pupil. Yet the attraction of the carefree and regressive life never left him; for even as he applied himself assiduously to his studies and excelled as a pupil, he continued to go around with school-hating chums, among them the seven bad boys who trick him into playing truant and going to the seashore. The further ambiguity here is that Pinocchio had good filial motives for going to the seashore; the boys' story that a marine monster was to be seen in the nearby waters had put him in hopes of learning something about his father, who at last report was presumed to have been swallowed by a sea monster. Nonetheless, Pinocchio is punished for his truancy by a short but terrifying second series of misadventures that conclude in an apparent reconciliation with the Fairy.

The third occasion involves a more clear-cut betrayal but no less ambiguous an attitude. Having been forgiven by his fairy godmother, Pinocchio returns to school and finishes the scholastic year, winning the highest honors. As a reward, the Fairy tells him that on the next day she will satisfy his wish to become a *ragazzo perbene*, that is, a 'proper' or 'true' boy in the sense of an authentic, flesh-and-blood boy, to be sure, but also a well-behaved, obedient boy of the kind the puppet, at this point, seems to have proved himself capable of being; for the Italian expression actually refers to respectability and conformity to a polite or "civilized" social code. An exultant Pinocchio goes around to invite all his companions to the celebration planned for the event. But again he will be denied; or rather, he will deny himself. He forfeits respectability and responsibility by surrendering to the temptation of life in Funland, a plan hatched by his closest friend and alter ego, Lampwick.

Thus we see that the star pupil Pinocchio has not yet completely rejected the attractions of the free-and-easy

life, indeed, of evil itself. Though *evil* may seem too strong a word to characterize Lampwick, in sound and meaning his Italian name, Lucignolo, calls to mind Lucifer, a name that immediately evokes notions of temptation and disobedience. It is worth recalling that in the nineteenth-century moral code for children, disobeying one's parents was considered tantamount to disobeying God. Lampwick's function is exactly analogous to that of the seven bad companions in the previous episode of truancy. But with how much more insidious an art does he achieve his end! Whereas Pinocchio recognized and resented the trick played upon him by the seven bad boys, Lampwick succeeds in breaking down his resistance and making him want what is bad for him. The "seven deadly sins" have been replaced by the single figure of one who would seem to be their master.

In introducing this personage, whose very nickname suggests something ungainly, Collodi fleetingly notes that his real name is Romeo, but neither explains nor further refers to this. Could it be that Collodi chose that name, so richly associated with romantic and sympathetic feelings, to hint at the secretly attractive side of Lampwick? It is he who leads a Pinocchio who is always ready to be led astray into making his gravest rejection of school and social responsibility as well as into committing his greatest blasphemy—the callous denial of his fairy godmother—just when it seems that he finally really does know better. Talking with Lampwick is the only time Pinocchio adopts a mocking attitude toward the authority represented by the mother-figure. One need only think of the aggressive mood and comical tone with which, at the outset of the book, the father-figure Geppetto is mocked by the puppet to sense that something more profoundly sacred to Collodi is being profaned when, in a great seduction scene, Pinocchio echoes Lampwick's words:

"Where do you expect to find a more whole-some place for us kids? There are no schools there; there are no teachers there; there are no books there. They never study in that blessed land."

"And what if the Fairy yells at me?"

"Let her yell. When she's tired of yelling, she'll calm down," said that scapegrace of a Lampwick.

"It's no use for you to tempt me! I've promised my good Fairy to be a sensible boy now, and I don't want to go back on my word."

"Well, farewell then, and give my best regards to the grammar schools . . . and the high schools too, if you meet them on the way."

"How soon will you be leaving?"

"In a little while."

"That's too bad! If it were only an hour before you leave, I might almost wait."

"And the Fairy?"

"I'm already late anyway, and to go home an hour sooner or an hour later doesn't matter."

"Poor Pinocchio! And what if the Fairy yells at you?"

"So what! I'll let her yell. When she's tired of yelling, she'll calm down."

"There it is!" shouted Lampwick, getting to his feet.

"Who is it?" asked Pinocchio in a low voice.

"It's the wagon that's coming to pick me up. Well, are you coming, yes or no?"

"But is it really true," the puppet asked, "that in that land kids never have to study?"

"Never, never, never!"

"What a wonderful land, what a wonderful land, what a wonderful land!"

The determining factor in persuading Pinocchio to renounce his imminent respectable real-boy status is Lampwick's insistence that in Funland there is no obli-

gation to study or attend school, that institution of constraint. But if all still seems innocent enough, we should look with our children's eyes at the ensuing events that draw Pinocchio into his most abject and humiliating adventures, but finally to his redemption as well. He will join Lampwick and the other boys who are to be driven to Funland by the simpering "little man" who is so much the most sinister character in the book, the real candidate for the role of the Devil in this episode, that with his appearance even Lampwick assumes but the ancillary role of an imp of Satan.

Lampwick has told Pinocchio that the departure time is midnight, which in popular superstitions and in the Romantic theater is the Devil's hour. The "little man" is not immediately presented as a physically repellent figure as is, say, Fagin in *Oliver Twist*, that "hideous old man [who] seemed like some loathsome reptile." Nonetheless, the adult reader senses something suspect in the jolly grotesqueness of his rotund smiling person. And before long we see that he is as ruthless as Fagin in the matter of exploiting children. In the light of what Pinocchio soon undergoes, the whole sequence appears as a version of the motif of selling one's soul to the Devil for a period of carefree pleasure, even though Pinocchio, unlike Faust, has made the pact unwittingly.

After five months of ease and play—with no school —Pinocchio, metamorphosed into a donkey, is sold by the "little man" to a circus ringmaster who beats him mercilessly in training him to dance and leap through hoops. But when Pinocchio the donkey stumbles and comes up lame, the irate ringmaster sells him in turn to a buyer who wants him only for his hide. Thrown into the sea by the buyer, who waits for him to drown so that he can draw him up and skin him, Pinocchio is set upon by a shoal of fish who ravenously devour him down to his original wooden core but cannot bite into him be-

yond that. Surfacing as a wiser though not yet sufficiently chastened puppet, he chides the buyer and swims off spunkily, only to find himself pursued by the Great Shark, who swallows him in a gulp that violently hurtles the puppet into his cavernous belly. This climactic adventure of initiation is one of the two or three most obviously archetypal images and events in Collodi's tale.

The motif of dying to be reborn, of descending to the depths in order to rise spiritually and morally renewed, has been depicted in the Jonah-in-the-whale stories of many lands. The question of Collodi's sources need not be taken up here, save to say that they included the Old Testament, Lucian, and Ariosto, but also—and perhaps more pertinent for our purposes—the popular puppet shows that Collodi and the children of his time knew so well.[13] Throughout his history, Pinocchio recognizes his errors and resolves to be good—obedient to his elders above all. Any one or several of his trials and ordeals might have sufficed to justify his conversion to orderly virtue. But there was always something inconclusive or insufficiently traumatic about the ordeals and

13. The sea monster in *Pinocchio* has more of the whale than the shark about him. Tempesti cautiously suggests a plausible reason for Collodi's choice of *pesce-cane* (shark) over *balena* (whale): the shark was much more readily associated with the idea of sharptoothed ferocity in the public's mind; see *Chi era il Collodi; Com'è fatto "Pinocchio"* (Milan, 1972), p. 117. Allan Gilbert points to the parallels between the episode of Pinocchio in the belly of the Great Shark and the episode in Ariosto's *Cinque Canti* (cantos excluded from the 1532 version of *Orlando Furioso*) in which the knight Ruggiero is swallowed by a whale; see "The Sea-Monster in Ariosto's *Cinque Canti* and in *Pinocchio*," *Italica* 32, no. 4 (December 1956): 260–63. A debt to Lucian's *A True Story*, long recognized by Italian critics, has been set forth again recently by Susan Gannon, "A Note on Collodi and Lucian," *Children's Literature* 8 (1980): 98–102. Although the sea monster of Lucian's tale obviously influenced Ariosto, Collodi's greater debt was to the Italian poet.

trials that allowed Pinocchio's ingrained waywardness to resurface as the occasion demanded. This proved possible even after his apparent death by hanging at the end of chapter 15, which, when published in the *Giornale per i bambini*, seemed so clearly the catastrophic end of the puppet's story that *fine* (the end) was appended to it.

Being swallowed alive and residing in the belly of a sea monster, however, is an adventure too specifically connected with regeneration to permit anything short of a definitive conversion. Moreover, it is significant that imagery of sea or water—a female element as myths and depth psychology tell us—becomes so prominent in the second part of Pinocchio's adventures, the part, that is, beginning with chapter 16 and the introduction of the Fairy, who will henceforth dominate the puppet's life. Pinocchio's sojourn in the belly of the Great Shark and his subsequent issuing from it—his rebirth or regeneration—causes him to be (re)born from a female, indeed, from a womb, if one likes. This maternal parturition complements or corrects the puppet's first birth, which was by means of the father-creator alone, much as in the Old Testament account of the creation of Adam.

This motif, then, allows Collodi to hasten to the happy ending of a story that, because it is built on episodic misadventures and the hero's proneness to fall into them, could otherwise have gone on indefinitely. Collodi is not concerned with representing the successive stages of a developing personality as in a true *Bildungsroman*, at least not in a consistent way. Indeed, the puppet is so ready to fall at any time that one might question whether he really learns from his experiences on the road, and whether his character actually develops, even as one admits the inevitability of the dramatic change that comes over him in the end. That is, it could be argued that Pinocchio does not really learn from the

hard knocks of life, but rather that his function as a quasi-picaresque character is to be available in a hostile world for misadventure upon misadventure from which Collodi's little readers might be expected to draw a lesson while they are being entertained.

Collodi, however, did not just suddenly hit upon the motif of the descent into the sea monster's belly; the motif fits too nicely as the culminating experience to a series of archetypal images. He must have had it in mind at least as early as chapters 23 and 24, when, in that other archetypal dimension of Pinocchio's story which is the quest for the originally rejected or abandoned father, he has the puppet swim in a raging sea in a heroic but vain attempt to reach old Geppetto. Interestingly enough, Geppetto had earlier set out in a small skiff in search of his runaway puppet, only to be swallowed up by a sea monster—the same Great Shark that gulps down Pinocchio. The two motifs—the dual quest of son and father for one another and the rebirth of Pinocchio—dovetail when the two characters meet in the bowels of the sea monster. And that Pinocchio, from the moment he realizes that he is in the Shark's belly, has begun to cast off his old self is evident: after some initial crying and calling for help, he does not, as he did in so many earlier crises, bemoan his fate and whimper his regrets for having failed to follow the advice of those who know better than he. We can grasp the change in him by recalling chapter 21, when the puppet, in a quasi-metamorphosis, was reduced to the condition of a chained watchdog. After whiningly berating himself for not having stayed at home with his poor father and for having preferred the life of a vagabond to that of a schoolboy, he sighs: " 'Oh, if only I could be born over again! . . . But it's too late now, and I have to put up with it.' " In the leviathan's belly, thanks to the benign irony of the author, he is in fact born anew.

Following the escape from the Great Shark, Pinocchio leads his old and enfeebled father in search of ref-
uge. On the way, they meet the Fox and the Cat, the
"assassins" who had hanged him and later gulled the
resuscitated but still naïve puppet into yielding his gold
coins by the great confidence trick of having him plant
them in the Field of Miracles. Now reduced to the lame-
ness, blindness, and general misery they had earlier
feigned, they receive neither sympathy nor alms, but
sermonizing proverbs from a wiser Pinocchio. It is true
that Pinocchio does not have alms to give. But not even
a kind word for the scoundrels? How different this behavior from the spontaneous charity of that "godless"
boy hero, Pinocchio's slightly older American contemporary who successfully resists all efforts to be "sivil-
ized" by the "persecuting good widow who wishes to
make a nice, truth-telling, respectable boy of him."[14]
Huck would have felt sorry for the Fox and the Cat just
as he did for the "Duke" and the "King" (who had
treated him so cruelly) when he saw them being run out
of town, tarred and feathered: "Well it made me sick to
see it; and I was sorry for them poor pitiful rascals, it
seemed like I couldn't feel any hardness against them
any more in the world. It was a dreadful thing to see.
Human beings can be awful cruel to one another."

Speaking in proverbs is new for Pinocchio and is another sure sign of the puppet-child's reformation in con-
sonance with an adult society of law-and-order and
general middle-class values. Pinocchio adopts the language in which society has rigidly codified "ancient"
wisdom and the behavior it demands, the language used

14. This is how Mark Twain describes Huck in the 1883 edition of
   Life on the Mississippi, where he introduced "The Raftsmen's Passage," part of the 1876 draft of *The Adventures of Huckleberry
   Finn* omitted from the novel in 1884 at the publisher's suggestion.

hitherto by Geppetto, who though poor is anything but a revolutionary, by the Fairy, and by the Talking Cricket, who more than a symbol of Pinocchio's conscience is a double of the father-figure.

It is the Cricket whom Pinocchio, accompanied by Geppetto, meets now as he enters the hut they have come upon. Earlier, the rebellious Pinocchio had "killed" the Cricket in the humble house where that domestic symbol par excellence of the patriarchal hearth had lived a hundred years. The murder took place when Geppetto was absent in prison, a victim of one of society's expedient travesties of justice that Collodi, conservative but pessimistic, sardonically enjoyed exposing. In this, their final meeting, with Geppetto present, the effective reconciliation with the father-figure, which was begun in the belly of the sea monster, is completed as Pinocchio offers himself up to the Cricket but asks for mercy for his poor father. The Cricket not only forgives Pinocchio but grants him the hospitality of the hut. Precisely while living in this humble hut Pinocchio will earn his final metamorphosis, by slaving for the market gardener Giangio in the kind of work usually performed by a beast of burden.[15]

The job of turning the beam of the windlass, in fact, last belonged to a donkey who worked so hard that he is now lying in the stable, near death. Pinocchio asks to see him and has an encounter that a reader might not have expected, for Collodi has told his little readers that he did not know what happened to Lampwick after the "little man" had sold him to a peasant. Because Lampwick's death, that of an unregenerate, coincides with

15. Here one thinks not only of the puppet's recent life as a donkey but also of the earlier Pinocchio on the Island of Busy Bees indignantly rejecting the offer of work made to him by the charcoal merchant: " 'I'll have you know that I've never been a jackass. I've never pulled a cart!' "

Pinocchio's rebirth, their brief reunion has great potential for drama or pathos. But when the market gardener sees Pinocchio shed a furtive tear over the dead Lampwick, he grumbles: " 'You feel so sorry for a jackass that didn't cost you anything? Then how should I feel, who paid hard cash for him?' " And when the puppet explains that the donkey was a former friend and schoolmate of his, Giangio guffaws in the crudest way. The scene is indicative of the work's radically secular morality and the no-nonsense world that Everyboy Pinocchio is preparing to enter as a full-fledged, no-nonsense boyadult.

Pinocchio's single tear shed over the dead Lampwick is the puppet's last farewell to frivolity and rebellion; and for it he is quickly overcome by a feeling of shame. Unlike the Bad Bad Boy who so cunningly and subvertingly suggested that the truly salutary life, the truly "civilized" life, for boys was to be found in hedonistic Funland, the Good Bad Boy is eventually redeemed and shaped into the exploitable boy-adult that Geppetto had in mind when he conceived him. Following more than five months of back-breaking service for Giangio and the side work of weaving baskets, Pinocchio receives a last mysterious visitation from the Fairy. And after once more proving the firmness of his love for her by further sacrifices, he will be rid of the slough of his puppet nature, appearing at last in the transfigured image of a radiant and respectable boy-adult.

One thinks of those fairy tales that tell of the metamorphosis of an ugly frog into a handsome prince after the incantation has been broken. But it is not Pinocchio's social status that changes. The puppet's transformation is the result of his unalterable acceptance of a rigid work ethic within a social structure that goes unquestioned. Rather than recounting a magical fromrags-to-riches tale, Collodi, even with an ironic and

parodic implementation of fairy-tale and picaresque elements, beats just that sort of foolish notion out of the boy-puppet. In this respect, *Pinocchio* as a whole is an anti-Cinderella story, just as its first fifteen chapters constitute a version of the cautionary tale of Little Red Riding Hood as told in Perrault's ironic but uncompromising version. The happy ending became mandatory once Collodi acceded to the demands of his little readers and his editor for more of Pinocchio. Only then, in fact, did the *Story of a Puppet* become *The Adventures of Pinocchio*, the original title demoted to a subtitle. This change was both appropriate and timely once Collodi's tale took on the character of an initiatory adventure story that in incorporating the first "story" would lead the protagonist from perilous innocence, by way of a journey through adventures, to a return home and a final rebirth into adulthood. It is this narrative pattern that allows *Pinocchio* to be compared with the *Odyssey* and any number of stories about adventures during journeys, stories which are inevitably rich with archetypal images and situations.[16] And to achieve this pattern Collodi introduces into the life of the puppet the benevolently stern Fairy by recasting the strange little blue-haired girl who had first appeared mysteriously as a death symbol.

Only while he is under the Fairy's tutelage is Pinocchio actually able to go to school; and for the purpose, she no longer appears as a little girl, a sister to the puppet, but rather as a grown-up, a young mother to him, with suggestions of a social bearing that lies somewhere between a lady of the middle class and a woman of the rural popular class. There was never any real chance of

16. A brief but sober analysis of parallels between the *Odyssey* and *Pinocchio* is given by Massimiliano Boni, *Un saggio e venti capricci su Pinocchio* (Bologna, 1977), pp. 84–92. But one must reject the notions of critics who would see Pinocchio as a Dantean Ulysses, fearlessly facing adventure because of a desire for experience and a love of knowledge.

Pinocchio's continuing in school while living with Geppetto, even had he not gone astray but arrived at school on that first day with the spelling-book purchased at so great a sacrifice. Education was the kind of luxury that poor Geppetto could not have offered his son for long. In the last phase of the puppet's adventures there is no talk of going to school. Learning is important, but Pinocchio must teach himself to read and write in the few spare hours he can allow himself. Meanwhile, the more urgent business of earning one's bread (and bread for father, too) must be attended to, a necessity that brings the reader back to the true reality of Pinocchio's world as it was at the beginning: a reality of hunger and a struggle to survive, which is not of concern to the puppet during his interludes with the magico-bourgeois Fairy. The social and economic differences between Geppetto and the Fairy in fact are one reason that this family *sui generis* can never live all three together in the same household. Moreover, given their roles as Pinocchio's pedagogues, in such a ménage Geppetto's presence could only be an embarrassment.

In this connection it is worth noting that in the fairy-tale tradition usually the mother or stepmother is the crueler parent—though not for pedagogic purposes—whereas the fairy godmother is almost always a benefactress. Pinocchio's Fairy, Collodi's internalized mother imago, blends the two concepts. Furthermore, the Fairy is both a magical presence, a role attributed to women in some patriarchal systems, and a down-to-earth pedagogue, a role that women of the middle class were increasingly called upon to assume in Collodi's Italy. The original conception of *Story of a Puppet*, in which Pinocchio is created or fashioned by a poor, old, and unmarried tradesman, and the exigencies of a plot line that has the protagonist on a quest for a father, could hardly allow for the simultaneous presence, much less the cohabitation, of two such disparate parental figures.

Indeed, the only way Collodi could include a mother figure in his story was to make her a Fairy, an attribute that has the additional advantage of precluding her staying on once father and son are reunited.

The magical and protective nature of the blue-haired Fairy is second only to Pinocchio's nose as a vexed question in Collodi's tale. Various interpretations have been made regarding the peculiarity of the color of her hair: blue, the color of the ineffable or the infinite, of the absolute and the unattainable; blue, the color of the Italian sky. Some readers have invoked the figure of the Virgin—so often depicted in art with a blue mantle—a reasonable notion unless stretched to infer a religious allegory and ascribe a Christological import to the puppet (son of a *carpenter* whose name is derived from *Joseph*!). That a fairy godmother—and, in the eyes of adoring children, real mothers—should acquire the characteristics of the Virgin in a country such as Italy, with its great cult of Mary and a rich iconographic tradition, is hardly surprising. Pinocchio's Fairy, however, is given to a punitive pedagogy that one can hardly associate with the gentle Virgin. The blue hair, moreover, is first attributed to the Little Girl with the waxen face, who appears as a death image in chapter 15, that is, before Collodi decided to give new life to his story and declared the Little Girl to be a Fairy.[17]

17. Among Collodi's many "sources," most of them consciously appropriated, are elements of the Christian gospel narration and the Catholic imagination. But these, without being satirized, are woven into a story whose ideological ground is secular without being overtly antireligious. At most, they are used with an easy nonchalance from which any hint of sacrilegious intent is wholly absent. Thus it is equally wrong to see Collodi's tale as either an antireligious fable or a religious parabolic tale. Nonetheless, for an acute reading of *Pinocchio* in a "minor Christological" or messianic key, see Franco Ferrucci, "Il teatro dei burattini," *Paragone*, no. 264 (August 1970), pp. 129–46; Ferrucci finds in Collodi's story an undeclared bourgeois Catholic "ideology."

Despite the Fairy's importance in the puppet's life, the story's ending confirms its initial frame of reference. However reduced, it is the patriarchal family that stands as an island of security in an uncertain Italy and in an egotistical, aggressively hostile world. In this respect Collodi shares a vision that is also at the core of *I Malavoglia*, the supreme family drama of Italian literature. Verga's 'Ntoni, whose rebellion and utopian dreams of making his fortune in the big city drag him into abject degradation and bring ruin upon the family, is not without his own moral rehabilitation in the end, though it comes too late to allow for his reinstatement in society. Nonetheless, his younger brother Alessi with humility and hard work restores the family, enacting a role parallel to that played by the reborn Pinocchio. With the bitter lesson of his brother's rebellion in mind, Alessi will be content to work hard just to maintain his station in the socioeconomic system. In contrast, one feels that Collodi's boy-adult will eventually raise himself a notch or two and might well become a small entrepreneur—a socioeconomic ascent that Manzoni indulgently yet realistically had allowed to his working-class hero, Renzo, at the end of *I promessi sposi*. Yet although the story's happy ending as such—the metamorphosis—is coherent, there remains something forced and contradictory in the fact that Pinocchio's poor boy's status is itself transfigured by Collodi's need to cater to his middle-class public.

That Pinocchio was destined to poverty as his true lot is so much the case that even before fashioning him from an ordinary piece of firewood, Geppetto, with an irony that is only deceptively blithe, in seeking a name for him that might bring him good luck can come up with nothing better than that of a family whose richest member was a beggar: "'What name shall I give him?' he said to himself. 'I'll call him Pinocchio. The name

will bring him good luck. I once knew a whole family of Pinocchios: the father was a Pinocchio, the mother was a Pinocchia, and the children were Pinocchios. And they all did well for themselves. The richest one of them begged for a living.'" Another such moment of deceptively blithe play on the theme of poverty occurs when the Master Puppeteer, Fire-Eater, asks Pinocchio about his father:

"What's your father's name?"
"Geppetto."
"And what's his trade?"
"That of a poor man."
"Does he earn much?"
"He earns enough never to have a cent in his pocket."

Yet the matter of poverty, for all Collodi's wry humor and sometimes cruel irony, is not a laughing matter for him; and perhaps the gravest line in the whole tale occurs early on when, as Pinocchio finds himself all ready to go to school except for the lack of a spelling-book, which a penniless and downcast Geppetto is unable to purchase, the author comments: "And although Pinocchio was a very good-humored boy, even he became sad, because poverty, when it is true poverty, is understood by everyone, even by children."

It is not surprising, then, that starvation anxieties and oral fantasies abound in *The Adventures of Pinocchio*; and food, or its absence, is so much the ruling image and theme that it is present even in the episodes involving the puppet's relationship with the Fairy, who does not hesitate to use food as a pedagogic weapon. Pinocchio yawns wide with hunger more than once. His first feeling of remorse for rebelling against his "father" comes early and connects with the specter of hunger: " 'The Talking Cricket was right. I was wrong to rebel against my father and run away from home . . . If my father

were here now, I wouldn't be yawning to death. Oh, what an awful sickness hunger is!' " On at least three occasions he eats things he first rejected: the skins and cores of the three pears Geppetto gives him for breakfast; the vetches found in the dovecote where the Pigeon flying him to the seashore pauses; the hay and straw he is forced to eat in his donkey existence. The vetches are a famine food; when the puppet finds them quite palatable despite what he calls his long-standing aversion to them, the Pigeon, sounding very much as Geppetto did at the end of the pedagogic lesson with the three pears, says to him: " 'Hunger knows neither fancies nor delicacies.' " Food also concerns Fire-Eater, who insists that his whole sheep must be properly roasted, even at the cost of using Pinocchio or, if need be, one of his own marionettes as firewood. And there is the unforgettable scene in The Red Crawfish Inn, where the Fox and the Cat, having declared themselves to be without appetite, proceed to gorge themselves at Pinocchio's expense while he uncharacteristically nibbles at no more than a bit of a walnut and a piece of bread because the thought of planting his gold pieces in the Field of Miracles in hopes of seeing them sprout into a richly laden money-tree has given the poor puppet a case of premature indigestion of gold coins.

If Collodi's hand were heavier, the cruelty of this joke would be intolerable, because the close alimentary association between money and eating, between poverty and starving, is the ground for the potentially tragic reality of Pinocchio's world. Of the many references to money in the story, it is enough to recall the emblematic example in which money-as-food and oral greediness are united in one image. When Pinocchio is pursued and seized by the "assassins" who demand his money or his life, he thrusts the gold pieces into his mouth and successfully resists all efforts the disguised Fox and Cat

make to pry open his mouth. He will literally be hanged first, but even then he manages to keep his coins. Hunger will drive the puppet to trespass on a farmer's property in order to eat a handful of grapes, a crime for which he is chained and made to serve as a watchdog. His punishment is in keeping with the inflexible bourgeois rule of the sacredness of private property, as is explained by the Firefly, who feels sympathy for him until she hears what he has done: " 'Hunger, my boy, is not a good reason for appropriating what is not ours.' "[18] Still more nightmarish is the episode in which the Green Fisherman, another father-as-ogre double, having hauled up Pinocchio in his net along with a bountiful catch, is just barely thwarted from committing child cannibalism. Thus on the occasion of his swimming ashore on the Island of Busy Bees, the puppet asks a passerby a question that is really a statement *in nuce* of Collodi's view of life in the real world: " 'Are there any villages on this island where one can eat without danger of being eaten?' "

This vision of the world *sub specie alimentaria* is a clue to what may be the root irony in the choice of the puppet's name. Before being forced by the success of Collodi's tale into its almost exclusive linguistic role as a referent for the tale's protagonist, *pinocchio* was the "standard" Italian word used to indicate the pine nut—that quite edible morsel which Collodi, using precisely

18. Such severity of punishment for what seem minor and even "justifiable" transgressions against private property was typical of the nineteenth century. In Luigi Alessandro Parravicini's *Giannetto* (1837), Italy's first "popular" children's book (really a heavily didactic scholastic text), during a visit to the city, Giannetto is brought by his father on a tour of the prison. Over each cell door an inscription indicates the infraction and the penalty. One of them reads: "Due anni di carcere a N.N. per avere salito il murello d'un giardino, e aver colà rubato una libbra di pesche" (Two years of prison to N.N. for having climbed over a garden wall to steal a pound of peaches).

that form rather than the more common Florentine *pi-nolo* (now the "standard" Italian term), once included in a ructatious evocation of foods in the marketplace of his native Florence.[19] And irony of ironies in this story destined to have a happy ending, the fundamental image of eating, indeed, the "eat-or-be-eaten" ethos, takes a positive turn in the episode of the traumatically redemptive ingestion of Pinocchio by the Great Shark. In the monster's belly, the puppet vigorously spurns the Tuna's suggestion that they both wait patiently to be digested. " 'But I don't want to be digested!' " says Pinocchio, in no mood for a Little Red Riding Hood ending. Sloshing his way to a dim light, which recalls the dim light in the dark of night that turned out to be the Cricket and was rejected by the puppet, he eventually comes across a hoary Geppetto who, *mirabile dictu*, is seated at a table illuminated by a candle stuck in a green wine bottle, munching toothlessly on fish in a scene that, as one critic has acutely observed, evokes the humble reality of a Tuscan trattoria. Surely it is as symptomatic as it is ironic that the chastened Pinocchio will, like Candide, find his salvation by working to cultivate a kitchen garden—not his own, however, but Giangio's.

Pinocchio's redemption is first signaled when he is restored to his original nature by the ravenous fish who furiously eat away his donkey hide but are unable to bite into his wood. Though the fish had been providentially sent by the Fairy, they nonetheless have their own autonomous feeding interests in mind when carrying out this mission. The episode recalls the earlier one in which the fish found the textbooks unpalatable, thus suggesting that for Collodi schoolbooks are not readily convertible into food, at least not for everyone, and certainly not in the Italy of his time. In this respect,

19. See note 10 to the text and translation.

Pinocchio's most revealing oral fantasy occurs when he returns to the Field of Miracles expecting to find that his four gold coins have sprouted into a full-grown money-tree. Along the way the puppet muses that once he is rich, among the things he wants to have in his mansion is a library whose bookshelves are chock-full of candied fruit, pies, *panettoni*, almond cakes, and cornets bursting with whipped cream! There can be little doubt about the choice to be made between "pane e libri" ("bread and books"), the title of a piece Collodi wrote in protesting the priorities of Italy's new government when it promulgated the law making elementary education obligatory.[20]

It is easy to accuse Collodi of conservative demagoguery when, in justification of his opposition to the law, he writes:

> As I see it, until now we have thought more about the heads than the stomachs of the classes that are needy and suffering. Now let us think a little more about their stomachs; and then let us see if by chance the sentiment of human dignity may not enter more readily into the bloodstream by way of bread than into the head by way of books and compulsory education.

But doubtless Collodi felt the law was unrealistic in a country where, as in *The Adventures of Pinocchio*, the overriding problem was the immediate and serious one of finding a way to eat, a problem only partially solved by the subsequent emigration of millions of Italian peasants to the Americas. Hence from his point of view it was the liberals who were guilty of demagogic subterfuge. The demagoguery was on both sides, and the

20. "Pane e libri," in *Tutto Collodi*, ed. Pietro Pancrazi (Florence, 1942), pp. 778–82.

fear of the social discontent that Collodi accused the liberals of responding to in an ineffectual and hypocritical way was probably felt by him even more, for at the time of his little masterpiece, Collodi was no longer the fiery republican of the Risorgimento years. Though disgruntled with the new Italy and the relegation of Florence and Tuscany to a secondary role in it, he did come to terms with it even while feeling himself more and more estranged. However, Collodi's post-Risorgimento conservatism is not to be understood as a repudiation of the idea of political unification. He was not the only Mazzinian republican to lose democratic ardor while coming more or less to terms with the nation newly unified under a monarch.[21] What is sure is that this writer of school texts for middle-class children did not believe that universal education in itself was a magical cure-all for the nation.

The same overriding problem of eating, coupled with an inveterate desire to remain unfettered and to avoid hard or honest work, is at the center of the life of the *ragazzo di strada*—the street kid—a species of urban humanity that held an enormous fascination for Collodi and with whom he felt a strong affinity. The vital link between this type and *The Adventures of Pinocchio* helps explain the ambiguity the adult reader senses in Collodi's attitude toward his protagonist, who is made to move in a dramatic tension between a desire for freedom and a need for order. Giannettino and Minuzzolo, with

21. An analogous case, and perhaps the best known, is that of the "national" poet Giosuè Carducci, who even in his "democratic" days was rigidly opposed to enforced literacy. For good observations on Collodi's ideology, see Carlo A. Madrignani, "Regionalismo, verismo e naturalismo in Toscana e nel Sud," in *La letteratura italiana: storia e testi: il secondo ottocento*, ed. C. Muscetta (Rome and Bari, 1975), 8:512; and Concetta D'Angeli, "L'ideologia 'moderata' di Carlo Lorenzini, detto Collodi," *La rassegna della letteratura italiana* 86, ser. 7, nos. 1–2 (gennaio–agosto 1982): 152–77.

their innocuous unruliness, are a far cry from the *ra-gazzo di strada* described by Collodi in an essay bearing that title.[22] Even Pinocchio himself is a tame version of this type, better represented by Lampwick. Of the street kid who has food on his mind more often than in his stomach and is capable of passing hours looking at the sumptuous displays in the windows of expensive restaurants, Collodi writes:

> A philosopher by temperament and training, there are only two things he seeks to avoid: carriages and work. Of the two, what he fears less are the carriages; and that is understandable. The worst that a carriage wheel can do is cripple a man; but work brutalizes him.

> Ever since he came into the world he has never known what is his; and he has always heard that what belongs to others must be respected in one case only—that is, when it is not possible to take it for oneself nonchalantly and without scandalizing the carabinieri or the police.

> In one of his economical aphorisms, the street kid says, "A people that smokes cigars down to the end, to the point of burning moustache and tongue, is a people reduced to begging, *obliged to eat a bit of dry bread and a slice of compulsory education*" [emphasis mine].

There is an inevitable ambiguity in the attraction an educated man of the city feels toward the peasant and the subproletarian. Collodi's attitude toward the street kid seems to lie somewhere between Manzoni's paternalistic and humorous but quite authentic attraction to his impatient and energetic protagonist Renzo, and Pier

22. "Il ragazzo di strada," in *Tutto Collodi*, pp. 607–18.

Paolo Pasolini's somewhat travailed exaltation of the vitalistic *ragazzi di vita*. As for the contradiction between the picaresque vitality so pronounced in Pinocchio and the street kid and their declarations of a *dolce far niente* credo, it is more apparent than real. When, early on, he testily rejects the Talking Cricket's advice that he learn a trade and make an honest living (since he will not hear of going to school), the puppet says that the only trade he has a disposition for is " 'that of eating, drinking, sleeping, having fun, and living the life of a vagabond from morning to night.' " This is the central article of faith that the street kid and Pinocchio have most in common. Both the Cricket and the Fairy, to whom Pinocchio recites this credo, warn him that those who follow it inevitably end up in jail or in the poorhouse. From their perspective, idleness is socially unproductive energy. But for the street kid and Pinocchio the vision of a life of ease represents a rejection of the demands of a society that would regiment them and set their anarchic and hedonistic vitality in order.

Thus Collodi's true idea of the street kid and, by extension, of Pinocchio is defined best by his humorous zoologico-kinetic collocation of that species on the evolutionary scale: "If the biologists were to study him [i.e., the street kid] in depth, they would make him the connecting link between the lizard and the goat." But Pinocchio differs from the street kid in his naïveté and inborn honesty, his penchant for lying notwithstanding. In contrast to the street kid's conscious and somewhat cynical indifference to the boundaries separating Thine and Mine, the puppet's transgressions are born of simple ignorance. His description of himself after refusing to collaborate with the thieving martens and initiating their capture is fundamentally accurate: " 'Now, you know, I may be a puppet with all the faults in the world, but one fault I'll never have is that of being in

39

cahoots with dishonest people and holding the sack for them.' "

Insofar as Collodi has orchestrated them, the pedagogic restraints imposed upon Pinocchio's spontaneous vitality and hedonistic instincts take other forms than hunger. Only somewhat less pervasive than the specter of hunger is the specter of death. Significantly, the same two kindred specters haunt not only the world of fairy tales, but also Manzoni's *I promessi sposi* and Verga's *I Malavoglia*, where they inspire a prose of tragic grandeur and pathos. For Collodi's child protagonist both specters bear upon the acute separation anxieties to which he is prey. Though the periodic evocation of death serves a positive function in calling Pinocchio and his little readers back to reality and order, its persistent return, sometimes in a key of funerary or black humor, reveals a preoccupation that far exceeds the patterning required by the tale's pedagogic purpose. Pinocchio dies twice: once by hanging, from which Collodi decided *post factum* to resuscitate him, and then by entombment in the belly of the marine monster, from which he emerges with new life.

But the most startling and puzzling representation of the specter of death comes with the first appearance of the Little Girl with blue hair, before Collodi turned her into the Fairy. After a wild runaround to evade the "assassins," the exhausted puppet bangs on the door of a little white house in the midst of the forest:

> Then there came to the window a beautiful Little Girl with blue hair and a face as white as a wax image who, with eyes closed and hands crossed over her breast, without moving her lips at all, said in a voice that seemed to come from the world beyond:
> "There is nobody in this house. They are all dead."

"Well, then you at least open up for me!" cried Pinocchio, weeping and imploring.

"I am dead, too."

"Dead? But then what are you doing there at the window?"

"I am waiting for the bier to come and take me away."

As soon as she said this, the Little Girl disappeared, and the window closed again without making a sound [chapter 15].

It is doubtful that a child would find comic relief from tension and anxiety in the Little Girl's reply to Pinocchio's question "'what are you doing there at the window [if you're dead]?'" As Emilio Garroni notes, the Little Girl's appearance and her role are unmotivated at this point in the story; although her repartee may make us laugh, her reply remains chilling precisely because of its incongruence or, as Garroni puts it, its incongruous congruence. Her witty retort, because of its obviousness and stereotypicality of language, may make the adult reader laugh even as it brings him pain at another level.[23] In the final analysis, then, the joke brings not mirth but fright.

We cannot know just what Collodi had in mind when he introduced the Little Girl as a ghostly harbinger of Pinocchio's own death by hanging. One attribute that remains consistent when she is transformed into the Fairy, sister-mother to the puppet, is the extraordinary cruelty of her pedagogy. The coffin motif, for example, is picked up in chapter 16 when Pinocchio is frightened into taking his medicine by the appearance of the four black rabbit pallbearers carrying *his* coffin into the room. And the motif of the Little Girl's death returns in chapter 23 when Pinocchio, making his way

23. Garroni, *Pinocchio uno e bino* (Rome and Bari, 1975), pp. 89–90.

back to her (as Fairy) after a period of truancy and mis-adventures, finds in place of the little white house a tombstone announcing that she has died of grief at being abandoned by her little brother Pinocchio. The self-lacerating expostulation Pinocchio utters at the tombstone of the presumably dead Fairy is the most explicit expression of the puppet's and perhaps Collodi's separation anxiety, as the puppet equally bewails the loss of his "father" and the death of his "mother."

That the anguish of separation is referred to both parents is in keeping with the themes of Pinocchio as orphan, the child's ambivalent feelings toward his parents, and the tension between asserting independence and the recognition of being, perhaps even the desire to be, dependent. When he later comes across the resuscitated and "grown-up" Fairy who offers to be his mother, Pinocchio's revealing and pathetic exclamation is: " 'For such a long time now I've yearned to have a mother, like all the other boys.' " And even when the puppet has bravely shouldered responsibility, Collodi introduces the motif of the son's dependence on the parents: the Tuna, who had escaped from the Great Shark's belly by following Pinocchio's lead and then comes to the rescue of the drowning puppet and Geppetto, is yet another version or double of the father.

In relation to both parent figures, in fact, Pinocchio's adventures involve a returning no less than a running away. Not long after running away from Geppetto, Pinocchio begins a quest for him with the twin desires to help and to be helped. His story thus is as much about being thwarted in his search for one or the other parent and his attempts to return "home" as it is about escaping from or resisting parental authority. In this sense, *The Adventures of Pinocchio* corresponds to the mainstream of children's literature since the mid–nineteenth century. Isabelle Jan, writing of home as the bright center

to which a child is instinctively drawn and which haunts his dreams when it is out of reach, notes that "about three quarters of the novels written for boys and girls since 1850 tell the story of a lost, abandoned orphan child in search of a family; during one hundred and fifty pages or so he hunts for his mother and father and ends up having found them—or an adequate substitute."[24] Collodi's tale is true to this pattern, in its unique fashion.

II

Where the word *Nose* occurs,—I declare,
by that word I mean a Nose, and nothing more or less
[*Tristram Shandy* 3:31].

For a puppet to behave as *it* might like
were indeed against nature; the movements
that are induced by personal appetites
are not free, but uncalculated and irregular
[Coomaraswamy, "Spiritual Paternity and the Puppet Complex"].

L'Italia è fatta; ora bisogna fare gli Italiani
[Massimo D'Azeglio].

Pinocchio is not merely the type of the motherless child; he is a foundling. The reader is not told how he happened to turn up in Master Cherry's shop as a stray log. Even at this embryonic stage Pinocchio begins to undergo harrowing adventures, for as soon as the practical-minded carpenter notices the piece of wood, he begins to whack away at it with the intention of turning it into a table leg; and when he hears a complaining voice

24. Jan, *On Children's Literature*, trans. Catherine Storr (London, 1973), p. 115. See also Ganna Ottevaere–van Praag, "Il tema della fuga nel libro per l'infanzia prima e dopo 'Pinocchio,'" in *Pinocchio oggi*, Fondazione Nazionale Carlo Collodi (Pescia, 1980), pp. 237–47.

from within it, he seizes the piece of wood with both hands and slams it around the walls of the room. By having a poor wood carver fashion a marionette out of the log and thereby become Pinocchio's putative father, Collodi is able almost from the outset to emblematize the basic clash between an adult utilitarian society and the desire for freedom in its children. Thus Pinocchio's resistance to being molded by his "betters" begins early. He kicks Geppetto in the shins when Master Cherry offers him—still an unshaped piece of wood—to the wood carver who has already made known his designs on him. And scarcely has Geppetto finished carving his eyes than the puppet begins to make faces at him.

But more notorious now than the prematurely mangled nose of Tristram Shandy or the rhetorically grandiose nose of Cyrano de Bergerac, it is Pinocchio's nose with its astonishing propensity to lengthen to alarming dimensions that presents the most clamorous expression of the puppet's filial rebellion. It should not be necessary here to disclaim with Sterne that "where the word *Nose* occurs, I declare, by that word I mean a Nose, and nothing more or less." Nonetheless, the refusal of most critics to admit to any sexual allusions in *Pinocchio* seems too rigidly exclusive. Fernando Tempesti, for example, dismisses the problem by a rhetorical question-*boutade*: "Che ci vuole a dire che il Campanile di Giotto è un simbolo fallico? Non certo fatica mentale" (What does it take to say that Giotto's tower is a phallic symbol? Certainly not any mental effort).[25] However, this quip overlooks the difference in behavior between Giotto's tower and Pinocchio's nose. And though Pinocchio seems for the most part to be prepubescent, even his age is not without a certain ambiguity. The boys crammed into the wagon going to Fun-

25. Tempesti, *Chi era il Collodi*, p. 98.

land are said to be between eight and twelve years old, but in Funland itself they are said to be between eight and fourteen. As for Pinocchio, the range of his activities and attitudes runs the gamut from infantile to adolescent. Both Enrico Mazzanti and Carlo Chiostri, the first two illustrators of *The Adventures of Pinocchio* as a book, in 1883 and 1901 respectively, show us a Pinocchio who in some scenes is assertively adolescent, a feature that is especially striking in the illustrated frontispieces of the two editions.[26]

At any rate, the abundance of jokes and popular superstitions concerning the symbolic equivalence between nose and penis justifies speculation on the matter in Pinocchio's case. The question is how much to make of it. Jung's statement that the penis is only a phallic symbol is much to the point here. When, no sooner than it has been formed, Pinocchio's nose lengthens inordinately and, it would seem, *voluntarily*, while a frantic Geppetto keeps cutting it back, the nose may be taken as a phallic symbol of aggressive self-assertion rather than mere sexuality. It is not necessary to look beyond this for serious Oedipal morbidities in Pinocchio's behavior toward Geppetto and the Fairy. Nor was Collodi

26. The frontispiece of the present work is Mazzanti's. Chiostri's frontispiece is shown on page 468 of this work. Actually Mazzanti's illustrations were preceded by a few vignettes done by Ugo Fleres for the serialized version of the *Giornale per i bambini*. They portray Pinocchio as a marionettelike figure who could not be mistaken for anything other than a full-fledged adolescent. The final illustration presents a metamorphosed or, better, a transfigured flesh-and-blood Pinocchio, as prim and proper as one could hope for, standing inside a display *P*, his arms resting on the lower part of the letter's loop, which has been straightened into a thick horizontal bar representing a desk-top or a lectern (see appendix, p. 463). This "Pinocchio" could almost be taken for a young schoolmaster. The illustrator has recently been identified by Rodolfo Biaggioni, "Pinocchio e l'illustratore perduto," *Schedario* (January–April 1981), p. 20.

writing either in celebration or in repression of the penis and sexual freedom, in any narrowly sexual or procreational sense.

But if Pinocchio is not quite prankish Puck, that impish image of the playful and fertile penis, neither is he too far removed a relation. For the marionette himself, and not just his nose, can be seen as a phallic expression of aggression, vitality, and spontaneity. The episodes of Geppetto cutting back Pinocchio's metonymic nose and the carabiniere catching the runaway puppet up by it are similar in their symbolic and thematic significance to the many other cases in which the hyperkinetic puppet is immobilized.[27] The same is true of the second instance—especially disturbing because of its still more sadistic comicality—of Pinocchio's nose being cut back to size. This time the nose lengthens when the puppet lies to the Fairy, and contrary to his impertinence in the scene with Geppetto, the father figure, here Pinocchio is clearly embarrassed and frightened: "His nose had grown so much that it could no longer pass through the door." Only after letting him cry and scream for more than half an hour does the Fairy summon a great flock of Woodpeckers who perch on the immodest nose and peck away until it is brought back to its usual size. In this incident, the *involuntary* elongation of the nose-

27. Pinocchio seems forever on the move, but he is also forever being immobilized. Such temporary immobilization of the hero is a standard convention in narratives of adventure and quest tales. Pinocchio is stopped short in his first flight by a carabiniere who catches him by the nose; his feet are burned off (a cruelly significant episode of punitive restraint that emphasizes the puppet's feet—emblematic of movement—which Geppetto restores with great art, despite his premonition that Pinocchio will again run away); he is tied up by Fire-Eater and later by the Green Fisherman; he is hanged by the Fox and the Cat; he is caught by the leg in an animal trap and then chained to a dog kennel; his foot is stuck in a door for hours; he is shut up in jail for four months; he is encased in the hulk of a donkey; he is entombed in the belly of the Great Shark.

penis seems a cruelly fantastic representation of poor Pinocchio's self-consciousness. The claustrophobic immobilization is caused by the puppet's sense of shame at lying and even more at being caught, once again by the "nose" as it were.

Commentators tend to pass over Pinocchio's first nasal escapade and think of the nose growing longer only as a punishment for the lies he tells the Fairy. Yet even the second case of spontaneous nose-lengthening occurs before the Fairy appears in the story, to wit, in chapter 5, when the hungry puppet rushes to the boiling kettle above the hearth only to discover that it is all just a painted scene. Here the lengthening of the nose is Collodi's caricatural representation of the Italian idiom *restare con un palmo di naso* (to remain with a hand's span of nose), which is used to express surprise and frustration or befuddlement. With the exception of the first episode, the phenomenon may, if one chooses, be understood in the terms applied by the Italian psychoanalyst E. Servadio, who refers only to the cases of lying. Servadio sees Pinocchio's nose-lengthening propensity as an example of castration *a contrariis*, a representation of a phenomenon or an idea by means of its opposite, as happens in certain witty or joking epithets and expressions. With Pinocchio in mind, he also suggests that a man whose penis were by some act of magic to become monstrously enlarged would feel no less stricken, ridiculed, and impotent than were he to have been castrated![28]

"Children's stories, because they are stories about children written by grown-ups, are predominantly nostalgic," writes Isabelle Jan.[29] Though Collodi seems neither to sentimentalize nor idealize the child, the nostal-

28. See Servadio, "Psicologia e simbolismo nelle *Avventure di Pinocchio*," in *Studi Collodiani*, pp. 573–79.
29. Jan, *On Children's Literature*, p. 124.

gia is surely there, albeit masked; and almost surely his need to exorcise it accounts for much of the ambiguity or secret tension felt by adult readers, most of whom are bound to smile indulgently at Pinocchio but not without some concern at his madcap flights and dangerously childish hopes. We are glad to return to the author a knowing wink of relief and complicity at his reassuring if severe curtailments of the puppet's misguided *élan vital*. For Collodi's ambivalence is also our own, an ambivalence that derives from the regressive pull of the child in us even as we enforce the role of responsible adults upon ourselves. Our idea of maturity and a workable social order necessitates the repression of the child whose amoral vitality and primordiality represent a threat to that idea. Thus we classify children and puppets as ontologically and socially inferior or inchoate beings who do not possess the fullness of humanity. It is no surprise, then, that children's stories are not only written by grown-ups but also are often about growing up.

To have given his protagonist an amphibological nature is the most genial stroke of all Collodi's inventiveness; for from this initial ambiguity, which literally equates a child with a puppet, there stems an endless chain of possible ironies, most of them quite consciously exploited, such as the fact that a "wood" child can be subjected to harsher "corporeal" punishment than a flesh-and-blood child. Although "real boys" and "puppets" are sometimes moralistically posed as opposites in the story, the reader often forgets that Pinocchio is a wooden marionette. His dual status as puppet and child has an apparent nonchalance but Collodi does not seem careless in using one term or the other in connection with Pinocchio. Among the most significant incidents that establish the equivalence of puppet and child is the early scene in which Geppetto carves the

puppet out of the stray piece of wood. No sooner does Pinocchio have arms and hands than he pulls off Geppetto's wig and mockingly puts it on his own head. Disconsolately, the wood carver says: " 'Scamp of a child, you aren't even finished and you're already beginning to lack respect for your father! That's bad, my boy, bad!' " Soon after, when the carabiniere is about to turn over the runaway puppet to Geppetto, the crowd that has gathered comments maliciously: " 'That Geppetto looks like a good man, but he's a real tyrant with *children*. If they leave that poor *puppet* in his hands, he's more than capable of hacking him to pieces' " (my emphasis). And when not Pinocchio but Geppetto is marched off to jail, the wood carver can only stammer: " 'Wicked *child*! And to think that I worked so hard to make him into a nice *puppet*!' "

Intentionally or not, Geppetto's utterance is particularly if ambiguously revelatory. The well-known derogatory connotations of *puppet*, of course, are intended to apply to Pinocchio, especially the strong Italian connotation of *burattino* as one whose actual words and deeds contradict his professed beliefs so that he seems to act without any moral sense of his behavior, much like an undisciplined child. Significantly, in the nineteenth century *ragazzo* (child) was used interchangeably with *burattino* in idioms expressing just this idea in connection with adults. Moreover, *burattino* was used to connote someone who is so lacking in will or opinions that his movements are regulated by someone else, as in the case of real puppets. From out of his poverty and his patriarchal vision, this is just what Geppetto wanted—a son who would be a puppet in his service:

> [GEPPETTO:] "This morning an idea popped into my head."
> [MASTER CHERRY:] "Let's hear it."
> [GEPPETTO:] "I thought of making myself a

fine wooden puppet; but a wonderful puppet who
can dance, and fence, and make daredevil leaps. I
intend to travel around the world with this puppet
so as to earn my crust of bread and a glass of
wine."

Even more important as an archetypal image or pattern than the redemptive imprisonment in the sea monster's belly is this image of the human being as a puppet
created by a Master Puppeteer. The Old Testament account of the creation of Adam is much in this vein but
allows the puppet to have a will and therefore a willfulness of his own. The man-as-puppet archetype also appears in Plato's discussion of how best to educate youths
so that they will become perfect citizens. Plato suggests
that the puppet, man, is pulled in various directions by
the strings of his passions, his likes and dislikes,
whereas he should let himself be guided (pulled) by the
golden cord of reason, "called by us the common law
of the state" (*Laws* 1:644). Plato's passage was undoubt-
edly known to Collodi, being one that would have
come up in the talk about puppets common among his
fellow drama critics in nineteenth-century Europe, particularly in Italy, where puppet theater, especially with
the use of marionettes, was vastly popular and never
exclusively juvenile in its appeal and repertoire.

One can easily imagine Collodi discussing Plato's
metaphor with his friend Pietro Coccoluto Ferrigni, the
influential Florentine drama critic and journalist who
published a full-length history of puppets, under the
pen name "Yorick, Son of Yorick," just one year after
the appearance of *Pinocchio* in book form. Indeed, Ferrigni cites Plato's passage with some flourish as proof
that in antiquity even the best spirits derived from puppet shows "the wisest precepts and the most efficacious
examples for directing us poor wretched mortals (prone
to rush into vices by roundabout ways and by shortcuts

alike) to the path of virtue."[30] As both Genesis and Plato's account make plain, there is a proper role for the puppet, man, and to stray from it is dangerous for the puppet and society. It is a mark of Collodi's unconventionality and ambiguity that he can make the theme reflect both his sense of a need for order and his recognition of the imperfections of the adult society that sets the rules for order.

While this twin vision of man-as-puppet resurfaces throughout the tale, it receives its most inventive treatment in chapter 10. When the ever-straying Pinocchio is irresistibly and atavistically drawn to the puppet show, the marionettes on stage ignore their predetermined roles and produce what amounts to a revolt in order to greet him enthusiastically as their brother-in-wood. Their conventional roles are described in ironic matter-of-fact tones by Collodi when he explains what Pinocchio sees upon first entering the theater:

> On the stage Harlequin and Punchinello were seen quarreling with one another, and as usual were threatening to exchange a load of slaps and thwacks at any moment.
> The spectators, completely absorbed, laughed so hard that it hurt as they listened to the squabble of the two puppets who were gesticulating and insulting each other as realistically as if they were two rational beings of this world.

One thinks of the less than edifying behavior of those two "adults" Master Cherry and Geppetto in chapter 2, when they insult and pommel each other in just such a fashion. The early episode indicates that from the outset Collodi was drawing upon the popular puppet shows of his time, although the subsequent changes in Gep-

---

30. Ferrigni, *La storia dei burattini* (Florence, 1884), p. 59. Ferrigni's statement is readily applicable to *Pinocchio*.

petto's character suggest that the author did not begin with a complete idea of his story. The slapstick element of puppet shows would have prepared any reader, child or adult, for the kind of violence that fills the pages of *Pinocchio*. But beyond that even, to a great extent *Pinocchio* is a transposition of the art of the puppet show to the written word, both in a number of specific episodes and, loosely, in an overall sense.[31]

The scene of joy that ensues when the marionettes step out of character, and out of their roles as "rational beings" intent on bashing one another, so as to proclaim Pinocchio one of their own is not tolerated by the audience of human spectators who become restless and begin to yell: " 'On with the show! On with the show!' "

31. The idea that *Pinocchio* owes its central invention of a living puppet to the puppet theater was first hinted at by Giuseppe De Robertis in "Pinocchio, o il teatro dei burattini," *Corriere di Milano*, March 14, 1948 (reprint, *Omaggio a Pinocchio*, Quaderni della Fondazione Carlo Collodi, no. 1 [Florence, 1967], pp. 29–32). Paul Hazard had earlier pointed to a kinship between Pinocchio and the Italian theater by suggesting that Collodi's puppet derives from the stock characters of the commedia dell'arte known as *maschere*: "Before he was called Pinocchio and amused youngsters, he was Harlequin, Punchinello, or Stenterello. He was one of the *maschere*, changeless characters that served as a fixed point for improvisation" (*Books, Children, and Men*, p. 115). Renato Bertacchini, author of the single most exhaustive study on Collodi, speaks of Pinocchio as the *maschera* of the wayward boy within the formula of the boy-as-puppet; see *Collodi narratore* (Pisa, 1961), p. 353. More recently, Tempesti sets forth a highly particularized and questionable thesis that relates not only the puppet but also the essence of Collodi's narrative style specifically with Stenterello, the live Florentine *maschera* who was given to linguistic funambulism and extravagance in general and was especially adept at building up situations in preparation for the delivery of witticisms; see *Chi era il Collodi*, pp. 60–81. Clearly, Collodi is an inveterate prankster with words, and Tempesti's view is useful up to a point. But the effort to explain the very "structure" of the tale in terms of the characteristics of Stenterello's verbal style (as a "structural model") leads to a one-sidedness in his interpretation.

Presumably, the spectators are adults, or adults and very small children, since it is a school day. The school-age boy with whom the puppet engages in conversation outside the theater serves as a foil and example to Pinocchio, to whom he has to read the announcement of the spectacle: a very proper boy with unbending good sense, authorized thereby to ridicule the puppet. Following the disruptive reunion of Pinocchio with his confreres, order is finally restored by an adult figure, Fire-Eater the Master Puppeteer, and the puppets are made to get on with the show. But in having the marionettes break out of their assigned roles, however briefly, Collodi has staged a remarkable version of the ancient theme of the revolt of the puppets—the revolt against authority par excellence. The enforced return to order, however, prefigures the story's ending.[32]

In the tale, Fire-Eater is the most significant double of the father; but he is also a double of the author Collodi who, of course, is the ultimate Master Puppeteer pulling all the strings until Pinocchio the puppet is replaced by the radiant boy he has become. But the "happy ending" of Pinocchio, in its very coherence, is an attempt to apply the coup de grâce to fantasy and the instinct to revolt that each new generation of children must express. Unchecked fantasy might keep us from contributing to society in a positive and useful way, or it might leave us defenseless in a world where the un-

32. In the issue carrying the penultimate installment of *Pinocchio*, the *Giornale per i bambini* published a play for marionettes representing stock figures of the commedia dell'arte tradition. At the play's end, the Venetian-speaking Harlequin is rejoicing that he and Columbine have been brought together by their own affection and volition and that they therefore have no need of strings attached to them. But he is suddenly jerked up and away by the hidden puppeteer, and as the curtain falls his last words are "El filo! El filo! El filo!" (The string! The string! The string!).

scrupulous always lie in wait. Pinocchio, for example, is chastised for his gullibility, that is, his fantasy, no less than for his disobedience, as is the case in the tradition of the Italian novella from the time of Boccaccio. And in keeping with this tradition, Collodi expresses no sympathy for Pinocchio as an underdog or as a victim of social injustice, though the latter is simultaneously satirized when the bleary-eyed gorilla judge, moved to the brink of tears by the puppet's account of how he has been cheated, declines to order a hunt for the swindlers but has the puppet thrown in jail for having let himself be duped.[33] But another danger lurks in fantasy. Precisely because it can be a liberating force, fantasy must be curbed, and Pinocchio's willingness to believe in utopian alternatives to hard work, such as the Field of Miracles and Funland, is itself as potentially explosive as it is foolish. Thus Collodi never lets *The Adventures of Pinocchio* be mistaken for a fantasy or a fairy tale, although he makes happy parodic use of fairy-tale modes and the fantastic.

As for the radiant boy who stands before the mirror at the story's end, one hesitates to call him Pinocchio, despite Collodi's retention of the name. The real Pinocchio stands propped against a chair, a lifeless marionette that the priggish and anomalous bourgeois "prince" now looks at and comments on with the story's closing words: "Pinocchio turned and looked at it; and after he

33. Collodi's sardonic sense of humor in connection with the real, or adult, world is also evident in the episode that brings Pinocchio's four months of imprisonment to a close. At the declaration of the general amnesty that empties the prisons, the jailer retains Pinocchio for not being among "the elect" until the puppet indignantly and cleverly tells him, without lying, that indeed he too is a "rogue." More than light-hearted ambiguity, this play on the double meaning of the word *rogue* is an expression of Collodi's deep pessimism concerning the real world and its "justice." This vision is shared in the nineteenth century by his predecessor, the religious Manzoni, and by his contemporary, the nonreligious Verga.

had looked at it for a while, he said to himself with a great deal of satisfaction: 'How funny I was when I was a puppet! And how glad I am now that I've become a proper boy!' " The discarded puppet so smugly scorned by the new Pinocchio may well be the story's cruelest image, and Collodi himself was among the first to feel uneasy about the tale's ending, especially Pinocchio's last statement, which he once told a friend he could not remember having written. Although some critics have surmised that Collodi's editor may have inserted the words, the manuscript copy leaves no doubt that it was Collodi who wrote them.[34] His subsequent uneasiness betrays the ambivalent attitude he had toward his wayward, unregimented puppet and the deep-rooted sympathy he had for the free-living street kid.

It may well be that Collodi later sought to atone for the ending of *Pinocchio* in his less fortunate sequel, *Pipì or the Little Pink Monkey* (1886), when he has the young simian's father say: " 'Watch out, Pipì! If you keep on aping men, sooner or later you'll become a man too. And then! Then you'll regret it bitterly; but it'll be too late!' "[35] In a reversal of the happy transformation of the puppet into a respectable miniature adult, Pipì is dressed as a human being and looks at himself in the mirror, as Pinocchio does after his final metamorphosis, only to howl in bitter protest: " 'Oh, how ugly I am . . . I'm no longer myself! . . . I'm no longer Pipì! . . . They've dressed me up like a man . . . and I've become an awful monster. I don't want to stay here anymore . . . I want

---

34. Of the original manuscript in Collodi's hand, only the last two chapters are extant. Tempesti makes a careful inquiry into the differences between the autograph of the two chapters and the printed text, differences that indicate considerable editing on the part of someone connected with the *Giornale per i bambini*; see *Chi era il Collodi*, pp. 119–33. But see also Pollidori's critical edition of *Pinocchio*, which includes a facsimile of the autograph.

35. *Tutto Collodi*, p. 201.

to go away . . . I want to go back home'" (p. 216). And although on this occasion he throws off the clothes and runs away, this poor monkey, like Pinocchio, will be saved at the end of the story, elegantly clothed and ready to accompany his young master.

Now, it can hardly be doubted that children readily accept and approve of Pinocchio's last and most marvelous metamorphosis. So too adults are bound to approve of it, if only because the alternative would be a character on the order of Peter Pan, the boy who expressly refuses to become a man. Barrie's play has its own sad, almost tragic ending: Peter fluttering about quite alone while Wendy and the other kids have decided to go about the business of growing up. In the final analysis *Peter Pan* voices a revolt against parents and adulthood. If we find it unacceptable, it is because the stubbornly sentimental refusal to bring fantasy—an impotent fantasy in this case—down to earth makes Barrie's cult of the child seem morbidly regressive.

A better antihero to the end and one with whom adults may prefer to identify themselves, Huckleberry Finn walks away from "sivilization" because, as he says, he has been there before. But the boy Huck has an innate humanity and a sense of morality that neither the infantile Peter Pan nor most of the grown-ups who make up "sivilization" know; moreover, the "territory" into which Huck walks was still available to him.[36] But perhaps we need only to see Pinocchio as an

---

36. *Huckleberry Finn* has its own controversial ending and came close to having a conclusion sadder even than that of *Pinocchio* or *Peter Pan*. In the closing chapters Huck, however uncomfortable he may be about it, yields to the puerile romanticism of Tom Sawyer, who persuades him to play at a humiliating game of saving the runaway slave whom Huck has not only befriended but already actually saved. Only at the very end does Mark Twain redeem Huck by having him turn his back on "sivilization."

adolescent here to realize the truth of Collodi's representation. For the new Pinocchio seems to be at the age when the adolescent, wanting to prove to himself and to others that he is a grown-up, rejects his former self, looking back on his earlier activities as "kid's stuff." In *Pinocchio*, civilization can be spelled with an *s* only in Funland, which Lampwick assures Pinocchio is the only place that offers a truly civilized life for boys, but where in fact the inhabitants are processed for an asinine existence. If, however reluctantly, we find Collodi's happy ending inevitable and right, it must be because as sane adults convinced of the need for social order, we too, despite our unchildlike intellectual capacity to accept the notion of a fortuitous order of things, like to stand on firm moral ground at the end of the story.

Yet the child-in-the-adult will occasionally feel a pull toward the freedom he thinks was his when he was really a child. Children, after all, look forward to adulthood as the Promised Land, whereas adults look back to childhood as the lost Eden. But it need be neither uncritical nostalgia, nor the bad conscience of an adult who has surrendered too completely, nor simply impish perversity that makes today's readers wonder who is more the puppet: the wayward and at times irreverent wooden marionette or the handsome boy-adult who takes hold of the golden cord, never to let go of it again and never again to deviate from the role he must play in society. A reader's resistance or disappointment may derive not from a desire for total retreat from the adult world, but rather from a sense of something excessive and small-minded in the thorough rejection of the puppet by the new Pinocchio. No amount of historicizing will keep us from finding him for his age and even for his times too young to be abandoning the child—that is, spontaneity, exuberance, and fantasy—so completely.

The fantastic in Collodi's hands is not "authentic" fantasy in that it is not posited in the service of alternatives to reality. *Pinocchio*'s author belongs to an illustrious line of Italian writers who display a deep-rooted rationalism, not to say skepticism, and a disposition to spoof at magic and the supernatural, or the fantastical. This attitude and manner are best known to us from the *Orlando Furioso*, at once the most fantastical and most reality-grounded work of Italian literature. In canto 24 of Ariosto's poem, the knight Astolfo rises astride a hippogryph to a mountaintop in Eden. There, before being carried in Elijah's chariot to the moon, where he will recover Orlando's lost wits, the knight is hosted by John the Evangelist and other saints, who see to it that the hippogryph is fed a proper ration of hay. Collodi's version of Ariosto's hippogryph is the great white Pigeon who, in carrying Pinocchio the thousand miles to the seashore, must stop on the way at a dovecote because he is thirsty; and whereas Astolfo was treated to fruits of Paradise, the ever-hungry Pinocchio must be content with vetch.

Such undercutting of the fantasy world begins with the first phrases of *Pinocchio*. The opening time-out-of-time formula prepares readers for the world of fantasy; Collodi, however, immediately shatters the fantasy and brings us back into a world of humble reality: "No, children, you are wrong. Once upon a time there was a piece of wood." In place of the expected king stands an ordinary piece of wood, token of a reality principle that denies not only the element of fantasy but also the predictable and the comfortable. But the *ex abrupto* reversal of fantasy is itself quickly followed by a reversal of the real—the piece of wood can feel and talk.

Yet even in the context of this new fantastic element the sense of concrete reality predominates; and in the matter-of-fact interplay between the two elements

throughout the tale the fantastic is never far removed from the familiar. The more unrealistic a matter or an event is, the more likely is Collodi to speak of it in clear, precise terms as though to authenticate its reality. Conversely, he uses homely or otherwise familiar similes to characterize something that at first appears as strange or extraordinary, thereby neutralizing the sense of the fantastic.[37] And when a descriptive detail is needed to support the action, Collodi calls it up out of nowhere: a hedge on the roadside is not mentioned until Pinocchio needs one to jump over, a pine tree appears when the puppet needs something to climb, and the wide canal-ditch filled with dirty water materializes so that the Fox and the Cat can fall into it. The effect might seem to be surrealistic or oneiric, but more often than not the prestidigitation does not arouse a lingering sense of wonder in the reader because the materialized object is one that naturally belongs in its setting.

A number of surrealistic appearances involve more than fleeting, suddenly evoked details, and many of them startle Pinocchio but quickly lose their strangeness by virtue of his immediate recovery and subsequent reaction to the object as merely an item in the realm of ordinary experience. The encounter with the fantastic, that is, does not undermine or distort the very human psychology of Pinocchio. The puppet is scared by the appearance of the black rabbit pallbearers, and he is momentarily nonplussed by a chick that flies out of the egg he intends to cook; but neither he nor the reader questions the reality of these incidents because Collodi does nothing to create the impression that such events are abnormal phenomena. This is so even in the extreme

37. See Vittorio Spinazzola, "Pinocchio e le risorse della fantasia," in *ACME* (Annali della Facoltà di Lettere e Filosofia dell'Università degli Studi di Milano) 22, no. 2 (maggio–agosto 1969): 138.

case of the evidently supernatural appearance of the "dead" Little Girl. Likewise, for all the archetypal or allegorical suggestiveness that the meeting with a great serpent may arouse in us, Pinocchio himself is simply frightened by it as he would be by any other "natural" menace in his path. The fantastic in this encounter too is deflated by an unheroic comic resolution that reminds readers familiar with Italian literature of Luigi Pulci's account of the death of the dwarf giant Margutte by a laughing fit. And when an iron knocker turns into a slippery eel that slithers away down the gutter, the puppet is not even taken aback; rather he shouts with human anger: " 'Oh, is that so? If the knocker has disappeared, I'll just go on knocking by kicking.' "

As for Collodi's landscapes and interiors, they are exclusively functional, their constituent elements conjured up only in the strictest relationship to the feelings and adventures of Pinocchio and, to a lesser degree, of a few other characters. For example, in Geppetto's humble abode objects continue to appear from chapter 3—where the three basic pieces, said to be all, are mentioned—through chapter 7; the accumulation of details is so gradual and so dependent on the puppet's activities, and not vice versa, that one is surprised at their number only after consciously undertaking a retrospective account of them. This technique most readily recalls fairy tales and folktales, which, like the language of the theater, do not generally profit by lengthy descriptive delays. "The absence of all desire to describe unessential details," writes Max Lüthi, "gives the European fairy tale its clarity and precision."[38] Such vivid clarity is achieved by a technique of isolation that ignores everything but the most significant or essential element of a

38. Lüthi, *Once Upon a Time: On the Nature of Fairy Tales* (Bloomington, 1976), p. 50.

scene or event, so that our attention is not allowed to stray from what matters. Although Lüthi is speaking of what he calls the "genuine" or naïvely told fairy tale or folktale of the oral tradition, writers of literary or art fairy tales also make good use of the technique, as does Collodi, who translated a number of the latter.

Related to the technique of the suddenly inserted descriptive notation and to the parodic implementation of the fairy-tale mode are Collodi's casual references to unexpected bits of information, as the occasion requires or allows, for the sake of giving a "plausible" explanation for an attitude or an action that advances the story. The episode of the white Pigeon and the vetch, for example, offers Collodi an opportunity to employ his ironic nonchalance by giving the puppet a fuller life history than the facts of his biography warrant: "All his life the puppet had never been able to stomach vetch. According to him, it nauseated him and turned his stomach; but that evening he ate so much of it that he nearly burst." So too the Great Shark, which like the Pigeon owes something to Ariosto, is cut down to familiar size by having a quite human ailment, one that allows Pinocchio and Geppetto to make their escape: "Now you should know that because the Shark was very old and suffered from asthma and palpitations of the heart, he was obliged to sleep with his mouth open."

Collodi, however, was not writing wholly in a fairy-tale mode, neither of the naïve nor the literary kind, and he did not hesitate to depict somewhat more detailed settings in order to create special effects of psychological, symbolic, or ironic import. Though casually introduced, the hellish night into which Pinocchio goes in search of food at the opening of chapter 6 is particularized by a brief but vivid description that prepares the reader for the puppet's misguided sally into town. Similarly, we have an efficacious, individualized description

of the pitch-black night into which Pinocchio walks when he leaves the Red Crawfish Inn, after an unforgettable circumstantial account of the Rabelaisian meal devoured by the Fox and the Cat. But the attention to particulars is largely focused on the representation of nature, which, true to the general hostility of the world in which Pinocchio moves, most often appears threatening.

In this respect, night plays an important role in the story, the blackest night of all being that which surrounds the puppet in the belly of the leviathan, suggesting a landscape of the inner life: "All around him there was total darkness, so deep and black a darkness that he felt as if he had gone headfirst into a full inkwell." Even this most pregnant darkness of all is playfully lightened by the bizarre yet familiar simile of the inkwell—an image that incidentally reminds us that Collodi's childhood audience is not the poor masses, but the literate middle-class minority familiar with school. Yet the simile, for all its playfulness, does not undercut the symbolic import of its referent.

Occasionally, nature does show a serene face, suggestive of a calm after a stormy or menacing escapade. The most symbolically laden of such moments occurs when Pinocchio and Geppetto, looking up through the wide open mouth of the sleeping sea monster through whose dark interior they have made their way, are able to see "quite a bit of starry sky and very bright moonlight." The sea is calm, and the night so clear that one can see as in daylight. When they jump from the leviathan's gaping mouth and begin to swim, "the sea [is] as smooth as oil and the moon [is] shining in all its splendor." But even here, the references to the weather are of the briefest sort. For the most part Collodi's "settings" are described with an economy that approaches the stage directions for a scene in a play or an opera, rather

than fulfilling one's expectations of a discursive literary narrative.

Though Collodi's descriptive notations are spare, not a few Italian readers have claimed that the environments in *Pinocchio* bear the unmistakable character of Tuscany, albeit a Tuscany *sui generis* without churches, monuments, or the Arno. In particular they point to a landscape that for all its generalized features is the product of a mid-nineteenth-century Tuscan mentality, accustomed to an intimate relationship with city, countryside, and sea.[39] Much of this impression may derive from Collodi's language, which some critics censure as irritatingly regional. Most notably, the contemporary Tuscan novelist Carlo Cassola finds the lively inventiveness of situation and action in *Pinocchio* to be vitiated by a characteristic recourse to linguistic provincialism and witticisms—the famous *arguzia toscana*.[40] But even if a psycholinguistic insularity and protective miniaturization of the world through the use of Tuscan is admitted, Cassola's complaint is too strong. In the nineteenth century, far more than at any other time, the perennial and thorny *questione della lingua*—the problem of molding a literary and, eventually, a spoken language for all Italians—had political as well as cultural implications. While the Risorgimento brought about an ever-increasing use of the national language as it emerged, the years immediately following political unification saw a revitalized interest in and a renewed use of the various dialects that constituted the native spoken languages of most Italians. In some cases the revived use of dialects reflected a desire to make Italians

---

39. Felice Del Beccaro, "Il paesaggio in *Pinocchio*," in *Omaggio a Pinocchio* (Florence, 1967), pp. 67–85; see also Luigi Santucci, *La letteratura infantile* (Milan, 1958), pp. 155–58.
40. Cassola, "Riflessioni su *Pinocchio*," in *Studi Collodiani*, p. 122.

more familiar with one another, an aim illustrated by Collodi in a series of instructional manuals, *Il viaggio per l'Italia di Giannettino* (1880, 1885, 1886), that offer examples of Italian dialects.

Among the most striking aspects of Italian cultural life has been this discrepancy between the national literary language and the different local forms of speech. Every major author of the nineteenth century, from Manzoni to Verga, had to face the task of transforming into the national language what in great part had come to him more spontaneously in a dialect. In this respect, no Italian writer seems as unself-conscious about his language as Collodi in *Pinocchio*. Of course, he was not trying to write a work of high literature, but neither did he intend a merely popular one; and he was too desirous of contributing to the creation of a standard national language to confine his idiom exclusively to a vernacular. Thus while he believed in the primacy of Florentine speech over all other dialects, he did not wish to restrict "Italian" to the parlance of his native city. (That his tale was to appear in a periodical published in Rome, which in 1870 became the nation's capital, further precluded any such notion.) His aim was to offer an Italian with a Tuscan bias or flavor. *Pinocchio*, after all, was written for the same middle-class public of children and adults for whom he wrote *Giannettino*, *Minuzzolo*, and *Il viaggio per l'Italia di Giannettino*, instructional texts that shared the civic-minded purpose of unifying Italians into one nation.

To be sure, one does not have to read very far in *Pinocchio* to happen upon one Tuscanism and another. Yet for all the local linguistic color of his little classic, Collodi has his chosen idiom under control—devoid of the extreme vernacular indulgence he allowed in some of his earlier polemical journalism and literary sketches. The compulsory but, from the standpoint of Italian,

pleonastic use of *gli* or *egli* as a subject pronoun before a verb beginning with a vowel is hardly overindulged. After the opening page, despite the familiar and even colloquial tone, Collodi as narrator does not resort to this *gli* or its feminine counterpart *la*. One can hardly object if he allows its use by the emotionally over-wrought puppet, when he sees his father in a storm-tossed skiff far out at sea and exclaims in his native tongue: "Gli è il mi' babbo! gli è il mi' babbo!" And when Pinocchio excitedly tells the Dolphin that his is the best father in the world, the pleonastic *gli* introduces one of the most Tuscan outbursts of all—"gli è il più babbo buono del mondo"—where the superlative *il più* is separated from its adjective *buono* by the noun that is modified. Such syntax is possible only in popular Florentine speech and will seem perverse to other Italians. Indeed some editors have taken it as a typographical error and have "corrected" the word order. Yet the local linguistic flavor of the tale in general, precisely as in the specific case of this pleonastic *gli*, is much more pronounced in the dialogues than in the narration. Some of the Tuscanisms used by Collodi have acquired the same meanings in standard Italian by virtue of the tale's popularity. Others have remained restricted to Tuscan usage, and a few have lost all currency so that today not even Florentines are absolutely sure of their precise meaning.[41]

As for the pervasive endearing diminutive *-ino*, which more than anything else in Florentine speech

41. Interestingly, the two cases of the pleonastic *gli* referred to occur in phrases in which the Tuscan word for father—*babbo*—occurs. In standard Italian the phrases would be rendered: "È mio padre! è mio padre!" and "È il padre più buono del mondo" (or "È il migliore padre del mondo"). *Babbo* (father, dad) has reached beyond Tuscany but not without great resistance; and both northerners and southerners would usually say *papà* in a similar sit-

might create the impression of a too cozy familiarizing of reality, Collodi's use of it, while admittedly frequent, is often far from casual and is apt to carry ironic weight in his deceptively blithe prose. The prevalence of this particular diminutive suffix in any Tuscan-intoned speech or narration is made still more inevitable because the diminutive is often used simply as an equivalent of the standard form of the word without any reference to size or affective value. This convention creates problems not only for the non-Italian, let alone translators, but also for the non-Florentine Italian. It is especially troublesome when one tries to capture the exact value of such recurrent key words in *Pinocchio* as *ciuchino* and *ragazzino*, which alternate with the standard forms *ciuco* (ass) and *ragazzo* (kid). Even a *vecchino* may be no more—or less—than a *vecchio* (old man).

Nonetheless, a diminutive or affective intimation clings to those words for which a neutral form is still in use. A process of eliminating a number of diminutives from Collodi's text can be traced in the editions following the first. How much, if anything, the author had to do with such changes in the editions printed in his lifetime cannot be determined. But certainly the *vecchino* who dumps an enormous basinful of water on the hungry Pinocchio awaiting a handout of food, the diabolically simpering *Omino* who travels around the world enticing boys to Funland, and the duped runaways who

---

uation. Indeed, for the inhabitants of some regions of southern Italy *babbo* is laughable inasmuch as it recalls *babbeo* (blockhead). Although the standard Italian *padre* is itself a Tuscan form and is sometimes used even in popular Tuscan speech, *babbo* is so natural for all speakers of the region, regardless of social, economic, or cultural differences that even the Fairy uses it spontaneously. The narrating voice in the tale also uses *babbo* most of the time, but *padre* does appear in a few instances, which seem to be dictated by the greater solemnity of the context.

eventually metamorphose into so many *ciuchini* are not endearing or "cute" figures. Precisely in connection with the asinized puppet, Collodi revels in one of his more circumstantial and ironic descriptions when he details the gaiety in which the "famous" *CIUCHINO PINOCCHIO* is bedecked at the time of his much heralded first appearance before the public. He concludes his description with the apparently endearing but actually ironic comment: "Era insomma un ciuchino da innamorare!" (In short, he was a [little] donkey to steal your heart away). There is often the same ironic interplay between the lively Tuscan flavor of Collodi's Italian and his sardonic world view as there is between the fantastic and the real.

Nothing beyond a reading of *Pipì o lo scimmiottino color di rosa* is needed to make one see that in *Pinocchio* Collodi was writing as much for himself and other adults as he was for children. For in *Pipì*, as Aldo Cibaldi notes, the language is often affectedly babyish, and an adult reader is conscious of an author who is deliberately catering to a specific audience of little readers.[42] Of course, there *is* a way of talking to children without falling into baby talk, especially when it is storytelling time. Given Collodi's presumed audience, it is this *spoken* storytelling manner that forms the basis of *Pinocchio*'s style: strong gestural and acoustic mimesis, hyperbolic adjectives and similes to magnify in contradistinction to diminutives, and interventions by a narrator who occasionally admonishes his little listeners or asks them to guess at events only to move on quickly with the story.

This oral mode is complemented by the dialogues, psychologically and linguistically attuned to characters

42. Cibaldi, *Storia della letteratura per l'infanzia e l'adolescenza* (Brescia, 1967), p. 165.

and situations, that constantly alternate with the narration and possess, like the narration, an essentiality that advances the action. The vibrancy and naturalness of Collodi's language never give way to cuteness or false naïveté. Even when his prose becomes more complex and ironically charged, through a tone or phrases that allude to a variety of literary traditions, there is little or no diminishing of the impression of spontaneity, so wittily and unself-consciously are the literary components integrated into the swift flow of oral storytelling.

Perhaps the most striking and lasting impression created by the prose of *Pinocchio* is in fact its rapidity.[43] This swiftness characterizes the tale throughout, at least until the adagio movement that accompanies the puppet's period of conversion. The puppet's paroxysmal résumés of his misadventures punctuate the narration, always following thematic pauses represented by his being checked in his reckless flights. However, the pauses themselves enhance the sense of rapidity by bringing into relief the swift narrative that precedes and follows. While a practical purpose is served by the rapid-fire résumés in a sporadically serialized story—to remind readers of important events after long intervals between installments—they counter the narrative pauses by giving a still greater sense of the rush of events.

The swiftness of the prose itself, in short, is an integral part of the story's principal motifs and images—the hyperkinetic marionette on the loose and on the road,

43. In agreement with Fredi Chiappelli, "Sullo stile del Lorenzini," *Letteratura* 1, nos. 5–6 (September–December 1953): 110–18, critics have rightly spoken of Collodi's linguistic sureness and the swiftness of his prose. Chiappelli relates Collodi's love of "swiftness" to an irresistible need for diversional variety, an accurate characterization which suggests at least one important reason that *Pinocchio* must be considered a "minor" classic when placed beside the novels of Manzoni and Verga.

forever tumbling into adventures.[44] The long stretches of time during which Pinocchio is not on the road are given the barest notice, except his stay in Funland—a waystop on the road, allowing for an implicitly moralizing description of the life that leads to one's becoming an ass—and the description of his redemptive life with Geppetto (chapter 36), which offers a lesson in what it takes to become a boy-adult. But the road is at the heart of the adventures. Aside from the actual and frequently mentioned country roads (and main road or highway) and town streets as such, the settings in which the puppet often finds himself are metaphorical extensions of the road, milieus in which the quest or journey motif is developed, although each may also have a singular symbolic value in the context of the tale. Thus there are the country fields, the air, the forest (with its own path), and in the last chapter, shore and sea.[45] The "road" is everything outside the security of home and school, and because the puppet, between his initial rebellion and his final reconciliation with his father (the end of the road and the quest), moves for the most part outside the confines of such security Collodi's tale is not merely "the story of a puppet" but "the adventures of Pinocchio."

---

44. Pinocchio's nervous energy, his frenetic mobility, and the chases or flights (by land, sea, and air) bring to mind the early silent comic cinema with its great chase scenes. In string puppets, of course, motion and action are of the essence.

45. The motif of the *strada*—the road—is given excellent treatment by Renato Bertacchini, "Epifanie e segni del paesaggio nelle *Avventure di Pinocchio*," in *C'era una volta un pezzo di legno: La simbologia di Pinocchio*, Fondazione Nazionale Carlo Collodi (Milan, 1981), pp. 113–38, which supplements Bertacchini's treatment of the concept of "adventures" in *Pinocchio* in his volume *Collodi narratore*. See also the fine article by Giorgio De Rienzo, "La fuga di Pinocchio," in *Narrativa Toscana dell'ottocento* (Florence, 1975), pp. 281–343.

Preface to
the Text and Translation

The Italian text given here is that of the critical edition published as the capstone of the centennial celebrations by the Fondazione Nazionale Carlo Collodi: *Le avventure di Pinocchio*, ed. Ornella Castellani Pollidori (Pescia, 1983). The concluding serial installment of *Pinocchio* was printed in the *Giornale per i bambini* on January 25, 1883. Within two weeks, in February, the first book edition was printed in Florence by Felice Paggi. The summarizing chapter headings, which have become an integral part of Collodi's text, were written for Paggi's edition. The four editions published by Paggi appeared successively in 1883, 1886, 1887, and 1888. The fifth edition, published by R. Bemporad e Figlio in 1890, came out shortly after Collodi's death.

For her critical edition, Pollidori has privileged Bemporad's edition, following her conviction that Collodi personally attended to the revision of the successive printings of his text until the year of his death. Despite her careful scrutiny of the several editions and the extant autograph of the last two chapters, her ascription of this responsibility to Collodi remains a conjecture. At the least, even she is obliged to acknowledge that others played some role in making emendations, not to mention the respective typesetters, who must be held accountable for a large number of errors. To judge from what we know of Collodi's life and working habits, however, it seems much more likely that his corrections were limited to those made in preparing the text for Paggi's first book edition. This opinion is shared by more than one editor, the most philologically sound of whom was Amerindo Camilli, responsible for an earlier

"critical edition" of *Pinocchio* (Florence, 1946). It is also the view of Fernando Tempesti who, in his edition published hard upon Pollidori's (Milan, 1983), rejects both her line of argument and her choice of a copy text. Tempesti's edition is important for its annotations on the language and style of *Pinocchio* and for its suggestive references to the theatrical aspects of the tale. But both Camilli and Tempesti make their own emendations of it, which is indicative of the serious flaws in the first edition.

Nonetheless, Pollidori's volume remains the definitive critical edition, complete with a splendid apparatus that includes all the variants, down to commas and capitals, from the serial printing to the fifth edition. (However, she was unable to locate the rarest of the rare early editions, the third. Thanks to the Fondazione, which recently acquired a photocopy, I was able to consult the third edition. Save for an additional full-page illustration, the text seems identical to the second edition.) Among its many riches, Pollidori's volume also includes a critique of the main editions of the tale after the author's death, a fine discussion of Collodi's language in relation to standard Italian, and a brief glossary of *fiorentinismi*. Though one may raise legitimate questions concerning her choice of the text to be privileged, the fifth edition does appear almost to have completed a process, begun with the second edition, of weeding out the errors of the first. Pollidori has carried this process still further, purging those errors intended as "corrections" that were introduced in the new printings down to the fifth edition itself. Without agreeing with all her restorations, one must acknowledge that she has thereby offered as clean a text as one can expect.

For purposes of the present bilingual volume, it should also be noted that the substantive differences between the fifth and the first edition, though sometimes significant, are not extensive. There is a slight increase

in the interpolation of brief explanatory phrases in apposition to certain words, a didactic measure meant for Collodi's little readers or listeners and one already evident in the tale's serialized version in the *Giornale*, especially beginning with chapter 16, that is, after Collodi decided to resuscitate his puppet and continue his adventures. There is also an endeavor to divest words of their Tuscan form in favor of the "national" language, a feature Tempesti holds was already programmatic in Collodi's revisions for the first edition. However, this tendency is countered by a less pronounced effort to accomplish just the reverse. The more significant discrepancies between the first and fifth editions, Pollidori's most important restorations, and her rare interventions—two, in chapter 30—are discussed in my notes to the text.

Since the appearance of the first English version of *Pinocchio* in 1892, the tale has received well over a hundred complete or nearly complete translations, abridgments, *rifacimenti*, and adaptations for the theater. The vast majority of them are reductive, by virtue of either abbreviating and adapting or giving monochromatic renderings that indicate no awareness of Collodi's situational and linguistic irony. One might think it less necessary to bowdlerize *Pinocchio* than, say, *Gulliver's Travels* in editions meant for young readers. Yet Collodi's tale has undergone a similar fate, primarily but not exclusively when rendered into English. Clearly, there is much in Collodi's tale that translators and adapters (including Walt Disney) have felt obliged to delete or change in order to make it a "proper" children's story. A partial account of some of the indignities and insensitive renditions *Pinocchio* has suffered in the United States, especially because of moral and pedagogic concerns, is provided by Richard Wunderlich and Thomas J. Morrissey, "The Desecration of *Pinocchio* in the United States," *Horn Book Magazine* 58, no. 2 (April

1982): 205–11, and "Pinocchio Before 1920: The Popular and Pedagogical Traditions," *Italian Quarterly* 23, no. 88 (Spring 1982): 61–72. In Italian there is Nancy D. Sachse's essay *Pinocchio in U.S.A.* (Pescia, 1981), which lists the translations and adaptations of *Pinocchio* published in the United States.

For the situation in Great Britain, one may consult Franklin Samuel Stych's *Pinocchio in Gran Bretagna e Irlanda* (Pescia, 1971) and "Anglosaxon Attitudes to Collodi in the Seventies," *Studi Collodiani*, Fondazione Nazionale Carlo Collodi (Pescia, 1976), pp. 581–85. Among the English versions noteworthy for their greater, though still relative, faithfulness to the original, in addition to the very first by Mary E. Murray (London, 1892) are those by Jane McIntyre (New York and London, 1959); E. Harden (1944; rpt. Middlesex, England, and Baltimore, 1974); Luisa Rapaccini (Florence, 1971); Jane Fior (London, 1975); and M. L. Rosenthal (New York, 1983). But even in these better versions— inaccuracies and omissions aside—what one misses most is a sufficient sense of Collodi's linguistic irony and word play and the oral and gestural storytelling qualities of the narrator's comments. The latter is lost in the translators' tendencies to break up the many longer sentences of the narration and even of Pinocchio's periodic breathless and somewhat asyntactical accounts of his misadventures. The translators thereby also inevitably lose the semantically charged swiftness of Collodi's prose. One reads these versions easily enough— they are well written—but one does not listen to them. Several translators also frequently expand or add to Collodi's own sometimes obstructive didactic interpolations, a tendency particularly troublesome in Rosenthal's version. Such alterations only augment the impression that the texts are intended to cater exclusively to young readers.

The present translation, the first based on Pollidori's critical edition, aims chiefly if not solely to be as philologically close to the letter, imagery, and syntax of Collodi's text as tolerable English allows. I can only hope that I have not stretched English too far in my determination not to stray far from this ideal, beyond which I have no philosophy of translation to expound. Everyone is familiar with the thought best expressed in the Italian *tradurre = tradire* or, if one is more aggressively ill-disposed, *traduttore = traditore*. Yet dare one must, consoled or haunted, as the case may be, by the truth expressed by Walter Benjamin in an essay on the subject: "There is no muse of philosophy, nor is there one of translation."

In the notes to the text and translation, the editions of *Pinocchio* prepared by Ornella Castellani Pollidori and Fernando Tempesti are referred to by the surnames of the respective editors. I have made ample use of the other fundamental critical instruments that no translator or scholar of Collodi's writings and language can do without. I refer to the following nineteenth-century dictionaries, three of them with a specifically declared Florentine or Tuscan bias: N. Tommaseo and B. Bellini, *Dizionario della lingua italiana* (Turin, 1865–1879); G. B. Giorgini and E. Broglio, *Novo vocabolario della lingua italiana secondo l'uso di Firenze* (Florence, 1877–1897); P. Petrocchi, *Novo dizionario universale della lingua italiana* (Milan, 1887–1891); G. Rigutini and P. Fanfani, *Vocabolario italiano della lingua parlata, novamente compilato da G. Rigutini e accresciuto di molte voci, maniere e significati* (Florence, 1893). I have of course also used recent dictionaries, the most important of which, in the eleven volumes that have been printed to date, has reached *oracolo*: S. Battaglia, *Grande dizionario della lingua italiana* (Turin, 1961–).

Brief Remarks
on the Illustrations

IN AN ABSOLUTE OR IDEAL SENSE, *Pinocchio* is betrayed
by any attempt at a figurative representation. Collodi's
paucity of descriptive detail—whether of settings or of
characters (humans and humanized animals, not to
mention the wooden puppet, or puppet-boy, whose
only truly distinctive physical trait is "an enormously
long nose")—and his ironic merger of realistic and fantastic elements seem to make the verbal text fundamentally recalcitrant to pictorial reduction and therefore
best left to the reader's (or listener's) imagination. Yet,
paradoxically, just this ambiguity and suggestiveness
make *Pinocchio* so tempting a challenge to illustrators.
Of Italian literary works, only Dante's *Divine Comedy*
has elicited a quantitatively comparable iconographic
tradition.

The decision to include here, interspersed in the text,
the illustrations that accompanied the first book edition
of *Le avventure di Pinocchio* derives from the wish to
present the tale as it appeared in its historicocultural
context and as most Italians since then have grown up
with it. For despite the more than 150 illustrators the
story has had in Italy alone, Enrico Mazzanti's illustrations have been reproduced, in part or in toto, in numerous printings of the story, although a number of the
sketches done by Carlo Chiostri for the 1901 edition are

1. In the appendix to the present volume are reproduced a few of
the most memorable of Chiostri's illustrations as well as the vignettes done by Ugo Fleres expressly for the tale when it appeared in serialized form in the *Giornale per i bambini*. Mazzanti
added illustrations to the second through fourth book editions,
until the original sixty-two had become eighty-three. The most

equally impressed in the Italian conscience.[1] Both Mazzanti and Chiostri have the merit of reflecting Collodi's world. In response to a story that is evocative and suggestive rather than descriptive, Chiostri seeks to introduce the fantastic into the heart of daily reality, while Mazzanti, moving in the opposite direction, "fantasticates" the real.[2] Though there is something broadly "European" about Mazzanti's illustrations—they reveal the influence of the great French and English illustrators of the nineteenth century—both men ground Collodi's story in a humble and basically "Tuscan" world. Beginning with Attilio Mussino's illustrations (often splendid in their own right, the first in color, and the first in which the Fox and the Cat are clothed and wholly anthropomorphized) for Bemporad's 1911 edition, the world that Collodi moved in disappears from the iconographic tradition, with the perhaps inevitable result that illustrators would henceforth vie with the author and obtrude their own versions of *Pinocchio* rather than try to second Collodi's text.

Mazzanti's participation in the first edition of Collodi's masterpiece resulted in a relationship that is on the level of such celebrated nineteenth-century "pairs" as Cruikshank/Dickens and Tenniel/Carroll. Mazzanti had the advantage of being Collodi's friend and of having already illustrated several of the author's books for children, including his translation of Perrault's fairy

---

interesting of these is the nocturnal scene of Pinocchio and Geppetto on the Tuna's back (chapter 36), introduced in the third edition as a full-page photogravure, traversal to the facing printed page. This and a few others of Mazzanti's illustrations included in later editions are reproduced in the appendix, p. 463.

2. See the fine remarks printed in the splendid catalogue produced for the exhibition held in Florence between September and December 1981: Valentino Baldacci and Andrea Rauch, *Pinocchio e la sua immagine* (Florence, 1981).

tales, published in 1875 by Paggi in Florence. One can safely assume that Collodi was aware of the nature of the illustrations Mazzanti was preparing for *Pinocchio*, and it is not hazardous to suggest that a true collaboration took place in the sense that the two men may have discussed at least some aspects of the pictorial interpretation. In any case, Mazzanti's "narrative" vein is clear enough. He does not insist, as Chiostri later does, on the moralizing side of the story. Rather, he frequently catches Collodi's ironical resolution even of scenes that have the potential or danger of falling into what would otherwise be sentimentalizing or terrifying, as when he follows the text to the letter, as it were, in his representation of Pinocchio's hanging: the puppet swings violently in the wind "like the clapper of a joyously ringing bell." The themes of swiftness and flight, thematically and syntactically central to Collodi's tale, are likewise felicitously drawn, sometimes most efficaciously by an original use of the technique of the silhouette. The silhouette is used to good effect also in rendering the nocturnal motif, as in the marvelous representation of the midnight appearance of the diabolical "little man" in his wagon. Fernando Mazzocca has rightly noted that Mazzanti sees *Pinocchio* essentially as an amusing *educazione sentimentale*, a picaresque journey with a happy ending: "Suffice it to place side by side the illustrated frontispiece—where the hero triumphs with an air somewhere between bravado and silly stubbornness—and the final illustration, where the cheerful, curly-haired boy points, without regrets, to the empty form of the puppet."[3]

3. Fernando Mazzocca, "Tra Romanticismo e Realismo: il Pinocchio 'europeo' di Mazzanti e il Pinocchio 'toscano' di Chiostri," in Fondazione Nazionale Carlo Collodi, *Studi Collodiani* (Pescia, 1976), p. 376; my translation.

Indeed, in that last illustration, the marionette—the "real" Pinocchio—stands propped against a chair, not only lifeless, but very much like the hanged and presumably dead Pinocchio at the end of chapter 15: "after giving a great shudder, he remained there as though frozen stiff."

In the present volume, Mazzanti's illustrations are reproduced in the English text. Details of these illustrations prepared by book designer Wolfgang Lederer for this edition appear in the Italian text.

Le Avventure
di Pinocchio

The Adventures
of Pinocchio
Story of a Puppet

CAPITOLO I

Come andò che Maestro Ciliegia,
falegname, trovò un pezzo di legno,
che piangeva e rideva come un bambino.

C'era una volta . . .

– Un re! – diranno subito i miei piccoli lettori.

– No, ragazzi, avete sbagliato. C'era una volta un pezzo di legno.

Non era un legno di lusso, ma un semplice pezzo da catasta, di quelli che d'inverno si mettono nelle stufe e nei caminetti per accendere il fuoco e per riscaldare le stanze.

Non so come andasse, ma il fatto gli è che un bel giorno questo pezzo di legno capitò nella bottega di un vecchio falegname, il quale aveva nome mastr'Antonio, se non che tutti lo chiamavano maestro Ciliegia, per via della punta del suo naso, che era sempre lustra e paonazza, come una ciliegia matura.

Appena maestro Ciliegia ebbe visto quel pezzo di legno, si rallegrò tutto; e dandosi una fregatina di mani per la contentezza, borbottò a mezza voce:

– Questo legno è capitato a tempo; voglio servirmene per fare una gamba di tavolino. –

Detto fatto, prese subito l'ascia arrotata per cominciare a levargli la scorza e a digrossarlo; ma quando fu lì per lasciare andare la prima asciata, rimase col braccio sospeso in aria, perché sentì una vocina sottile sottile, che disse raccomandandosi:

– Non mi picchiar tanto forte! –

Figuratevi come rimase quel buon vecchio di maestro Ciliegia!

Girò gli occhi smarriti intorno alla stanza per vedere

CHAPTER I

How it happened that Master Cherry,
a carpenter, found a piece of wood
that laughed and cried like a little boy.

Once upon a time, there was . . .

"A king!" my little readers will say right away.

No, children, you are wrong. Once upon a time there was a piece of wood.[1]

It wasn't expensive wood, just the ordinary kind that we take from a woodpile in the winter and put in the stove or the fireplace in order to get a fire going and warm up the rooms.

I don't know how it came about, but the fact of the matter is that one fine day this piece of wood turned up in the workshop of an old carpenter whose name was Master Anthony,[2] although everybody called him Master Cherry on account of the tip of his nose, which was shiny and purplish like a ripe cherry.

As soon as Master Cherry saw the piece of wood he was overjoyed, and rubbing his hands with satisfaction he muttered in a low voice:

"This piece of wood has turned up at the right time: I think I'll use it to make a table-leg."

Without further ado he quickly grasped his sharpened hatchet so as to begin to remove the bark and whittle the wood down. But just as he was about to strike the first blow he stopped, with his arm raised high, because he heard a thin little voice say pleadingly:

"Don't hit me so hard!"

Imagine how startled good old Master Cherry was.

He rolled his frightened eyes around the room to see

di dove mai poteva essere uscita quella vocina, e non vide nessuno! Guardò sotto il banco, e nessuno; guardò dentro un armadio che stava sempre chiuso, e nessuno; guardò nel corbello dei trucioli e della segatura, e nessuno; aprì l'uscio di bottega per dare un'occhiata anche sulla strada, e nessuno. O dunque? . . .

– Ho capito; – disse allora ridendo e grattandosi la parrucca – si vede che quella vocina me la son figurata io. Rimettiamoci a lavorare. –

E ripresa l'ascia in mano, tirò giù un solennissimo colpo sul pezzo di legno.

– Ohi! tu m'hai fatto male! – gridò rammaricandosi la solita vocina.

Questa volta maestro Ciliegia restò di stucco, cogli occhi fuori del capo per la paura, colla bocca spalancata e colla lingua giù ciondoloni fino al mento, come un mascherone da fontana.

Appena riebbe l'uso della parola, cominciò a dire tremando e balbettando dallo spavento:

just where that little voice could have come from, but he didn't see anyone. He looked under the workbench: nobody! He looked inside a cabinet that was always shut tight: nobody! He looked in the basket used for shavings and sawdust: nobody! He opened the door of his workshop to have a look out on the street too, but there was nobody. Well then? . . .

"I get it," he said then, laughing and scratching his wig. "It's obvious that I imagined that little voice. Let's get back to work now."

And taking up the hatchet again, he came down with a powerful blow on the piece of wood.

"Ouch! you've hurt me!" the same little voice cried out, complainingly.

This time Master Cherry was petrified, and he stood there with his eyes bulging out of his head with fright, his mouth wide open, and his tongue hanging down his chin, like a fountain gargoyle.[3]

As soon as he found his tongue again, all trembling and stammering with fear, he began:

85

– Ma di dove sarà uscita questa vocina che ha detto *ohi*? . . . Eppure qui non c'è anima viva. Che sia per caso questo pezzo di legno che abbia imparato a piangere e a lamentarsi come un bambino? Io non lo posso credere. Questo legno eccolo qui; è un pezzo di legno da caminetto, come tutti gli altri, e a buttarlo sul fuoco, c'è da far bollire una pentola di fagioli . . . O dunque? Che ci sia nascosto dentro qualcuno? Se c'è nascosto qualcuno, tanto peggio per lui. Ora l'accomodo io! –

E così dicendo, agguantò con tutte e due le mani quel povero pezzo di legno, e si pose a sbatacchiarlo senza carità contro le pareti della stanza.

Poi si messe in ascolto, per sentire se c'era qualche vocina che si lamentasse. Aspettò due minuti, e nulla; cinque minuti, e nulla; dieci minuti, e nulla!

– Ho capito; – disse allora sforzandosi di ridere e arruffandosi la parrucca – si vede che quella vocina che ha detto *ohi*, me la son figurata io! Rimettiamoci a lavorare. –

E perché gli era entrata addosso una gran paura, si provò a canterellare per farsi un po' di coraggio.

Intanto, posata da una parte l'ascia, prese in mano la pialla, per piallare e tirare a pulimento il pezzo di legno; ma nel mentre che lo piallava in su e in giù, sentì la solita vocina che gli disse ridendo:

– Smetti! tu mi fai il pizzicorino sul corpo! –

Questa volta il povero maestro Ciliegia cadde giù come fulminato. Quando riaprì gli occhi, si trovò seduto per terra.

Il suo viso pareva trasfigurito, e perfino la punta del naso, di paonazza come era quasi sempre, gli era diventata turchina dalla gran paura.

"But where could that little voice that said 'Ouch!' have come from? . . . I mean, there's not a living soul here. Could it by chance be that this piece of wood has learned how to cry and complain like a child? I can't believe it. This piece of wood—look at it here. It's a piece of firewood like any other; and if I threw it on the fire it would be enough to boil a pot of beans. So then? . . . Could someone be hidden inside it? Well, if someone is hidden there, so much the worse for him. I'll fix him for good now!"

And as he was saying this, he seized that poor piece of wood with his two hands and began to slam it mercilessly against the walls of the room.

Then he paused to listen, to hear if there was a thin voice complaining. He waited two minutes, but there was no sound. Five minutes: still nothing. Ten minutes: and still nothing.

"I get it," he said then, forcing a laugh and ruffling his wig; "it's obvious that I simply imagined the little voice that said 'Ouch.' Let's get back to work!"

And because a great scare had come over him, he tried humming to himself in a low voice in order to keep his courage up.

In the meantime, having put the hatchet to one side, he took up his plane in order to shave and smooth down the piece of wood; but even as he was planing up and down, he heard the same little voice say to him, laughing:

"Stop! You're tickling my belly!"[4]

This time poor Master Cherry fell down as if he had been struck by a bolt of lightning. When he opened his eyes again, he found himself sitting on the ground.

His face seemed disfigured,[5] and even the tip of his nose, which was almost always purplish, had turned blue with fright.

CAPITOLO II

*Maestro Ciliegia regala il pezzo di legno
al suo amico Geppetto, il quale lo prende per fabbricarsi
un burattino maraviglioso, che sappia
ballare, tirar di scherma e fare i salti mortali.*

In quel punto fu bussato alla porta.

– Passate pure, – disse il falegname, senza aver la forza
di rizzarsi in piedi.

Allora entrò in bottega un vecchietto tutto arzillo, il
quale aveva nome Geppetto; ma i ragazzi del vicinato,
quando lo volevano far montare su tutte le furie, lo chiamavano col soprannome di Polendina, a motivo della
sua parrucca gialla, che somigliava moltissimo alla polendina di granturco.

Geppetto era bizzosissimo. Guai a chiamarlo Polendina! Diventava subito una bestia, e non c'era più verso
di tenerlo.

– Buon giorno, mastr'Antonio, – disse Geppetto.
– Che cosa fate costì per terra?

– Insegno l'abbaco alle formicole.

– Buon pro vi faccia.

– Chi vi ha portato da me, compar Geppetto?

– Le gambe. Sappiate, mastr'Antonio, che son venuto da voi, per chiedervi un favore.

– Eccomi qui, pronto a servirvi, – replicò il falegname, rizzandosi su i ginocchi.

– Stamani m'è piovuta nel cervello un'idea.

– Sentiamola.

– Ho pensato di fabbricarmi da me un bel burattino
di legno: ma un burattino maraviglioso, che sappia ballare, tirare di scherma e fare i salti mortali. Con questo
burattino voglio girare il mondo, per buscarmi un tozzo
di pane e un bicchier di vino: che ve ne pare?

CHAPTER II

*Master Cherry makes a gift of the piece of wood
to his friend Geppetto who takes it in order
to carve himself a marvelous puppet who would be able
to dance, fence, and make daredevil leaps.*

Just then there was a knock at the door.

"Come right in," said the carpenter, without strength enough to stand up.

Then into the workshop stepped a little old man, quite spry and perky, whose name was Geppetto; however, the boys of the neighborhood, when they wanted to drive him wild with rage, called him by the nickname Polendina on account of his yellow wig, which very much resembled polenta made with Indian corn.[6]

Now, Geppetto was very hot-tempered. Woe if you called him Polendina! He'd fly off the handle, and there was no way of holding him down.

"Good day, Master Anthony," said Geppetto. "What are you doing there on the ground?"

"I'm teaching the ants how to count."

"Much good may it do you."

"Who brought you here, friend Geppetto?"

"My legs! Master Anthony, I must tell you that I've come to you for a favor."

"Here I am, at your service," replied the carpenter, climbing up on his knees.

"This morning an idea popped into my head."

"Let's hear it."

"I thought of making myself a fine wooden puppet; but a wonderful puppet who can dance, and fence, and make daredevil leaps. I intend to travel around the world with this puppet so as to earn my crust of bread and a glass of wine. What do you think about it?"

– Bravo Polendina! – gridò la solita vocina, che non si capiva di dove uscisse.

A sentirsi chiamar Polendina, compar Geppetto diventò rosso come un peperone dalla bizza, e voltandosi verso il falegname, gli disse imbestialito:

– Perché mi offendete?

– Chi vi offende?

– Mi avete detto Polendina! . . .

– Non sono stato io.

– Sta' un po' a vedere che sarò stato io! Io dico che siete stato voi.

– No!

– Sì!

– No!

– Sì! –

E riscaldandosi sempre più, vennero dalle parole ai fatti, e acciuffatisi fra di loro, si graffiarono, si morsero e si sbertucciarono.

Finito il combattimento, mastr'Antonio si trovò fra le mani la parrucca gialla di Geppetto, e Geppetto si accòrse di avere in bocca la parrucca brizzolata del falegname.

– Rendimi la mia parrucca! – gridò mastr'Antonio.

– E tu rendimi la mia, e rifacciamo la pace. –

I due vecchietti, dopo aver ripreso ognuno di loro la propria parrucca, si strinsero la mano e giurarono di rimanere buoni amici per tutta la vita.

– Dunque, compar Geppetto, – disse il falegname in segno di pace fatta – qual è il piacere che volete da me?

– Vorrei un po' di legno per fabbricare il mio burattino; me lo date? –

Mastr'Antonio, tutto contento, andò subito a prendere sul banco quel pezzo di legno che era stato cagione a lui di tante paure. Ma quando fu lì per consegnarlo all'amico, il pezzo di legno dètte uno scossone e sgu-

"Bravo, Polendina!" cried the same little voice that came from no one knew where.

On hearing himself called Polendina, friend Geppetto became as red with rage as a hot pepper, and turning on the carpenter, he said furiously:

"Why are you insulting me?"

"Who's insulting you?"

"You called me Polendina."

"It wasn't me."[7]

"Then I suppose it was me! I say it was you."

"No!"

"Yes!"

"No!"

"Yes!"

And becoming more and more heated, they went from words to deeds, and grabbing one another they scratched, bit, and mauled each other.

When the battle was over, Master Anthony found himself with Geppetto's yellow wig in his hands, and Geppetto realized that he had the carpenter's grizzled wig in his mouth.

"Give me back my wig," shouted Master Anthony.

"And you give me back mine, then we'll make peace."

After each of them had got back his own wig, the two old men shook hands and swore to remain good friends for the rest of their lives.

"Now then, friend Geppetto," said the carpenter as a token of the peace they had made, "what's the favor you want from me?"

"I'd like some wood to make my puppet. Will you give it to me?"

Delighted, Master Anthony went quickly to his workbench to get the piece of wood that had given him such an awful scare. But just as he was handing it over to his friend, the piece of wood gave a strong jolt, and,

sciandogli violentemente dalle mani, andò a battere con forza negli stinchi impresciuttiti del povero Geppetto.

– Ah! gli è con questo bel garbo, mastr'Antonio, che voi regalate la vostra roba? M'avete quasi azzoppito! . . .

– Vi giuro che non sono stato io!

– Allora sarò stato io! . . .

– La colpa è tutta di questo legno . . .

– Lo so che è del legno: ma siete voi che me l'avete tirato nelle gambe!

– Io non ve l'ho tirato!

– Bugiardo!

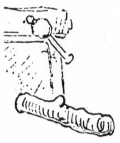

– Geppetto non mi offendete; se no vi chiamo Polendina! . . .

– Asino!

– Polendina!

– Somaro!

– Polendina!

– Brutto scimmiotto!

– Polendina! –

A sentirsi chiamar Polendina per la terza volta, Gep-

bolting suddenly out of his hands, banged against the thin and shriveled shins of poor Geppetto.

"Ah! So that's the courteous way you make a present of your goods? You've almost crippled me."

"I swear it wasn't me!"

"Then I suppose I did it."

"It's all the fault of this piece of wood."

"I know it's the wood's fault; but it was you who threw it at my legs."

"I didn't throw it at you."

"Liar!"

"Geppetto, don't insult me, or else I'll call you Polendina! . . ."

"Ass!"

"Polendina!"

"Jackass!"

"Polendina!"

"Baboon!"

"Polendina!"

Hearing himself called Polendina for the third time,

petto perse il lume degli occhi, si avventò sul falegname, e lì se ne dettero un sacco e una sporta.

A battaglia finita, mastr'Antonio si trovò due graffi di più sul naso, e quell'altro due bottoni di meno al giubbetto. Pareggiati in questo modo i loro conti, si strinsero la mano e giurarono di rimanere buoni amici per tutta la vita.

Intanto Geppetto prese con sé il suo bravo pezzo di legno, e ringraziato mastr'Antonio, se ne tornò zoppicando a casa.

Geppetto went wild and hurled himself at the carpenter; and right there they went at one another hammer and tongs.

When the battle was over, Master Anthony had two more scratches on his nose, and his foe had two buttons fewer on his jacket. Having evened the score in this way, they shook hands and swore to remain good friends for the rest of their lives.

And so Geppetto took his precious[8] piece of wood with him, and having thanked Master Anthony, he hobbled on home.

CAPITOLO III

*Geppetto, tornato a casa, comincia subito a fabbricarsi
il burattino e gli mette il nome di Pinocchio.
Prime monellerie del burattino.*

La casa di Geppetto era una stanzina terrena, che piglia-
va luce da un sottoscala. La mobilia non poteva essere
più semplice: una seggiola cattiva, un letto poco buono
e un tavolino tutto rovinato. Nella parete di fondo si
vedeva un caminetto col fuoco acceso; ma il fuoco era
dipinto, e accanto al fuoco c'era dipinta una pentola che
bolliva allegramente e mandava fuori una nuvola di
fumo, che pareva fumo davvero.

Appena entrato in casa, Geppetto prese subito gli arnesi e si pose a intagliare e a fabbricare il suo burattino.

– Che nome gli metterò? – disse fra sé e sé. – Lo voglio
chiamar Pinocchio. Questo nome gli porterà fortuna.
Ho conosciuto una famiglia intera di Pinocchi: Pinocchio il padre, Pinocchia la madre e Pinocchi i ragazzi, e
tutti se la passavano bene. Il più ricco di loro chiedeva
l'elemosina. –

Quando ebbe trovato il nome al suo burattino, allora
cominciò a lavorare a buono, e gli fece subito i capelli,
poi la fronte, poi gli occhi.

Fatti gli occhi, figuratevi la sua maraviglia quando si
accòrse che gli occhi si movevano e che lo guardavano
fisso fisso.

Geppetto, vedendosi guardare da quei due occhi di
legno, se n'ebbe quasi per male, e disse con accento risentito:

– Occhiacci di legno, perché mi guardate? –
Nessuno rispose.

CHAPTER III

After returning home, Geppetto begins at once to make his puppet and names him Pinocchio. The first pranks of the puppet.

Geppetto's home was a small room on the ground floor that got its light from the areaway under a staircase.[9] The furnishings couldn't have been more modest: a rickety chair, a broken-down bed and a battered table. At the back wall you could see a fireplace with a fire burning; but it was a painted fire, and along with the fire there was painted a kettle that boiled merrily and sent up a cloud of steam that really looked like steam.

Once inside, Geppetto immediately got his tools and began to carve and shape his puppet.

"What name shall I give him?" he said to himself. "I'll call him Pinocchio.[10] The name will bring him good luck. I once knew a whole family of Pinocchios: the father was a Pinocchio, the mother was a Pinocchia, and the children were Pinocchios. And they all did well for themselves. The richest one of them begged for a living."

Having found a name for his puppet, he then began to work in earnest, and quickly made his hair, then his forehead, and then his eyes.

When the eyes were done, just imagine his astonishment when he realized that those eyes moved and that they were staring him straight in the face.

Seeing himself looked at by those two eyes of wood, Geppetto took a little offense and said in an irritated tone:

"Spiteful wooden eyes, why are you looking at me?"

Nobody answered.

Allora, dopo gli occhi, gli fece il naso; ma il naso, appena fatto, cominciò a crescere: e cresci, cresci, cresci, diventò in pochi minuti un nasone che non finiva mai.

Il povero Geppetto si affaticava a ritagliarlo; ma più lo ritagliava e lo scorciva, e più quel naso impertinente diventava lungo.

Dopo il naso gli fece la bocca.

La bocca non era ancora finita di fare, che cominciò subito a ridere e a canzonarlo.

– Smetti di ridere! – disse Geppetto impermalito; ma fu come dire al muro.

– Smetti di ridere, ti ripeto! – urlò con voce minacciosa.

Allora la bocca smesse di ridere, ma cacciò fuori tutta la lingua.

Geppetto, per non guastare i fatti suoi, finse di non avvedersene, e continuò a lavorare. Dopo la bocca, gli fece il mento, poi il collo, poi le spalle, lo stomaco, le braccia e le mani.

Appena finite le mani, Geppetto sentì portarsi via la

Then, after the eyes he made him a nose. But as soon as the nose was made, it began to grow; and it grew and grew and grew so that in a few minutes it became an endless nose.

Poor Geppetto kept struggling to cut it back; but the more he cut and shortened it, the longer that impudent nose became.

After the nose he made him a mouth.

The mouth wasn't even done when it quickly began to laugh and mock him.

"Stop laughing!" said Geppetto out of sorts; but it was like talking to the wall.

"Stop laughing, I repeat!" he roared in a threatening voice.

The mouth stopped laughing then; but it stuck its tongue out all the way.

So as not to spoil what he was doing, Geppetto pretended not to notice this and went on working. After the mouth, he made his chin, then his neck, then his shoulders, his trunk, his arms and his hands.

As soon as the hands were finished, Geppetto felt his

99

parrucca dal capo. Si voltò in su, e che cosa vide? Vide la sua parrucca gialla in mano del burattino.

– Pinocchio! . . . rendimi subito la mia parrucca! –

E Pinocchio, invece di rendergli la parrucca, se la messe in capo per sé, rimanendovi sotto mezzo affogato.

A quel garbo insolente e derisorio, Geppetto si fece tristo e melanconico, come non era stato mai in vita sua: e voltandosi verso Pinocchio, gli disse:

– Birba d'un figliuolo! Non sei ancora finito di fare, e già cominci a mancar di rispetto a tuo padre! Male, ragazzo mio, male! –

E si rasciugò una lacrima.

Restavano sempre da fare le gambe e i piedi.

Quando Geppetto ebbe finito di fargli i piedi, sentì arrivarsi un calcio sulla punta del naso.

– Me lo merito! – disse allora fra sé. – Dovevo pensarci prima! Oramai è tardi! –

Poi prese il burattino sotto le braccia e lo posò in terra, sul pavimento della stanza, per farlo camminare.

Pinocchio aveva le gambe aggranchite e non sapeva muoversi, e Geppetto lo conduceva per la mano per insegnargli a mettere un passo dietro l'altro.

Quando le gambe gli si furono sgranchite, Pinocchio cominciò a camminare da sé e a correre per la stanza; finché, infilata la porta di casa, saltò nella strada e si dètte a scappare.

E il povero Geppetto a corrergli dietro senza poterlo raggiungere, perché quel birichino di Pinocchio andava a salti come una lepre, e battendo i suoi piedi di legno sul lastrico della strada, faceva un fracasso, come venti paia di zoccoli da contadini.

– Piglialo! piglialo! – urlava Geppetto; ma la gente che era per la via, vedendo questo burattino di legno, che correva come un barbero, si fermava incantata a guardarlo, e rideva, rideva e rideva, da non poterselo figurare.

wig being snatched from his head. He looked up, and what did he see? He saw his yellow wig in the puppet's hands.

"Pinocchio! . . . give me back my wig at once."

But instead of giving back the wig, Pinocchio put it on his own head, nearly suffocating underneath it.

At that insolent and mocking behavior, Geppetto became sadder and more dejected than he had ever been in his life; and turning to Pinocchio, he said:

"Scamp of a child, you aren't even finished and you're already beginning to lack respect for your father! That's bad, my boy, bad!"

And he wiped away a tear.

The legs and feet still remained to be done.

When Geppetto finished making him feet, he felt a kick land on the tip of his nose.

"I deserve it!" he said to himself then. "I should have thought of it before; now it's too late."

Then he took the puppet under his arms and put him down on the floor of the room in order to make him walk.

Pinocchio's legs were stiff, and he didn't know how to move; so Geppetto led him by the hand, teaching him how to take one step after the other.

When his legs were limbered, Pinocchio began to walk on his own and then to run around the room; and then, having rushed out the door, he jumped into the street and set off on the run.

And there was poor Geppetto running after him without being able to catch up, because that imp of a Pinocchio bounded along like a hare; and as his wooden feet struck the pavement, he made a clatter like twenty pairs of peasants' clogs.

"Catch him! Catch him!" shouted Geppetto; but the passersby, seeing a wooden puppet running like a racehorse, just stood still in amazement to watch him, and laughed and laughed and laughed beyond belief.

Alla fine, e per buona fortuna, capitò un carabiniere il quale, sentendo tutto quello schiamazzo, e credendo si trattasse di un puledro che avesse levata la mano al padrone, si piantò coraggiosamente a gambe larghe in mezzo alla strada, coll'animo risoluto di fermarlo e d'impedire il caso di maggiori disgrazie.

Ma Pinocchio, quando si avvide da lontano del carabiniere, che barricava tutta la strada, s'ingegnò di passargli, per sorpresa, framezzo alle gambe, e invece fece fiasco.

Il carabiniere, senza punto smuoversi, lo acciuffò pulitamente per il naso (era un nasone spropositato, che pareva fatto apposta per essere acchiappato dai carabinieri), e lo riconsegnò nelle proprie mani di Geppetto; il quale, a titolo di correzione, voleva dargli subito una buona tiratina d'orecchi. Ma figuratevi come rimase quando, nel cercargli gli orecchi, non gli riuscì di poterli trovare: e sapete perché? perché, nella furia di scolpirlo, si era dimenticato di farglieli.

At last, by a lucky chance, a carabiniere happened along. Hearing all that racket and thinking it was a colt running wildly out of control, he set himself bravely with legs wide apart in the middle of the street, determined to stop it and prevent anything worse from happening.

But when Pinocchio, from a distance, noticed that the carabiniere was blocking the whole street, he planned to surprise him by passing between his legs; but he botched it.

Without budging at all, the carabiniere snatched him neatly by the nose (it was an enormously long nose that seemed made expressly to be seized by carabinieri) and handed him over to Geppetto who, for the sake of discipline, immediately wanted to box his ears. But just imagine how he felt when, looking for his ears, he wasn't able to find them. And do you know why? Because in his haste to carve him, he had forgotten to make them.

Allora lo prese per la collottola, e, mentre lo riconduceva indietro, gli disse tentennando minacciosamente il capo:

– Andiamo subito a casa. Quando saremo a casa, non dubitare che faremo i nostri conti! –

Pinocchio, a questa antifona, si buttò per terra, e non volle più camminare. Intanto i curiosi e i bighelloni principiavano a fermarsi lì dintorno e a far capannello.

Chi ne diceva una, chi un'altra.

– Povero burattino! – dicevano alcuni – ha ragione a non voler tornare a casa! Chi lo sa come lo picchierebbe quell'omaccio di Geppetto! . . . –

E gli altri soggiungevano malignamente:

– Quel Geppetto pare un galantuomo! ma è un vero tiranno coi ragazzi! Se gli lasciano quel povero burattino fra le mani, è capacissimo di farlo a pezzi! . . . –

Insomma, tanto dissero e tanto fecero, che il carabiniere rimesse in libertà Pinocchio, e condusse in prigione quel pover'uomo di Geppetto. Il quale, non avendo parole lì per lì per difendersi, piangeva come un vitellino, e nell'avviarsi verso il carcere, balbettava singhiozzando:

– Sciagurato figliuolo! E pensare che ho penato tanto a farlo un burattino per bene! Ma mi sta il dovere! Dovevo pensarci prima! . . . –

Quello che accadde dopo, è una storia così strana da non potersi quasi credere, e ve la racconterò in quest'altri capitoli.

So he took him by the scruff of the neck and as he led him back, he said, shaking his head threateningly:

"Let's go straight home. And when we're home, you can be sure that we'll settle our accounts!"

Hearing this tune, Pinocchio threw himself to the ground and refused to walk any further. Meanwhile the curious and the idlers began to stop and gather around them in a group.

Some said one thing; some said another.

"Poor puppet," some said, "he's right not to want to go home. Who knows how that awful Geppetto would beat him!"

And the others added maliciously:

"That Geppetto looks like a good man, but he's a real tyrant with children. If they leave that poor puppet in his hands, he's more than capable of hacking him to pieces."

In short, they made such a hue and cry that the carabiniere set Pinocchio free again and marched poor old Geppetto off to prison. And he, not finding words to defend himself just then, cried like a calf; and on the way to jail he stammered amid his sobbing:

"Wicked child! And to think that I worked so hard to make him into a nice puppet! But it serves me right. I should have known better."

What happened afterward is so strange a story that it is hardly to be believed; but I will tell you about it in the following chapters.

CAPITOLO IV

La storia di Pinocchio col Grillo-parlante,
dove si vede come i ragazzi cattivi hanno a noja di sentirsi
correggere da chi ne sa più di loro.

Vi dirò dunque, ragazzi, che mentre il povero Geppetto era condotto senza sua colpa in prigione, quel monello di Pinocchio, rimasto libero dalle grinfie del carabiniere, se la dava a gambe giù attraverso ai campi, per far più presto a tornarsene a casa; e nella gran furia del correre saltava greppi altissimi, siepi di pruni e fossi pieni d'acqua, tale e quale come avrebbe potuto fare un capretto o un leprottino inseguito dai cacciatori.

Giunto dinanzi a casa, trovò l'uscio di strada socchiuso. Lo spinse, entrò dentro, e appena ebbe messo tanto di paletto, si gettò a sedere per terra, lasciando andare un gran sospirone di contentezza.

Ma quella contentezza durò poco, perché sentì nella stanza qualcuno che fece:

– Crì-crì-crì!

– Chi è che mi chiama? – disse Pinocchio tutto impaurito.

– Sono io! –

Pinocchio si voltò, e vide un grosso grillo che saliva lentamente su su per il muro.

– Dimmi, Grillo, e tu chi sei?

– Io sono il Grillo-parlante, e abito in questa stanza da più di cent'anni.

– Oggi però questa stanza è mia – disse il burattino – e se vuoi farmi un vero piacere, vattene subito, senza nemmeno voltarti indietro.

– Io non me ne anderò di qui, – rispose il Grillo – se prima non ti avrò detto una gran verità.

CHAPTER IV

The story of Pinocchio and the Talking Cricket,
wherein we see that bad boys don't like to be
corrected by those who know better than they do.

So, children, I will tell you that while poor Geppetto was being led blameless to prison, that little urchin Pinocchio was no sooner out of the claws of the carabiniere than he took to his heels, cutting across the fields in order to get back home more quickly. And in his great haste, he jumped over high embankments, briar hedges, and gushing streams, just like a kid-goat or a young hare chased by hunters.

When he arrived in front of the house he found the street door ajar, so he pushed it open and went in; and as soon as he had bolted the door tight, he sat plunk on the floor, heaving a deep sigh of satisfaction.

But his satisfaction didn't last long, for he heard someone in the room go:

"Crick-crick-crick."

"Who's calling me?" said Pinocchio, thoroughly frightened.

"It is I."

Pinocchio turned around and saw a large Cricket crawling slowly up the wall.

"Tell me, Cricket, just who are you?"

"I'm the Talking Cricket, and I've lived in this room for over a hundred years."

"Now, however, this room is mine," said the puppet, "and if you want to do me a real favor, get out of here right away without even looking back."

"I will not go from here," replied the Cricket, "without first telling you a great truth."

– Dimmela e spicciati.

– Guai a quei ragazzi che si ribellano ai loro genitori, e che abbandonano capricciosamente la casa paterna. Non avranno mai bene in questo mondo; e prima o poi dovranno pentirsene amaramente.

– Canta pure, Grillo mio, come ti pare e piace: ma io so che domani, all'alba, voglio andarmene di qui, perché se rimango qui, avverrà a me quel che avviene a tutti gli altri ragazzi, vale a dire mi manderanno a scuola, e per amore o per forza mi toccherà a studiare; e io, a dirtela in confidenza, di studiare non ne ho punto voglia, e mi diverto più a correre dietro alle farfalle e a salire su per gli alberi a prendere gli uccellini di nido.

– Povero grullerello! Ma non sai che, facendo così, diventerai da grande un bellissimo somaro, e che tutti si piglieranno gioco di te?

– Chetati, Grillaccio del mal'augurio! – gridò Pinocchio.

Ma il Grillo, che era paziente e filosofo, invece di aversi a male di questa impertinenza, continuò con lo stesso tono di voce:

– E se non ti garba di andare a scuola, perché non impari almeno un mestiere, tanto da guadagnarti onestamente un pezzo di pane?

– Vuoi che te lo dica? – replicò Pinocchio, che cominciava a perdere la pazienza. – Fra i mestieri del mondo non ce n'è che uno solo che veramente mi vada a genio.

– E questo mestiere sarebbe?

– Quello di mangiare, bere, dormire, divertirmi e fare dalla mattina alla sera la vita del vagabondo.

– Per tua regola – disse il Grillo-parlante con la sua solita calma – tutti quelli che fanno codesto mestiere, finiscono quasi sempre allo spedale o in prigione.

– Bada, Grillaccio del mal'augurio! . . . se mi monta la bizza, guai a te! . . .

"Tell me and hurry up."

"Woe to those children who disobey their parents and wilfully leave home. They will never come to any good in this world, and sooner or later they'll be bitterly sorry for it."

"Sing on all you want, my *dear* Cricket; but I know that I'm going away tomorrow at dawn, because if I stay here, what happens to all the other kids will happen to me. I mean to say that they'll send me to school, and whether I like it or not I'll have to study; but confidentially, I don't have the slightest desire to study, and I get more pleasure from chasing butterflies and climbing up trees to get baby birds."

"Poor little simpleton! Don't you know that if you do that, you'll grow up to be a perfect jackass and everyone will poke fun at you?"[11]

"Shut up, wretched Cricket of doom!" shouted Pinocchio.

But the Cricket, who was both patient and a philosopher, instead of taking offense at such impudence, went on in the same tone of voice:

"And if it doesn't suit you to go to school, why don't you at least learn a trade so that you can earn your slice of bread honestly?"

"Do you want me to tell you why?" replied Pinocchio, who was beginning to lose his temper. "Of all the trades in the world there's really only one that's to my liking."

"And what trade would that be?"

"That of eating, drinking, sleeping, having fun, and living the life of a vagabond from morning to night."

"For your information," said the Talking Cricket with his usual calm, "everyone who follows that trade is bound to end up in the poorhouse[12] or in prison."

"Watch out, wretched Cricket of doom! If I get mad, it'll be too bad for you."

– Povero Pinocchio! mi fai proprio compassione! . . .

– Perché ti faccio compassione?

– Perché sei un burattino e, quel che è peggio, perché hai la testa di legno. –

A queste ultime parole, Pinocchio saltò su tutt'infuriato e preso di sul banco un martello di legno, lo scagliò contro il Grillo-parlante.

Forse non credeva nemmeno di colpirlo; ma disgraziatamente lo colse per l'appunto nel capo, tanto che il povero Grillo ebbe appena il fiato di fare *crì-crì-crì*, e poi rimase lì stecchito e appiccicato alla parete.

"Poor Pinocchio, I really feel sorry for you."

"Why do you feel sorry for me?"

"Because you're a puppet and, what's worse, because you've got a wooden head."

At these words, Pinocchio jumped up in a fury, and taking a mallet from the workbench, he hurled it at the Talking Cricket.

Maybe he didn't even mean to hit him, but unluckily he caught him squarely on the head, so that the poor Cricket barely had enough breath to utter a crick-crick-crick, after which he remained there stark dead and stuck on the wall.

CAPITOLO V

*Pinocchio ha fame e cerca un uovo per farsi
una frittata; ma sul più bello, la frittata
gli vola via dalla finestra.*

Intanto cominciò a farsi notte, e Pinocchio, ricordandosi che non aveva mangiato nulla, sentì un'uggiolina allo stomaco, che somigliava moltissimo all'appetito.

Ma l'appetito nei ragazzi cammina presto, e di fatti, dopo pochi minuti, l'appetito diventò fame, e la fame, dal vedere al non vedere, si convertì in una fame da lupi, in una fame da tagliarsi col coltello.

Il povero Pinocchio corse subito al focolare, dove c'era una pentola che bolliva, e fece l'atto di scoperchiarla, per vedere che cosa ci fosse dentro: ma la pentola era dipinta sul muro. Immaginatevi come restò. Il suo naso, che era già lungo, gli diventò più lungo almeno quattro dita.

Allora si dètte a correre per la stanza e a frugare per tutte le cassette e per tutti i ripostigli in cerca di un po' di pane, magari un po' di pan secco, un crosterello, un osso avanzato al cane, un po' di polenta muffita, una lisca di pesce, un nocciolo di ciliegia, insomma qualche cosa da masticare: ma non trovò nulla, il gran nulla, proprio nulla.

E intanto la fame cresceva, e cresceva sempre: e il povero Pinocchio non aveva altro sollievo che quello di sbadigliare, e faceva degli sbadigli così lunghi, che qualche volta la bocca gli arrivava fino agli orecchi. E dopo avere sbadigliato, sputava, e sentiva che lo stomaco gli andava via.

Allora piangendo e disperandosi, diceva:

– Il Grillo-parlante aveva ragione. Ho fatto male a

CHAPTER V

Pinocchio gets hungry and looks for an egg
to make himself an omelette; but lo and behold,
the omelette flies away from him and out the window.

In the meantime night started to fall, and remembering that he hadn't eaten anything, Pinocchio felt a little pang in his stomach that very much resembled a twinge of appetite.

But a child's appetite grows fast, and in fact after a few minutes his appetite became hunger; and in the twinkle of an eye he had become as hungry as a wolf: a hunger so thick that you could cut it with a knife.[13]

Poor Pinocchio ran quickly to the hearth where a kettle was boiling and reached out to uncover it so as to see what was in it; but the kettle was painted on the wall. You can imagine how he felt. His nose, which was already long, grew still longer by at least some four inches.

Then he began to run around the room, rummaging in all the drawers and nooks and corners, looking for a piece of bread, even stale bread, a small crust, a bone left by a dog, a bit of moldy polenta, a fish bone, a cherry pit: in short, something to chew on. But he found nothing, a whole lot of nothing, plain nothing.

And meanwhile his hunger grew and grew all the time; but the only relief poor Pinocchio got came from yawning. He yawned so wide that sometimes his mouth opened as far back as his ears; and after yawning, he would spit, until he felt as if his stomach were caving in.[14]

Then, weeping in despair, he said:

"The Talking Cricket was right. I was wrong to rebel

rivoltarmi al mio babbo e a fuggire di casa . . . Se il mio babbo fosse qui, ora non mi troverei a morire di sbadigli! Oh! che brutta malattia che è la fame! –

Quand'ecco che gli parve di vedere nel monte della spazzatura qualche cosa di tondo e di bianco, che somigliava tutto a un uovo di gallina. Spiccare un salto e gettarvisi sopra, fu un punto solo. Era un uovo davvero.

La gioia del burattino è impossibile descriverla: bisogna sapersela figurare. Credendo quasi che fosse un sogno, si rigirava quest'uovo fra le mani, e lo toccava e lo baciava, e baciandolo diceva:

– E ora come dovrò cuocerlo? Ne farò una frittata! . . . No, è meglio cuocerlo nel piatto! . . . O non sarebbe più saporito se lo friggessi in padella? O se invece lo cuocessi a uso uova a bere? No, la più lesta di tutte è di cuocerlo nel piatto o nel tegamino: ho troppo voglia di mangiarmelo! –

Detto fatto, pose un tegamino sopra un caldano pieno di brace accesa: messe nel tegamino, invece d'olio o di burro, un po' d'acqua: e quando l'acqua principiò a fumare, *tac!* . . . spezzò il guscio dell'uovo, e fece l'atto di scodellarvelo dentro.

Ma invece della chiara e del torlo scappò fuori un pulcino tutto allegro e complimentoso, il quale facendo una bella riverenza disse:

– Mille grazie, signor Pinocchio, d'avermi risparmiata la fatica di rompere il guscio! Arrivedella, stia bene e tanti saluti a casa! –

Ciò detto, distese le ali, e, infilata la finestra che era aperta, se ne volò via a perdita d'occhio.

Il povero burattino rimase lì, come incantato, cogli occhi fissi, colla bocca aperta e coi gusci dell'uovo in mano. Riavutosi, peraltro, dal primo sbigottimento, cominciò a piangere, a strillare, a battere i piedi in terra per la disperazione, e piangendo diceva:

against my father and run away from home . . . If my father were here now, I wouldn't be yawning to death. Oh, what an awful sickness hunger is!"

But just then he thought he saw on top of the rubbish pile something round and white that looked quite like a hen's egg. In a flash he leaped and pounced on it. It really was an egg.

It's impossible to describe the puppet's joy; you have to be able to imagine it. Almost thinking it was a dream, he turned the egg over and over in his hands, fondling it and kissing it; and as he kissed it, he said:

"And now how shall I cook it? I'll make an omelette with it . . . No, it's better to cook it on a griddle . . . But wouldn't it be tastier if I fried it in a skillet? What if, instead, I made a soft-boiled egg?[15] No, the fastest way of all is to cook it on a griddle or in a small pan. I can't wait to eat it."

No sooner said than done. He put a small pan on a brazier full of burning embers; in place of butter and oil he put a little water in the pan, and when the water began to steam, crack! . . . he broke the shell of the egg and made as if to drop it in.

But instead of the white of the egg and the yolk, a little chick all perky and ceremonious jumped out and, making a fine bow, said:

"A thousand thanks, Signor Pinocchio, for saving me the trouble of breaking the shell. Bye, bye, for now;[16] keep well, and best regards to all at home."

Having said this, he spread his wings and, passing through the open window, flew away far out of sight.

The poor puppet stood there as if bewitched, eyes gaping, mouth wide open, and the two halves of the eggshell in his hands. However, when he had recovered from the first shock, he began to cry, to scream, to stamp his feet on the ground in desperation; and weeping all the time, he said:

115

– Eppure il Grillo-parlante aveva ragione! Se non fossi scappato di casa e se il mio babbo fosse qui, ora non mi troverei a morire di fame! Oh! che brutta malattia che è la fame! . . . –

E perché il corpo gli seguitava a brontolare più che mai, e non sapeva come fare a chetarlo, pensò di uscir di casa e di dare una scappata al paesello vicino, nella speranza di trovare qualche persona caritatevole, che gli facesse l'elemosina di un po' di pane.

"The Talking Cricket was really right, then. If I hadn't run away and if my father were here now, I wouldn't be starving to death. Oh! What an awful sickness hunger is!"

And because his stomach went on grumbling more than ever and he didn't know what to do to quiet it, he decided to make a quick dash to the nearby village in the hope of finding some kind person who might give him a bit of bread.

CAPITOLO VI

Pinocchio si addormenta coi piedi sul caldano,
e la mattina dopo si sveglia
coi piedi tutti bruciati.

Per l'appunto era una nottataccia d'inferno. Tonava forte forte, lampeggiava come se il cielo pigliasse fuoco, e un ventaccio freddo e strapazzone, fischiando rabbiosamente e sollevando un immenso nuvolo di polvere, faceva stridere e cigolare tutti gli alberi della campagna.

Pinocchio aveva una gran paura dei tuoni e dei lampi: se non che la fame era più forte della paura: motivo per cui accostò l'uscio di casa, e presa la carriera, in un centinaio di salti arrivò fino al paese, colla lingua fuori e col fiato grosso, come un cane da caccia.

Ma trovò tutto buio e tutto deserto. Le botteghe erano chiuse; le porte di casa chiuse; le finestre chiuse, e nella strada nemmeno un cane. Pareva il paese dei morti.

Allora Pinocchio, preso dalla disperazione e dalla fame, si attaccò al campanello d'una casa, e cominciò a sonare a distesa, dicendo dentro di sé:

– Qualcuno si affaccerà. –

Difatti si affacciò un vecchino, col berretto da notte in capo, il quale gridò tutto stizzito:

– Che cosa volete a quest'ora?

– Che mi fareste il piacere di darmi un po' di pane?

– Aspettami costì che torno subito, – rispose il vecchino, credendo di aver da fare con qualcuno di quei ragazzacci rompicolli che si divertono di notte a sonare i campanelli delle case, per molestare la gente per bene, che se la dorme tranquillamente.

CHAPTER VI

*Pinocchio falls asleep with his feet
on the brazier and wakes up the next morning
with his feet all burned off.*

It so happened that it was a horrid, hellish night.[17] It thundered mightily, lightning flashed as though the sky were catching fire, and a cold, blustery wind whistled wildly as it raised a huge cloud of dust and made all the trees in the countryside screech and creak.

Pinocchio was terribly afraid of thunder and lightning. But his hunger was stronger than his fear. So he set the door ajar, and going at full speed, in about a hundred leaps and bounds he reached the village panting heavily and with his tongue hanging out, just like a hunting dog.

But he found everything dark and deserted. The shops were closed; the doors were closed; the windows were closed; and not even a stray dog was in the streets. It looked like the land of the dead.

Driven by despair and hunger, Pinocchio then tugged at the bellcord of a house and rang uninterruptedly, telling himself:

"Someone is bound to look out."

In fact, a little old man with a nightcap on his head looked out the window and shouted angrily:

"What do you want at this hour?"

"Would you be so kind as to give me some bread?"

"Wait where you are; I'll be right back," answered the little old man, thinking that he had to do with one of those young rowdies who amuse themselves at night by ringing doorbells just to annoy respectable people who are sleeping peacefully.

Dopo mezzo minuto la finestra si riaprì, e la voce del solito vecchino gridò a Pinocchio:

– Fatti sotto e para il cappello. –

Pinocchio si levò subito il suo cappelluccio; ma mentre faceva l'atto di pararlo, sentì pioversi addosso un'enorme catinellata d'acqua che lo annaffiò tutto dalla testa ai piedi, come se fosse un vaso di giranio appassito.

Tornò a casa bagnato come un pulcino e rifinito dalla stanchezza e dalla fame: e perché non aveva più forza da reggersi ritto, si pose a sedere, appoggiando i piedi fradici e impillaccherati sopra un caldano pieno di brace accesa.

E lì si addormentò; e nel dormire, i piedi che erano di legno gli presero fuoco, e adagio adagio gli si carbonizzarono e diventarono cenere.

E Pinocchio seguitava a dormire e a russare, come se i suoi piedi fossero quelli d'un altro. Finalmente sul far del giorno si svegliò, perché qualcuno aveva bussato alla porta.

– Chi è? – domandò sbadigliando e stropicciandosi gli occhi.

– Sono io! – rispose una voce.

Quella voce era la voce di Geppetto.

In half a minute the window opened again, and the voice of that same little old man called out to Pinocchio:

"Come closer and hold out your hat."

Pinocchio took off his shabby little hat[18] at once, but just as he was holding it out, he felt an enormous basin-ful of water pour down on him, drenching him from head to foot as though he were a pot of withering geraniums.

He returned home wet as a chick and quite worn out with fatigue and hunger; and because he no longer even had the strength to stand up, he sat down, putting his soaked and mud-spattered feet on top of a brazier full of burning embers.

And there he fell asleep; and while he slept his feet, which were made of wood, caught fire and little by little burned and turned to ashes.

But Pinocchio went on sleeping and snoring as though his feet belonged to someone else. Finally, at daybreak he woke up because somebody had knocked at the door.

"Who is it?" he asked, yawning and rubbing his eyes.

"It's me!" answered a voice.

It was the voice of Geppetto.

CAPITOLO VII

Geppetto torna a casa,
e dà al burattino la colazione che
il pover'uomo aveva portata per sé.

Il povero Pinocchio, che aveva sempre gli occhi fra il sonno, non s'era ancora avvisto dei piedi che gli si erano tutti bruciati: per cui appena sentì la voce di suo padre, schizzò giù dallo sgabello per correre a tirare il paletto; ma invece, dopo due o tre traballoni, cadde di picchio tutto lungo disteso sul pavimento.

E nel battere in terra fece lo stesso rumore, che avrebbe fatto un sacco di mestoli, cascato da un quinto piano.

– Aprimi! – intanto gridava Geppetto dalla strada.

– Babbo mio, non posso – rispondeva il burattino piangendo e ruzzolandosi per terra.

– Perché non puoi?

– Perché mi hanno mangiato i piedi.

– E chi te li ha mangiati?

– Il gatto – disse Pinocchio, vedendo il gatto che colle zampine davanti si divertiva a far ballare alcuni trucioli di legno.

– Aprimi, ti dico! – ripeté Geppetto – se no, quando vengo in casa, il gatto te lo do io!

– Non posso star ritto, credetelo. Oh! povero me! povero me, che mi toccherà a camminare coi ginocchi per tutta la vita! . . . –

Geppetto, credendo che tutti questi piagnistei fossero un'altra monelleria del burattino, pensò bene di farla finita, e arrampicatosi su per il muro, entrò in casa dalla finestra.

Da principio voleva dire e voleva fare; ma poi,

CHAPTER VII

*Geppetto returns home and gives
the puppet the breakfast that the poor man
had brought for himself.*

Poor Pinocchio, whose eyes were still sleepy, hadn't yet realized that his feet were all burned off; so as soon as he heard his father's voice he jumped down from his stool in order to run and unbolt the door; but after two or three lurches all at once he fell flat on the floor.

And in striking the floor, he made the same racket that a sackful of wooden ladles would have made in falling from the fifth story.[19]

"Open up for me!" Geppetto shouted meanwhile from the street.

"Dear father, I can't," replied the puppet, crying and rolling about on the floor.

"Why can't you?"

"Because they've eaten my feet."

"And who ate them?"

"The cat," said Pinocchio, seeing the cat who was amusing itself by kicking up some wood shavings with its front paws.

"Let me in, I say!" repeated Geppetto. "If not, when I get in I'll give you the cat all right!"

"I can't stand up, believe me. Oh, poor me, poor me. I'll have to walk on my knees all my life!"

Thinking that all that whining was another of the puppet's pranks, Geppetto decided to put a stop to it; so, climbing up the wall he entered the house by the window.

At first he had intended to treat him harshly, but

quando vide il suo Pinocchio sdraiato in terra e rimasto senza piedi davvero, allora sentì intenerirsi; e presolo subito in collo, si dètte a baciarlo e a fargli mille carezze e mille moine, e, coi luccioloni che gli cascavano giù per le gote, gli disse singhiozzando:

– Pinocchiuccio mio! Com'è che ti sei bruciato i piedi?

– Non lo so, babbo, ma credetelo che è stata una nottata d'inferno e me ne ricorderò fin che campo. Tonava, balenava e io avevo una gran fame, e allora il Grillo-parlante mi disse: «Ti sta bene: sei stato cattivo, e te lo meriti» e io gli dissi: «Bada, Grillo!...» e lui mi disse: «Tu sei un burattino e hai la testa di legno» e io gli tirai un manico di martello, e lui morì, ma la colpa fu sua, perché io non volevo ammazzarlo, prova ne sia che messi un tegamino sulla brace accesa del caldano, ma il pulcino scappò fuori e disse: «Arrivedella... e tanti saluti a casa.» E la fame cresceva sempre, motivo per cui quel vecchino col berretto da notte, affacciandosi alla

when he saw his very own Pinocchio stretched out on the floor and really without feet, he felt his heart melt, and quickly picking him up in his arms, he kissed and fondled him with a thousand blandishments. And as big tears rolled down his cheeks, he said amidst his sobbing:

"My poor little Pinocchio, how is it that you burned your feet off?"

"I don't know, father, but believe me, it was a hellish night, and I'll remember it as long as I live. It was thundering and lightning and I was very hungry, and then the Talking Cricket said to me, 'It serves you right; you've been wicked, and you deserve it,' and I said to him, 'Watch out, Cricket! . . .' and he said to me, 'You're a puppet and you've got a wooden head,' and I threw a hammer handle at him and he died, but it was his fault, because I didn't want to kill him, the proof being that I put a little pan on the burning embers of the brazier, but the chick jumped out and said: 'Bye bye and best regards to all at home' and I got more and more hungry, on account of which that little old man with the

finestra mi disse: «Fatti sotto e para il cappello» e io con quella catinellata d'acqua sul capo, perché il chiedere un po' di pane non è vergogna, non è vero? me ne tornai subito a casa, e perché avevo sempre una gran fame, messi i piedi sul caldano per rasciugarmi, e voi siete tornato, e me li sono trovati bruciati, e intanto la fame l'ho sempre e i piedi non li ho più! ih! . . . ih! . . . ih! . . . ih! . . . –

E il povero Pinocchio cominciò a piangere e a berciare così forte, che lo sentivano da cinque chilometri lontano.

Geppetto, che di tutto quel discorso arruffato aveva capito una cosa sola, cioè che il burattino sentiva morirsi dalla gran fame, tirò fuori di tasca tre pere, e porgendogliele, disse:

– Queste tre pere erano la mia colazione: ma io te le do volentieri. Mangiale, e buon pro ti faccia.

– Se volete che le mangi, fatemi il piacere di sbucciarle.

– Sbucciarle? – replicò Geppetto meravigliato. – Non avrei mai creduto, ragazzo mio, che tu fossi così boccuccia e così schizzinoso di palato. Male! In questo mondo, fin da bambini, bisogna avvezzarsi abboccati e a saper mangiar di tutto, perché non si sa mai quel che ci può capitare. I casi son tanti! . . .

– Voi direte bene – soggiunse Pinocchio – ma io non mangerò mai una frutta, che non sia sbucciata. Le bucce non le posso soffrire. –

E quel buon uomo di Geppetto, cavato fuori un coltellino, e armatosi di santa pazienza, sbucciò le tre pere, e pose tutte le bucce sopra un angolo della tavola.

Quando Pinocchio in due bocconi ebbe mangiata la prima pera, fece l'atto di buttar via il torsolo: ma Geppetto gli trattenne il braccio, dicendogli:

– Non lo buttar via: tutto in questo mondo può far comodo.

nightcap, looking out the window, said to me: 'Come closer and hold out your hat' and with that basinful of water on my head (because it's not a disgrace to ask for a piece of bread, is it?) I returned home and because I was still very hungry I put my feet on the brazier to dry out, and you came back and I found them burned off, and in the meantime I'm still hungry and my feet are all gone. Boo . . . hoo . . . hoo! . . ."

And poor Pinocchio began to cry and wail so loudly that they could hear him five miles away.[20]

Geppetto understood only one thing in all that rigamarole, and that is that the puppet was dying of hunger; so he took three pears from his pocket, and handing them over to him he said:

"These three pears were for my breakfast, but I'm glad to give them to you. Eat them, and may they do you good."

"If you want me to eat them, do me the favor of peeling them."

"Peeling them?" replied Geppetto, taken aback. "My boy, I would never have believed that you were so fussy and finicky.[21] That's bad! In this world, from the time we are children we have to get used to eating anything and everything, because we never know what may befall us. So many things can happen!"

"You may be right," Pinocchio retorted, "but I'll never eat fruit that's not peeled. I can't stand the skins."

And so good old Geppetto took out a small knife, and fortifying himself with saintly patience he peeled the three pears, putting the skins on the corner of the table.

After he had eaten the first pear in just two bites, Pinocchio was about to throw away the core; but Geppetto held back his arm and said:

"Don't throw it away: in this world everything may come in handy."

– Ma io il torsolo non lo mangio davvero! . . . –
gridò il burattino, rivoltandosi come una vipera.

– Chi lo sa! I casi son tanti! . . . – ripeté Geppetto,
senza riscaldarsi.

Fatto sta che i tre torsoli, invece di esser gettati fuori
dalla finestra, vennero posati sull'angolo della tavola in
compagnia delle bucce.

Mangiate o, per dir meglio, divorate le tre pere, Pinocchio fece un lunghissimo sbadiglio e disse piagnu-
colando:

– Ho dell'altra fame!

– Ma io, ragazzo mio, non ho più nulla da darti.

– Proprio nulla, nulla?

– Ci avrei soltanto queste bucce e questi torsoli di
pera.

– Pazienza! – disse Pinocchio, – se non c'è altro, mangerò una buccia. –

E cominciò a masticare. Da principio storse un po' la
bocca: ma poi una dietro l'altra, spolverò in un soffio
tutte le bucce: e dopo le bucce anche i torsoli, e quan-
d'ebbe finito di mangiare ogni cosa, si batté tutto contento le mani sul corpo, e disse gongolando:

– Ora sì che sto bene!

– Vedi dunque – osservò Geppetto – che avevo ragione io quando ti dicevo che non bisogna avvezzarsi né
troppo sofistici né troppo delicati di palato. Caro mio,
non si sa mai quel che ci può capitare in questo mondo.
I casi son tanti!! . . . –

"But I am certainly not going to eat the core," the puppet yelled, recoiling like a viper.

"Who knows! So many things can happen . . ." Geppetto said again, without losing his temper.

And so the three cores, instead of being thrown out the window, were placed on the corner of the table along with the peelings.

Having eaten, or rather devoured, the three pears, Pinocchio gave a long and deep yawn and whimpered:

"I'm still hungry."

"But, my child, I don't have anything else to give you."

"Really, nothing at all?"

"All I have are these pear cores and peelings."

"Patience!" said Pinocchio, "if there's nothing else, I'll eat some peelings."

And he began to chew on them. At first he made faces; but then one after another he polished off all the peelings, and after the peelings the cores too. And when he had finished eating everything, he clapped his stomach with satisfaction and said gleefully:

"*Now* I feel better."

"So you see," Geppetto remarked, "I was right when I told you that we shouldn't become too choosy or too finicky in our tastes. My dear boy, we can never be sure about what may befall us in this world. So many things can happen!"

CAPITOLO VIII

Geppetto rifà i piedi a Pinocchio,
e vende la propria casacca per comprargli l'Abbecedario.

Il burattino, appena che si fu levata la fame, cominciò subito a bofonchiare e a piangere, perché voleva un paio di piedi nuovi.

Ma Geppetto, per punirlo della monelleria fatta, lo lasciò piangere e disperarsi per una mezza giornata: poi gli disse:

– E perché dovrei rifarti i piedi? Forse per vederti scappar di nuovo da casa tua?

– Vi prometto – disse il burattino singhiozzando – che da oggi in poi sarò buono . . .

– Tutti i ragazzi – replicò Geppetto – quando vogliono ottenere qualcosa, dicono così.

– Vi prometto che anderò a scuola, studierò e mi farò onore . . .

– Tutti i ragazzi, quando vogliono ottenere qualcosa, ripetono la medesima storia.

– Ma io non sono come gli altri ragazzi! Io sono più buono di tutti, e dico sempre la verità. Vi prometto, babbo, che imparerò un'arte, e che sarò la consolazione e il bastone della vostra vecchiaia. –

Geppetto che, sebbene facesse il viso di tiranno, aveva gli occhi pieni di pianto e il cuore grosso dalla passione nel vedere il suo povero Pinocchio in quello stato compassionevole, non rispose altre parole: ma, presi in mano gli arnesi del mestiere e due pezzetti di legno stagionato, si pose a lavorare di grandissimo impegno.

E in meno d'un'ora, i piedi erano bell'e fatti: due piedini svelti, asciutti e nervosi, come se fossero modellati da un artista di genio.

CHAPTER VIII

*Geppetto makes new feet for Pinocchio and sells
his own jacket to buy him a spelling-book.*

As soon as he satisfied his hunger, the puppet began to
grumble and cry, because he wanted a new pair of feet.

But Geppetto, to punish him for the mischief he had
done, let him cry and wail for half a day. Then he said
to him:

"And why should I make your feet over again? So I
can see you run away from home again?"

"I promise," said the puppet, sobbing, "that from
now on I'll be good."

"All children, when they want something, say the
same thing," replied Geppetto.

"I promise that I'll go to school, I'll study and make
you proud of me."

"All children, when they want something, repeat the
same story."

"But I'm not like other children! I'm better than all
of them, and I always tell the truth. I promise you, father, that I'll learn a trade and be the comfort and staff
of your old age."

Although he put on a tyrant's look, Geppetto's eyes
filled with tears and his heart swelled with compassion
on seeing his poor Pinocchio in such a pitiful state. So
he said nothing more; but taking up his tools and two
small pieces of seasoned wood, he set to work in the
greatest earnest.

And in less than an hour the feet were all done; two
nimble little feet, slender and sinewy, as though carved
by a supreme artist.

Allora Geppetto disse al burattino:

– Chiudi gli occhi e dormi! –

E Pinocchio chiuse gli occhi e fece finta di dormire. E nel tempo che si fingeva addormentato, Geppetto con un po' di colla sciolta in un guscio d'uovo gli appiccicò i due piedi al loro posto, e glieli appiccicò così bene, che non si vedeva nemmeno il segno dell'attaccatura.

Appena il burattino si accòrse di avere i piedi, saltò giù dalla tavola dove stava disteso, e principiò a fare mille sgambetti e mille capriòle, come se fosse ammattito dalla gran contentezza.

– Per ricompensarvi di quanto avete fatto per me – disse Pinocchio al suo babbo – voglio subito andare a scuola.

– Bravo ragazzo.

– Ma per andare a scuola ho bisogno d'un po' di vestito. –

Geppetto, che era povero e non aveva in tasca nemmeno un centesimo, gli fece allora un vestituccio di carta fiorita, un paio di scarpe di scorza d'albero e un berrettino di midolla di pane.

Pinocchio corse subito a specchiarsi in una catinella piena d'acqua e rimase così contento di sé, che disse pavoneggiandosi:

– Paio proprio un signore!

– Davvero, – replicò Geppetto – perché, tienlo a mente, non è il vestito bello che fa il signore, ma è piuttosto il vestito pulito.

– A proposito, – soggiunse il burattino – per andare alla scuola mi manca sempre qualcosa: anzi mi manca il più e il meglio.

– Cioè?

– Mi manca l'Abbecedario.

– Hai ragione: ma come si fa per averlo?

– È facilissimo: si va da un libraio e si compra.

– E i quattrini?

Then Geppetto said to the puppet:

"Close your eyes and go to sleep."

So he closed his eyes and pretended to sleep. And while Pinocchio pretended to be sleeping, Geppetto took some glue he had melted in an eggshell and stuck the feet in place; and he stuck them on so well that you couldn't even see any sign of the seam.

As soon as the puppet realized that he had feet, he jumped down from the table where he had been lying and started to skip and caper all around as though he had gone wild with joy.

"To pay you back for all you've done for me," Pinocchio said to his father, "I'll start school right away."

"Splendid, my boy!"

"But to go to school I need some clothes."

Geppetto, who was poor and didn't even have a penny in his pocket, then made him a modest little suit out of flowered paper, a pair of shoes out of tree bark, and a cap out of bread crumb.

Pinocchio immediately ran to look at himself in a basin full of water and felt so pleased with himself that he said, as proud as a peacock:

"I look like a real gentleman!"

"Quite so," replied Geppetto. "Because, and keep this in mind, it's not fine clothes that make a gentleman, but clean ones."

"By the way," the puppet continued, "to go to school, there's still something I need; in fact, I lack the most important and most necessary thing of all."

"And what's that?"

"I don't have a spelling-book."

"You're right; but how can we get one?"

"It's quite easy; we'll go to a bookstore and buy one."

"And the money?"

– Io non ce l'ho.

– Nemmeno io – soggiunse il buon vecchio, facendosi tristo.

E Pinocchio, sebbene fosse un ragazzo allegrissimo, si fece tristo anche lui: perché la miseria, quando è miseria davvero, la intendono tutti: anche i ragazzi.

– Pazienza! – gridò Geppetto tutt'a un tratto rizzandosi in piedi; e infilatasi la vecchia casacca di frustagno, tutta toppe e rimendi, uscì correndo di casa.

Dopo poco tornò: e quando tornò, aveva in mano l'Abbecedario per il figliuolo, ma la casacca non l'aveva più. Il pover'uomo era in maniche di camicia, e fuori nevicava.

– E la casacca, babbo?

– L'ho venduta.

– Perché l'avete venduta?

– Perché mi faceva caldo. –

Pinocchio capì questa riposta a volo, e non potendo frenare l'impeto del suo buon cuore, saltò al collo di Geppetto e cominciò a baciarlo per tutto il viso.

"I don't have any."

"Neither have I," added the good old man, saddened.

And although Pinocchio was a very good-humored boy, even he became sad, because poverty, when it is true poverty, is understood by everyone, even by children.

"Never mind!" Geppetto exclaimed all of a sudden, getting to his feet; and slipping on his old fustian jacket[22] full of darns and patches, he rushed out of the house.

After a short while he returned; and when he returned, he was holding the spelling-book for his son in his hands, but he no longer had his jacket. The poor man was in shirt sleeves, and it was snowing outside.

"And your jacket, father?"

"I sold it."

"Why did you sell it?"

"Because it made me hot."

Pinocchio caught the meaning of this answer at once, and being unable to restrain his heart's true impulse, he threw his arms around Geppetto's neck and covered his face with kisses.

CAPITOLO IX

Pinocchio vende l'Abbecedario
per andare a vedere il teatrino dei burattini.

Smesso che fu di nevicare, Pinocchio, col suo bravo Abbecedario nuovo sotto il braccio, prese la strada che menava alla scuola: e strada facendo, fantasticava nel suo cervellino mille ragionamenti e mille castelli in aria uno più bello dell'altro.

E discorrendo da sé solo, diceva:

– Oggi, alla scuola, voglio subito imparare a leggere: domani poi imparerò a scrivere, e domani l'altro imparerò a fare i numeri. Poi, colla mia abilità, guadagnerò molti quattrini e coi primi quattrini che mi verranno in tasca, voglio subito fare al mio babbo una bella casacca di panno. Ma che dico di panno? Gliela voglio fare tutta d'argento e d'oro, e coi bottoni di brillanti. E quel pover'uomo se la merita davvero: perché, insomma, per compràrmi i libri e per farmi istruire, è rimasto in maniche di camicia . . . a questi freddi! Non ci sono che i babbi che sieno capaci di certi sacrifizi! . . . –

Mentre tutto commosso diceva così, gli parve di sentire in lontananza una musica di pifferi e di colpi di gran cassa: pì-pì-pì, pì-pì-pì, zum, zum, zum, zum.

Si fermò e stette in ascolto. Quei suoni venivano di fondo a una lunghissima strada traversa, che conduceva a un piccolo paesetto fabbricato sulla spiaggia del mare.

– Che cosa sia questa musica? Peccato che io debba andare a scuola, se no . . . –

E rimase lì perplesso. A ogni modo, bisognava prendere una risoluzione: o a scuola, o a sentire i pifferi.

– Oggi anderò a sentire i pifferi, e domani a scuola:

CHAPTER IX

*Pinocchio sells his spelling-book
in order to go and see the puppet show.*

When it had stopped snowing, Pinocchio, with his fine new spelling-book under his arm, set out for school, and on the way his little head dreamed up a thousand thoughts and built a thousand castles in the air, each more beautiful than the last.

And talking to himself, he said:

"Today, at school, I'll learn how to read right away, tomorrow I'll learn how to write, and the day after tomorrow I'll learn arithmetic. Then with my skill I'll make lots of money, and with the first money that I get in my pocket I'll buy my father a beautiful woolen jacket.[23] But what am I talking about, wool? I'll get him one all of silver and gold, with diamond buttons. And the poor man really deserves it, because, after all, in order to buy me books and have me educated he's left in shirt sleeves . . . in the middle of winter! Only fathers are capable of such sacrifices."

While, greatly moved, he was saying this, he thought he heard in the distance a music of fifes and the thump of a bass drum: fi-fi-fi, fi-fi-fi, boom, boom, boom.

He stopped and stood listening. The sounds came from the other end of a very long crossroad that led to a small village built by the seashore.

"What can that music be? It's too bad I have to go to school; otherwise . . ."

And he stood there, undecided. Nonetheless, it was necessary for him to make a decision: to go to school or to listen to the fifes.

"Today I'll go and hear the fifes, and tomorrow I'll

per andare a scuola c'è sempre tempo – disse finalmente quel monello, facendo una spallucciata.

Detto fatto, infilò giù per la strada traversa e cominciò a correre a gambe. Più correva e più sentiva distinto il suono dei pifferi e dei tonfi della gran-cassa: pì-pì-pì, pì-pì-pì, pì-pì-pì, zum, zum, zum, zum.

Quand'ecco che si trovò in mezzo a una piazza tutta piena di gente, la quale si affollava intorno a un gran baraccone di legno e di tela dipinta di mille colori.

– Che cos'è quel baraccone? – domandò Pinocchio, voltandosi a un ragazzetto che era lì del paese.

– Leggi il cartello, che c'è scritto, e lo saprai.

– Lo leggerei volentieri, ma per l'appunto oggi non so leggere.

– Bravo bue! Allora te lo leggerò io. Sappi dunque che in quel cartello a lettere rosse come il fuoco, c'è scritto: GRAN TEATRO DEI BURATTINI . . .

– È molto che è incominciata la commedia?

– Comincia ora.

– E quanto si spende per entrare?

– Quattro soldi. –

Pinocchio, che aveva addosso la febbre della curiosità, perse ogni ritegno e disse, senza vergognarsi, al ragazzetto col quale parlava:

– Mi daresti quattro soldi fino a domani?

– Te li darei volentieri – gli rispose l'altro canzonandolo – ma oggi per l'appunto non te li posso dare.

– Per quattro soldi, ti vendo la mia giacchetta – gli disse allora il burattino.

– Che vuoi che mi faccia di una giacchetta di carta fiorita? Se ci piove su, non c'è più verso di cavarsela da dosso.

– Vuoi comprare le mie scarpe?

go to school. There's always time to go to school," the little scamp finally said, shrugging his shoulders.

Without further ado, he took the crossroad and began to run hard. The more he ran, the more distinctly he heard the sound of the fifes and the thump of the bass drum: fi-fi-fi, fi-fi-fi, fi-fi-fi, boom, boom, boom, boom.

And suddenly he found himself in the middle of a square full of people crowding around a large booth made of wood and canvas painted in a thousand colors.

"What's that large booth?" asked Pinocchio, turning to a small boy who was from the village.

"Read the poster where it's written, and you'll know."

"I'd like to read it, but it just so happens that today I can't read."

"Good for you, dumb ox! Then I'll read it to you. For your information, on that poster with flaming-red letters it says: GREAT PUPPET SHOW."

"Is it long since the show began?"

"It's just beginning now."

"How much does it cost to get in?"

"Four pennies."

Pinocchio, who was burning with curiosity, lost all reserve, and without feeling ashamed he asked the small boy with whom he was talking:

"Would you give me four pennies until tomorrow?"

"I'd be glad to give them to you," the other boy answered, mocking him, "but it just so happens that today I can't give them to you."

"I'll sell you my jacket for four pennies," the puppet said to him then.

"What do you expect me to do with a jacket of flowered paper? If it rains on it, there's no way of taking it off."

"Do you want to buy my shoes?"

– Sono buone per accendere il fuoco.

– Quanto mi dai del berretto?

– Bell'acquisto davvero! Un berretto di midolla di pane! C'è il caso che i topi me lo vengano a mangiare in capo! –

Pinocchio era sulle spine. Stava lì lì per fare un'ultima offerta: ma non aveva coraggio: esitava, tentennava, pativa. Alla fine disse:

– Vuoi darmi quattro soldi di quest'Abbecedario nuovo?

– Io sono un ragazzo, e non compro nulla dai ragazzi – gli rispose il suo piccolo interlocutore, che aveva più giudizio di lui.

– Per quattro soldi l'Abbecedario lo prendo io – gridò un rivenditore di panni usati, che s'era trovato presente alla conversazione.

E il libro fu venduto lì su due piedi. E pensare che quel pover'uomo di Geppetto era rimasto a casa, a tremare dal freddo in maniche di camicia, per comprare l'Abbecedario al figliuolo!

"They're only good for lighting a fire."

"How much will you give me for my cap?"

"A great bargain, for sure! A cap made of bread crumb! The chances are that the mice would come and eat it right off my head."

Pinocchio was on pins and needles. He was on the verge of making a final offer, but he didn't have the heart; he hesitated, wavered, writhed with anguish. At last he said:

"Will you give me four pennies for this new spelling-book?"

"I'm just a boy, and I don't buy anything from other boys," replied his little interlocutor who had more sense than he had.

"For four pennies I'll take the spelling-book," cried out a ragman who had been present during the conversation.

And so the book was sold right there on the spot. And to think that poor old Geppetto had remained at home shivering with cold in his shirt sleeves just to buy that spelling-book for his son!

CAPITOLO X

I burattini riconoscono il loro fratello Pinocchio,
e gli fanno una grandissima festa; ma sul più bello,
esce fuori il burattinaio Mangiafoco,
e Pinocchio corre il pericolo di fare una brutta fine.

Quando Pinocchio entrò nel teatrino delle marionette, accadde un fatto che destò una mezza rivoluzione.

Bisogna sapere che il sipario era tirato su e la commedia era già incominciata.

Sulla scena si vedevano Arlecchino e Pulcinella, che bisticciavano fra di loro e, secondo il solito, minacciavano da un momento all'altro di scambiarsi un carico di schiaffi e di bastonate.

La platea, tutta attenta, si mandava a male dalle grandi risate, nel sentire il battibecco di quei due burattini, che gestivano e si trattavano d'ogni vituperio con tanta verità, come se fossero proprio due animali ragionevoli e due persone di questo mondo.

Quando all'improvviso, che è che non è, Arlecchino smette di recitare, e voltandosi verso il pubblico e accennando colla mano qualcuno in fondo alla platea, comincia a urlare in tono drammatico:

– Numi del firmamento! sogno o son desto? Eppure quello laggiù è Pinocchio! . . .

– È Pinocchio davvero! – grida Pulcinello.

– È proprio lui! – strilla la signora Rosaura, facendo capolino di fondo alla scena.

– È Pinocchio! è Pinocchio! – urlano in coro tutti i burattini, uscendo a salti fuori dalle quinte. – È Pinocchio! È il nostro fratello Pinocchio! Evviva Pinocchio! . . .

– Pinocchio, vieni quassù da me! – grida Arlecchino

CHAPTER X

*The puppets recognize their brother Pinocchio
and give him a joyous welcome; but just then
the puppeteer, Fire-Eater, turns up and
Pinocchio runs the risk of coming to a bad end.*

When Pinocchio entered the puppet theater, an incident occurred that caused a near riot.

First, you have to know that the curtain was already up and the show had already begun.

On the stage Harlequin and Punchinello were seen quarreling with one another, and as usual were threatening to exchange a load of slaps and thwacks at any moment.

The spectators, completely absorbed, laughed so hard that it hurt as they listened to the squabble of the two puppets who were gesticulating and insulting each other as realistically as if they were two rational beings of this world.

But all of a sudden, just like that, Harlequin stops acting, and turning toward the audience and pointing to someone in the rear of the pit, begins to exclaim melodramatically:

"Gods above! Do I wake or dream? But surely that is Pinocchio down there."

"It's really Pinocchio," yells Punchinello.

"It's actually *him*," screams Signora Rosaura, peeping out from the back of the stage.

"It's Pinocchio! It's Pinocchio!" shout all the puppets in chorus, leaping out from the wings. "It's Pinocchio! It's our brother Pinocchio! Long live Pinocchio!"

"Pinocchio, come up here to me!" shouts Harlequin,

– vieni a gettarti fra le braccia dei tuoi fratelli di legno! –

A questo affettuoso invito, Pinocchio spicca un salto, e di fondo alla platea va nei posti distinti; poi con un altro salto, dai posti distinti monta sulla testa del direttore d'orchestra, e di lì schizza sul palcoscenico.

È impossibile figurarsi gli abbracciamenti, gli strizzoni di collo, i pizzicotti dell'amicizia e le zuccate della vera e sincera fratellanza, che Pinocchio ricevé in mezzo a tanto arruffìo dagli attori e dalle attrici di quella compagnia drammatico-vegetale.

Questo spettacolo era commovente, non c'è che dire: ma il pubblico della platea, vedendo che la commedia non andava più avanti, s'impazientì e prese a gridare:

– Vogliamo la commedia, vogliamo la commedia! –

Tutto fiato buttato via, perché i burattini, invece di continuare la recita, raddoppiarono il chiasso e la grida, e, postosi Pinocchio sulle spalle, se lo portarono in trionfo davanti ai lumi della ribalta.

Allora uscì fuori il burattinaio, un omone così brutto, che metteva paura soltanto a guardarlo. Aveva una barbaccia nera come uno scarabocchio d'inchiostro, e tanto lunga che gli scendeva dal mento fino a terra: basta dire che, quando camminava, se la pestava coi piedi. La sua bocca era larga come un forno, i suoi occhi parevano due lanterne di vetro rosso, col lume acceso di dietro; e con le mani schioccava una grossa frusta, fatta di serpenti e di code di volpe attorcigliate insieme.

All'apparizione inaspettata del burattinaio, ammutolirono tutti: nessuno fiatò più. Si sarebbe sentito volare una mosca. Quei poveri burattini, maschi e femmine, tremavano come tante foglie.

"come and throw yourself into the arms of your brothers-in-wood!"

At this warm invitation Pinocchio makes a bound from the back of the pit to the front section; then with another bound, from the front section he lands on the head of the orchestra conductor; and from there he springs onto the stage.

It's impossible to imagine all the hugging, the tight clasps around the neck, the friendly pinches and the raps on the head given in true brotherly affection, that Pinocchio received in the midst of all that confusion from the actors and actresses of the dramatico-vegetal company.

It was a moving sight, no doubt about it; but the audience, seeing that the show wasn't getting on, became restless and began to yell:

"On with the show! On with the show!"

It was all a waste of breath, because instead of going on with the performance, the puppets redoubled the fracas and their shouts; and raising Pinocchio up on their shoulders, they carried him in triumph before the footlights.[24]

But then the puppeteer came out, a man so huge and ugly that just to look at him gave one a fright. He had a fearsome beard, as black as an inkblot and so long that it reached from his chin down to the ground. Just think that he stepped on it when he walked. His mouth was as wide as an oven, his eyes looked like two lanterns of red glass with the flame burning inside them, and in his hands he held a big whip (which he would crack) made of snakes and foxtails twisted together.

At the unexpected appearance of the puppeteer, everyone turned mute; no one even breathed anymore. You could have heard a fly go by. Those poor puppets, male and female alike, trembled like so many leaves in the wind.

– Perché sei venuto a mettere lo scompiglio nel mio teatro? – domandò il burattinaio a Pinocchio, con un vocione d'Orco gravemente infreddato di testa.

– La creda, illustrissimo, che la colpa non è stata mia! . . .

– Basta così! Stasera faremo i nostri conti. –

Difatti, finita la recita della commedia, il burattinaio andò in cucina, dov'egli s'era preparato per cena un bel montone, che girava lentamente infilato nello spiede. E perché gli mancavano le legna per finirlo di cuocere e di rosolare, chiamò Arlecchino e Pulcinella e disse loro:

– Portatemi di qua quel burattino, che troverete attaccato al chiodo. Mi pare un burattino fatto di un legname molto asciutto, e sono sicuro che, a buttarlo sul fuoco, mi darà una bellissima fiammata all'arrosto. –

Arlecchino e Pulcinella da principio esitarono; ma impauriti da un'occhiataccia del loro padrone, obbedirono: e dopo poco tornarono in cucina, portando sulle braccia il povero Pinocchio, il quale, divincolandosi come un'anguilla fuori dell'acqua, strillava disperatamente:

– Babbo mio, salvatemi! Non voglio morire, no, non voglio morire! . . . –

"What do you mean by coming here to create a riot in my theater?" the puppeteer asked Pinocchio, in the booming voice of an ogre with a bad head cold.

"Believe me, most illustrious Sir, it wasn't my fault."

"That's enough! We'll settle our accounts tonight."

In fact, when the performance was over, the puppeteer went into the kitchen where a fine large sheep he had prepared himself for dinner was slowly turning on the spit. Now, because he lacked the firewood to finish roasting and browning it, he called Harlequin and Punchinello and said to them:

"Bring me the puppet that you'll find hanging on the nail. It seems to me that he's a puppet made of very dry wood, and if I throw him on the fire I'm sure he'll make a beautiful blaze for the roast."

At first Harlequin and Punchinello hesitated, but being terrified at the fierce look of their master, they obeyed; and in a little while they came back into the kitchen carrying poor Pinocchio, who was wriggling like an eel out of water and screaming desperately:

"Dear Father, save me! I don't want to die, no, I don't want to die."

CAPITOLO XI

Mangiafoco starnutisce e perdona a Pinocchio,
il quale poi difende dalla morte il suo amico Arlecchino.

Il burattinaio Mangiafoco (ché questo era il suo nome) pareva un uomo spaventoso, non dico di no, specie con quella sua barbaccia nera che, a uso grembiale, gli copriva tutto il petto e tutte le gambe; ma nel fondo poi non era un cattiv'uomo. Prova ne sia che quando vide portarsi davanti quel povero Pinocchio, che si dibatteva per ogni verso, urlando «Non voglio morire, non voglio morire!», principiò subito a commuoversi e a impietosirsi; e dopo aver resistito un bel pezzo, alla fine non ne poté più, e lasciò andare un sonorissimo starnuto.

A quello starnuto, Arlecchino, che fin allora era stato afflitto e ripiegato come un salcio piangente, si fece tutto allegro in viso e chinatosi verso Pinocchio, gli bisbigliò sottovoce:

– Buone nuove, fratello! Il burattinaio ha starnutito, e questo è segno che s'è mosso a compassione per te, e oramai sei salvo. –

Perché bisogna sapere che, mentre tutti gli uomini, quando si sentono impietositi per qualcuno, o piangono, o per lo meno fanno finta di rasciugarsi gli occhi, Mangiafoco, invece, ogni volta che s'inteneriva davvero aveva il vizio di starnutire. Era un modo come un altro, per dare a conoscere agli altri la sensibilità del suo cuore.

Dopo avere starnutito, il burattinaio, seguitando a fare il burbero, gridò a Pinocchio:

– Finiscila di piangere! I tuoi lamenti mi hanno messo un'uggiolina qui in fondo allo stomaco . . . sento uno

CHAPTER XI

Fire-Eater sneezes and forgives Pinocchio,
who then saves his friend Harlequin from death.

The puppeteer Fire-Eater (for that was his name) seemed a fearsome man, I don't deny it, especially with that awful black beard of his which covered all his chest and legs like an apron; but deep down he wasn't a bad man. The proof is that as soon as he saw poor Pinocchio brought before him, struggling as hard as he could and screaming: "I don't want to die, I don't want to die!" he was immediately touched and began to feel pity for him. And after having resisted for quite awhile, he just couldn't stand it any longer and let out a powerful sneeze.

At that sneeze Harlequin, who until then had been dejected and drooping like a weeping willow tree, showed a cheerful face, and leaning toward Pinocchio he whispered softly:

"Good news, brother! The puppeteer sneezed, and that's a sign that he's taking pity on you. So now you're saved."

Because, you see, whereas all other persons who feel sorry for someone either cry or at least pretend to dry their tears, whenever Fire-Eater was really touched, he had the bad habit of sneezing. It was as good a way as another of letting people know he had a heart with feelings.

After he had sneezed, the puppeteer, continuing to appear grumpy, shouted at Pinocchio:

"Stop crying! Your wailing has given me a funny feeling in the pit of my stomach . . . I feel a spasm, that

spasimo, che quasi quasi . . . *Etcì! Etcì!* – e fece altri due starnuti.

– Felicità! – disse Pinocchio.

– Grazie. E il tuo babbo e la tua mamma sono sempre vivi? – gli domandò Mangiafoco.

– Il babbo, sì: la mamma non l'ho mai conosciuta.

– Chi lo sa che dispiacere sarebbe per il tuo vecchio padre, se ora ti facessi gettare fra que' carboni ardenti! Povero vecchio! lo compatisco! . . . *Etcì, etcì, etcì* – e fece altri tre starnuti.

– Felicità! – disse Pinocchio.

– Grazie! Del resto bisogna compatire anche me, perché, come vedi, non ho più legna per finire di cuocere quel montone arrosto, e tu, dico la verità, in questo caso mi avresti fatto un gran comodo! Ma ormai mi sono impietosito e ci vuol pazienza. Invece di te, metterò a bruciare sotto lo spiede qualche burattino della mia Compagnia. Olà, giandarmi! –

A questo comando comparvero subito due giandarmi di legno, lunghi lunghi, secchi secchi, col cappello a lucerna in testa e colla sciabola sfoderata in mano.

Allora il burattinaio disse loro con voce rantolosa:

– Pigliatemi lì quell'Arlecchino, legatelo ben bene, e poi gettatelo a bruciare sul fuoco. Io voglio che il mio montone sia arrostito bene! –

Figuratevi il povero Arlecchino! Fu tanto il suo spavento, che le gambe gli si ripiegarono e cadde bocconi per terra.

Pinocchio, alla vista di quello spettacolo straziante, andò a gettarsi ai piedi del burattinaio, e piangendo dirottamente e bagnandogli di lacrime tutti i peli della lunghissima barba, cominciò a dire con voce supplichevole:

– Pietà, signor Mangiafoco! . . .

– Qui non ci son signori! – replicò duramente il burattinaio.

almost, almost . . . Atchoo! atchoo!" and he sneezed again twice.

"Bless you!" said Pinocchio.

"Thank you! And your father and mother, are they still alive?" Fire-Eater asked him.

"My father is; but I never knew my mother."

"Who knows how grieved your old father would be if now I had you thrown on those burning coals! Poor old man, I feel sorry for him! . . . Atchoo, atchoo, atchoo!" and he sneezed three more times.

"Bless you!" said Pinocchio.

"Thank you! All the same, you have to feel sorry for me too, because as you can see I don't have any more firewood to finish roasting my mutton, and to tell the truth, in these circumstances you would have been a great convenience to me. But now I've been moved to pity and that's that. Instead of you, I'll have a puppet of my Company burned on the spit. Ho there, gendarmes!"[25]

At this command, two wooden gendarmes appeared on the spot, very tall and lean, with three-cornered hats on their heads and unsheathed swords in their hands.

Then the puppeteer said to them in a wheezing voice:

"Seize Harlequin there, tie him up tight, and then throw him on the fire to burn. I want my mutton to be well roasted."

Imagine poor Harlequin! He was so terrified that his legs folded under him and he fell flat on his face.

At that heartrending sight, Pinocchio threw himself at the puppeteer's feet, weeping in torrents and drenching the hair of that enormously long beard. Then he said in a pleading voice:

"Have pity, Signor Fire-Eater!"

"There are no signori here," replied the puppeteer harshly.

– Pietà, signor Cavaliere! . . .
– Qui non ci sono cavalieri!
– Pietà, signor Commendatore! . . .
– Qui non ci sono commendatori!
– Pietà, Eccellenza! . . . –

A sentirsi chiamare Eccellenza, il burattinaio fece subito il bocchino tondo, e diventato tutt'a un tratto più umano e più trattabile, disse a Pinocchio:

– Ebbene, che cosa vuoi da me?
– Vi domando grazia per il povero Arlecchino! . . .

– Qui non c'è grazia che tenga. Se ho risparmiato te, bisogna che faccia mettere sul fuoco lui, perché io voglio che il mio montone sia arrostito bene.

– In questo caso – gridò fieramente Pinocchio, rizzandosi e gettando via il suo berretto di midolla di pane – in questo caso conosco qual è il mio dovere. Avanti, signori giandarmi! Legatemi e gettatemi là fra quelle fiamme. No, non è giusta che il povero Arlecchino, il vero amico mio, debba morire per me! –

Queste parole, pronunziate con voce alta e con accento eroico, fecero piangere tutti i burattini che erano

"Have pity, Sir Knight!"

"There are no knights here."

"Have pity, Sir Commendatore!"

"There are no commendatori here."

"Have pity, Excellency!"[26]

On hearing himself called Excellency, the puppeteer quickly pursed his lips, and suddenly becoming more gentle and affable, he said to Pinocchio:

"Well then, what do you want of me?"

"I beg mercy of you for poor Harlequin."

"There's no place for mercy here. Since I've spared you, I must have him put on the fire, because I want my mutton to be well roasted."

"In that case," cried Pinocchio boldly, getting up and throwing off his cap of crumb, "in that case I know where my duty lies. Come gendarmes! Bind me and throw me on those flames there. No, it is not right that poor Harlequin, my true friend, should die for me."

These words, uttered in a clear, heroic tone, made all the puppets present at that scene cry. Even the gen-

presenti a quella scena. Gli stessi giandarmi, sebbene fossero di legno, piangevano come due agnellini di latte.

Mangiafoco, sul principio, rimase duro e immobile come un pezzo di ghiaccio: ma poi, adagio adagio, cominciò anche lui a commuoversi e a starnutire. E fatti quattro o cinque starnuti, aprì affettuosamente le braccia e disse a Pinocchio:

– Tu sei un gran bravo ragazzo! Vieni qua da me e dammi un bacio. –

Pinocchio corse subito, e arrampicandosi come uno scoiattolo su per la barba del burattinaio, andò a posargli un bellissimo bacio sulla punta del naso.

– Dunque la grazia è fatta? – domandò il povero Arlecchino, con un fil di voce che si sentiva appena.

– La grazia è fatta! – rispose Mangiafoco: poi soggiunse sospirando e tentennando il capo:

– Pazienza! Per questa sera mi rassegnerò a mangiare il montone mezzo crudo: ma un'altra volta, guai a chi toccherà! . . . –

Alla notizia della grazia ottenuta, i burattini corsero tutti sul palcoscenico e, accesi i lumi e i lampadari come in serata di gala, cominciarono a saltare e a ballare. Era l'alba e ballavano sempre.

darmes, although they were made of wood, cried like two newborn lambs.

At first, Fire-Eater remained hard and unyielding, like a block of ice; but then he too began slowly to melt and then to sneeze. And after four or five sneezes, he opened his arms affectionately and said to Pinocchio:

"You're really a wonderful lad. Come here and give me a kiss."

Pinocchio ran quickly, and scampering up the puppeteer's beard like a squirrel, he planted a hearty kiss on the tip of his nose.

"Mercy is granted then?" asked poor Harlequin, in a faint voice that could hardly be heard.

"Mercy is granted," answered Fire-Eater; then, with a sigh as he shook his head, he added:

"So be it! For tonight I'll resign myself to eating my mutton half-cooked; but the next time it'll be too bad for whoever happens to come along."

At the news that mercy had been obtained, all the puppets ran onto the stage, and having lit the lamps and chandeliers as if for an evening gala performance, they began to leap and dance. Dawn came, and they were still dancing.

CAPITOLO XII

Il burattinaio Mangiafoco regala cinque monete d'oro
a Pinocchio perché le porti al suo babbo Geppetto:
e Pinocchio, invece, si lascia abbindolare
dalla Volpe e dal Gatto e se ne va con loro.

Il giorno dipoi Mangiafoco chiamò in disparte Pinocchio e gli domandò:

– Come si chiama tuo padre?

– Geppetto.

– E che mestiere fa?

– Il povero.

– Guadagna molto?

– Guadagna tanto quanto ci vuole per non aver mai un centesimo in tasca. Si figuri che per comprarmi l'Abbecedario della scuola dové vendere l'unica casacca che aveva addosso: una casacca che, fra toppe e rimendi, era tutta una piaga.

– Povero diavolo! Mi fa quasi compassione. Ecco qui cinque monete d'oro. Va' subito a portargliele e salutalo tanto da parte mia. –

Pinocchio, com'è facile immaginarselo, ringraziò mille volte il burattinaio: abbracciò, a uno a uno, tutti i burattini della compagnia, anche i giandarmi; e fuori di sé dalla contentezza, si mise in viaggio per ritornarsene a casa sua.

Ma non aveva fatto ancora mezzo chilometro, che incontrò per la strada una Volpe zoppa da un piede e un Gatto cieco da tutt'e due gli occhi che se ne andavano là là, aiutandosi fra di loro, da buoni compagni di sventura. La Volpe, che era zoppa, camminava appoggiandosi al Gatto: e il Gatto, che era cieco, si lasciava guidare dalla Volpe.

CHAPTER XII

The puppeteer, Fire-Eater, gives Pinocchio
five gold pieces to take to his father Geppetto;
but Pinocchio lets himself be duped
by the Fox and the Cat and goes off with them.

The next day Fire-Eater called Pinocchio to one side and asked him:

"What's your father's name?"

"Geppetto."

"And what's his trade?"

"That of a poor man."

"Does he earn much?"

"He earns enough never to have a cent in his pocket. Just think that in order to buy me a spelling-book for school he had to sell the only jacket he had; a jacket so full of darns and patches that it was a calamity."

"Poor devil, I almost feel sorry for him. Here's five gold coins. Go and take them to him right away, and give him my best wishes."

As you can well imagine, Pinocchio thanked the puppeteer a thousand times. He embraced all the puppets of the Company one by one, even the gendarmes, and then, beside himself with joy, he set out for home.

But he hadn't yet gone half a mile when he met a Fox, lame in one foot, and a Cat, blind in both eyes, who were making their way very slowly, helping one another like good comrades in misfortune. The Fox, who was lame, walked leaning on the Cat, and the Cat, who was blind, was led by the Fox.

– Buon giorno, Pinocchio – gli disse la Volpe, salutandolo garbatamente.

– Com'è che sai il mio nome? – domandò il burattino.

– Conosco bene il tuo babbo.

– Dove l'hai veduto?

– L'ho veduto ieri sulla porta di casa sua.

– E che cosa faceva?

– Era in maniche di camicia e tremava dal freddo.

– Povero babbo! Ma, se Dio vuole, da oggi in poi non tremerà più! . . .

– Perché?

– Perché io sono diventato un gran signore.

– Un gran signore tu? – disse la Volpe, e cominciò a ridere di un riso sguaiato e canzonatore: e il Gatto rideva anche lui, ma per non darlo a vedere, si pettinava i baffi colle zampe davanti.

– C'è poco da ridere – gridò Pinocchio impermalito. – Mi dispiace davvero di farvi venire l'acquolina in bocca, ma queste qui, se ve ne intendete, sono cinque bellissime monete d'oro. –

E tirò fuori le monete avute in regalo da Mangiafoco.

"Good day, Pinocchio," said the Fox, greeting him politely.

"How is it that you know my name?" asked the puppet.

"I know your father well."

"Where did you last see him?"

"I saw him yesterday in the doorway of his house."

"And what was he doing?"

"He was in shirt sleeves, shivering with cold."

"Poor father! But, God willing, from now on he won't shiver any more."

"Why not?"

"Because I've become a wealthy man."

"A wealthy man, you?" said the Fox, and he began to laugh in a coarse and mocking manner.[27] And the Cat was laughing too, but so as not to show it he stroked his whiskers with his forepaws.

"There's nothing to laugh at," cried Pinocchio, peevishly. "I'm really sorry to make your mouths water, but these, if you know anything about it, are five beautiful gold coins."

And he pulled out the coins he had received as a gift from Fire-Eater.

Al simpatico suono di quelle monete, la Volpe per un moto involontario allungò la gamba che pareva rattrappita, e il Gatto spalancò tutt'e due gli occhi che parvero due lanterne verdi: ma poi li richiuse subito, tant'è vero che Pinocchio non si accòrse di nulla.

– E ora – gli domandò la Volpe – che cosa vuoi farne di codeste monete?

– Prima di tutto – rispose il burattino – voglio comprare per il mio babbo una bella casacca nuova, tutta d'oro e d'argento e coi bottoni di brillanti: e poi voglio comprare un Abbecedario per me.

– Per te?

– Davvero: perché voglio andare a scuola e mettermi a studiare a buono.

– Guarda me! – disse la Volpe. – Per la passione sciocca di studiare ho perduto una gamba.

– Guarda me! – disse il Gatto. – Per la passione sciocca di studiare ho perduto la vista di tutti e due gli occhi. –

In quel mentre un Merlo bianco, che se ne stava appollaiato sulla siepe della strada, fece il suo solito verso e disse:

– Pinocchio, non dar retta ai consigli dei cattivi compagni: se no, te ne pentirai! –

Povero Merlo, non l'avesse mai detto! Il Gatto, spiccando un gran salto, gli si avventò addosso, e senza dargli nemmeno il tempo di dire *ohi*, se lo mangiò in un boccone, con le penne e tutto.

Mangiato che l'ebbe e ripulitosi la bocca, chiuse gli occhi daccapo, e ricominciò a fare il cieco come prima.

– Povero Merlo! – disse Pinocchio al Gatto – perché l'hai trattato così male?

– Ho fatto per dargli una lezione. Così un'altra volta imparerà a non metter bocca nei discorsi degli altri. –

At the agreeable ring of those coins, the Fox, with an involuntary movement, stretched out the paw that was supposed to be crippled, and the Cat opened both eyes so wide that they looked like two green lanterns; but then he closed them again so quickly that Pinocchio didn't notice anything.

"And now," the Fox asked him, "what do you expect to do with those coins of yours?"

"First of all," the puppet answered, "I intend to buy my father a fine new jacket made all of gold and silver, and with diamond buttons; and then I want to buy a spelling-book for myself."

"For yourself?"

"That's right. Because I want to go to school and study hard."

"Look at me!" said the Fox. "Because of a foolish passion for study I lost a paw."

"Look at me!" said the Cat. "Because of a foolish passion for study I lost the sight of both eyes."

At that moment a White Blackbird, who was perched on the hedge by the road, began his usual chirping and said:

"Pinocchio, don't listen to the advice of bad companions, or you'll regret it!"

Poor Blackbird, would that he had never said it! With a sudden leap the Cat pounced on him and without even giving him the time to say "oh" devoured him in one gulp, feathers and all.

After he had eaten him and wiped his mouth, the Cat closed his eyes again and began once more to pretend that he was blind as before.

"Poor Blackbird," said Pinocchio to the Cat, "why did you treat him so badly?"[28]

"I did it to teach him a lesson. Now the next time he'll know better than to stick his beak into other people's affairs."

Erano giunti più che a mezza strada quando la Volpe, fermandosi di punto in bianco, disse al burattino:

– Vuoi raddoppiare le tue monete d'oro?

– Cioè?

– Vuoi tu, di cinque miserabili zecchini, farne cento, mille, duemila?

– Magari! e la maniera?

– La maniera è facilissima. Invece di tornartene a casa tua, dovresti venir con noi.

– E dove mi volete condurre?

– Nel paese dei Barbagianni. –

Pinocchio ci pensò un poco, e poi disse risolutamente:

– No, non ci voglio venire. Oramai sono vicino a casa, e voglio andarmene a casa, dove c'è il mio babbo che m'aspetta. Chi lo sa, povero vecchio, quanto ha sospirato ieri, a non vedermi tornare. Pur troppo io sono stato un figliolo cattivo, e il Grillo-parlante aveva ragione quando diceva: «i ragazzi disobbedienti non possono aver bene in questo mondo». E io l'ho provato a mie spese, perché mi sono capitate dimolte disgrazie, e anche ieri sera in casa di Mangiafoco, ho corso pericolo . . . Brrr! mi viene i bordoni soltanto a pensarci!

– Dunque – disse la Volpe – vuoi proprio andare a casa tua? Allora va' pure, e tanto peggio per te.

– Tanto peggio per te! – ripeté il Gatto.

– Pensaci bene, Pinocchio, perché tu dai un calcio alla fortuna.

– Alla fortuna! – ripeté il Gatto.

– I tuoi cinque zecchini, dall'oggi al domani sarebbero diventati duemila.

– Duemila! – ripeté il Gatto.

– Ma com'è mai possibile che diventino tanti? – domandò Pinocchio, restando a bocca aperta dallo stupore.

They had gone more than halfway to Geppetto's house, when all of a sudden the Fox stopped and said to the puppet:

"Do you want to double your gold coins?"

"What do you mean?"

"Do you want to turn those miserable five gold pieces into a hundred or a thousand or two thousand?"

"You bet! But how?"

"The way to do it is quite easy. Instead of going back home, you'd only have to come with us."

"And where do you want to take me?"

"To Dodoland."

Pinocchio thought about it for a moment, and then said resolutely:

"No, I won't come. I'm nearly home now, and I want to continue home where my father's waiting for me. Who knows how sad the poor old man was yesterday not seeing me come back. Unfortunately, I've been a bad son, and the Talking Cricket was right when he said: 'Disobedient children can't come to any good in this world.' And I've learned it the hard way, because a lot of bad things have happened to me; and just last night in Fire-Eater's house I was in danger of . . . Brrr! I get goose pimples just thinking of it!"

"So then," the Fox said, "you really want to go home? Well, go ahead then, and so much the worse for you."

"So much the worse for you!" repeated the Cat.

"Think it over, Pinocchio, because you're throwing away a golden opportunity."

"A golden opportunity!" repeated the Cat.

"Your five gold pieces could have become two thousand overnight."

"Two thousand!" repeated the Cat.

"But how is it possible for them to become that many?" asked Pinocchio, his mouth agape in astonishment.

– Te lo spiego subito – disse la Volpe. – Bisogna sapere che nel paese dei Barbagianni c'è un campo benedetto, chiamato da tutti il Campo dei miracoli. Tu fai in questo campo una piccola buca e ci metti dentro, per esempio, uno zecchino d'oro. Poi ricopri la buca con un po' di terra: l'annaffi con due secchie d'acqua di fontana, ci getti sopra una presa di sale, e la sera te ne vai tranquillamente a letto. Intanto, durante la notte, lo zecchino germoglia e fiorisce, e la mattina dopo, di levata, ritornando nel campo, che cosa trovi? Trovi un bell'albero carico di tanti zecchini d'oro quanti chicchi di grano può avere una bella spiga nel mese di giugno.

– Sicché dunque – disse Pinocchio sempre più sbalordito – se io sotterrassi in quel campo i miei cinque zecchini, la mattina dopo quanti zecchini ci troverei?

– È un conto facilissimo – rispose la Volpe – un conto che puoi farlo sulla punta delle dita. Poni che ogni zecchino ti faccia un grappolo di cinquecento zecchini: moltiplica il cinquecento per cinque, e la mattino dopo ti trovi in tasca duemilacinquecento zecchini lampanti e sonanti.

– Oh che bella cosa! – gridò Pinocchio, ballando dall'allegrezza. – Appena che questi zecchini li avrò raccolti, ne prenderò per me duemila e gli altri cinquecento di più li darò in regalo a voialtri due.

– Un regalo a noi? – gridò la Volpe sdegnandosi e chiamandosi offesa. – Dio te ne liberi!

– Te ne liberi! – ripeté il Gatto.

– Noi – riprese la Volpe – non lavoriamo per il vile interesse: noi lavoriamo unicamente per arricchire gli altri.

– Gli altri! – ripeté il Gatto.

– Che brave persone! – pensò dentro di sé Pinocchio: e dimenticandosi lì sul tamburo, del suo babbo, della casacca nuova, dell'Abbecedario e di tutti i buoni proponimenti fatti, disse alla Volpe e al Gatto:

– Andiamo subito, io vengo con voi. –

"I'll explain it to you right away," said the Fox. "You see, in Dodoland there's a blessed field known to everybody as the Field of Miracles. In this field you dig a little hole and you put, say, a gold piece in it. Then you cover the hole over again with some earth, water it with two bucketsful of spring water, sprinkle a pinch of salt over it, and in the evening you go peacefully to bed. Meanwhile, during the night the gold piece sprouts and blossoms, and as soon as you're up the next morning, you go back to the field and what do you find? You find a beautiful tree laden with as many gold pieces as a good ear of corn has grains in the month of June."

"Why then," said Pinocchio, more amazed than ever, "if I buried my five gold pieces in that field, how many would I find there the next morning?"

"That's easy enough to figure out," answered the Fox, "you can do it on your fingers. Suppose that each gold piece makes a bunch of five hundred; multiply the five hundred by five, and the next morning there you are with two thousand five hundred shiny, clinking gold pieces in your pocket."

"Oh, how wonderful!" shouted Pinocchio, dancing for joy. "As soon as I've picked the gold pieces I'll keep two thousand for myself, and I'll give the remaining five hundred to you two as a present."

"A present for us?" cried the Fox, taking offense and claiming to be insulted. "Heaven forbid!"

"Forbid!" repeated the Cat.

"We," continued the Fox, "we do not work for miserable personal gain; we work only to enrich others."

"Others!" repeated the Cat.

"What wonderful people!" Pinocchio thought to himself. And forgetting on the spot all about his father, the new jacket, the spelling-book, and all the good resolutions he had made, he said to the Fox and the Cat:

"Let's get going! I'm coming with you."

CAPITOLO XIII

L'osteria del «Gambero Rosso».

Cammina, cammina, cammina, alla fine sul far della sera arrivarono stanchi morti all'osteria del Gambero Rosso.

– Fermiamoci un po' qui – disse la Volpe – tanto per mangiare un boccone e per riposarci qualche ora. A mezzanotte poi ripartiremo per essere domani, all'alba, nel Campo dei miracoli. –

Entrati nell'osteria, si posero tutti e tre a tavola: ma nessuno di loro aveva appetito.

Il povero Gatto, sentendosi gravemente indisposto di stomaco, non poté mangiare altro che trentacinque triglie con salsa di pomodoro e quattro porzioni di trippa alla parmigiana: e perché la trippa non gli pareva condita abbastanza, si rifece tre volte a chiedere il burro e il formaggio grattato!

La Volpe avrebbe spelluzzicato volentieri qualche cosa anche lei: ma siccome il medico le aveva ordinato una grandissima dieta, così dové contentarsi di una semplice lepre dolce e forte con un leggerissimo contorno di pollastre ingrassate e di galletti di primo canto. Dopo la lepre, si fece portare per tornagusto un cibreino di pernici, di starne, di conigli, di ranocchi, di lucertole e d'uva paradisa; e poi non volle altro. Aveva tanta nausea per il cibo, diceva lei, che non poteva accostarsi nulla alla bocca.

Quello che mangiò meno di tutti fu Pinocchio. Chiese uno spicchio di noce e un cantuccio di pane, e lasciò nel piatto ogni cosa. Il povero figliuolo, col pensiero sempre fisso al Campo dei miracoli, aveva preso un'indigestione anticipata di monete d'oro.

CHAPTER XIII

The Red Crawfish Inn.

And walk and walk and walk,[29] until toward evening they finally arrived dead tired at the Red Crawfish Inn.

"Let's stop here for a while," said the Fox, "just to have a bite to eat and rest for a few hours. Then at midnight we'll start out again, so as to be at the Field of Miracles tomorrow at dawn."

Entering the inn, the three of them sat down at a table, but none of them was hungry.

The poor Cat, suffering from a badly upset stomach, was only able to eat thirty-five red mullets with tomato sauce and four portions of tripe à la Parmesan; and because the tripe didn't seem savory enough, he didn't hesitate to ask for the butter and grated cheese three times.

The Fox also would have been glad to pick at something; but seeing that the doctor had put him on a strict diet, he had to limit himself to hare in sweet-and-sour sauce, meagerly garnished with plump pullets and prime cockerels. After the hare, as an entremets[30] he ordered a small fricassée of partridges, rabbits, frogs, lizards, and dried sweet paradise grapes. Following this, he took nothing else. He felt such nausea at the thought of food, so he said, that he couldn't bring anything to his mouth.

It was Pinocchio who ate least of all. He asked for a quarter of a walnut and a small piece of bread crust, but he left everything on his plate. With his mind fixed on the Field of Miracles, the poor boy had got a case of anticipatory indigestion from gold coins.

Quand'ebbero cenato, la Volpe disse all'oste:

– Datemi due buone camere, una per il signor Pinocchio e un'altra per me e per il mio compagno. Prima di ripartire stiacceremo un sonnellino. Ricordatevi però che a mezzanotte vogliamo essere svegliati per continuare il nostro viaggio.

– Sissignori – rispose l'oste, e strizzò l'occhio alla Volpe e al Gatto, come dire: «Ho mangiata la foglia e ci siamo intesi! . . .»

Appena che Pinocchio fu entrato nel letto, si addormentò a colpo e principiò a sognare. E sognando gli pareva di essere in mezzo a un campo, e questo campo era pieno di arboscelli carichi di grappoli, e questi grappoli erano carichi di zecchini d'oro che, dondolandosi mossi dal vento, facevano *zin*, *zin*, *zin*, quasi volessero dire «chi ci vuole, venga a prenderci.» Ma quando Pinocchio fu sul più bello, quando, cioè, allungò la mano per prendere a manciate tutte quelle belle monete e mettersele in

After they had supped, the Fox said to the innkeeper: "Let us have two nice rooms, one for Signor Pinocchio and another for me and my companion. Before starting out again we'll squeeze out a few winks. But remember that at midnight we want to be awakened so we can continue our journey."

"Yessir," replied the innkeeper, and he winked at the Fox and the Cat, as if to say: "I get it, and you can count on me."

As soon as Pinocchio got into bed, he fell right to sleep and began to dream. And in his dream he saw himself in the middle of a field; and the field was full of small trees laden with clusters, and the clusters were laden with gold pieces that went *clinkety-clink* swaying in the wind, as if to say: "Whoever wants us, come and get us." But just when Pinocchio was at the best part, that is, when he stretched out his hands to take fistfuls of those beautiful coins and put them in his pocket, he was

tasca, si trovò svegliato all'improvviso da tre violentissimi colpi dati nella porta di camera.

Era l'oste che veniva a dirgli che la mezzanotte era sonata.

– E i miei compagni sono pronti? – gli domandò il burattino.

– Altro che pronti! Sono partiti due ore fa.

– Perché mai tanta fretta?

– Perché il Gatto ha ricevuto un'imbasciata, che il suo gattino maggiore, malato di geloni ai piedi, stava in pericolo di vita.

– E la cena l'hanno pagata?

– Che vi pare? Quelle lì sono persone troppo educate, perché facciano un affronto simile alla signoria vostra.

– Peccato! Quest'affronto mi avrebbe fatto tanto piacere! – disse Pinocchio, grattandosi il capo. Poi domandò:

– E dove hanno detto di aspettarmi quei buoni amici?

– Al Campo dei miracoli, domattina, allo spuntare del giorno. –

Pinocchio pagò uno zecchino per la cena sua e per quella dei suoi compagni, e dopo partì.

Ma si può dire che partisse a tastoni, perché fuori dell'osteria c'era un buio così buio che non ci si vedeva da qui a lì. Nella campagna all'intorno non si sentiva alitare una foglia. Solamente, di tanto in tanto, alcuni uccellacci notturni, traversando la strada da una siepe all'altra, venivano a sbattere le ali sul naso di Pinocchio, il quale facendo un salto indietro per la paura, gridava: – Chi va là? – e l'eco delle colline circostanti ripeteva in lontananza: – Chi va là? chi va là? chi va là? –

Intanto, mentre camminava, vide sul tronco di un albero un piccolo animaletto che riluceva di una luce pallida e opaca, come un lumino da notte dentro una lampada di porcellana trasparente.

– Chi sei? – gli domandò Pinocchio.

rudely awakened by three loud knocks on the door of his room.

It was the innkeeper, who had come to tell him that midnight had struck.

"And are my companions ready?" the puppet asked him.

"I'll say they're ready! They left two hours ago."

"Why in such a hurry?"

"Because the Cat received a message saying that his eldest kitten, suffering from chilblains, was near death."

"Did they pay for the supper?"

"How can you think that? They are too well bred to insult your lordship like that!"

"What a pity! I would have been glad to receive such an insult!" said Pinocchio, scratching his head. Then he asked:

"And where did those good friends of mine say they would wait for me?"

"In the Field of Miracles, at the crack of dawn."

Pinocchio paid a gold piece for his supper and for that of his companions, and then went on his way.

But you can say that he went gropingly, because outside the inn it was dark, so dark that it was impossible to see a step ahead. All around in the countryside not even a leaf was heard rustling. Only a few scary night birds, crossing the road now and then from one hedge to the other, hit their wings against Pinocchio's nose. Jumping back in fright, he shouted: "Who goes there!" And in the distance the echo from the surrounding hills repeated: Who goes there? Who goes there? Who goes there?

In the meantime, as he walked on, he saw a tiny creature on the trunk of a tree, glowing with a dim and pale light, like a nightcandle inside a transparent china lamp.

"Who are you?" Pinocchio asked.

– Sono l'ombra del Grillo-parlante – rispose l'animaletto con una vocina fioca fioca, che pareva venisse dal mondo di là.

– Che vuoi da me? – disse il burattino.

– Voglio darti un consiglio. Ritorna indietro e porta i quattro zecchini, che ti sono rimasti, al tuo povero babbo, che piange e si dispera per non averti più veduto.

– Domani il mio babbo sarà un gran signore, perché questi quattro zecchini diventeranno duemila.

– Non ti fidare, ragazzo mio, di quelli che promettono di farti ricco dalla mattina alla sera. Per il solito o sono matti o imbroglioni! Dài retta a me, ritorna indietro.

– E io invece voglio andare avanti.

– L'ora è tarda! . . .

– Voglio andare avanti.

– La nottata è scura . . .

– Voglio andare avanti.

– La strada è pericolosa . . .

– Voglio andare avanti.

– Ricordati che i ragazzi che vogliono fare di capriccio e a modo loro, prima o poi se ne pentono.

– Le solite storie. Buona notte, Grillo.

– Buona notte, Pinocchio, e che il cielo ti salvi dalla guazza e dagli assassini. –

Appena dette queste ultime parole, il Grillo-parlante si spense a un tratto, come si spenge un lume soffiandoci sopra, e la strada rimase più buia di prima.

"I am the ghost of the Talking Cricket," answered the tiny creature, in a faint little voice that seemed to come from the world beyond.

"What do you want with me?" said the puppet.

"I want to give you a piece of advice. Go back and take the four gold pieces you still have left to your poor father, who is weeping in despair at not seeing you any more."

"Tomorrow my father will be a wealthy man, because these four gold pieces are going to become two thousand."

"My boy, don't trust people who promise to make you rich overnight. Usually, they are either madmen or swindlers. Listen to me; go back."

"And instead, I want to go on."

"The hour is late!"

"I want to go on."

"The night is dark . . ."

"I want to go on."

"The way is dangerous . . ."

"I want to go on."

"Remember that children who want their own way regret it sooner or later."

"The same old story. Good night, Cricket."

"Good night, Pinocchio, and may Heaven protect you from the dampness and the assassins."

No sooner had he spoken these last words than the Talking Cricket suddenly went out, as a candle goes out when you blow on it, and the road was left darker than before.

CAPITOLO XIV

Pinocchio, per non aver dato retta
ai buoni consigli del Grillo-parlante,
s'imbatte negli assassini.

— Davvero – disse fra sé il burattino rimettendosi in viaggio – come siamo disgraziati noi altri poveri ragazzi! Tutti ci sgridano, tutti ci ammoniscono, tutti ci dànno dei consigli. A lasciarli dire, tutti si metterebbero in capo di essere i nostri babbi e i nostri maestri; tutti: anche i Grilli-parlanti. Ecco qui: perché io non ho voluto dar retta a quell'uggioso di Grillo, chi lo sa quante disgrazie, secondo lui, mi dovrebbero accadere! Dovrei incontrare anche gli assassini! Meno male che agli assassini io non ci credo, né ci ho creduto mai. Per me gli assassini sono stati inventati apposta dai babbi, per far paura ai ragazzi che vogliono andar fuori la notte. E poi se anche li trovassi qui sulla strada, mi darebbero forse soggezione? Neanche per sogno. Anderei loro sul viso, gridando: «Signori assassini, che cosa vogliono da me? Si rammentino che con me non si scherza! Se ne vadano dunque per i fatti loro, e zitti!» A questa parlantina fatta sul serio, quei poveri assassini, mi par di vederli, scapperebbero via come il vento. Caso poi fossero tanto ineducati da non volere scappare, allora scapperei io, e così la farei finita . . . –

Ma Pinocchio non poté finire il suo ragionamento, perché in quel punto gli parve di sentire dietro di sé un leggerissimo fruscìo di foglie.

Si voltò a guardare, e vide nel buio due figuracce nere, tutte imbacuccate in due sacchi da carbone, le quali correvano dietro a lui a salti e in punta di piedi, come se fossero due fantasmi.

CHAPTER XIV

For not listening to the good advice
of the Talking Cricket,
Pinocchio runs into the assassins.

"Really," said the puppet to himself, resuming his journey, "how unlucky we poor boys are! Everybody scolds us, everybody criticizes us, everybody gives us advice. If they had their way, they'd all take it into their heads to be our fathers and teachers, all of them, even Talking Crickets. Now, for example, just because I wouldn't listen to that gloomy Cricket, who knows, according to him, how many disasters must befall me. I'm even supposed to run into assassins! It's a good thing I don't believe in assassins; and I never have believed in them either. As far as I'm concerned, assassins were invented on purpose by fathers just to frighten children who want to go out at night. And besides, even if I happened to meet them here on the road, do you think they'd scare me? Not in the least. I'd go right up to them and shout: 'You assassins there, what do you want with me? Take heed that I'm not to be trifled with. So go on about your business, and shush!' I can just see those poor assassins rush off like the wind at such sharp talk. But if they happened to be so ill-mannered as not to run off, then I'd run away, and that would be the end of that!"

But Pinocchio wasn't able to finish his discourse, because just then he thought he heard a slight rustling of leaves behind him.

He turned around to look, and there, in the darkness, he saw two horrid black shapes, all loosely wrapped in charcoal sacks. They were chasing after him in leaps on tiptoe, like two ghosts.

– Eccoli davvero! – disse dentro di sé: e non sapendo dove nascondere i quattro zecchini, se li nascose in bocca e precisamente sotto la lingua.

Poi si provò a scappare. Ma non aveva ancora fatto il primo passo, che sentì agguantarsi per le braccia e intese due voci orribili e cavernose, che gli dissero:

– O la borsa o la vita! –

Pinocchio non potendo rispondere con le parole, a motivo delle monete che aveva in bocca, fece mille salamelecchi e mille pantomime, per dare ad intendere a quei due incappati, di cui si vedevano soltanto gli occhi attraverso i buchi dei sacchi, che lui era un povero burattino e che non aveva in tasca nemmeno un centesimo falso.

– Via, via! Meno ciarle e fuori i denari! – gridarono minacciosamente i due briganti.

E il burattino fece col capo e colle mani un segno, come dire: «Non ne ho.»

– Metti fuori i denari o sei morto – disse l'assassino più alto di statura.

– Morto! – ripeté l'altro.

– E dopo ammazzato te, ammazzeremo anche tuo padre!

– Anche tuo padre!

– No, no, no, il mio povero babbo no! – gridò Pi-

"They're really here!" he said to himself; and not knowing where to hide his four gold pieces, he put them in his mouth, right under his tongue.

Then he tried to run away. But he hadn't yet taken the first step when he felt himself grabbed by the arms and heard two horrible, deep voices saying to him:

"Your money or your life!"

Unable to reply in words because of the coins he had in his mouth, Pinocchio made a thousand salaams and gestures, trying to convince those two shrouded figures, whose eyes alone could be seen through the holes in the sacks, that he was just a poor puppet and that he didn't have so much as a bad penny in his pocket.

"Come on! Less blab, and out with your money!" the two brigands cried threateningly.

But the puppet made a sign with his head and hands as if to say: "I don't have any."

"Hand over your money or you're a dead man!" said the taller of the two assassins.

"A dead man!" replied the other.

"And after we've killed you, we'll kill your father, too."

"Your father, too!"

"No, no, no, not my poor father!" cried Pinocchio

nocchio con accento disperato: ma nel gridare così, gli zecchini gli sonarono in bocca.

– Ah furfante! dunque i danari te li sei nascosti sotto la lingua? Sputali subito! –

E Pinocchio, duro!

– Ah! tu fai il sordo? Aspetta un po', ché penseremo noi a farteli sputare! –

Difatti uno di loro afferrò il burattino per la punta del naso e quell'altro lo prese per la bazza, e lì cominciarono a tirare screanzatamente uno per in qua e l'altro per in là, tanto da costringerlo a spalancare la bocca: ma non ci fu verso. La bocca del burattino pareva inchiodata e ribadita.

Allora l'assassino più piccolo di statura, cavato fuori un coltellaccio, provò a conficcarglielo a guisa di leva e di scalpello fra le labbra: ma Pinocchio, lesto come un lampo, gli azzannò la mano coi denti, e dopo avergliela con un morso staccata di netto, la sputò; e figuratevi la sua meraviglia quando, invece di una mano, si accòrse di avere sputato in terra uno zampetto di gatto.

Incoraggito da questa prima vittoria, si liberò a forza dalle unghie degli assassini, e saltata la siepe della strada, cominciò a fuggire per la campagna. E gli assassini a correre dietro a lui, come due cani dietro una lepre: e quello che aveva perduto uno zampetto correva con una gamba sola, né si è saputo mai come facesse.

Dopo una corsa di quindici chilometri, Pinocchio non ne poteva più. Allora, vistosi perso, si arrampicò su per il fusto di un altissimo pino e si pose a sedere in vetta ai rami. Gli assassini tentarono di arrampicarsi anche loro, ma giunti a metà del fusto sdrucciolarono e, ricascando a terra, si spellarono le mani e i piedi.

Non per questo si dettero per vinti: ché anzi, raccolto un fastello di legna secche a piè del pino, vi appiccarono il fuoco. In men che non si dice, il pino cominciò a bruciare e a divampare come una candela agitata dal vento.

in an anguished voice; but in crying out like that, the gold pieces clinked in his mouth.

"Aha, you scoundrel! So you've hidden the money under your tongue. Spit it out, right away!"

But Pinocchio stood firm.

"Ah! So you're playing deaf, are you? Just wait a moment, we'll get you to spit it out."

With that, one of them gripped the puppet by the end of his nose and the other seized him by the chin; then they began to tug rudely, one down and the other up, trying to force him to open his mouth. But no way. It was as if the puppet's mouth had been nailed and riveted.

Then the shorter assassin pulled out a horrid knife and tried to stick it between the puppet's lips like a lever or a chisel; but Pinocchio, as quick as a flash, dug his teeth into his hand, and after biting it clean off, he spat it out. Imagine his astonishment when he realized that instead of a hand he had spat a cat's paw to the ground.

Taking heart at this initial victory, he struggled free from the claws of the assassins, and jumping over the hedge by the roadside, he began to flee across the fields—and the assassins after him like two dogs pursuing a hare. The one who had lost a paw ran on one leg alone, and nobody ever knew how he managed it.

After a race of fifteen miles, Pinocchio was worn out. Then, out of desperation, he scrambled up the trunk of a very tall pine tree and settled down in the topmost branches. The assassins tried to climb up, too, but when they got halfway up the trunk, they slipped and fell back to the ground, badly scraping their hands and feet.

Despite that, they didn't give up; in fact, after gathering a bundle of dry sticks at the foot of the pine, they set fire to it. In no time at all the tree took fire and began to blaze like a candle in the wind. Seeing the flames ris-

Pinocchio, vedendo che le fiamme salivano sempre più e non volendo far la fine del piccione arrosto, spiccò un bel salto di vetta all'albero, e via a correre daccapo attraverso ai campi e ai vigneti. E gli assassini dietro, sempre dietro, senza stancarsi mai.

Intanto cominciava a baluginare il giorno e si rincorrevano sempre; quand'ecco che Pinocchio si trovò improvvisamente sbarrato il passo da un fosso largo e profondissimo, tutto pieno di acquaccia sudicia, color del caffè e latte. Che fare? «Una, due, tre!» gridò il burattino, e slanciandosi con una gran rincorsa, saltò dall'altra parte. E gli assassini saltarono anche loro, ma non avendo preso bene la misura, *patatunfete!* . . . cascarono giù nel bel mezzo del fosso. Pinocchio che sentì il tonfo e gli schizzi dell'acqua, urlò ridendo e seguitando a correre:

– Buon bagno, signori assassini! –

E già si figurava che fossero bell'e affogati, quando invece, voltandosi a guardare, si accòrse che gli correvano dietro tutti e due, sempre imbacuccati nei loro sacchi, e grondanti acqua come due panieri sfondati.

ing higher and higher, and not wanting to end up like a roasted pigeon, Pinocchio made a great leap from the top of the tree, and away he ran again across fields and vineyards—and the assassins behind him, always giving chase, without ever tiring.

Meanwhile day was beginning to break, and the chase was still on, when suddenly Pinocchio found his way blocked by a wide and very deep ditch, full of filthy water, brownish in color. What to do? "One, two, three!" cried the puppet, and taking a running start he vaulted to the other bank. The assassins jumped too, but having misjudged the distance, *splash!* . . . they fell right into the middle of the ditch. Pinocchio, who heard the plunge and the splashing of water, cried out with laughter, running all the time:

"Have a nice bath, my dear assassins."

He was already thinking that they were good and drowned when, turning around to look, he saw instead that they were both running after him, still wrapped in their sacks and streaming with water like two bottomless baskets.

CAPITOLO XV

Gli assassini inseguono Pinocchio;
e dopo averlo raggiunto,
lo impiccano a un ramo della Quercia grande.

Allora il burattino, perdutosi d'animo, fu proprio sul punto di gettarsi in terra e di darsi per vinto, quando, nel girare gli occhi all'intorno, vide fra mezzo al verde cupo degli alberi biancheggiare in lontananza una casina candida come la neve.

– Se io avessi tanto fiato da arrivare fino a quella casa, forse sarei salvo! – disse dentro di sé.

E senza indugiare un minuto, riprese a correre per il bosco a carriera distesa. E gli assassini sempre dietro.

Dopo una corsa disperata di quasi due ore, finalmente, tutto trafelato, arrivò alla porta di quella casina e bussò.

Nessuno rispose.

Tornò a bussare con maggior violenza, perché sentiva avvicinarsi il rumore dei passi e il respiro grosso e affannoso de' suoi persecutori. Lo stesso silenzio.

Avvedutosi che il bussare non giovava a nulla, cominciò per disperazione a dare calci e zuccate nella porta. Allora si affacciò alla finestra una bella Bambina, coi capelli turchini e il viso bianco come un'immagine di cera, gli occhi chiusi e le mani incrociate sul petto, la quale, senza muover punto le labbra, disse con una vocina che pareva venisse dall'altro mondo:

– In questa casa non c'è nessuno. Sono tutti morti.

– Aprimi almeno tu! – gridò Pinocchio piangendo e raccomandandosi.

– Sono morta anch'io.

CHAPTER XV

The assassins pursue Pinocchio,
and after catching him they hang him
from a branch of the Great Oak tree.

Having lost heart now, the puppet was just about to throw himself to the ground and give up when, looking around through the midst of the dark green of the trees, he saw a little house as white as snow gleaming in the distance.

"If only I had enough breath to reach that house, maybe I'd be saved," he said to himself.

And without hesitating a minute, he resumed running through the forest at full speed, the assassins still right behind him.

And after a wild chase of almost two hours, gasping for breath, he finally reached the door of that little house and knocked.

Nobody answered.

He knocked again, harder, because he could hear his tormentors' footsteps nearing and their heavy labored breath. The same silence.

Realizing that knocking did no good, in desperation he began to kick the door and bang his head against it. Then there came to the window a beautiful Little Girl with blue hair[31] and a face as white as a wax image who, with eyes closed and hands crossed over her breast, without moving her lips at all, said in a voice that seemed to come from the world beyond:

"There is nobody in this house. They are all dead."

"Well, then you at least open up for me!" cried Pinocchio, weeping and imploring.

"I am dead, too."

– Morta? e allora che cosa fai costì alla finestra?

– Aspetto la bara che venga a portarmi via. –

Appena detto così, la Bambina disparve, e la finestra si richiuse senza far rumore.

– O bella Bambina dai capelli turchini, – gridava Pinocchio – aprimi per carità. Abbi compassione di un povero ragazzo inseguito dagli assass . . . –

Ma non poté finir la parola, perché sentì afferrarsi per il collo, e le solite due vociacce che gli brontolarono minacciosamente:

– Ora non ci scappi più! –

Il burattino, vedendosi balenare la morte dinanzi agli occhi, fu preso da un tremito così forte, che nel tremare, gli sonavano le giunture delle sue gambe di legno e i quattro zecchini che teneva nascosti sotto la lingua.

– Dunque? – gli domandarono gli assassini – vuoi aprirla la bocca, sì o no? Ah? non rispondi? . . . Lascia fare: ché questa volta te la faremo aprir noi! . . . –

E cavati fuori due coltellacci lunghi lunghi e affilati come rasoi, *zaff* e *zaff* . . . , gli affibbiarono due colpi nel mezzo alle reni.

Ma il burattino per sua fortuna era fatto d'un legno durissimo, motivo per cui le lame, spezzandosi, andarono in mille schegge e gli assassini rimasero col manico dei coltelli in mano, a guardarsi in faccia.

– Ho capito – disse allora un di loro – bisogna impiccarlo! Impicchiamolo!

– Impicchiamolo! – ripeté l'altro.

Detto fatto, gli legarono le mani dietro le spalle, e, passatogli un nodo scorsoio intorno alla gola, lo attaccarono penzoloni al ramo di una grossa pianta detta la Quercia grande.

"Dead? But then what are you doing there at the window?"

"I am waiting for the bier to come and take me away."

As soon as she said this, the Little Girl disappeared, and the window closed again without making a sound.

"O beautiful Little Girl with blue hair," cried Pinocchio, "open for me, for mercy's sake. Have pity on a poor boy chased by assass—"

But he was unable to finish the word, because he felt himself being grasped by the neck and heard the same two terrible voices that growled threateningly at him:

"Now you won't get away from us again."

Seeing death flash before his eyes, the puppet was seized by such a violent fit of trembling that the joints of his wooden legs and the four gold coins hidden under his tongue resounded.

"Well then?" the assassins asked him, "will you open your mouth, yes or no? Ah, you won't answer? . . . It doesn't matter, because this time we'll make you open it."

And drawing out two very long horrible knives sharpened like razors, *zack zack*, they let him have two blows in the small of the back.

But to the puppet's good fortune he was made of such extremely hard wood that the blades snapped and splintered into a thousand pieces, and the assassins were left with the knife-handles in their hands, looking into one another's face.

"I get it," said one of them then: "We have to hang him. Let's hang him!"

"Let's hang him!" repeated the other.

Without further ado they tied his hands behind his back; and after passing a slip noose around his neck they strung him up to the branch of a big tree called the Great Oak.

Poi si posero là, seduti sull'erba, aspettando che il burattino facesse l'ultimo sgambetto: ma il burattino, dopo tre ore, aveva sempre gli occhi aperti, la bocca chiusa e sgambettava più che mai.

Annoiati finalmente di aspettare, si voltarono a Pinocchio e gli dissero sghignazzando:

– Addio a domani. Quando domani torneremo qui, si spera che ci farai la garbatezza di farti trovare bell'e morto e con la bocca spalancata. –

E se ne andarono.

Intanto s'era levato un vento impetuoso di tramontana, che soffiando e mugghiando con rabbia, sbatacchiava in qua e in là il povero impiccato, facendolo dondolare violentemente come il battaglio d'una campana che suona a festa. E quel dondolìo gli cagionava acutissimi spasimi, e il nodo scorsoio, stringendosi sempre più alla gola, gli toglieva il respiro.

Then they settled down there on the grass, waiting for the puppet to kick his last; but after three hours the puppet had his eyes open, his mouth shut, and he was kicking harder than ever.

At last, tired of waiting, they turned to Pinocchio, and laughing sarcastically they said to him:

"Good-bye until tomorrow. When we come back here tomorrow we hope that you'll do us the courtesy of letting yourself be found good and dead, and with your mouth wide open."

And they went away.

Meanwhile a strong north wind had come up, which, blowing and howling furiously, slammed the poor hanged puppet back and forth, causing him to swing violently like the clapper of a joyously ringing bell. And that swinging caused him the sharpest spasms while the slip noose, tightening more and more around his throat, was choking him.

A poco a poco gli occhi gli si appannarono; e sebbene sentisse avvicinarsi la morte, pure sperava sempre che da un momento all'altro sarebbe capitata qualche anima pietosa a dargli aiuto. Ma quando, aspetta aspetta, vide che non compariva nessuno, proprio nessuno, allora gli tornò in mente il suo povero babbo . . . e balbettò quasi moribondo:

– Oh babbo mio! se tu fossi qui! . . . –

E non ebbe fiato per dir altro. Chiuse gli occhi, aprì la bocca, stirò le gambe e, dato un grande scrollone, rimase lì come intirizzito.

Little by little his eyes grew dim; and although he felt death approaching, he nonetheless still continued to hope that at any moment some compassionate soul would pass by and help him. But when, after waiting and waiting, he saw that nobody showed up, absolutely nobody, then he remembered his poor father again . . . and almost at death's door, he stuttered:[32]

"Oh, dear father! . . . if only you were here!"

And he had no breath to say anything else. He closed his eyes, opened his mouth, stretched out his legs, and, after giving a great shudder, he remained there as though frozen stiff.

CAPITOLO XVI

*La bella Bambina dai capelli turchini
fa raccogliere il burattino:
lo mette a letto, e chiama
tre medici per sapere se sia vivo o morto.*

In quel mentre che il povero Pinocchio impiccato dagli assassini a un ramo della Quercia grande, pareva oramai più morto che vivo, la bella Bambina dai capelli turchini si affacciò daccapo alla finestra, e impietositasi alla vista di quell'infelice che, sospeso per il collo, ballava il trescone alle ventate di tramontana, batté per tre volte le mani insieme, e fece tre piccoli colpi.

A questo segnale si sentì un gran rumore di ali che volavano con foga precipitosa, e un grosso Falco venne a posarsi sul davanzale della finestra.

– Che cosa comandate, mia graziosa Fata? – disse il Falco abbassando il becco in atto di riverenza (perché bisogna sapere che la Bambina dai capelli turchini non era altro in fin dei conti che una bonissima Fata, che da più di mill'anni abitava nelle vicinanze di quel bosco).

CHAPTER XVI

The beautiful Little Girl with blue hair
has the puppet taken down;
she puts him to bed and calls in three doctors
to learn whether he is dead or alive.

While poor Pinocchio, strung up by the assassins to a branch of the Great Oak, by now seemed more dead than alive, the beautiful Little Girl with blue hair came to the window again; and being moved to pity at the sight of the poor wretch, who, as he dangled by the neck was dancing a jig to the gusts of the north wind, she struck her hands together three times and made three faint claps.

At this signal was heard a loud whir of wings in precipitate flight, and a large Falcon came and perched on the windowsill.

"What is your command, my gracious Fairy?" said the Falcon, lowering his beak in a sign of reverence (because you should know, after all, that the Little Girl with blue hair was nothing other than a good Fairy who for more than a thousand years had been living near that forest).

– Vedi tu quel burattino attaccato penzoloni a un ramo della Quercia grande?

– Lo vedo.

– Orbene: vola subito laggiù; rompi col tuo fortissimo becco il nodo che lo tiene sospeso in aria, e posalo delicatamente sdraiato sull'erba, a piè della Quercia. –

Il Falco volò via e dopo due minuti tornò, dicendo:

– Quel che mi avete comandato, è fatto.

– E come l'hai trovato? Vivo o morto?

– A vederlo pareva morto, ma non dev'essere ancora morto perbene, perché appena gli ho sciolto il nodo scorsoio che lo stringeva intorno alla gola, ha lasciato andare un sospiro, balbettando a mezza voce: «Ora mi sento meglio! . . .» –

Allora la Fata, battendo le mani insieme, fece due piccoli colpi, e apparve un magnifico Can-barbone, che camminava ritto sulle gambe di dietro, tale e quale come se fosse un uomo.

Il Can-barbone era vestito da cocchiere in livrea di gala. Aveva in capo un nicchiettino a tre punte gallonato

"Do you see that puppet hanging from a branch of the Great Oak?"

"I see him."

"Now then, fly swiftly there; with your strong beak break the knot that holds him suspended in the air, and gently lay him on the grass at the foot of the Oak."

The Falcon flew off and in two minutes returned, saying:

"What you have commanded me is done."

"And how did you find him? Dead or alive?"

"To look at him, he seemed dead; but he probably isn't quite dead yet, because as soon as I undid the noose that was choking him, he let out a sigh and murmured: 'I feel better now.'"

Striking her hands, the Fairy then made two faint claps and there appeared a magnificent Poodle who walked upright on his hind legs, just exactly as if he were a man.

The Poodle was dressed as a coachman in his finest livery. He wore a gold-braided three-cornered hat on

d'oro, una parrucca bianca coi riccioli che gli scende-
vano giù per il collo, una giubba color di cioccolata coi
bottoni di brillanti e con due grandi tasche per tenervi
gli ossi, che gli regalava a pranzo la padrona, un paio di
calzon corti di velluto cremisi, le calze di seta, gli scar-
pini scollati, e di dietro una specie di fodera da ombrelli,
tutta di raso turchino, per mettervi dentro la coda,
quando il tempo cominciava a piovere.

– Su da bravo, Medoro! – disse la Fata al Can-barbone. – Fa' subito attaccare la più bella carrozza della mia
scuderia e prendi la via del bosco. Arrivato che sarai
sotto la Quercia grande, troverai disteso sull'erba un
povero burattino mezzo morto. Raccoglilo con garbo,
posalo pari pari su i cuscini della carrozza e portamelo
qui. Hai capito? –

Il Can-barbone, per fare intendere che aveva capito,
dimenò tre o quattro volte la fodera di raso turchino,
che aveva dietro, e partì come un barbero.

Di lì a poco, si vide uscire dalla scuderia una bella
carrozzina color dell'aria, tutta imbottita di penne di
canarino e foderata nell'interno di panna montata e di
crema coi savoiardi. La carrozzina era tirata da cento
pariglie di topini bianchi, e il Can-barbone, seduto a cassetta, schioccava la frusta a destra e a sinistra, come un
vetturino quand'ha paura di aver fatto tardi.

Non era ancora passato un quarto d'ora, che la carrozzina tornò, e la Fata, che stava aspettando sull'uscio
di casa, prese in collo il povero burattino, e portatolo in
una cameretta che aveva le pareti di madreperla, mandò
subito a chiamare i medici più famosi del vicinato.

E i medici arrivarono subito uno dopo l'altro: arrivò,
cioè, un Corvo, una Civetta e un Grillo-parlante.

– Vorrei sapere da lor signori – disse la Fata, rivol-
gendosi ai tre medici riuniti intorno al letto di Pinocchio
– vorrei sapere da lor signori se questo disgraziato burattino sia vivo o morto! . . . –

his head, a white wig with curls that came down to his neck, a chocolate-colored jacket with diamond buttons and two large pockets to hold the bones that his mistress gave him at dinner, a pair of crimson velvet breeches, silk stockings, pumps, and a sort of umbrella case made of blue satin, to put his tail into when it began to rain.

"Quick, my good Medoro," said the Fairy to the Poodle. "Harness the most beautiful carriage in my coachhouse and take the forest road. When you arrive under the Great Oak, you will find a poor puppet stretched out half-dead on the grass. Pick him up gently, lay him with care on the cushions in the carriage, and bring him here to me. Do you understand?"

The Poodle, to show that he had understood, wagged the deep-blue satin case he had behind him three or four times and set off like a racehorse.

In a little while, out of the coachhouse came a beautiful little carriage the color of air, all padded with canary feathers, and lined on the inside with whipped cream and ladyfingers in custard.[33] The carriage was drawn by a hundred pairs of white mice, and the Poodle, sitting on the box, cracked his whip left and right, like a driver who is afraid of being late.

A quarter of an hour hadn't yet gone by when the little carriage returned. Then the Fairy, who was waiting at the door of the house, took the poor puppet in her arms; and after carrying him into a little room that had mother-of-pearl walls, she immediately sent for the most distinguished doctors in the neighborhood.

And the doctors arrived quickly, one after the other: that is, there arrived a Raven, an Owl, and a Talking Cricket.

"I want to know from you gentlemen," said the Fairy, addressing the three doctors gathered around Pinocchio's bed, "I want to know from you gentlemen whether this unfortunate puppet is dead or alive."

A quest'invito, il Corvo, facendosi avanti per il primo, tastò il polso a Pinocchio, poi gli tastò il naso, poi il dito mignolo dei piedi: e quand'ebbe tastato ben bene, pronunziò solennemente queste parole:

— A mio credere il burattino è bell'e morto: ma se per disgrazia non fosse morto, allora sarebbe indizio sicuro che è sempre vivo!

— Mi dispiace — disse la Civetta — di dover contraddire il Corvo, mio illustre amico e collega: per me, invece, il burattino è sempre vivo; ma se per disgrazia non fosse vivo, allora sarebbe segno che è morto davvero.

— E lei non dice nulla? — domandò la Fata al Grillo-parlante.

— Io dico che il medico prudente, quando non sa quello che dice, la miglior cosa che possa fare, è quella di stare zitto. Del resto quel burattino lì, non m'è fisono-mia nuova: io lo conosco da un pezzo! —

At this invitation the Raven, coming forward first, felt Pinocchio's pulse, then he felt his nose, then the little toe of each foot; and when he had felt all over thoroughly, he solemnly pronounced these words:

"In my opinion, the puppet is good and dead; but if, by some misfortune, he should not be dead, then it would be a sure indication that he is still alive."

"I am sorry," said the Owl, "to have to contradict my illustrious friend and colleague, the Raven. For me, on the contrary, the puppet is still alive; but if, by some misfortune, he should not be alive, then it would be an indication that he is indeed dead."

"And have you nothing to say?" the Fairy asked the Talking Cricket.

"I say that the best thing the prudent doctor can do when he doesn't know what he's talking about is to keep quiet. Besides, that puppet's face is not new to me, I have known him for some time."

Pinocchio, che fin allora era stato immobile come un vero pezzo di legno, ebbe una specie di fremito convulso, che fece scuotere tutto il letto.

– Quel burattino lì – seguitò a dire il Grillo-parlante – è una birba matricolata . . . –

Pinocchio aprì gli occhi e li richiuse subito.

– È un monellaccio, uno svogliato, un vagabondo . . . –

Pinocchio si nascose la faccia sotto i lenzuoli.

– Quel burattino lì è un figliuolo disubbidiente, che farà morire di crepacuore il suo povero babbo! . . . –

A questo punto si sentì nella camera un suono soffocato di pianti e di singhiozzi. Figuratevi come rimasero tutti, allorché, sollevati un poco i lenzuoli, si accòrsero che quello che piangeva e singhiozzava era Pinocchio.

– Quando il morto piange, è segno che è in via di guarigione – disse solennemente il Corvo.

– Mi duole di contraddire il mio illustre amico e collega – soggiunse la Civetta – ma per me quando il morto piange, è segno che gli dispiace a morire. –

Pinocchio, who until then had been motionless like a true piece of wood, was seized with a kind of convulsive shudder that made the whole bed shake.

"That puppet there," continued the Talking Cricket, "is a confirmed rascal."

Pinocchio opened his eyes and closed them again quickly.

"He's a nasty urchin, a loafer, a vagabond . . ."

Pinocchio hid his face under the sheets.

"That puppet there is a disobedient child who will make his poor father die of heartbreak."

At this point, there was heard in the room a stifled sound of crying and sobbing. Imagine how surprised they all were when, upon lifting the sheets up a little, they discovered that it was Pinocchio who was crying and sobbing.

"When the deceased cries, it is an indication that he is on the road to recovery," said the Raven solemnly.

"It grieves me to contradict my illustrious friend and colleague," added the Owl, "but for me, when the deceased cries, it is an indication that he is sorry to die."

CAPITOLO XVII

Pinocchio mangia lo zucchero,
ma non vuol purgarsi:
però quando vede i becchini che vengono
a portarlo via, allora si purga.
Poi dice una bugia e per gastigo gli cresce il naso.

Appena i tre medici furono usciti di camera, la Fata si accostò a Pinocchio, e, dopo averlo toccato sulla fronte, si accòrse che era travagliato da un febbrone da non si dire.

Allora sciolse una certa polverina bianca in un mezzo bicchier d'acqua, e porgendolo al burattino, gli disse amorosamente:

– Bevila, e in pochi giorni sarai guarito. –

Pinocchio guardò il bicchiere, storse un po' la bocca, e poi dimandò con voce di piagnisteo:

– È dolce o amara?

– È amara, ma ti farà bene.

– Se è amara non la voglio.

– Da' retta a me: bevila.

– A me l'amaro non mi piace.

– Bevila: e quando l'avrai bevuta, ti darò una pallina di zucchero, per rifarti la bocca.

– Dov'è la pallina di zucchero?

– Eccola qui – disse la Fata, tirandola fuori da una zuccheriera d'oro.

– Prima voglio la pallina di zucchero, e poi beverò quell'acquaccia amara . . .

– Me lo prometti?

– Sì . . . –

La Fata gli dètte la pallina, e Pinocchio, dopo averla

CHAPTER XVII

*Pinocchio eats the sugar, but refuses
to swallow his medicine; however, when he sees
the undertakers coming to take him away,
he swallows the medicine. Then he tells a lie,
and as a punishment his nose grows longer.*

As soon as the three doctors had left the room, the Fairy came up to Pinocchio; and when she touched him on the forehead, she realized that he was running an incredibly high fever.

So she dissolved a certain fine white powder in half a glass of water,[34] and handing it to the puppet she said tenderly:

"Drink it, and in a few days you will be better."

Pinocchio looked at the glass, made a wry face, and then asked in a whining voice:

"Is it sweet or bitter?"

"It's bitter, but it will do you good."

"If it's bitter, I don't want it."

"Listen to me. Drink it."

"I don't like bitter things."

"Drink it; and after you have drunk it, I'll give you a lump of sugar to take away the taste."

"Where's the lump of sugar?"

"Here it is," said the Fairy, taking it out of a gold sugar bowl.

"First I want the lump of sugar, and then I'll drink that awful, bitter stuff."

"Is that a promise?"

"Yes."

The Fairy gave him the sugar lump and, after

sgranocchiata e ingoiata in un àttimo, disse leccandosi i labbri:

– Bella cosa se anche lo zucchero fosse una medicina! . . . Mi purgherei tutti i giorni.

– Ora mantieni la promessa e bevi queste poche gocciole d'acqua, che ti renderanno la salute. –

Pinocchio prese di mala voglia il bicchiere in mano e vi ficcò dentro la punta del naso: poi se l'accostò alla bocca: poi tornò a ficcarci la punta del naso: finalmente disse:

– È troppo amara! troppo amara! Io non la posso bere.

– Come fai a dirlo se non l'hai nemmeno assaggiata?

– Me lo figuro! L'ho sentita all'odore. Voglio prima un'altra pallina di zucchero . . . e poi la beverò! –

Allora la Fata, con tutta la pazienza di una buona mamma, gli pose in bocca un altro po' di zucchero; e dopo gli presentò daccapo il bicchiere.

– Così non la posso bere! – disse il burattino, facendo mille smorfie.

– Perché?

– Perché mi dà noia quel guanciale che ho laggiù su i piedi. –

La Fata gli levò il guanciale.

– È inutile! Nemmeno così la posso bere.

– Che cos'altro ti dà noia?

– Mi dà noia l'uscio di camera, ch è mezzo aperto. –

La Fata andò, e chiuse l'uscio di camera.

– Insomma – gridò Pinocchio, dando in uno scoppio di pianto – quest'acquaccia amara, non la voglio bere, no, no, no! . . .

– Ragazzo mio, te ne pentirai . . .

– Non me n'importa . . .

– La tua malattia è grave . . .

– Non me n'importa . . .

– La febbre ti porterà in poche ore all'altro mondo . . .

crunching[35] and swallowing it down in a flash, Pinocchio said, licking his lips:

"How wonderful it would be if sugar were also medicine! . . . I'd take it every day."

"Now keep your promise and drink these few drops of water that will make you well again."

Pinocchio took the glass in his hands reluctantly and stuck the tip of his nose in it; then he brought it to his lips; then he put the tip of his nose in it again; finally he said:

"It's too too bitter! I can't drink it."

"How can you tell, if you haven't even tried it?"

"I can tell because I've smelled it! First I want another lump of sugar . . . and then I'll drink it."

So the Fairy, with all the patience of a good mother, put another bit of sugar into his mouth, after which she handed him the glass again.

"I can't drink it this way," said the puppet, making all kinds of faces.

"Why not?"

"Because that cushion there on my feet bothers me."

The Fairy took away the cushion.

"It's no use! Even like that, I can't drink it."

"What else bothers you?"

"The door of the room, which is half open, bothers me."

The Fairy got up and closed the door.

"The fact is," cried Pinocchio, bursting into tears, "I don't want to drink that awful bitter stuff. I won't, I won't, I won't."

"My boy, you'll be sorry."

"I don't care."

"You are seriously ill."

"I don't care."

"The fever will carry you off to the next world in a few short hours."

– Non me n'importa . . .

– Non hai paura della morte?

– Nessuna paura! . . . Piuttosto morire, che bevere quella medicina cattiva. –

A questo punto, la porta della camera si spalancò, ed entrarono dentro quattro conigli neri come l'inchiostro, che portavano sulle spalle una piccola bara da morto.

– Che cosa volete da me? – gridò Pinocchio, rizzandosi tutto impaurito a sedere sul letto.

– Siamo venuti a prenderti – rispose il coniglio più grosso.

– A prendermi? . . . Ma io non sono ancora morto! . . .

– Ancora no: ma ti restano pochi minuti di vita, avendo tu ricusato di bevere la medicina, che ti avrebbe guarito della febbre! . . .

– O Fata mia, o Fata mia! – cominciò allora a strillare il burattino – datemi subito quel bicchiere . . . Spiccia-

"I don't care."

"Aren't you afraid of dying?"

"Not in the least afraid! Better to die than drink that terrible medicine."

At that very moment the door of the room opened wide and in came four rabbits as black as ink, carrying a small coffin on their shoulders.

"What do you want from me?" cried Pinocchio, sitting up straight in terror.

"We have come to get you," replied the biggest rabbit.

"To get me? . . . But I'm not dead yet!"

"Not yet; but you have only a few minutes of life left, since you refused to drink the medicine that would have cured you of the fever."

"O my Fairy, my Fairy," the puppet then began to scream, "give me the glass right away. Hurry, for Heav-

tevi, per carità, perché non voglio morire, no . . . non voglio morire. –

E preso il bicchiere con tutte e due le mani, lo votò in un fiato.

– Pazienza! – dissero i conigli. – Per questa volta abbiamo fatto il viaggio a ufo. – E tiratisi di nuovo la piccola bara sulle spalle, uscirono di camera bofonchiando e mormorando fra i denti.

Fatto sta che di lì a pochi minuti, Pinocchio saltò giù dal letto, bell'e guarito; perché bisogna sapere che i burattini di legno hanno il privilegio di ammalarsi di rado e di guarire prestissimo.

E la Fata, vedendolo correre e ruzzare per la camera, vispo e allegro come un gallettino di primo canto, gli disse:

– Dunque la mia medicina t'ha fatto bene davvero?

– Altro che bene! Mi ha rimesso al mondo! . . .

– E allora come mai ti sei fatto tanto pregare a berla?

– Egli è che noi ragazzi siamo tutti così! Abbiamo più paura delle medicine che del male.

– Vergogna! I ragazzi dovrebbero sapere che un buon medicamento preso a tempo, può salvarli da una grave malattia e fors'anche dalla morte . . .

– Oh! ma un'altra volta non mi farò tanto pregare! Mi rammenterò di quei conigli neri, con la bara sulle spalle . . . e allora piglierò subito il bicchiere in mano, e giù! . . .

– Ora vieni un po' qui da me, e raccontami come andò che ti trovasti fra le mani degli assassini.

– Gli andò, che il burattinaio Mangiafoco mi dètte cinque monete d'oro, e mi disse: «To', portale al tuo babbo!», e io, invece, per la strada trovai una Volpe e un Gatto, due persone molto per bene, che mi dissero: «Vuoi che codeste monete diventino mille e duemila? Vieni con noi, e ti condurremo al Campo dei miracoli.»

en's sake; I don't want to die, no, I don't want to die!"

And clutching the glass with both hands, he emptied it in one gulp.

"Well, so much for that!" said the rabbits. "We've made the trip for nothing this time." And lifting the little coffin up on their shoulders again, they went out of the room, snorting and muttering under their breath.

And the fact is that in a few minutes Pinocchio hopped out of bed, all better; because, you see, wooden puppets have the privilege of rarely getting sick and of getting better very quickly.

And the Fairy, seeing him run and romp around the room as brisk and cheerful as a cockerel just beginning to crow, said to him:

"So then my medicine really did you some good?"

"More than good! It brought me back to life."

"Then why did you have to be begged so much to drink it?"

"It's just that we boys are all like that. We're more afraid of medicine than of being sick."

"Shame on you! Children should know that a good medicine taken in time can save them from a serious illness and perhaps even from death."

"Oh, but the next time I won't make such a fuss. I'll remember those black rabbits with the coffin on their shoulders . . . and then I'll take the glass in my hands right away, and down it'll go!"

"Now come over here to me and tell me how it happened that you came into the hands of the assassins."

"What happened was that Fire-Eater the puppeteer gave me some gold coins and said: 'Here, take these to your father,' but instead I met a Fox and a Cat on the way, two very nice people, who said: 'Do you want those five coins to turn into a thousand or even two thousand? Come with us, and we'll take you to the Field of Miracles.' So I said: 'Let's go'; and they said: 'Let's

E io dissi: «Andiamo;» e loro dissero: «Fermiamoci qui all'osteria del Gambero rosso, e dopo la mezzanotte ripartiremo.» E io, quando mi svegliai, loro non c'erano più, perché erano partiti. Allora io cominciai a camminare di notte, che era un buio che pareva impossibile, per cui trovai per la strada due assassini dentro due sacchi da carbone, che mi dissero: «Metti fuori i quattrini;» e io dissi: «non ce n'ho;» perché le monete d'oro me l'ero nascoste in bocca, e uno degli assassini si provò a mettermi le mani in bocca, e io con un morso gli staccai la mano e poi la sputai, ma invece di una mano sputai uno zampetto di gatto. E gli assassini a corrermi dietro, e io corri che ti corro, finché mi raggiunsero, e mi legarono per il collo a un albero di questo bosco col dire: «Domani torneremo qui, e allora sarai morto e colla bocca aperta, e così ti porteremo via le monete d'oro che hai nascoste sotto la lingua.»

– E ora le quattro monete dove le hai messe? – gli domandò la Fata.

– Le ho perdute! – rispose Pinocchio; ma disse una bugia, perché invece le aveva in tasca.

Appena detta la bugia il suo naso, che era già lungo, gli crebbe subito due dita di più.

– E dove le hai perdute?

– Nel bosco qui vicino. –

A questa seconda bugia, il naso seguitò a crescere.

– Se le hai perdute nel bosco vicino – disse la Fata – le cercheremo e le ritroveremo: perché tutto quello che si perde nel vicino bosco, si ritrova sempre.

– Ah! ora che mi rammento bene – replicò il burattino imbrogliandosi – le quattro monete non le ho perdute, ma senza avvedermene, le ho inghiottite mentre bevevo la vostra medicina. –

stop here at the Red Crawfish Inn, and after midnight we'll go on again.' But then I, when I woke up they weren't there any more, because they had left. So then I began to make my way at night where it was so dark you wouldn't believe it, so that on the way I met two assassins inside two charcoal sacks, who said to me: 'Hand over your money,' and I said to them: 'I don't have any,' because those four gold coins, well, I had hidden them in my mouth, so one of the assassins tried to get his hands in my mouth, so I bit his hand off and spat it out, but instead of a hand I spat out a cat's paw. And the assassins were chasing after me while I was running with all my might to stay ahead of them until they caught me and tied me by the neck to a tree in this forest, saying: 'Tomorrow we'll come back here, and then you'll be dead with your mouth open, and that way we'll take away the gold coins that you've hidden under your tongue.'"

"And now where have you put the four coins?" the Fairy asked him.

"I've lost them," replied Pinocchio; but he was telling a lie, because in fact he had them in his pocket.

As soon as he had told the lie, his nose, which was already rather long, immediately grew another two inches.

"And where did you lose them?"

"In the forest nearby."

At this second lie, his nose grew still more.

"If you lost them in the forest nearby," said the Fairy, "we'll look for them and find them again; because everything that is lost in the nearby forest is always found again."

"Ah, now that I think of it," replied the puppet, getting confused, "I didn't lose the four coins, but without realizing it I swallowed them while I was drinking your medicine."

A questa terza bugia, il naso gli si allungò in un modo così straordinario, che il povero Pinocchio non poteva più girarsi da nessuna parte. Se si voltava di qui, batteva il naso nel letto o nei vetri della finestra, se si voltava di là, lo batteva nelle pareti o nella porta di camera, se alzava un po' più il capo, correva il rischio di ficcarlo in un occhio alla Fata.

E la Fata lo guardava e rideva.

– Perché ridete? – gli domandò il burattino, tutto confuso e impensierito di quel suo naso che cresceva a occhiate.

– Rido della bugia che hai detto.

– Come mai sapete che ho detto una bugia?

– Le bugie, ragazzo mio, si riconoscono subito, perché ve ne sono di due specie: vi sono le bugie che hanno le gambe corte, e le bugie che hanno il naso lungo: la tua per l'appunto è di quelle che hanno il naso lungo. –

Pinocchio, non sapendo più dove nascondersi per la vergogna, si provò a fuggire di camera; ma non gli riuscì. Il suo naso era cresciuto tanto, che non passava più dalla porta.

At this third lie, his nose grew so extraordinarily long that poor Pinocchio could no longer turn around. If he turned this way he bumped his nose against the bed or the windowpanes; if he turned that way, he bumped it against the wall or the door of the room; if he raised his head a little, he ran the risk of poking it into one of the Fairy's eyes.

And the Fairy looked at him and laughed.

"Why are you laughing?" the puppet asked her, quite embarrassed and worried about that nose of his that was growing before his very eyes.

"I'm laughing at the lie you told."

"How do you know that I've told a lie?"

"Lies, my dear boy, are quickly discovered; because there are two kinds. There are lies with short legs, and lies with long noses. Yours is clearly of the long-nosed variety."

Pinocchio, not knowing where to hide himself for shame, tried to run from the room; but he couldn't. His nose had grown so much that it could no longer pass through the door.

CAPITOLO XVIII

Pinocchio ritrova la Volpe e il Gatto,
e va con loro a seminare le quattro monete
nel Campo de' miracoli.

Come potete immaginarvelo, la Fata lasciò che il burattino piangesse e urlasse una buona mezz'ora, a motivo di quel suo naso che non passava più dalla porta di camera; e lo fece per dargli una severa lezione e perché si correggesse dal brutto vizio di dire le bugie, il più brutto vizio che possa avere un ragazzo. Ma quando lo vide trasfigurato e cogli occhi fuori della testa dalla gran disperazione, allora, mossa a pietà, batté le mani insieme, e a quel segnale entrarono in camera dalla finestra un migliaio di grossi uccelli chiamati *Picchi*, i quali, posatisi tutti sul naso di Pinocchio, cominciarono a beccarglielo tanto e poi tanto, che in pochi minuti quel naso enorme e spropositato si trovò ridotto alla sua grandezza naturale.

– Quanto siete buona, Fata mia, – disse il burattino, asciugandosi gli occhi – e quanto bene vi voglio!

– Ti voglio bene anch'io – rispose la Fata – e se tu vuoi rimanere con me, tu sarai il mio fratellino e io la tua buona sorellina . . .

– Io resterei volentieri . . . ma il mio povero babbo?

– Ho pensato a tutto. Il tuo babbo è stato digià avvertito: e prima che faccia notte, sarà qui.

– Davvero? – gridò Pinocchio, saltando dall'allegrezza. – Allora, Fatina mia, se vi contentate, vorrei andargli incontro! Non vedo l'ora di poter dare un bacio a quel povero vecchio, che ha sofferto tanto per me!

– Va' pure, ma bada di non ti sperdere. Prendi la via del bosco, e sono sicura che lo incontrerai. –

Pinocchio partì: e appena entrato nel bosco, comin-

CHAPTER XVIII

Pinocchio comes across the Fox
and the Cat again and goes with them to sow
the four coins in the Field of Miracles.

As you can well imagine, the Fairy let the puppet cry and yell for a good half hour over that nose of his which could no longer get through the door of the room; and she did it to give him a severe lesson so that he would rid himself of the ugly habit of telling lies, the worst fault a boy can have. But when she saw him disfigured and with his eyes popping out of his head in wild despair, she was moved to pity and clapped her hands; and at that signal, in through the window came about a thousand large birds called Woodpeckers who perched on Pinocchio's nose and set about pecking at it in such good measure that in a few minutes that huge, exaggerated nose was brought back to its natural size.

"How good you are, my Fairy," said the puppet, drying his eyes, "and how much I love you!"

"I love you too," replied the Fairy, "and if you want to stay with me, you shall be my little brother, and I your good little sister."[36]

"I'd be glad to stay . . . but my poor father?"

"I have thought of everything. Your father has already been told, and before nightfall he'll be here."

"Really?" cried Pinocchio, jumping with joy. "Then, my dear little Fairy, if it's all right with you, I would like to go and meet him on the way. I can't wait to kiss that poor old man who has suffered so much on my account."

"Go ahead, but be sure not to go astray. Take the forest path, and I'm sure that you will meet him."

Pinocchio set out, and as soon as he entered the for-

ciò a correre come un capriòlo. Ma quando fu arrivato a un certo punto, quasi in faccia alla Quercia grande, si fermò, perché gli parve di aver sentito gente fra mezzo alle frasche. Difatti vide apparire sulla strada, indovinate chi? . . . la Volpe e il Gatto, ossia i due compagni di viaggio coi quali aveva cenato all'osteria del Gambero rosso.

– Ecco il nostro caro Pinocchio! – gridò la Volpe, abbracciandolo e baciandolo. – Come mai sei qui?

– Come mai sei qui? – ripeté il Gatto.

– È una storia lunga – disse il burattino – e ve la racconterò a comodo. Sappiate però che l'altra notte, quando mi avete lasciato solo sull'osteria, ho trovato gli assassini per la strada . . .

– Gli assassini? . . . Oh povero amico! E che cosa volevano?

– Mi volevano rubare le monete d'oro.

– Infami! . . . – disse la Volpe.

– Infamissimi! – ripeté il Gatto.

– Ma io cominciai a scappare – continuò a dire il burattino – e loro sempre dietro: finché mi raggiunsero e m'impiccarono a un ramo di quella quercia . . . –

E Pinocchio accennò la Quercia grande, che era lì a due passi.

– Si può sentir di peggio? – disse la Volpe. – In che mondo siamo condannati a vivere! Dove troveremo un rifugio sicuro noi altri galantuomini? –

Nel tempo che parlavano così, Pinocchio si accòrse che il Gatto era zoppo dalla gamba destra davanti, perché gli mancava in fondo tutto lo zampetto cogli unghioli: per cui gli domandò:

– Che cosa hai fatto del tuo zampetto? –

Il Gatto voleva rispondere qualche cosa, ma s'imbrogliò. Allora la Volpe disse subito:

– Il mio amico è troppo modesto, e per questo non risponde. Risponderò io per lui. Sappi dunque che

est, he started to run like a deer. But when he came to a certain spot, almost in front of the Great Oak, he stopped, because he thought he heard someone amid the foliage. In fact, he saw appear on the road—guess who?—the Fox and the Cat, that is, the two traveling companions with whom he had supped at the Red Crawfish Inn.

"Here's our dear Pinocchio!" cried the Fox, embracing and kissing him. "How do you happen to be here?"

"How do you happen to be here?" repeated the Cat.

"It's a long story," said the puppet, "and I'll tell you about it when it's more convenient. But I can tell you now that the other night, after you left me alone at the inn, I met the assassins on the road."

"The assassins? . . . Oh, my poor friend! But what did they want?"

"They wanted to steal my gold coins."

"Villains!" said the Fox.

"Villainous villains!" repeated the Cat.

"But I began to run," the puppet went on, "and they kept after me until they caught me and hanged me from a branch of that oak tree."

And Pinocchio pointed to the Great Oak, which was right close by.

"Have you ever heard anything so awful!" said the Fox. "What a world we are condemned to live in! Is there no haven for honest men such as we?"[37]

While they were talking in this way, Pinocchio noticed that the Cat limped on his right foreleg, because his whole paw, claws and all, was missing from the end of it; so he asked him:

"What have you done with your paw?"

The Cat tried to answer something, but became confused. So then the Fox said quickly:

"My friend is too modest, and that's why he doesn't answer. I will answer for him. You see, an hour ago on

215

un'ora fa abbiamo incontrato sulla strada un vecchio lupo, quasi svenuto dalla fame, che ci ha chiesto un po' d'elemosina. Non avendo noi da dargli nemmeno una lisca di pesce, che cosa ha fatto l'amico mio, che ha davvero un cuore di Cesare? Si è staccato coi denti uno zampetto delle sue gambe davanti e l'ha gettato a quella povera bestia, perché potesse sdigiunarsi. –

E la Volpe, nel dir così, si asciugò una lagrima.

Pinocchio, commosso anche lui, si avvicinò al Gatto, sussurrandogli negli orecchi:

– Se tutti i gatti ti somigliassero, fortunati i topi! . . .

– E ora che cosa fai in questi luoghi? – domandò la Volpe al burattino.

– Aspetto il mio babbo, che deve arrivare qui di momento in momento.

– E le tue monete d'oro?

– Le ho sempre in tasca, meno una che la spesi all'osteria del Gambero rosso.

– E pensare che, invece di quattro monete, potrebbero diventare domani mille e duemila! Perché non dài retta al mio consiglio? Perché non vai a seminarle nel Campo dei miracoli?

– Oggi è impossibile: vi anderò un altro giorno.

– Un altro giorno sarà tardi! . . . – disse la Volpe.

– Perché?

– Perché quel campo è stato comprato da un gran signore, e da domani in là non sarà più permesso a nessuno di seminarvi i denari.

– Quant'è distante di qui il Campo dei miracoli?

– Due chilometri appena. Vuoi venire con noi? Fra mezz'ora sei là: semini subito le quattro monete: dopo pochi minuti ne raccogli duemila, e stasera ritorni qui colle tasche piene. Vuoi venire con noi? –

Pinocchio esitò un poco a rispondere, perché gli tornò in mente la buona Fata, il vecchio Geppetto e gli

the road we met an old wolf, nearly fainting from hunger, who begged us for alms. Not having so much as a fishbone to give him, what did my friend, who truly has the heart of a Caesar, do?[38] With his own teeth he bit off a paw from one of his forelegs and cast it to the poor beast so that he might break his fast."

And in relating this, the Fox wiped away a tear.

Pinocchio, who was also moved, went up to the Cat, whispering in his ear:

"If all cats were like you, how lucky the mice would be!"

"But now what are you doing in these parts?" the Fox asked the puppet.

"I'm waiting for my father who should be coming by at any moment."

"And your gold coins?"

"I still have them in my pocket, except one that I spent at the Red Crawfish Inn."

"And to think that instead of four coins, tomorrow they could be a thousand or even two thousand! Why don't you listen to my advice? Why don't you go and sow them in the Field of Miracles?"

"Today it's impossible; I'll go there another day."

"Another day will be too late," said the Fox.

"Why?"

"Because the field has been bought by a rich gentleman, and beginning tomorrow nobody will be allowed to sow money there."

"How far is the Field of Miracles from here?"

"Hardly two miles. Do you want to come with us? In half an hour you're there, you sow the four coins right away, after a few minutes you gather two thousand of them, and this evening you return here with your pockets full. Do you want to come with us?"

Pinocchio hesitated a little before answering, because he thought of the good Fairy, old Geppetto, and the

217

avvertimenti del Grillo-parlante; ma poi finì col fare come fanno tutti i ragazzi senza un fil di giudizio e senza cuore; finì, cioè, col dare una scrollatina di capo, e disse alla Volpe e al Gatto:

– Andiamo pure: io vengo con voi. –

E partirono.

Dopo aver camminato una mezza giornata arrivarono a una città che aveva nome «Acchiappa-citrulli». Appena entrato in città, Pinocchio vide tutte le strade popolate di cani spelacchiati, che sbadigliavano dall'appetito, di pecore tosate, che tremavano dal freddo, di

galline rimaste senza cresta e senza bargigli, che chiedevano l'elemosina d'un chicco di granturco, di grosse farfalle, che non potevano più volare, perché avevano venduto le loro bellissime ali colorite, di pavoni tutti scodati, che si vergognavano a farsi vedere, e di fagiani che zampettavano cheti cheti, rimpiangendo le loro scintillanti penne d'oro e d'argento, oramai perdute per sempre.

In mezzo a questa folla di accattoni e di poveri vergognosi, passavano di tanto in tanto alcune carrozze signo-

warnings of the Talking Cricket; but then he ended by doing what all boys do who haven't a shred of sense and are heartless: that is, he ended by shrugging his shoulders and saying to the Fox and the Cat:

"Let's go; I'm coming with you."

And they went on their way.

After walking for half a day, they came to a town called Catchafool.[39] As soon as he entered the town, Pinocchio saw all the streets crowded with mangy dogs yawning with hunger, fleeced sheep shivering with

cold, hens bereft of crest and wattle begging for a kernel of corn, large butterflies no longer able to fly because they had sold their beautiful colored wings, tailless peacocks ashamed to be seen, and pheasants who waddled about silently, mourning their brilliant feathers of gold and silver lost forevermore.

In the midst of this crowd of beggars and downcast poor, from time to time an elegant carriage would pass

rili con dentro o qualche Volpe, o qualche Gazza ladra, o qualche uccellaccio di rapina.

– E il Campo dei miracoli dov'è? – domandò Pinocchio.

– È qui a due passi. –

Detto fatto traversarono la città e, usciti fuori dalle mura, si fermarono in un campo solitario che, su per giù, somigliava a tutti gli altri campi.

– Eccoci giunti – disse la Volpe al burattino. – Ora chinati giù a terra, scava con le mani una piccola buca nel campo, e mettici dentro le monete d'oro. –

Pinocchio obbedì. Scavò la buca, ci pose le quattro monete d'oro che gli erano rimaste: e dopo ricoprì la buca con un po' di terra.

– Ora poi – disse la Volpe – va' alla gora qui vicina, prendi una secchia d'acqua e annaffia il terreno dove hai seminato. –

Pinocchio andò alla gora, e perché non aveva lì per lì una secchia, si levò di piedi una ciabatta e, riempitala d'acqua, annaffiò la terra che copriva la buca. Poi domandò:

– C'è altro da fare?

– Nient'altro – rispose la Volpe. – Ora possiamo andar via. Tu poi ritorna qui fra una ventina di minuti, e troverai l'arboscello già spuntato dal suolo e coi rami tutti carichi di monete. –

Il povero burattino, fuori di sé dalla gran contentezza, ringraziò mille volte la Volpe e il Gatto, e promise loro un bellissimo regalo.

– Noi non vogliamo regali – risposero que' due malanni. – A noi ci basta di averti insegnato il modo di arricchire senza durar fatica, e siamo contenti come pasque. –

Ciò detto salutarono Pinocchio, e augurandogli una buona raccolta, se ne andarono per i fatti loro.

by, with either a fox or a thieving mapgie, or a horrid bird of prey inside.

"But where is the Field of Miracles?" asked Pinocchio.

"It's right nearby here."

Without further ado, they crossed the city, and going out beyond the walls they stopped in an isolated field which looked more or less like any other field.

"And here we are," said the Fox to the puppet. "Now stoop to the ground, dig a little hole in the field with your hands, and put the gold coins in it."

Pinocchio obeyed; he dug the hole, put his remaining four gold coins inside, and then covered the hole over again with some earth.

"Now, then," said the Fox, "go to the nearby ditch, get a bucket of water, and sprinkle the ground where you sowed."

Pinocchio went to the ditch and since he didn't have a bucket on hand just then, he took off one of his clogs, and after filling it with water he sprinkled the earth that covered the hole. Then he asked:

"Is there anything else to be done?"

"Nothing else," replied the Fox. "We can go away now. Then you come back here in about twenty minutes, and you'll find the little tree has already come up through the soil, with its branches all laden with coins."

The poor puppet, beside himself with joy, thanked the Fox and the Cat a thousand times and promised them a beautiful gift.

"We do not desire gifts," replied those two rogues. "It's enough for us to have taught you how to become rich without effort, and for that we are as happy as a holiday."[40]

So saying, they bade farewell to Pinocchio, and wishing him a rich harvest they went off about their business.

CAPITOLO XIX

Pinocchio è derubato delle sue monete d'oro,
e per gastigo, si busca quattro mesi di prigione.

Il burattino, ritornato in città, cominciò a contare i minuti a uno a uno; e, quando gli parve che fosse l'ora, riprese subito la strada che menava al Campo dei miracoli.

E mentre camminava con passo frettoloso, il cuore gli batteva forte e gli faceva tic, tac, tic, tac, come un orologio da sala, quando corre davvero. E intanto pensava dentro di sé:

«E se invece di mille monete, ne trovassi su i rami dell'albero duemila? . . . E se invece di duemila, ne trovassi cinquemila? e se invece di cinquemila, ne trovassi centomila? Oh che bel signore, allora, che diventerei! . . . Vorrei avere un bel palazzo, mille cavallini di legno e mille scuderie, per potermi baloccare, una cantina di rosoli e di alchermes, e una libreria tutta piena di canditi, di torte, di panattoni, di mandorlati e di cialdoni colla panna.»

Così fantasticando, giunse in vicinanza del campo, e lì si fermò a guardare se per caso avesse potuto scorgere qualche albero coi rami carichi di monete: ma non vide nulla. Fece altri cento passi in avanti, e nulla: entrò sul campo . . . andò proprio su quella piccola buca, dove aveva sotterrato i suoi zecchini, e nulla. Allora diventò pensieroso e, dimenticando le regole del Galateo e della buona creanza, tirò fuori una mano di tasca e si dètte una lunghissima grattatina di capo.

In quel mentre sentì fischiarsi negli orecchi una gran

CHAPTER XIX

*Pinocchio is robbed of his gold coins, and
as a punishment he gets four months in prison.*

Having returned to the city, the puppet began to count the minutes one by one, and when he thought it was time, he quickly went back to the road that led to the Field of Miracles.

And as he hurried along his heart was beating fast and going *tick-tock*, *tick-tock*, like a grandfather clock when it's really running strong. Meanwhile he thought to himself:

"And if instead of a thousand coins, I found two thousand in the branches of the tree? And if instead of two thousand I found five thousand? And if instead of five thousand I found a hundred thousand? Oh! What a wealthy gentleman I'd become then! I'd get myself a beautiful palace, a thousand little wooden horses and a thousand stables to play with, a cellar full of rosolio cordials and alkermes liqueurs, and a library chock-full of candied fruit, pies, *panettoni*, almond cakes, and rolled wafers filled with whipped cream."

While he was building these castles in the air, he came near the field and stopped to see if by chance he could make out a tree with its branches laden with coins; but he didn't see anything. He went ahead another hundred steps: still nothing. He entered the field, went right up to the little hole where he had buried his gold pieces: still nothing. Then he became worried; and forgetting all the rules of etiquette[41] and good manners, he took his hand out of his pocket and stood there scratching his head for a long time.

Suddenly a great screech of laughter pierced his ears;

risata: e voltatosi in su, vide sopra un albero un grosso Pappagallo che si spollinava le poche penne che aveva addosso.

– Perché ridi? – gli domandò Pinocchio con voce di bizza.

– Rido, perché nello spollinarmi mi sono fatto il solletico sotto le ali. –

Il burattino non rispose. Andò alla gora e riempita d'acqua la solita ciabatta, si pose novamente ad annaffiare la terra, che ricopriva le monete d'oro.

Quand'ecco che un'altra risata, anche più impertinente della prima, si fece sentire nella solitudine silenziosa di quel campo.

– Insomma – gridò Pinocchio, arrabbiandosi – si può sapere, Pappagallo mal educato, di che cosa ridi?

and looking up he saw a large Parrot in a tree, pecking the fleas from the few feathers he still had on him.

"What are you laughing at?" Pinocchio asked, peevishly.

"I'm laughing because in pecking the fleas from my feathers I tickled myself under my wings."

The puppet said nothing. He went to the ditch and after filling that same clog of his with water set about once more to sprinkle the earth that covered his gold coins.

But then—another burst of laughter, even more impudent than the first, resounded in the deep silence of that lonely field.

"All right, then," shouted Pinocchio, getting quite angry, "may I know, ill-bred Parrot, what you are laughing at?"

– Rido di quei barbagianni, che credono a tutte le scioccherie e che si lasciano trappolare da chi è più furbo di loro.

– Parli forse di me?

– Sì, parlo di te, povero Pinocchio; di te che sei così dolce di sale da credere che i denari si possano seminare e raccogliere nei campi, come si seminano i fagiuoli e le zucche. Anch'io l'ho creduto una volta, e oggi ne porto le pene. Oggi (ma troppo tardi!) mi son dovuto persuadere che per mettere insieme onestamente pochi soldi bisogna saperseli guadagnare o col lavoro delle proprie mani o coll'ingegno della propria testa.

– Non ti capisco – disse il burattino, che già cominciava a tremare dalla paura.

– Pazienza! Mi spiegherò meglio – soggiunse il Pappagallo. – Sappi dunque che, mentre tu eri in città, la Volpe e il Gatto sono tornati in questo campo: hanno preso le monete d'oro sotterrate, e poi sono fuggiti come il vento. E ora chi li raggiunge, è bravo! –

Pinocchio restò a bocca aperta, e non volendo credere alle parole del Pappagallo, cominciò colle mani e colle unghie a scavare il terreno che aveva annaffiato. E scava, scava, scava, fece una buca così profonda, che ci sarebbe entrato per ritto un pagliaio: ma le monete non c'erano più.

Preso allora dalla disperazione, tornò di corsa in città e andò difilato in tribunale, per denunziare al giudice i due malandrini, che lo avevano derubato.

Il giudice era uno scimmione della razza dei Gorilla: un vecchio scimmione rispettabile per la sua grave età, per la sua barba bianca e specialmente per i suoi occhiali d'oro, senza vetri, che era costretto a portare continuamente, a motivo d'una flussione d'occhi, che lo tormentava da parecchi anni.

Pinocchio, alla presenza del giudice, raccontò per filo e per segno l'iniqua frode, di cui era stato vittima; dètte

"I'm laughing at those dodoes who believe all kinds of nonsense and let themselves be tricked by anyone who is more cunning than they are."

"Are you speaking of me, by any chance?"

"Yes, I'm speaking of you, poor Pinocchio, of you who are so lacking in salt[42] as to believe that money can be sown and harvested in the fields, like beans and pumpkins. There was a time when I believed that too, but I'm paying for it now. Now (when it's too late!) I've come to realize that in order to put together a little money honestly, we must know how to earn it with the labor of our own hands or the wit of our own brains."

"I don't know what you mean," said the puppet, who was already beginning to tremble with fear.

"All right! I'll explain myself better," continued the Parrot. "You see, while you were in town the Fox and the Cat came back to this field, took the gold coins buried here and then fled like the wind. And whoever catches up with them now will be quite a fellow."

Pinocchio stood there with his mouth open; and not wanting to believe the Parrot's words, with his hands and nails he began to dig up the ground he had watered. And—dig, dig, dig,—he made such a deep hole that a haystack would have fit upright in it; but the coins were no longer there.

Seized with panic then, he rushed back to town and went straight to the Court House to denounce the two brigands before the judge.

The judge was a big ape of the gorilla family, elderly and venerable for his advanced years and his white beard, but above all for his gold-rimmed spectacles without lenses, which he was obliged to wear all the time on account of an inflammation of the eyes that had been plaguing him for many years.

Before the judge, Pinocchio recounted in great detail the events of the iniquitous fraud of which he had been

227

il nome, il cognome e i connotati dei malandrini, e finì chiedendo giustizia.

Il giudice lo ascoltò con molta benignità; prese vivissima parte al racconto: s'intenerì, si commosse: e quando il burattino non ebbe più nulla da dire, allungò la mano e sonò il campanello.

A quella scampanellata comparvero subito due can mastini vestiti da giandarmi.

Allora il giudice, accennando Pinocchio ai giandarmi, disse loro:

– Quel povero diavolo è stato derubato di quattro monete d'oro: pigliatelo dunque, e mettetelo subito in prigione. –

Il burattino, sentendosi dare questa sentenza fra capo e collo, rimase di princisbecco e voleva protestare: ma i giandarmi, a scanso di perditempi inutili, gli tapparono la bocca e lo condussero in gattabuia.

E lì v'ebbe a rimanere quattro mesi: quattro lunghissimi mesi: e vi sarebbe rimasto anche di più se non si fosse dato un caso fortunatissimo. Perché bisogna sapere che il giovane Imperatore che regnava nella città di Acchiappa-citrulli, avendo riportato una bella vittoria

the victim; he gave the first names, the surnames, and a description of the brigands, and then finished by asking for justice.

The judge listened to him very sympathetically, took a keen interest in the tale, was touched and deeply moved, and when the puppet had nothing else to say he stretched out his hand and rang a bell.

At that loud ringing, two mastiffs quickly appeared, dressed as gendarmes.

Then the judge, pointing out Pinocchio to the gendarmes, said:

"This poor devil has been robbed of four gold coins; so seize him and put him in prison right away."

Hearing himself sentenced this way, like a bolt out of the blue, the puppet was dumbfounded and wanted to protest;[43] but the gendarmes, so as not to waste time needlessly, stopped his mouth up and led him away to the clink.

And there he stayed for four months, four long long months; and he would have remained there even longer had not something quite fortunate occurred. For you must know that the young Emperor who reigned over the town of Catchafool, having won a splendid victory

contro i suoi nemici, ordinò grandi feste pubbliche, luminarie, fuochi artificiali, corse di barberi e di velocipedi, e in segno di maggiore esultanza, volle che fossero aperte anche le carceri e mandati fuori tutti i malandrini.

– Se escono di prigione gli altri, voglio uscire anch'io – disse Pinocchio al carceriere.

– Voi no, – rispose il carceriere – perché voi non siete del bel numero . . .

– Domando scusa; – replicò Pinocchio – sono un malandrino anch'io.

– In questo caso avete mille ragioni – disse il carceriere; e levandosi il berretto rispettosamente e salutandolo, gli aprì le porte della prigione e lo lasciò scappare.

over his enemies, ordered great public rejoicing with illuminations, fireworks, and horse and cycle races; and, as a token of the greatest jubilation, he ordered that the prisons also be opened and all the rogues set free.

"If the others are getting out of prison, I want to go out too," said Pinocchio to the jailer.

"Not you," replied the jailer, "because you're not one of the select company."

"I beg your pardon," Pinocchio retorted; "I'm a rogue too."

"In that case, you are absolutely right," said the jailer; and removing his cap respectfully while bowing to him, he opened the prison gates for him and let him run away.

CAPITOLO XX

Liberato dalla prigione,
si avvia per tornare a casa della Fata;
ma lungo la strada trova un Serpente orribile,
e poi rimane preso alla tagliuola.

Figuratevi l'allegrezza di Pinocchio quando si sentì libero. Senza stare a dire che è e che non è, uscì subito fuori della città e riprese la strada, che doveva ricondurlo alla Casina della Fata.

A cagione del tempo piovigginoso, la strada era diventata tutta un pantano e ci si andava fino a mezza gamba. Ma il burattino non se ne dava per inteso. Tormentato dalla passione di rivedere il suo babbo e la sua sorellina dai capelli turchini, correva a salti come un can levriero, e nel correre le pillacchere gli schizzavano fin sopra il berretto. Intanto andava dicendo fra sé e sé: «Quante disgrazie mi sono accadute . . . E me le merito! perché io sono un burattino testardo e piccoso . . . e voglio far sempre tutte le cose a modo mio, senza dar retta a quelli che mi voglion bene e che hanno mille volte più giudizio di me! . . . Ma da questa volta in là, faccio proponimento di cambiar vita e di diventare un ragazzo ammodo e ubbidiente . . . Tanto ormai ho bell'e visto che i ragazzi, a essere disubbidienti, ci scapitano sempre e non ne infilano mai una per il su' verso. E il mio babbo mi avrà aspettato? . . . Ce lo troverò a casa della Fata? È tanto tempo, pover'uomo, che non lo vedo più, che mi struggo di fargli mille carezze e di finirlo dai baci! E la Fata mi perdonerà la brutta azione che le ho fatta? . . . E pensare che ho ricevuto da lei tante attenzioni e tante cure amorose . . . e pensare che se oggi son sempre

CHAPTER XX

*Freed from prison, he sets out to return
to the Fairy's house; but along the way
he meets a horrible Serpent and then
gets caught in an animal trap.*

Imagine Pinocchio's joy when he felt himself free. Without the slightest hesitation he rapidly left the town and again took the road that should have led him back to the Fairy's house.

But because a slight drizzle was falling, the whole road had become knee-deep in mud. But the puppet didn't care about that. Wild to see his father and his little blue-haired sister again, he ran in leaps and bounds like a greyhound; and as he ran, the mud splashed up and bespattered him all the way up to his cap. Meanwhile, he was saying to himself:

"How many bad things have happened to me! . . . But I deserve them, because I'm a stubborn and willful puppet . . . and I always want things my own way without listening to those who love me and have a thousand times more sense than I have . . . But from now on, I make a resolution to change my ways and become a well-behaved and obedient boy. Besides, by now I've seen only too well that when boys are disobedient they always pay for it and things never turn out right for them . . . Who knows if my father has waited for me? I wonder if I'll find him at the Fairy's house? Poor man, it's been so long since I last saw him that I'm dying to hug him over and over, and to smother him with kisses . . . And will the Fairy forgive me for the terrible thing I've done to her? . . . And to think that I received so much attention and loving care from her; to think that

vivo, lo debbo a lei! . . . Ma si può dare un ragazzo più ingrato e più senza cuore di me? . . .»

Nel tempo che diceva così, si fermò tutt'a un tratto spaventato, e fece quattro passi indietro.

Che cosa aveva veduto?

Aveva veduto un grosso Serpente, disteso attraverso alla strada, che aveva la pelle verde, gli occhi di fuoco e la coda appuntata, che gli fumava come una cappa di camino.

Impossibile immaginarsi la paura del burattino: il quale, allontanatosi più di mezzo chilometro, si mise a sedere sopra un monticello di sassi, aspettando che il Serpente se ne andasse una buona volta per i fatti suoi e lasciasse libero il passo della strada.

Aspettò un'ora; due ore; tre ore: ma il Serpente era sempre là, e, anche di lontano, si vedeva il rosseggiare de' suoi occhi di fuoco e la colonna di fumo che gli usciva dalla punta della coda.

Allora Pinocchio, figurandosi di aver coraggio, si avvicinò a pochi passi di distanza, e facendo una vocina dolce, insinuante e sottile, disse al Serpente:

if I'm still alive today I owe it to her! . . . Can there be a more ungrateful and heartless boy than I am?"

While he was saying this, he suddenly stopped in terror and took four steps backward.

What had he seen?

He had seen a large Serpent stretched out across the road. It had green skin, fiery eyes, and a pointed tail that smoked like a chimney stack.

You couldn't imagine the puppet's fear; after retreating more than half a mile he sat down on a small pile of stones and waited for the Serpent to go off for good about his business and leave the way free.

He waited an hour, two hours, three hours. But the Serpent was still there, and even from a distance you could see the red glow of his fiery eyes and the column of smoke that was rising from the pointed end of his tail.

Then Pinocchio, trying to seem brave, approached to within a few steps and, speaking in a soft ingratiating voice, said to the Serpent:

235

– Scusi, signor Serpente, che mi farebbe il piacere di tirarsi un pochino da una parte, tanto da lasciarmi passare? –

Fu lo stesso che dire al muro. Nessuno si mosse.

Allora riprese colla solita vocina:

– Deve sapere, signor Serpente, che io vado a casa, dove c'è il mio babbo che mi aspetta e che è tanto tempo che non lo vedo più! . . . Si contenta dunque che io seguiti per la mia strada? –

Aspettò un segno di risposta a quella dimanda: ma la risposta non venne: anzi il Serpente, che fin allora pareva arzillo e pieno di vita, diventò immobile e quasi irrigidito. Gli occhi gli si chiusero e la coda gli smesse di fumare.

– Che sia morto davvero? . . . – disse Pinocchio, dandosi una fregatina di mani dalla gran contentezza; e senza mettere tempo in mezzo, fece l'atto di scavalcarlo,

per passare dall'altra parte della strada. Ma non aveva ancora finito di alzare la gamba, che il Serpente si rizzò all'improvviso come una molla scattata: e il burattino,

"Excuse me, Signor Serpent, I wonder if you would do me the favor of moving over a little bit, just enough to let me go by?"

It was the same as talking to the wall. Nobody moved.

Then he began again in the same soft voice:

"Consider, Signor Serpent, that I am going home where my father is waiting for me, and that I haven't seen him for such a long time. Is it all right with you, then, if I continue on my way?"

He waited for some sign of an answer to this request, but no answer came. On the contrary, the Serpent, who until then had seemed active and full of life, became motionless and rather stiff. His eyes closed and his tail stopped smoking.

"Can he really be dead?" said Pinocchio, rubbing his hands together with glee. And without wasting any

time, he made as if to jump over him so as to get to the other side of the road. But he hadn't yet finished lifting his leg when the Serpent suddenly shot up like a released

nel tirarsi indietro spaventato, inciampò e cadde per terra.

E per l'appunto cadde così male, che restò col capo conficcato nel fango della strada e con le gambe ritte su in aria.

Alla vista di quel burattino, che sgambettava a capo fitto con una velocità incredibile, il Serpente fu preso da una tal convulsione di risa, che ridi, ridi, ridi, alla fine, dallo sforzo del troppo ridere, gli si strappò una vena sul petto: e quella volta morì davvero.

Allora Pinocchio ricominciò a correre per arrivare a casa della Fata avanti che si facesse buio. Ma lungo la strada, non potendo più reggere ai morsi terribili della fame, saltò in un campo coll'intenzione di cogliere poche ciocche d'uva moscadella. Non l'avesse mai fatto!

Appena giunto sotto la vite, *crac* . . . sentì stringersi le gambe da due ferri taglienti, che gli fecero vedere quante stelle c'erano in cielo.

Il povero burattino era rimasto preso a una tagliuola appostata là da alcuni contadini per beccarvi alcune grosse faine, che erano il flagello di tutti i pollai del vicinato.

spring; and as the puppet drew back in terror, he stumbled and fell to the ground.

And in fact, he fell so awkwardly that he landed with his head stuck in the mud and his legs straight up in the air.

At the sight of that upside-down puppet frantically kicking his heels, the Serpent was seized with such a fit of laughter that he laughed and laughed and laughed until, from the strain of too much laughing, he burst a blood vessel in his chest; and then he really died.

Then Pinocchio began to run again, trying to reach the Fairy's house before it turned dark. But on the way, not being able to bear the terrible pangs of hunger, he jumped into a field, intending to pick a few bunches of muscat grapes. Would that he had never done it!

As soon as he reached the vines—*Crack!*—he felt his legs clamped tightly between two sharp irons that made him see all the stars there were in the heavens.

The poor puppet had been caught in a trap set there by some peasants to catch a few large martens that were the scourge of all the chicken coops in the neighborhood.

CAPITOLO XXI

Pinocchio è preso da un contadino,
il quale lo costringe a far da can di guardia a un pollajo.

Pinocchio, come potete figurarvelo, si dètte a piangere, a strillare, a raccomandarsi: ma erano pianti e grida inutili, perché lì all'intorno non si vedevano case e dalla strada non passava anima viva.

Intanto si fece notte.

Un po' per lo spasimo della tagliuola che gli segava gli stinchi, e un po' per la paura di trovarsi solo e al buio in mezzo a quei campi, il burattino principiava quasi a svenirsi; quando a un tratto, vedendosi passare una lucciola di sul capo, la chiamò e le disse:

– O Lucciolina, mi faresti la carità di liberarmi da questo supplizio? . . .

– Povero figliuolo! – replicò la Lucciola, fermandosi impietosita a guardarlo. – Come mai sei rimasto colle gambe attanagliate fra codesti ferri arrotati?

– Sono entrato nel campo per cogliere due grappoli di quest'uva moscadella, e . . .

– Ma l'uva era tua?

– No . . .

– E allora chi t'ha insegnato a portar via la roba degli altri? . . .

– Avevo fame . . .

– La fame, ragazzo mio, non è una buona ragione per potersi appropriare la roba che non è nostra . . .

– È vero, è vero! – gridò Pinocchio piangendo – ma un'altra volta non lo farò più. –

A questo punto il dialogo fu interrotto da un piccolissimo rumore di passi, che si avvicinavano. Era il pa-

CHAPTER XXI

*Pinocchio is caught by a peasant who forces him
to work as a watchdog for his poultry-yard.*

Pinocchio, as you can imagine, began to cry, to scream, to plead; but his tears and cries were of no use, because no houses were to be seen anywhere around there, and not a living soul passed by along the road.

Meanwhile, night came on.

Partly because of the intense pain caused by the animal trap that was sawing at his shinbones, and partly because of his fear at finding himself alone in the dark in the middle of those fields, the puppet was almost on the verge of fainting, when all of a sudden he saw a Firefly passing by overhead and called out to her:

"Oh, dear little Firefly, would you be so kind as to free me from this torture?"

"Poor little fellow!" replied the Firefly, stopping to look at him with pity. "How did you ever get your legs clamped between those sharp irons?"

"I came into the field to pick a few bunches of these muscatel grapes, and . . ."

"But were the grapes yours?"

"No . . ."

"Then who taught you to take other people's things?"

"I was hungry . . ."

"Hunger, my boy, is not a good reason for appropriating what is not ours."

"That's true, that's true," cried Pinocchio in tears, "but the next time I won't do it anymore."

At that moment their conversation was interrupted by a light sound of approaching footsteps. It was the

drone del campo che veniva in punta di piedi a vedere se
qualcuna di quelle faine, che gli mangiavano di notte-
tempo i polli, fosse rimasta presa al trabocchetto della
tagliuola.

E la sua maraviglia fu grandissima quando, tirata
fuori la lanterna di sotto al pastrano, s'accòrse che, invece di una faina, c'era rimasto preso un ragazzo.

– Ah, ladracchiolo! – disse il contadino incollerito –
dunque sei tu che mi porti via le galline?

– Io no, io no! – gridò Pinocchio, singhiozzando. –
Io sono entrato nel campo per prendere soltanto due
grappoli d'uva!

– Chi ruba l'uva è capacissimo di rubare anche i polli.
Lascia fare a me, che ti darò una lezione da ricordartene
per un pezzo. –

E aperta la tagliuola, afferrò il burattino per la collottola e lo portò di peso fino a casa, come si porterebbe un
agnellino di latte.

Arrivato che fu sull'aia dinanzi alla casa, lo scaraventò in terra: e tenendogli un piede sul collo, gli disse:

owner of the field, who was coming on tiptoe to see if any of the martens that ate his chickens at night had been caught in the trap he had laid.

And his astonishment was quite great when after taking his lantern out from under his overcoat he found that, instead of a marten, a boy had been caught.

"Ah, you little thief!" said the peasant in a rage, "so it's you who steals my hens."

"Not me, not me!" cried Pinocchio, sobbing. "I only came into the field to get a few bunches of grapes."

"Anyone who steals grapes is quite capable of stealing chickens too. Leave it to me! I'll teach you a lesson you'll remember for a long time."

And opening the trap, he grabbed the puppet by the scruff of the neck and carried him bodily all the way home, just as you would carry a little lamb.

When he reached the threshing floor in front of the house, he flung him to the ground, and keeping one foot on his neck, he said:

– Oramai è tardi e voglio andare a letto. I nostri conti li aggiusteremo domani. Intanto, siccome oggi m'è morto il cane che mi faceva la guardia di notte, tu prenderai subito il suo posto. Tu mi farai da cane di guardia. –

Detto fatto, gl'infilò al collo un grosso collare tutto coperto di spunzoni di ottone, e glielo strinse in modo, da non poterselo levare passandoci la testa di dentro. Al collare c'era attaccata una lunga catenella di ferro: e la catenella era fissata nel muro.

– Se questa notte – disse il contadino – cominciasse a piovere, tu puoi andare a cuccia in quel casotto di legno, dove c'è sempre la paglia che ha servito di letto per quattr'anni al mio povero cane. E se per disgrazia venissero i ladri, ricordati di stare a orecchi ritti e di abbaiare. –

Dopo quest'ultimo avvertimento, il contadino entrò in casa chiudendo la porta con tanto di catenaccio: e il povero Pinocchio rimase accovacciato sull'aia più morto che vivo, a motivo del freddo, della fame e della paura. E di tanto in tanto cacciandosi rabbiosamente le mani dentro al collare, che gli serrava la gola, diceva piangendo:

– Mi sta bene! . . . Pur troppo mi sta bene! Ho voluto fare lo svogliato, il vagabondo . . . ho voluto dar retta ai cattivi compagni, e per questo la fortuna mi perseguita sempre. Se fossi stato un ragazzino per bene, come ce n'è tanti; se avessi avuto voglia di studiare e di lavorare, se fossi rimasto in casa col mio povero babbo, a quest'ora non mi troverei qui, in mezzo ai campi, a fare il cane di guardia alla casa di un contadino. Oh se potessi rinascere un'altra volta! . . . Ma oramai è tardi, e ci vuol pazienza! . . . –

Fatto questo piccolo sfogo, che gli venne proprio dal cuore, entrò dentro il casotto e si addormentò.

"It's late now, and I want to go to bed. We'll settle our accounts tomorrow. Meanwhile, since the dog that kept watch for me at night died today, you'll take his place right away. You'll be my watchdog."

Without further ado he slipped a big collar covered with brass spikes around the puppet's neck and tightened it so much that Pinocchio couldn't slip it off by pulling his head through it. A long iron chain was attached to the collar; and the chain was fastened to the wall.

"If it begins to rain tonight," said the peasant, "you can go lie down in that wooden doghouse where there's still the same straw that was my poor dog's bed for four years. And if by ill chance those thieves should come, remember to keep your ears cocked and bark."

After this final warning, the peasant went into the house, securing the door with an enormous bolt, while poor Pinocchio remained crouched on the threshing-floor yard, more dead than alive with cold, hunger, and fear. And from time to time, thrusting his hands furiously inside the collar that squeezed his throat, he would say, weeping:

"It serves me right! Unfortunately, it serves me right! I wanted to be a lazybones, a vagabond; I preferred to listen to bad companions, and that's why fortune continues to hound me. If I had been a proper boy, the way so many others are, if I had been willing to study and work, if I had stayed at home with my poor father, I wouldn't find myself here now in the middle of the country, being a watchdog at a peasant's house. Oh, if only I could be born over again! . . . But it's too late now, and I have to put up with it."

Having given vent to these feelings that came right from his heart, he went into the doghouse and fell asleep.

CAPITOLO XXII

Pinocchio scuopre i ladri,
e in ricompensa di essere stato fedele vien posto in libertà.

Ed era già più di due ore che dormiva saporitamente; quando verso la mezzanotte fu svegliato da un bisbiglio e da un pissi-pissi di vocine strane, che gli parve di sentire nell'aia. Messa fuori la punta del naso dalla buca del casotto, vide riunite a consiglio quattro bestiuole di pelame scuro, che parevano gatti. Ma non erano gatti: erano faine, animaletti carnivori, ghiottissimi specialmente d'uova e di pollastrine giovani. Una di queste faine, staccandosi dalle sue compagne, andò alla buca del casotto e disse sottovoce:

– Buona sera, Melampo.

– Io non mi chiamo Melampo – rispose il burattino.

– O dunque chi sei?

– Io sono Pinocchio.

– E che cosa fai costì?

– Faccio il cane di guardia.

– O Melampo dov'è? dov'è il vecchio cane, che stava in questo casotto?

– È morto questa mattina.

– Morto? Povera bestia! . . . Era tanto buono! . . . Ma giudicandoti dalla fisonomia, anche te mi sembri un cane di garbo.

– Domando scusa, io non sono un cane! . . .

– O chi sei?

– Io sono un burattino.

– E fai da cane di guardia?

– Pur troppo: per mia punizione! . . .

CHAPTER XXII

Pinocchio catches the thieves,
and as a reward for his loyalty he is set free.

And he had already been sleeping soundly for more than two hours when, toward midnight, he was awakened by the whispering and low chatter of unfamiliar, soft voices that he thought he heard coming from the threshing floor. Sticking the tip of his nose out of the hole of the doghouse, he saw four small, dark-coated creatures who looked like cats consulting in a huddle. But they were not cats: they were martens, little flesh-eating animals, particularly fond of eggs and plump young chickens.[44] One of these martens, leaving his companions, went up to the hole of the doghouse and said softly:

"Good evening, Melampus."

"My name isn't Melampus," answered the puppet.

"Well, who are you then?"

"I'm Pinocchio."

"And what are you doing there?"

"I'm being the watchdog."

"Well, where's Melampus then? Where's the old dog who used to live in this doghouse?"

"He died this morning."

"He died? Poor creature! He was so good! . . . Still, judging by your looks, you seem to be a pretty decent dog too."

"I beg your pardon; I'm not a dog."

"Well, what are you?"

"I'm a puppet."

"And you're acting as a watchdog?"

"Unfortunately, yes; as a punishment."

– Ebbene, io ti propongo gli stessi patti, che avevo col defunto Melampo: e sarai contento.

– E questi patti sarebbero?

– Noi verremo una volta la settimana, come per il passato, a visitare di notte questo pollaio, e porteremo via otto galline. Di queste galline, sette le mangeremo noi, e una la daremo a te, a condizione, s'intende bene, che tu faccia finta di dormire e non ti venga mai l'estro di abbaiare e di svegliare il contadino.

– E Melampo faceva proprio così? – domandò Pinocchio.

– Faceva così, e fra noi e lui, siamo andati sempre d'accordo. Dormi dunque tranquillamente, e stai sicuro che prima di partire di qui, ti lasceremo sul casotto una gallina bell'e pelata per la colazione di domani. Ci siamo intesi bene?

– Anche troppo bene! . . . – rispose Pinocchio: e tentennò il capo in un certo modo minaccioso, come se avesse voluto dire: – Fra poco ci riparleremo! . . . –

Quando le quattro faine si credettero sicure del fatto loro, andarono difilato al pollaio, che rimaneva appunto vicinissimo al casotto del cane; e aperta a furia di denti e di unghioli la porticina di legno, che ne chiudeva l'entrata, vi sgusciarono dentro, una dopo l'altra. Ma non erano ancora finite d'entrare, che sentirono la porticina richiudersi con grandissima violenza.

Quello che l'aveva richiusa era Pinocchio; il quale, non contento de averla richiusa, vi posò davanti per maggior sicurezza una grossa pietra, a guisa di puntello.

E poi cominciò ad abbaiare: e, abbaiando proprio come se fosse un cane di guardia, faceva colla voce: *bù-bù-bù-bù.*

A quell'abbaiata, il contadino saltò il letto, e preso il fucile e affacciatosi alla finestra, domandò:

– Che c'è di nuovo?

– Ci sono i ladri! – rispose Pinocchio.

"Well then, I'll offer you the same deal that I had with the late Melampus. And you're bound to be satisfied."

"And this deal, what would it be?"

"As in the past, we'll come once a week at night to pay a visit to this chicken coop, and we'll make off with eight hens. Of these hens, we'll eat seven and give one to you on condition, of course, that you pretend to be asleep and never get the notion to bark and wake up the peasant."

"And Melampus really did that?" asked Pinocchio.

"He did; and we always got along well. So sleep peacefully, and rest assured that before going away from here we'll leave you a ready-plucked hen on the dog-house for tomorrow's breakfast. Do we understand each other?"

"Only too well!" replied Pinocchio; and he shook his head in a threatening sort of way, as if to say: "We'll soon see about that."

When the four martens felt sure they had things their way, they went straight to the chicken coop, which was located just by the doghouse; and when by dint of their teeth and claws they had opened the small wooden gate that closed the entrance way, they slipped inside one after the other. But no sooner had they finished going in than they heard the gate slam shut behind them.

It was Pinocchio who had shut it; and not satisfied with just shutting it, he propped a big rock against it as an additional precaution.

Then he began to bark; and barking just as if he really were a watchdog, he made his voice go bow-wow-wow.

At that loud barking the peasant sprang out of bed, and after getting his gun and looking out the window, he asked:

"What's up now?"

"The thieves are here," answered Pinocchio.

– Dove sono?

– Nel pollaio.

– Ora scendo subito. –

E difatti, in men che si dice *amen*, il contadino scese: entrò di corsa nel pollaio, e dopo avere acchiappate e rinchiuse in un sacco le quattro faine, disse loro con accento di vera contentezza:

– Alla fine siete cascate nelle mie mani! Potrei punirvi, ma sì vil non sono! Mi contenterò, invece, di portarvi domani all'oste del vicino paese, il quale vi spellerà e vi cucinerà a uso lepre dolce e forte. È un onore che non vi meritate, ma gli uomini generosi, come me, non badano a queste piccolezze! . . . –

Quindi, avvicinatosi a Pinocchio, cominciò a fargli molte carezze, e, fra le altre cose, gli domandò:

– Com'hai fatto a scoprire il complotto di queste quattro ladroncelle? E dire che Melampo, il mio fido Melampo, non s'era mai accorto di nulla! . . . –

Il burattino, allora, avrebbe potuto raccontare quel che sapeva; avrebbe potuto, cioè, raccontare i patti ver-

"Where are they?"

"In the chicken coop."

"I'll be right down."

And in fact, faster than you can say "Amen," the peasant came down and rushed into the chicken coop; and after seizing the four martens and stuffing them in a sack he said with real satisfaction:

"At last you have fallen into my hands! I could punish you, but I am not that base.[45] Instead, I'll just take you to the innkeeper in the nearby village tomorrow, and he'll skin you and cook you like hare in sweet-and-sour sauce. It's an honor you don't deserve, but magnanimous men like me don't quibble over such trifles."

Then, going up to Pinocchio he began to compliment him enthusiastically, and among other things, he asked him:

"How did you manage to discover the plot of these four petty thieves? And to think that Melampus, my faithful Melampus, never noticed anything!"

The puppet could have told him everything he knew

gognosi che passavano fra il cane e le faine: ma ricorda-
tosi che il cane era morto, pensò subito dentro di sé: – A
che serve accusare i morti? . . . I morti son morti, e la
miglior cosa che si possa fare è quella di lasciarli in
pace! . . .

– All'arrivo delle faine sull'aia, eri sveglio o dormi-
vi? – continuò a chiedergli il contadino.

– Dormivo – rispose Pinocchio – ma le faine mi
hanno svegliato coi loro chiacchiericci, e una è venuta
fin qui al casotto per dirmi: «Se prometti di non abbaiare, e di non svegliare il padrone, noi ti regaleremo
una pollastra bell'e pelata! . . .» Capite, eh? Avere la
sfacciataggine di fare a me una simile proposta! Perché
bisogna sapere che io sono un burattino, che avrò tutti i
difetti di questo mondo: ma non avrò mai quello di star
di balla e di reggere il sacco alla gente disonesta! –

– Bravo ragazzo! – gridò il contadino, battendogli sur
una spalla. – Cotesti sentimenti ti fanno onore: e per
provarti la mia grande soddisfazione, ti lascio libero fin
d'ora di tornare a casa. –

E gli levò il collare da cane.

then: that is, he could have told about the shameful pact that existed between the dog and the martens. But remembering that the dog was dead, he immediately thought to himself: "What's the good of accusing the dead? The dead are dead, and the best thing we can do is to leave them in peace."

"When the martens came into the yard, were you awake or were you sleeping?" the peasant went on to ask him.

"I was sleeping," replied Pinocchio, "but the martens woke me up with their chatter; and one of them came right up to the doghouse here to say to me: 'If you promise not to bark and not to wake up the owner, we'll make you a present of a ready-plucked young hen.' Can you imagine, huh? The nerve of making such a proposal to me! Now, you know, I may be a puppet with all the faults in the world, but one fault I'll never have is that of being in cahoots with dishonest people and holding the sack for them!"

"Good for you, my boy!" cried the peasant, slapping him on the back. "Such sentiments do you honor; and to show you how grateful I am, I'm letting you go free right now to return home."

And he removed the dog collar from him.

CAPITOLO XXIII

Pinocchio piange la morte della bella
Bambina dai capelli turchini: poi trova
un Colombo, che lo porta sulla riva del mare,
e lì si getta nell'acqua per andare
in aiuto del suo babbo Geppetto.

Appena Pinocchio non sentì più il peso durissimo e umiliante di quel collare intorno al collo, si pose a scappare attraverso ai campi, e non si fermò un solo minuto finché non ebbe raggiunta la strada maestra, che doveva ricondurlo alla Casina della Fata.

Arrivato sulla strada maestra, si voltò in giù a guardare nella sottoposta pianura, e vide benissimo, a occhio nudo, il bosco, dove disgraziatamente aveva incontrato la Volpe e il Gatto: vide, fra mezzo agli alberi, inalzarsi la cima di quella Quercia grande, alla quale era stato appeso ciondoloni per il collo: ma, guarda di qui, guarda di là, non gli fu possibile di vedere la piccola casa della bella Bambina dai capelli turchini.

Allora ebbe una specie di tristo presentimento; e datosi a correre con quanta forza gli rimaneva nelle gambe, si trovò in pochi minuti sul prato, dove sorgeva una volta la Casina bianca. Ma la Casina bianca non c'era più. C'era, invece, una piccola pietra di marmo, sulla

CHAPTER XXIII

Pinocchio mourns the death of the beautiful
Little Girl with blue hair; then he meets
a Pigeon who carries him to the seashore
where he leaps into the water
to go to the rescue of his father Geppetto.

As soon as Pinocchio no longer felt the heavy and humiliating weight of that dog collar around his neck, he
set out on the run across the fields and didn't stop for a
single moment until he had reached the main road that
should have led him to the Fairy's house.

Once he was on the main road, he turned to look
down on the plain below, and with his naked eye he
could easily see the forest where, to his misfortune, he
had met the Fox and the Cat. There he saw, rising amid
the trees, the top of the Great Oak from which he had
been left dangling by the neck; but though he looked
here, there, and everywhere, he couldn't see the house
of the Little Girl with the blue hair.

Then he felt a sort of sad foreboding; and running
with all the strength he had left in his legs, in a few minutes he was in the meadow where the little white house
once stood. But the little white house was no longer

quale si leggevano in carattere stampatello queste dolorose parole:

QUI GIACE

LA BAMBINA DAI CAPELLI TURCHINI

MORTA DI DOLORE

PER ESSERE STATA ABBANDONATA DAL SUO

FRATELLINO PINOCCHIO

Come rimanesse il burattino, quand'ebbe compitate alla peggio quelle parole, lo lascio pensare a voi. Cadde bocconi a terra, e coprendo di mille baci quel marmo mortuario, dètte in un grande scoppio di pianto. Pianse tutta la notte, e la mattina dopo, sul far del giorno, pian-

geva sempre, sebbene negli occhi non avesse più lacrime: e le sue grida e i suoi lamenti erano così strazianti ed acuti, che tutte le colline all'intorno ne ripetevano l'eco.

E piangendo diceva:

«O Fatina mia, perché sei morta? . . . perché, invece di te, non sono morto io, che sono tanto cattivo, mentre tu eri tanto buona? . . . E il mio babbo dove sarà? O Fatina mia, dimmi dove posso trovarlo, ché voglio stare sempre con lui, e non lasciarlo più! più! più! . . . O Fatina mia, dimmi che non è vero che sei morta! . . . Se davvero mi vuoi bene . . . se vuoi bene al tuo fratellino, rivivisci . . . ritorna viva come prima! . . . Non ti dispiace a vedermi solo, abbandonato da tutti? . . . Se ar-

there. Instead, there was a small marble slab on which one could read in block letters these sorrowful words:

HERE LIES

THE LITTLE GIRL WITH THE BLUE HAIR

WHO DIED OF GRIEF

FOR HAVING BEEN ABANDONED BY HER

LITTLE BROTHER PINOCCHIO

I leave it to you to imagine how the puppet felt after he had struggled to make out those words. He fell face-down to the ground; and covering the tombstone with a thousand kisses, he burst into a flood of tears. He wept throughout the night, and at daybreak the next morning

he was still weeping, although he had no tears left in his eyes. And his cries and wails were so heartrending and piercing that the hills all around resounded with their echo. And weeping, he said:

"Oh, my little Fairy, why did you die? Why didn't I die instead of you, I who am so wicked, while you were so good? . . . And my father, where can he be? Oh, my little Fairy, tell me where I can find him, because I want to stay with him always and never leave him again, never! never! . . . Oh, my little Fairy, tell me it's not true that you're dead! If you really love me, if you love your little brother, live again, come back to life as before! Aren't you sorry to see me alone and abandoned by

rivano gli assassini, mi attaccheranno daccapo al ramo dell'albero . . . e allora morirò per sempre. Che vuoi che io faccia qui solo in questo mondo? Ora che ho perduto te e il mio babbo, chi mi darà da mangiare? Dove anderò a dormire la notte? Chi mi farà la giacchettina nuova? Oh! sarebbe meglio, cento volte meglio, che morissi anch'io! Sì, voglio morire! ih! ih! ih! . . .»

E mentre si disperava a questo modo, fece l'atto di volersi strappare i capelli: ma i suoi capelli, essendo di legno, non poté nemmeno levarsi il gusto di ficcarci dentro le dita.

Intanto passò su per aria un grosso Colombo, il quale soffermatosi, a ali distese, gli gridò da una grande altezza:

– Dimmi, bambino, che cosa fai costaggiù?

– Non lo vedi? piango! – disse Pinocchio alzando il capo verso quella voce e strofinandosi gli occhi colla manica della giacchetta.

– Dimmi – soggiunse allora il Colombo – non conosci per caso fra i tuoi compagni, un burattino, che ha nome Pinocchio?

– Pinocchio? . . . Hai detto Pinocchio? – ripeté il burattino saltando subito in piedi. – Pinocchio sono io! –

Il Colombo, a questa risposta, si calò velocemente e venne a posarsi a terra. Era più grosso di un tacchino.

– Conoscerai dunque anche Geppetto! – domandò al burattino.

– Se lo conosco! È il mio povero babbo! Ti ha forse parlato di me? Mi conduci da lui? ma è sempre vivo? rispondimi per carità; è sempre vivo?

– L'ho lasciato tre giorni fa sulla spiaggia del mare.

– Che cosa faceva?

– Si fabbricava da sé una piccola barchetta, per traversare l'Oceano. Quel pover'uomo sono più di quattro

everyone? If the assassins come, they'll string me up again to the branch of the tree, and then I'll die forever. What can you expect me to do here alone in this world? Now that I have lost you and my father, who will feed me? Where will I go to sleep at night? Who will make me a nice new jacket? Oh, it would be better, a hundred times better, if I died too! Yes, I want to die! . . . Boo-hoo-hoo!"[46]

And while he was wailing in this fashion, he made as if to tear out his hair; but since his hair was of wood, he couldn't even have the satisfaction of thrusting his fingers into it.

At that moment a large Pigeon passed by overhead and, hovering with outspread wings, called out to him from a great height:

"Tell me, child, what are you doing down there?"

"Can't you see? I'm crying!" said Pinocchio, raising his head up toward that voice and rubbing his eyes with the sleeve of his jacket.

"Tell me," the Pigeon added then, "among your comrades, do you by any chance know a puppet named Pinocchio?"

"Pinocchio? . . . Did you say Pinocchio?" the puppet replied, jumping quickly to his feet. "I'm Pinocchio!"

At this answer the Pigeon descended rapidly and alighted on the ground. He was bigger than a turkey.

"Then you probably know Geppetto, too?" he asked the puppet.

"Know him! He's my poor father! Did he speak to you about me? Will you lead me to him? Is he still alive? Answer me, for pity's sake: is he still alive?"

"I left him three days ago on the seashore."

"What was he doing?"

"He was building a little boat by himself, so as to cross the Ocean. The poor man, for more than four

mesi che gira per il mondo in cerca di te: e non avendoti potuto mai trovare, ora si è messo in capo di cercarti nei paesi lontani del nuovo mondo.

– Quanto c'è di qui alla spiaggia? – domandò Pinocchio con ansia affannosa.

– Più di mille chilometri.

– Mille chilometri? O Colombo mio, che bella cosa potessi avere le tue ali! . . .

– Se vuoi venire, ti ci porto io.

– Come?

– A cavallo sulla mia groppa. Sei peso dimolto?

– Peso? tutt'altro! Son leggiero come una foglia. –

E lì, senza stare a dir altro, Pinocchio saltò sulla groppa al Colombo; e messa una gamba di qui e l'altra di là, come fanno i cavallerizzi, gridò tutto contento:

months he has been going everywhere looking for you; and since he hasn't been able to find you, he has taken it into his head to look for you in the far-off lands of the New World."

"How far is it from here to the shore?" asked Pinocchio in breathless anxiety.

"More than a thousand miles."

"A thousand miles? O dear Pigeon, how wonderful it would be if I had your wings!"

"If you want to go, I'll take you there."

"How?"

"Astride my back. Are you very heavy?"

"Heavy? Quite the contrary! I'm as light as a leaf."

And without another word, Pinocchio jumped on the Pigeon's back and, putting a leg on each side of him the way horsemen do, he shouted happily:

«Galoppa, galoppa, cavallino, ché mi preme di arrivar presto! . . .»

Il Colombo prese l'àire e in pochi minuti arrivò col volo tanto in alto, che toccava quasi le nuvole. Giunto a quell'altezza straordinaria, il burattino ebbe la curiosità di voltarsi in giù a guardare: e fu preso da tanta paura e da tali giracapi che, per evitare il pericolo di venir di sotto, si avviticchiò colle braccia, stretto stretto, al collo della sua piumata cavalcatura.

Volarono tutto il giorno. Sul far della sera, il Colombo disse:

– Ho una gran sete!

– E io una gran fame! – soggiunse Pinocchio.

– Fermiamoci a questa colombaia pochi minuti; e dopo ci rimetteremo in viaggio, per essere domattina all'alba sulla spiaggia del mare. –

Entrarono in una colombaia deserta, dove c'era soltanto una catinella piena d'acqua e un cestino ricolmo di vecce.

Il burattino, in tempo di vita sua, non aveva mai potuto patire le vecce: a sentir lui, gli facevano nausea, gli rivoltavano lo stomaco: ma quella sera ne mangiò a strippapelle, e quando l'ebbe quasi finite, si voltò al Colombo e gli disse:

– Non avrei mai creduto che le vecce fossero così buone!

– Bisogna persuadersi, ragazzo mio, – replicò il Colombo – che quando la fame dice davvero e non c'è altro da mangiare, anche le vecce diventano squisite! La fame non ha capricci né ghiottonerie! –

Fatto alla svelta un piccolo spuntino, si riposero in viaggio, e via! La mattina dopo arrivarono sulla spiaggia del mare.

Il Colombo posò a terra Pinocchio, e non volendo nemmeno la seccatura di sentirsi ringraziare per aver fatto una buona azione, riprese subito il volo e sparì.

"Gallop, gallop, little horse, for I am eager to get there fast!"

The Pigeon took flight, and in a few minutes he had soared so high that he almost touched the clouds. When he had reached that extraordinary height, the puppet, out of curiosity, turned to look down; but he was seized by so great a fright and such giddiness that, to keep from falling off, he flung his arms as tightly as he could around the neck of his plumed mount.

They flew all day. Toward evening the Pigeon said:

"I'm very thirsty."

"And I'm very hungry," added Pinocchio.

"Let's stop for a few minutes at this dovecote, and then we'll continue our journey so as to be at the seashore by dawn tomorrow."

They went into an empty dovecote where there was nothing but a basin full of water and a basket brimful of vetch.

All his life the puppet had never been able to tolerate vetch. According to him, it nauseated him and turned his stomach; but that evening he ate so much of it that he nearly burst, and when he had almost finished he turned and said to the Pigeon:

"I would never have believed that vetch was so good."

"We have to realize, my boy, that when we are really hungry, and there is nothing else to eat, even vetch can be delicious! Hunger knows neither fancies nor delicacies!"[47]

After a quick snack they set out on their journey again, and away they went! The next morning they arrived at the seashore.

The Pigeon put Pinocchio down, and not wanting to be bothered with hearing himself thanked for having done a good deed, he flew off again at once and disappeared.

La spiaggia era piena di gente che urlava e gesticolava, guardando verso il mare.

– Che cos'è accaduto? – domandò Pinocchio a una vecchina.

– Gli è accaduto che un povero babbo, avendo perduto il figliuolo, gli è voluto entrare in una barchetta per andare a cercarlo di là dal mare; e il mare oggi è molto cattivo e la barchetta sta per andare sott'acqua . . .

– Dov'è la barchetta?

– Eccola laggiù, diritta al mio dito – disse la vecchia, accennando una piccola barca che, veduta a quella distanza, pareva un guscio di noce con dentro un omino piccino piccino.

Pinocchio appuntò gli occhi da quella parte, e dopo aver guardato attentamente, cacciò un urlo acutissimo gridando:

– Gli è il mi' babbo! gli è il mi' babbo! –

Intanto la barchetta, sbattuta dall'infuriare dell'onde, ora spariva fra i grossi cavalloni, ora tornava a galleggiare: e Pinocchio, ritto sulla punta di un alto scoglio, non finiva più dal chiamare il suo babbo per nome, e dal fargli molti segnali colle mani e col moccichino da naso e perfino col berretto che aveva in capo.

E parve che Geppetto, sebbene fosse molto lontano dalla spiaggia, riconoscesse il figliuolo, perché si levò il berretto anche lui e lo salutò e, a furia di gesti, gli fece capire che sarebbe tornato volentieri indietro; ma il mare era tanto grosso, che gl'impediva di lavorare col remo e di potersi avvicinare alla terra.

Tutt'a un tratto venne una terribile ondata, e la barca sparì. Aspettarono che la barca tornasse a galla; ma la barca non si vide più tornare.

– Pover'omo – dissero allora i pescatori, che erano raccolti sulla spiaggia; e brontolando sottovoce una preghiera, si mossero per tornarsene alle loro case.

Quand'ecco che udirono un urlo disperato, e voltan-

The shore was crowded with people yelling and gesticulating as they looked out to sea.

"What's happened?" Pinocchio asked a little old lady.

"What's happened is that a poor father, having lost
his child, has insisted on going out in a little boat to look
for him beyond the sea; but the waters are very rough
today and the boat is about to go under."

"Where's the boat?"

"There it is, out there, in line with my finger," said
the old woman, pointing to a small boat which, seen
from that distance, looked like a nutshell with a tiny
little man in it.

Pinocchio fixed his gaze in that direction and, after
looking hard, let out a piercing cry:

"It's my father! it's my father!"

Meanwhile the little boat, tossed about by the fury
of the waves, would now disappear amid the large bil-
lows and now reappear above them. And Pinocchio,
standing on the top of a high rock, never stopped calling
his father's name and making him a lot of signs with his
hands, his handkerchief,[48] and even with the cap he had
on his head.

And although Geppetto was very far from shore, it
seemed that he recognized his son, because he too took
off his cap and waved at him; and with a flurry of gestures he gave him to understand that he would gladly
have come back, but the sea was so rough that it kept
him from maneuvering the oars and from being able to
approach land.

All of a sudden there was a mighty wave, and the
boat disappeared. Everyone waited for it to resurface,
but the boat was not seen again.

"Poor man!" said the fishermen then, who were assembled on the shore; and muttering a prayer under
their breath, they started to go back home.

But just then they heard a desperate cry, and turning

dosi indietro, videro un ragazzetto che, di vetta a uno scoglio, si gettava in mare gridando:

– Voglio salvare il mio babbo! –

Pinocchio, essendo tutto di legno, galleggiava facilmente e nuotava come un pesce. Ora si vedeva sparire sott'acqua, portato dall'impeto dei flutti, ora riappariva fuori con una gamba o con un braccio, a grandissima distanza dalla terra. Alla fine lo persero d'occhio e non lo videro più.

– Povero ragazzo! – dissero allora i pescatori, che erano raccolti sulla spiaggia; e brontolando sottovoce una preghiera, tornarono alle loro case.

around they saw a little boy jumping from the top of a reef into the sea and shouting:

"I want to save my father!"

Being all of wood, Pinocchio floated easily and swam like a fish. At one moment they saw him disappear under the water, borne down by the rush of the waves, and the next moment he reappeared above with a leg or an arm, at a vast distance from land. Finally, they lost sight of him and saw him no more.

"Poor boy!" said the fishermen then, who were assembled on the shore; and muttering a prayer under their breath, they went home.

CAPITOLO XXIV

Pinocchio arriva all'isola delle «Api industriose»
e ritrova la Fata.

Pinocchio, animato dalla speranza di arrivare in tempo a dare aiuto al suo povero babbo, nuotò tutta quanta la notte.

E che orribile nottata fu quella! Diluviò, grandinò, tuonò spaventosamente e con certi lampi, che pareva di giorno.

Sul far del mattino, gli riuscì di vedere poco distante una lunga striscia di terra. Era un'isola in mezzo al mare.

Allora fece di tutto per arrivare a quella spiaggia: ma inutilmente. Le onde, rincorrendosi e accavallandosi, se lo abballottavano fra di loro, come se fosse stato un fuscello o un filo di paglia. Alla fine, e per sua buona fortuna, venne un'ondata tanto prepotente e impetuosa, che lo scaraventò di peso sulla rena del lido.

Il colpo fu così forte che, battendo in terra, gli crocchiarono tutte le costole e tutte le congiunture: ma si consolò subito col dire:

– Anche per questa volta l'ho scampata bella! –

Intanto a poco a poco il cielo si rasserenò; il sole apparve fuori in tutto il suo splendore, e il mare diventò tranquillissimo e buono come un olio.

Allora il burattino distese i suoi panni al sole per rasciugarli, e si pose a guardare di qua e di là se per caso avesse potuto scorgere su quella immensa spianata d'acqua una piccola barchetta con un omino dentro. Ma dopo aver guardato ben bene, non vide altro dinanzi a sé che cielo, mare e qualche vela di bastimento, ma così lontana lontana, che pareva una mosca.

– Sapessi almeno come si chiama quest'isola! – an-

CHAPTER XXIV

Pinocchio arrives at the island of Busy Bees
and finds the Fairy again.

Spurred on by the hope of arriving in time to help his poor father, Pinocchio swam the whole night through.

And what an awful night it was! The rain fell in torrents, it hailed, it thundered fearfully, and the lightning was such that it seemed daytime.

Toward morning he was able to see a long strip of land not far off. It was an island in the middle of the sea.

Then he strove with all his might to get to that shore, but in vain. The waves, chasing after one another and tumbling over one another, tossed him all about as if he were a twig or a piece of straw. At last, and a good thing for him, there came a wave so powerful and violent that it dashed him bodily onto the sands of the beach.

He was dashed so hard that in hitting the ground all his ribs and joints cracked; but he quickly consoled himself, saying:

"This time, too, I've had a narrow escape!"

Meanwhile the sky cleared up little by little, the sun came out in all its splendor, and the sea became quite calm and as smooth as oil.

Then the puppet spread his clothes out to dry in the sun and began to look this way and that to see if he could discern on that vast expanse of water a little boat with a little man in it. But although he looked hard and long, he saw nothing in front of him but sky and sea and the occasional sail of a ship, but so very far away that it seemed no bigger than a fly.

"If only I knew the name of this island!" he kept say-

dava dicendo. – Sapessi almeno se quest'isola è abitata da gente di garbo, voglio dire da gente che non abbia il vizio di attaccare i ragazzi ai rami degli alberi! ma a chi mai posso domandarlo? a chi, se non c'è nessuno? . . . –

Quest'idea di trovarsi solo, solo, solo, in mezzo a quel gran paese disabitato, gli messe addosso tanta malinconia, che stava lì lì per piangere; quando tutt'a un tratto vide passare, a poca distanza dalla riva, un grosso pesce, che se ne andava tranquillamente per i fatti suoi, con tutta la testa fuori dell'acqua.

Non sapendo come chiamarlo per nome, il burattino gli gridò a voce alta, per farsi sentire:

– Ehi, signor pesce, che mi permetterebbe una parola?

– Anche due – rispose il pesce, il quale era un Delfino così garbato, come se ne trovano pochi in tutti i mari del mondo.

– Mi farebbe il piacere di dirmi se in quest'isola vi sono dei paesi dove si possa mangiare, senza pericolo d'esser mangiati?

– Ve ne sono sicuro – rispose il Delfino. – Anzi, ne troverai uno poco lontano di qui.

ing. "If only I knew whether this island is inhabited by civilized people; I mean, by people who don't have the bad habit of stringing up boys from tree branches! But who can I possibly ask? Who, if there isn't anybody here?"

The thought of being alone, utterly alone, in the midst of that great uninhabited land put him in such low spirits that he was on the verge of crying. But just then he saw a large fish passing by a little way offshore, going along quietly about his business with all of his head above water.

Not knowing how to call him by name, the puppet called out to him in a loud voice, to make himself heard:

"Ho there, Signor Fish; may I have a word with you?"

"Even two," replied the fish, who was a Dolphin, and so polite that very few of his kind are to be found in all the seas of the world.

"Would you be so kind as to tell me whether there are any villages on this island where one can eat without danger of being eaten?"

"Indeed there are," answered the Dolphin. "In fact, you will find one not far from here."

– E che strada si fa per andarvi?

– Devi prendere quella viottola là, a mancina, e camminare sempre diritto al naso. Non puoi sbagliare.

– Mi dica un'altra cosa. Lei che passeggia tutto il giorno e tutta la notte per il mare, non avrebbe incontrato per caso una piccola barchettina con dentro il mi' babbo?

– E chi è il tuo babbo?

– Gli è il più babbo buono del mondo, come io sono il figliuolo più cattivo che si possa dare.

– Colla burrasca che ha fatto questa notte – rispose il Delfino – la barchetta sarà andata sott'acqua.

– E il mio babbo?

– A quest'ora l'avrà inghiottito il terribile pesce-cane, che da qualche giorno è venuto a spargere lo sterminio e la desolazione nelle nostre acque.

– Che è grosso dimolto questo pesce-cane? – domandò Pinocchio, che di già cominciava a tremare dalla paura.

– Se gli è grosso! . . . – replicò il Delfino. – Perché tu possa fartene un'idea, ti dirò che è più grosso di un casamento di cinque piani, ed ha una boccaccia così larga e profonda, che ci passerebbe comodamente tutto il treno della strada ferrata colla macchina accesa.

– Mamma mia! – gridò spaventato il burattino; e rivestitosi in fretta e furia, si voltò al Delfino e gli disse:

– Arrivedella, signor pesce: scusi tanto l'incomodo e mille grazie della sua garbatezza. –

Detto ciò, prese subito la viottola e cominciò a camminare di un passo svelto: tanto svelto, che pareva quasi che corresse. E a ogni più piccolo rumore che sentiva, si voltava subito a guardare indietro, per la paura di vedersi inseguire da quel terribile pesce-cane grosso come una casa di cinque piani e con un treno della strada ferrata in bocca.

Dopo aver camminato più di mezz'ora, arrivò a un

"And which way do I go to get there?"

"You take that path there on the left and just keep following your nose. You can't go wrong."

"Tell me another thing. You who go through the sea all day and all night, you wouldn't by any chance have come across a small little boat with my father in it?"

"And who is your father?"

"Oh, he's the best father in the world, while I'm the worst son that can be had."

"With the storm we had last night," the Dolphin answered, "the little boat must have gone under."

"And my father?"

"By now he has probably been swallowed by the terrible Shark who has been spreading death and destruction in our waters over the last few days."

"Why, is he very big, this Shark?" asked Pinocchio, who was already beginning to quake with fear.

"Is he big! . . ." replied the Dolphin. "So that you can have an idea of his size, I'll tell you that he is bigger than a five-story building, and has a horrible mouth so wide and deep that a whole railway train with its engine running could easily pass through it."

"Good Heavens!" the puppet exclaimed, terrified; and putting his clothes back on in a great hurry he turned to the Dolphin and said:

"Good-bye, Signor Fish; please excuse me for the trouble I've given you, and a thousand thanks for your kindness."

And so saying, he immediately took to the path and began walking at a fast pace—so fast that he seemed almost to be running. And at the slightest sound he heard, he would turn around quickly to look behind him for fear of being pursued by that terrible Shark as big as a five-story building and with a railway train in his mouth.

After half an hour on the road, he came to a small

piccolo paese detto «il paese delle Api industriose». Le strade formicolavano di persone che correvano di qua e di là per le loro faccende: tutti lavoravano, tutti avevano qualche cosa da fare. Non si trovava un ozioso o un vagabondo, nemmeno a cercarlo col lumicino.

– Ho capito; – disse subito quello svogliato di Pinocchio – questo paese non è fatto per me! Io non son nato per lavorare! –

Intanto la fame lo tormentava; perché erano oramai passate ventiquattr'ore che non aveva mangiato più nulla; nemmeno una pietanza di vecce.

Che fare?

Non gli restavano che due modi per potersi sdigiunare: o chiedere un po' di lavoro, o chiedere in elemosina un soldo o un boccon di pane.

A chiedere l'elemosina si vergognava: perché il suo babbo gli aveva predicato sempre che l'elemosina hanno il diritto di chiederla solamente i vecchi e gl'infermi. I veri poveri, in questo mondo, meritevoli di assistenza e di compassione, non sono altro che quelli che, per ragione d'età o di malattia, si trovano condannati a non potersi più guadagnare il pane col lavoro delle proprie mani. Tutti gli altri hanno l'obbligo di lavorare: e se non lavorano e patiscono la fame, tanto peggio per loro.

In quel frattempo, passò per la strada un uomo tutto sudato e trafelato, il quale da sé solo tirava con gran fatica due carretti carichi di carbone.

Pinocchio, giudicandolo dalla fisonomia per un buon uomo, gli si accostò e, abbassando gli occhi dalla vergogna, gli disse sottovoce:

– Mi fareste la carità di darmi un soldo, perché mi sento morir dalla fame?

– Non un soldo solo – rispose il carbonaio – ma te ne do quattro, a patto che tu m'aiuti a tirare fino a casa questi due carretti di carbone.

– Mi meraviglio! – rispose il burattino quasi offeso;

town called Busy-Bee Town. The streets were swarming with people rushing to and fro about their business. Everyone was working; everyone had something to do. Not a single idler or vagabond was to be found, not even if you looked with a lamp for one.

"I see," said that lazybones Pinocchio right away; "this place isn't meant for me. I wasn't born to work."

Meanwhile he was in the throes of hunger, because by now twenty-four hours had gone by without his having eaten anything, not even a dish of vetch.

What was he to do?

There were but two ways left for him to get something in his stomach: either by asking for a little work or by begging for a penny or a piece of bread.

He was ashamed to go begging, because his father had always taught him that only the old and the infirm had a right to ask for charity. The truly poor in this world, those worthy of help and compassion, are only those who by reason of age or infirmity are condemned to being unable to earn their bread with their own hands.[49] Everyone else has the duty of working; and if they don't work and go hungry, so much the worse for them.

At that moment, a man came down the street, perspiring and panting heavily as he struggled to pull two carts full of charcoal by himself.

Judging him by his looks to be a kind man, Pinocchio went up to him, and lowering his eyes for shame, said to him in a low voice:

"Would you be so kind as to give me a penny, because I feel I'm dying of hunger?"

"Not just one penny," replied the coal merchant, "but I'll give you four, provided that you help me to pull home these two carts of charcoal."

"I'm amazed!" answered the puppet, rather indig-

– per vostra regola io non ho fatto mai il somaro: io non ho mai tirato il carretto!

– Meglio per te! – rispose il carbonaio. – Allora, ragazzo mio, se ti senti davvero morir dalla fame, mangia due belle fette della tua superbia, e bada di non prendere un'indigestione. –

Dopo pochi minuti passò per la via un muratore, che portava sulle spalle un corbello di calcina.

– Fareste, galantuomo, la carità d'un soldo a un povero ragazzo, che sbadiglia dall'appetito?

– Volentieri; vieni con me a portar calcina – rispose il muratore – e invece d'un soldo, te ne darò cinque.

– Ma la calcina è pesa – replicò Pinocchio – e io non voglio durar fatica.

– Se non vuoi durar fatica, allora, ragazzo mio, divertiti a sbadigliare, e buon pro ti faccia. –

In men di mezz'ora passarono altre venti persone: e a tutte Pinocchio chiese un po' d'elemosina, ma tutte gli risposero:

– Non ti vergogni? Invece di fare il bighellone per la strada, va' piuttosto a cercarti un po' di lavoro, e impara a guadagnarti il pane! –

Finalmente passò una buona donnina che portava due brocche d'acqua.

– Vi contentate, buona donna, che io beva una sorsata d'acqua alla vostra brocca? – disse Pinocchio, che bruciava dall'arsione della sete.

– Bevi pure, ragazzo mio! – disse la donnina, posando le due brocche in terra.

Quando Pinocchio ebbe bevuto come una spugna, borbottò a mezza voce, asciugandosi la bocca:

– La sete me la son levata! Così mi potessi levar la fame! . . . –

La buona donnina, sentendo queste parole, soggiunse subito:

nantly. "I'll have you know that I've never been a jack-ass. I've never pulled a cart!"

"Good for you," replied the coal merchant. "And so then, my boy, if you're really dying of hunger, eat two good slices of your pride, and watch out that you don't get indigestion."

A few minutes later, a bricklayer passed by carrying a bucket of mortar on his shoulders.

"Good sir, would you be so kind as to give a penny to a poor boy who's yawning with hunger?"

"With pleasure. Come with me to carry mortar," the bricklayer answered, "and instead of one penny I'll give you five."

"But mortar is heavy," replied Pinocchio, "and I don't like hard work."

"If you don't like hard work, my boy, then have fun yawning, and a lot of good may it do you."

In less than half an hour another twenty persons passed by, and Pinocchio begged all of them for a little something, but they all answered:

"Aren't you ashamed of yourself? Instead of hanging around the streets like a loafer, go and look for some work, and learn to earn your bread."

Finally, a kindly woman passed by, carrying two water jugs.

"Kind woman, would you let me have a swallow of water from your jug?" said Pinocchio, who was parched with thirst.

"Go ahead and drink, my boy," said the kindly woman as she set the two jugs on the ground.

After Pinocchio had drunk like a sponge, he mumbled in a low voice while wiping his mouth:

"I've gotten rid of my thirst. If only I could get rid of my hunger now!"

Hearing these words, the kindly woman added quickly:

– Se mi aiuti a portare a casa una di queste brocche d'acqua, ti darò un bel pezzo di pane. –

Pinocchio guardò la brocca e non rispose né sì né no.

– E insieme col pane ti darò un bel piatto di cavolfiore condito coll'olio e coll'aceto – soggiunse la buona donna.

Pinocchio dètte un'altra occhiata alla brocca, e non rispose né sì né no.

– E dopo il cavolfiore ti darò un bel confetto ripieno di rosolio. –

Alle seduzioni di quest'ultima ghiottoneria, Pinocchio non seppe più resistere, e fatto un animo risoluto, disse:

– Pazienza! vi porterò la brocca fino a casa! –

La brocca era molto pesa, e il burattino, non avendo forza da portarla colle mani, si rassegnò a portarla in capo.

Arrivati a casa, la buona donnina fece sedere Pinocchio a una piccola tavola apparecchiata, e gli pose davanti il pane, il cavolfiore condito e il confetto.

Pinocchio non mangiò, ma diluviò. Il suo stomaco pareva un quartiere rimasto vuoto e disabitato da cinque mesi.

"If you help me to carry one of these water jugs to my home, I will give you a nice piece of bread."

Pinocchio looked at the jug without answering yes or no.

"And along with the bread, I will give you a nice dish of cauliflower seasoned with oil and vinegar," added the kindly woman.

Pinocchio gave another look at the pitcher, but didn't say yes or no.

"And after the cauliflower, I will give you a nice sugared candy filled with rosolio."

The temptation of this last dainty Pinocchio was unable to resist and, his mind made up, he said:

"All right, then! I'll carry the jug home for you."

The jug was very heavy, and since the puppet didn't have enough strength to carry it in his hands, he had to carry it on his head.

After reaching home, the kindly woman sat Pinocchio down at a small table that was already laid and put the bread, the seasoned cauliflower, and the candy before him.

Pinocchio didn't eat; rather he bolted everything down. His stomach was like a lodging that had been left vacant and uninhabited for five months.

Calmati a poco a poco i morsi rabbiosi della fame, allora alzò il capo per ringraziare la sua benefattrice: ma non aveva ancora finito di fissarla in volto, che cacciò un lunghissimo *ohhh!* di maraviglia, e rimase là incantato, cogli occhi spalancati, colla forchetta per aria e colla bocca piena di pane e di cavolfiore.

– Che cos'è mai tutta questa meraviglia? – disse ridendo la buona donna.

– Egli è . . . – rispose balbettando Pinocchio – egli è . . . egli è . . . , che voi mi somigliate . . . voi mi rammentate . . . sì, sì, sì, la stessa voce . . . gli stessi occhi . . . gli stessi capelli . . . sì, sì, sì . . . anche voi avete i capelli turchini . . . come lei! . . . O Fatina mia! . . . o Fatina mia! . . . ditemi che siete voi, proprio voi! . . . Non mi fate più piangere! Se sapeste! Ho pianto tanto, ho patito tanto! . . . –

E nel dir così, Pinocchio piangeva dirottamente, e gettatosi ginocchioni per terra, abbracciava i ginocchi di quella donnina misteriosa.

Having gradually appeased his violent hunger pangs, he raised his head to thank his benefactress; but he had scarcely looked up into her face when he let out a very long "o-o-o-oh" of surprise, and sat there spellbound, with his eyes wide open, his fork in the air, his mouth full of bread and cauliflower.

"What in the world is all this surprise?" said the kindly woman, laughing.

"It's . . ." stammered Pinocchio, "it's . . . it's . . . just that you resemble . . . you remind me of . . . yes, yes, the same voice . . . the same eyes . . . the same hair . . . yes, yes . . . you have blue hair, too . . . like her! . . . Oh, my little Fairy, oh, my little Fairy! . . . tell me that it's you, really you! Don't make me cry any more! If you only knew! . . . I've cried so much, I've suffered so much! . . ."

As he said this, Pinocchio was shedding floods of tears; and then he fell on his knees to the floor and clasped his arms around the knees of that mysterious woman.

CAPITOLO XXV

Pinocchio promette alla Fata
di esser buono e di studiare,
perché è stufo di fare il burattino
e vuol diventare un bravo ragazzo.

In sulle prime, la buona donnina cominciò col dire che lei non era la piccola Fata dai capelli turchini: ma poi, vedendosi oramai scoperta e non volendo mandare più in lungo la commedia, finì per farsi riconoscere, e disse a Pinocchio:

– Birba d'un burattino! Come mai ti sei accorto che ero io?

– Gli è il gran bene che vi voglio, quello che me l'ha detto.

– Ti ricordi, eh? Mi lasciasti bambina, e ora mi ritrovi donna; tanto donna, che potrei quasi farti da mamma.

– E io l'ho caro dimolto, perché così, invece di sorellina, vi chiamerò la mia mamma. Gli è tanto tempo che mi struggo di avere una mamma come tutti gli altri ragazzi! . . . Ma come avete fatto a crescere così presto?

– È un segreto.

– Insegnatemelo: vorrei crescere un poco anch'io. Non lo vedete? Sono sempre rimasto alto come un soldo di cacio.

– Ma tu non puoi crescere – replicò la Fata.

– Perché?

– Perché i burattini non crescono mai. Nascono burattini, vivono burattini e muoiono burattini.

– Oh! sono stufo di far sempre il burattino! – gridò Pinocchio, dandosi uno scappellotto. – Sarebbe ora che diventassi anch'io un uomo . . .

CHAPTER XXV

*Pinocchio promises the Fairy that he will be
good and go to school, because he is
sick and tired of being a puppet
and wants to become a good boy.*

At first the kindly woman began by saying that she was
not the little Fairy with the blue hair, but then, seeing
that she had been found out, and not wanting to prolong
the game, she finally admitted her identity and said to
Pinocchio:

"You scamp of a puppet, how did you ever realize it
was I?"

"It's the great love I have for you that told me so."

"Do you remember? When you left me, I was a little
girl, and now you find me a woman, such a grown-up
woman that I could almost be your mother."

"I'm really glad about that, because now, instead of
calling you my little sister, I'll call you my mother. For
such a long time now I've yearned to have a mother, like
all the other boys . . . But how did you manage to grow
up so fast?"

"It's a secret."

"Teach it to me; I'd like to grow a little too. Don't
you see? I'm still no taller than knee-high to a grasshopper."[50]

"But you can't grow," replied the Fairy.

"Why not?"

"Because puppets never grow. They are born as puppets, they live as puppets, and they die as puppets."

"Oh, I'm sick and tired of always being a puppet!"
cried Pinocchio, rapping himself on the head. "It's
about time that I too became a man."

– E lo diventerai, se saprai meritarlo . . .

– Davvero? E che posso fare per meritarmelo?

– Una cosa facilissima: avvezzarti a essere un ragazzino perbene.

– O che forse non sono?

– Tutt'altro! I ragazzi perbene sono ubbidienti, e tu invece . . .

– E io non ubbidisco mai.

– I ragazzi perbene prendono amore allo studio e al lavoro, e tu . . .

– E io, invece, faccio il bighellone e il vagabondo tutto l'anno.

– I ragazzi perbene dicono sempre la verità . . .

– E io sempre le bugie.

– I ragazzi perbene vanno volentieri alla scuola . . .

– E a me la scuola mi fa venire i dolori di corpo. Ma da oggi in poi voglio mutar vita.

– Me lo prometti?

– Lo prometto. Voglio diventare un ragazzino perbene, e voglio essere la consolazione del mio babbo . . . Dove sarà il mio povero babbo a quest'ora?

– Non lo so.

– Avrò mai la fortuna di poterlo rivedere e abbracciare?

– Credo di sì: anzi ne sono sicura. –

A questa risposta fu tale e tanta la contentezza di Pinocchio, che prese le mani alla Fata e cominciò a baciargliele con tanta foga, che pareva quasi fuori di sé. Poi, alzando il viso e guardandola amorosamente, le domandò:

– Dimmi, mammina: dunque non è vero che tu sia morta?

– Par di no – rispose sorridendo la Fata.

– Se tu sapessi che dolore e che serratura alla gola che provai, quando lessi *qui giace* . . .

– Lo so: ed è per questo che ti ho perdonato. La sin-

"And you will become one, when you learn to deserve it."

"Really? And what can I do to deserve it?"

"Something quite simple: learn how to be a proper boy."

"But isn't that what I already am?"

"Far from it! Proper boys are obedient, and you instead—"

"Instead, I never obey."

"Proper boys are fond of studying and working, you instead—"

"Instead, I'm just a loafer and a vagabond all year round."

"Proper boys always tell the truth—"

"And I tell lies all the time."

"Proper boys are glad to go to school—"

"And school gives me a bellyache. Still, as of today I'm going to turn over a new leaf."

"Do you promise me?"

"I promise. I want to become a proper boy, and I want to be the comfort of my father . . . Oh, where can my poor father be now?"

"I don't know."

"Will I ever be lucky enough to see him again and hug him?"

"I think so; in fact, I'm sure of it."

At this answer Pinocchio's joy was so great that he took the Fairy's hands and began to kiss them with such fervor that he seemed beside himself. Then, lifting his face and looking at her lovingly, he asked her:

"Tell me, mother dear, it's not true then that you died?"

"It doesn't seem so," replied the Fairy, smiling.

"If you only knew the grief I felt, and the lump I had in my throat, when I read 'HERE LIES . . .'"

"I know, and that's why I've forgiven you. The sin-

cerità del tuo dolore mi fece conoscere che tu avevi il cuore buono: e dai ragazzi buoni di cuore, anche se sono un po' monelli e avvezzati male, c'è sempre da sperar qualcosa: ossia, c'è sempre da sperare che rientrino sulla vera strada. Ecco perchè son venuta a cercarti fin qui. Io sarò la tua mamma . . .

– Oh! che bella cosa! – gridò Pinocchio saltando dall'allegrezza.

– Tu mi ubbidirai e farai sempre quello che ti dirò io.

– Volentieri, volentieri, volentieri!

– Fino da domani – soggiunse la Fata – tu comincerai coll'andare a scuola. –

Pinocchio diventò subito un po' meno allegro.

– Poi sceglierai a tuo piacere un'arte o un mestie-re . . . –

Pinocchio diventò serio.

– Che cosa brontoli fra i denti? – domandò la Fata con accento risentito.

– Dicevo . . . – mugolò il burattino a mezza voce – che oramai per andare a scuola mi pare un po' tardi . . .

– Nossignore. Tieni a mente che per istruirsi e per imparare non è mai tardi.

– Ma io non voglio fare né arti né mestieri . . .

– Perché?

– Perché a lavorare mi par fatica.

– Ragazzo mio, – disse la Fata – quelli che dicono così, finiscono quasi sempre o in carcere o allo spedale. L'uomo, per tua regola, nasca ricco o povero, è obbligato in questo mondo a far qualcosa, a occuparsi, a lavorare. Guai a lasciarsi prendere dall'ozio! L'ozio è una bruttissima malattia e bisogna guarirla subito, fin da bambini: se no, quando siamo grandi, non si guarisce più. –

Queste parole toccarono l'animo di Pinocchio, il

cerity of your sorrow made me realize that you had a good heart; and there's always something to hope for from boys with good hearts, even if they are a little mischievous and spoiled. That is, there's always the hope that they may mend their ways. That's why I've come all the way here to look for you. I shall be your mother . . ."

"Oh, how wonderful!" exclaimed Pinocchio, jumping for joy.

"You'll obey me and always do what I tell you."

"I will, I will, I will!"

"As of tomorrow," added the Fairy, "you'll begin to go to school."

At once Pinocchio became a little less elated.

"Then you'll choose a profession or trade to your liking."

Pinocchio became glum.

"What are you muttering under your breath?" asked the Fairy in an irritated tone.

"I was saying . . ." the puppet whimpered in an undertone, "that it seems a little late for me to start school now . . ."

"No sir! Bear in mind that it's never too late to study and to learn."

"But I don't want to follow any profession or trade!"

"Why is that?"

"Because work seems like drudgery to me."

"My boy," said the Fairy, "people who talk that way almost always end up in jail or in the poorhouse. Let me tell you that whether one is born rich or poor, one has the duty to do something in this world, to keep busy, to work. Woe to those who yield to idleness! Idleness is a horrible disease, and it has to be cured early, in childhood; otherwise, when we are grown-up, we never get over it."

Pinocchio was very much moved by these words,

quale rialzando vivacemente la testa, disse alla Fata:

– Io studierò, io lavorerò, io farò tutto quello che mi dirai, perché, insomma, la vita del burattino mi è venuta a noia, e voglio diventare un ragazzo a tutti i costi. Me l'hai promesso, non è vero?

– Te l'ho promesso, e ora dipende da te. –

and lifting his head decisively, he said to the Fairy:

"I'll study, I'll work, I'll do everything you tell me to do, because I'm really fed up with a puppet's life, and I want to become a boy,[51] no matter what. You've promised me, haven't you?"

"I have promised you, and now it's up to you."

CAPITOLO XXVI

Pinocchio va co' suoi compagni di scuola
in riva al mare, per vedere il terribile Pesce-cane.

Il giorno dopo Pinocchio andò alla Scuola comunale.

Figuratevi quelle birbe di ragazzi, quando videro entrare nella loro scuola un burattino! Fu una risata, che non finiva più. Chi gli faceva uno scherzo, chi un altro: chi gli levava il berretto di mano: chi gli tirava il giubbettino di dietro: chi si provava a fargli coll'inchiostro due grandi baffi sotto il naso, e chi si attentava perfino a legargli dei fili ai piedi e alle mani, per farlo ballare.

Per un poco Pinocchio usò disinvoltura e tirò via; ma finalmente, sentendosi scappar la pazienza, si rivolse a quelli che più lo tafanavano e si pigliavano gioco di lui, e disse loro a muso duro:

– Badate, ragazzi: io non son venuto qui per essere il vostro buffone. Io rispetto gli altri e voglio esser rispettato.

– Bravo berlicche! Hai parlato come un libro stampato! – urlarono quei monelli, buttandosi via dalle matte

CHAPTER XXVI

*Pinocchio goes to the seashore with
his schoolmates to see the terrible Shark.*

The next day Pinocchio went to the public school.

Just imagine those devilish boys when they saw a puppet walk into their school! There was no end of laughter. They played all sorts of tricks on him. One snatched his cap out of his hand, another tugged at his jacket from behind; one of them tried to make a big mustache in ink under his nose, and someone even tried to tie strings to his hands and feet to make him dance.

For a while Pinocchio took it all in stride and didn't pay too much attention to it; but then, feeling his patience was running out, he turned to the ones who were pestering him and making fun of him most and, with a hard look, he said:

"Watch out, fellows; I didn't come here to play the fool for you. I respect others, and I want to be respected."

"Good for you, wise guy![52] You talk like a printed book!" those little rogues yelled, rolling over with wild

risate: e uno di loro, più impertinente degli altri, allungò la mano coll'idea di prendere il burattino per la punta del naso.

Ma non fece a tempo: perché Pinocchio stese la gamba sotto la tavola e gli consegnò una pedata negli stinchi.

– Ohi! che piedi duri! – urlò il ragazzo stropicciandosi il livido che gli aveva fatto il burattino.

– E che gomiti! . . . anche più duri dei piedi! – disse un altro che, per i suoi scherzi sguaiati, s'era beccata una gomitata nello stomaco.

Fatto sta che dopo quel calcio e quella gomitata, Pinocchio acquistò subito la stima e la simpatia di tutti i ragazzi di scuola: e tutti gli facevano mille carezze e tutti gli volevano un ben dell'anima.

E anche il maestro se ne lodava, perché lo vedeva attento, studioso, intelligente, sempre il primo a entrare nella scuola, sempre l'ultimo a rizzarsi in piedi, a scuola finita.

Il solo difetto che avesse era quello di bazzicare troppi compagni: e fra questi, c'erano molti monelli conosciutissimi per la loro poca voglia di studiare e di farsi onore.

Il maestro lo avvertiva tutti i giorni, e anche la buona Fata non mancava di dirgli e di ripetergli più volte:

– Bada, Pinocchio! Quei tuoi compagnacci di scuola finiranno prima o poi col farti perdere l'amore allo studio e, forse forse, col tirarti addosso qualche grossa disgrazia.

– Non c'è pericolo! – rispondeva il burattino, facendo una spallucciata, e toccandosi coll'indice in mezzo alla fronte, come per dire: «C'è tanto giudizio qui dentro!»

Ora avvenne che un bel giorno, mentre camminava verso la scuola, incontrò un branco dei soliti compagni, che, andandogli incontro, gli dissero:

laughter. And one who was bolder than the rest stretched out his hand with the intention of grabbing the puppet by the tip of his nose.

But he wasn't quick enough, because Pinocchio thrust his leg under the study bench and gave him a kick in the shins.

"Ouch, what hard feet!" howled the boy, rubbing the bruise that the puppet had caused him.

"And what elbows! . . . even harder than his feet!" said another, who had got a good poke in the stomach for his rude taunts.

So it was that after that kick and that elbow poke, Pinocchio soon won the respect and the affection of all the boys in the school; they all played up to him and were just wild about him.

Even the teacher spoke highly of him, because he saw that he was attentive, studious, and bright, always the first to arrive at school and always the last to get up and leave when school was over.

His one fault was that he went around with too many companions, a good number of whom were urchins well known for their indifference to study and doing well.

His teacher would warn him every day, and the good Fairy too didn't fail to tell him over and over again:

"Be careful, Pinocchio! Sooner or later those good-for-nothing comrades of yours will succeed in making you lose your love for study and may even get you into some serious trouble."

"There's no danger of that!" the puppet would answer, shrugging his shoulders and touching the middle of his forehead with his index finger, as if to say: "There's a lot of good sense in here."

Now it happened that on a certain day while he was walking to school, he met a pack of his usual comrades, who came up to him and said:

– Sai la gran notizia?

– No.

– Qui nel mare vicino è arrivato un Pesce-cane, grosso come una montagna.

– Davvero? . . . Che sia quel medesimo Pesce-cane di quando affogò il mio povero babbo?

– Noi andiamo alla spiaggia per vederlo. Vuoi venire anche tu?

– Io no: io voglio andare a scuola.

– Che t'importa della scuola? Alla scuola ci anderemo domani. Con una lezione di più o con una di meno, si rimane sempre gli stessi somari.

– E il maestro che dirà?

– Il maestro si lascia dire. È pagato apposta per brontolare tutti i giorni.

– E la mia mamma?

– Le mamme non sanno mai nulla – risposero quei malanni.

– Sapete che cosa farò? – disse Pinocchio. – Il Pesce-cane voglio vederlo per certe mie ragioni . . . ma anderò a vederlo dopo la scuola.

– Povero giucco! – ribatté uno del branco. – Che credi che un pesce di quella grossezza voglia star lì a fare il comodo tuo? Appena s'è annoiato, piglia il dirizzone per un'altra parte, e allora chi s'è visto s'è visto.

– Quanto tempo ci vuole di qui alla spiaggia? – domandò il burattino.

– Fra un'ora, siamo bell'e andati e tornati.

– Dunque, via! e chi più corre, è più bravo! – gridò Pinocchio.

Dato così il segnale della partenza, quel branco di monelli, coi loro libri e i loro quaderni sotto il braccio, si messero a correre attraverso ai campi: e Pinocchio era sempre avanti a tutti: pareva che avesse le ali ai piedi.

Di tanto in tanto, voltandosi indietro, canzonava i

"Have you heard the great news?"

"No."

"A Shark as big as a mountain has shown up in the sea not far from here."

"Really? . . . I wonder if it could be the same Shark as the one when my poor father drowned."

"We're going down to the beach to see him. Do you want to come too?"

"Not me! I want to go to school."

"What do you care about school? We'll go to school tomorrow. With one lesson more or less, we'll still be the same jackasses."

"But what will the teacher say?"

"Let the teacher say whatever he likes. He gets paid to grumble all day."

"And my mother?"

"Mothers never know anything," answered those troublemakers.

"Do you know what I'll do?" said Pinocchio, "I have my own good reasons for wanting to see the Shark . . . but I'll go to see him after school."

"You poor numbskull!" countered one of the gang. "Do you think that a fish as big as that is going to hang around and wait for you? As soon as he gets bored with one place, he makes a beeline for another, and that's the end of that."

"How long does it take from here to the beach?" the puppet asked.

"In an hour we can be there and back."

"Let's go, then! And the first one there is the winner!" shouted Pinocchio.

At this signal to start, that pack of urchins set out on the run across the fields with their textbooks and copybooks under their arms. But Pinocchio kept ahead of them all as though he had wings on his feet.

Once in a while, he turned around to poke fun at his

suoi compagni rimasti a una bella distanza, e nel vederli
ansanti, trafelati, polverosi e con tanto di lingua fuori,
se la rideva proprio di cuore. Lo sciagurato, in quel momento, non sapeva a quali paure e a quali orribili disgrazie andava incontro! . . .

comrades who were far behind; and seeing them gasping for breath, all covered with dust and with their
tongues hanging out, he laughed with all his might. The
poor wretch little knew at that moment what terrors
and horrible misfortunes he was heading toward.

CAPITOLO XXVII

*Gran combattimento fra Pinocchio
e i suoi compagni: uno de' quali essendo rimasto ferito,
Pinocchio viene arrestato dai carabinieri.*

Giunto che fu sulla spiaggia, Pinocchio dètte subito una grande occhiata sul mare; ma non vide nessun Pesce-cane. Il mare era tutto liscio come un gran cristallo da specchio.

– O il Pesce-cane dov'è? – domandò, voltandosi ai compagni.

– Sarà andato a far colazione – rispose uno di loro, ridendo.

– O si sarà buttato sul letto per fare un sonnellino – aggiunse un altro, ridendo più forte che mai.

Da quelle risposte sconclusionate e da quelle risatacce grulle, Pinocchio capì che i suoi compagni gli avevano fatto una brutta celia, dandogli ad intendere una cosa che non era vera, e pigliandosela a male, disse loro con voce di bizza:

– E ora? che sugo ci avete trovato a darmi ad intendere la storiella del Pesce-cane?

– Il sugo c'è sicuro! . . . – risposero in coro quei monelli.

– E sarebbe?

– Quello di farti perdere la scuola e di farti venire con noi. Non ti vergogni a mostrarti tutti i giorni così preciso e così diligente alla lezione? Non ti vergogni a studiar tanto, come fai?

– E se io studio, che cosa ve ne importa?

– A noi ce ne importa moltissimo, perché ci costringi a fare una brutta figura col maestro . . .

– Perché?

CHAPTER XXVII

*A great battle between Pinocchio
and his comrades, and when one is wounded,
Pinocchio is arrested by the carabinieri.*

When he got to the beach, Pinocchio immediately gave a sweeping look over the sea, but he saw no Shark. The sea was all smooth, like the surface of a great mirror.

"Well, where's the Shark?" he asked, turning to his comrades.

"He must have gone to have breakfast," answered one of them, laughing.

"Or maybe he hopped into bed to take a nap," added another, laughing still louder.

From their nonsensical answers and their silly jeers, Pinocchio realized that his comrades had played a mean trick on him in giving him to understand something that wasn't true; and taking offense, he said in an irritated voice:

"Well, then? What good did you get out of making me believe that humbug about the Shark?"

"A lot of good, that's for sure!" those rascals answered in a chorus.

"And what would it be?"

"Making you miss school and come with us. Aren't you ashamed of appearing so well prepared and so conscientious every day in class? Aren't you ashamed of studying so hard, the way you do?"

"And what does it matter to you if I study?"

"It matters a whole lot to us, because you make us look bad in front of the teacher."

"Why?"

– Perché gli scolari che studiano, fanno sempre scomparire quelli, come noi, che non hanno voglia di studiare. E noi non vogliamo scomparire! Anche noi abbiamo il nostro amor proprio! . . .

– E allora che cosa devo fare per contentarvi?

– Devi prendere a noia, anche tu, la scuola, la lezione
e il maestro, che sono i nostri tre grandi nemici.

– E se io volessi seguitare a studiare?

– Noi non ti guarderemo più in faccia, e alla prima
occasione ce la pagherai! . . .

– In verità mi fate quasi ridere – disse il burattino con
una scrollatina di capo.

– Ehi, Pinocchio! – gridò allora il più grande di quei
ragazzi, andandogli sul viso. – Non venir qui a fare lo
smargiasso: non venir qui a far tanto il galletto! . . .
perché se tu non hai paura di noi, neanche noi abbiamo
paura di te! Ricordati che tu sei solo e noi siamo sette.

– Sette come i peccati mortali – disse Pinocchio con
una gran risata.

– Avete sentito? Ci ha insultati tutti! Ci ha chiamato
col nome di peccati mortali! . . .

– Pinocchio! chiedici scusa dell'offesa . . . o se no,
guai a te! . . .

– Cucù! – fece il burattino, battendosi coll'indice sulla
punta del naso, in segno di canzonatura.

– Pinocchio! la finisce male! . . .

– Cucù!

– Ne toccherai quanto un somaro! . . .

– Cucù!

– Ritornerai a casa col naso rotto! . . .

– Cucù!

– Ora il cucù te lo darò io! – gridò il più ardito di quei
monelli. – Prendi intanto quest'acconto, e serbalo per la
cena di stasera. –

E nel dir così gli appiccicò un pugno nel capo.

Ma fu, come si suol dire, botta e risposta; perché il

"Because pupils who study hard always make those of us who don't like to study look bad. And we don't want to look bad. We have our pride too."

"And so what am I supposed to do to please you?"

"You too have got to hate school, and lessons, and the teacher: our three great enemies."

"And what if I want to go on studying?"

"We won't even look at you again, and we'll make you pay for it at the first chance."

"Really, you make me almost want to laugh," said the puppet with a little toss of his head.

"Hey, Pinocchio," shouted the biggest of the boys, going right up to him. "Don't play the big shot around here; don't be such a show-off! . . . because if you're not afraid of us, we're not afraid of you, either. Remember that you're alone, and there are seven of us."

"Seven, like the seven deadly sins," said Pinocchio with a hearty laugh.

"Did you hear that? He insulted all of us! He called us the seven deadly sins!"

"Pinocchio, apologize to us for that insult, or else it'll be too bad for you!"

"Cuckoo!" went the puppet, tapping the tip of his nose with his forefinger, as a sign he was mocking them.

"Pinocchio, there's going to be trouble!"

"Cuckoo!"

"You'll get the beating of a jackass!"

"Cuckoo!"

"You'll go home with a broken nose!"

"Cuckoo!"

"I'll give you a cuckoo!" yelled the boldest of the urchins. "Take this to start with, and keep it for your supper tonight."

And as he said this, he pasted a blow on the puppet's head.

But it was tit for tat, as the saying goes, because the

burattino, com'era da aspettarselo, rispose subito con un altro pugno: e lì, da un momento all'altro, il combattimento diventò generale e accanito.

Pinocchio, sebbene fosse solo, si difendeva come un eroe. Con quei suoi piedi di legno durissimo lavorava così bene, da tener sempre i suoi nemici a rispettosa distanza. Dove i suoi piedi potevano arrivare e toccare, ci lasciavano sempre un livido per ricordo.

Allora i ragazzi, indispettiti di non potersi misurare col burattino a corpo a corpo, pensarono bene di metter mano ai proiettili; e sciolti i fagotti de' loro libri di scuola, cominciarono a scagliare contro di lui i *Sillabari*, le *Grammatiche*, i *Giannettini*, i *Minuzzoli*, i *Racconti* del Thouar, il *Pulcino* della Baccini e altri libri scolastici: ma

il burattino, che era d'occhio svelto e ammalizzito, faceva sempre civetta a tempo, sicché i volumi, passandogli di sopra al capo, andavano tutti a cascare nel mare.

Figuratevi i pesci! I pesci, credendo che quei libri fossero roba da mangiare, correvano a frotte a fior d'acqua; ma dopo avere abboccata qualche pagina o qualche frontespizio, la risputavano subito, facendo con la bocca una certa smorfia, che pareva volesse dire: «Non è roba per noi: noi siamo avvezzi a cibarci molto meglio!»

Intanto il combattimento s'inferociva sempre più, quand'ecco che un grosso Granchio, che era uscito fuori

puppet, as was to be expected, answered right away
with another blow; and in no time at all the battle became general and furious.

Although he was alone, Pinocchio defended himself
heroically. With those hard wooden feet he managed so
well that he kept his foes at a respectful distance. Wher-
ever his feet could reach and strike, they left a bruise as
a reminder.

Then the boys, vexed at not being able to fight close
up with the puppet, decided to take up missiles; and un-
doing their bundles of books, they began to hurl their
primers, their grammars, their *Giannettinos* and *Minuz-
zolos*, Thouar's *Stories*, Mme Baccini's *Little Chick*, and

other schoolbooks.[53] But the puppet, who had quick
and sharp eyes, always ducked in time, so that all the
books sailed over his head and landed in the sea.

Just imagine the fish! Thinking that those books were
something good to eat, the fish hurried in shoals to the
surface of the water; but after nibbling at a few pages or
at a frontispiece, they spat them out, making the sort of
face that seemed to say: "That's not for us; we're used
to feeding on much better fare."

Meanwhile, the battle was getting fiercer all the time,
when suddenly a big Crab, who had come out of the

dall'acqua e s'era adagio adagio arrampicato fin sulla spiaggia, gridò con una vociaccia di trombone infreddato:

– Smettetela, birichini che non siete altro! Queste guerre manesche fra ragazzi e ragazzi raramente vanno a finir bene. Qualche disgrazia accade sempre! . . . –

Povero Granchio! Fu lo stesso che avesse predicato al vento. Anzi quella birba di Pinocchio, voltandosi indietro a guardarlo in cagnesco, gli disse sgarbatamente:

– Chetati, Granchio dell'uggia! Faresti meglio a succiare due pasticche di lichene per guarire da codesta infreddatura di gola. Va' piuttosto a letto e cerca di sudare! . . . –

In quel frattempo i ragazzi, che avevano finito oramai di tirare tutti i loro libri, occhiarono lì a poca distanza il fagotto dei libri del burattino, e se ne impadronirono in men che non si dice.

Fra questi libri, v'era un volume rilegato in cartoncino grosso, colla costola e colle punte di cartapecora. Era un *Trattato di Aritmetica*. Vi lascio immaginare se era peso di molto!

Uno di quei monelli agguantò quel volume, e presa di mira la testa di Pinocchio, lo scagliò con quanta forza aveva nel braccio: ma invece di cogliere il burattino, colse nella testa uno dei compagni; il quale diventò bianco come un panno lavato, e non disse altro che queste parole:

– O mamma mia, aiutatemi . . . perché muoio! . . . –

Poi cadde disteso sulla rena del lido.

Alla vista di quel morticino, i ragazzi spaventati si dettero a scappare a gambe, e in pochi minuti non si videro più.

Ma Pinocchio rimase lì; e sebbene per il dolore e per lo spavento, anche lui fosse più morto che vivo, nondimeno corse a inzuppare il suo fazzoletto nell'acqua del

water and climbed very slowly right onto the beach, blared out in a harsh voice like a trombone with a cold:

"Stop it, you good-for-nothing rascals! These fist-fights between boys seldom come to any good. Something bad always happens."

Poor Crab! It was just as if he had preached to the wind. In fact, that scamp of a Pinocchio, turning around with a fierce look, spoke rudely to him:

"Shut up, tedious Crab! You'd do better to suck on a couple of lichen drops to cure that hoarse throat of yours. Why don't you go to bed and try to sweat it off!"

In the meantime, the boys, who had now finished throwing all their own books, caught sight of the puppet's bundle of books nearby, and in no time at all they got hold of it.

Among the books there was a volume bound in thick cardboard, with its spine and corners in parchment. It was a *Manual of Arithmetic*. I leave it to you to imagine how heavy it was!

One of those urchins grabbed the volume and, taking aim at Pinocchio's head, let it fly with all his might. But instead of hitting the puppet, it struck the head of one of his own comrades, who turned as white as a sheet and could only say:

"Oh mother, help me . . . I'm dying!"

Then he fell full-length on the sand.

At the sight of that poor little inert figure, the frightened boys took to their heels in a hurry; and in a few moments they were out of sight.

But Pinocchio stayed behind; and although he was more dead than alive from grief and fright, he nonetheless ran to soak his handkerchief in the sea and began to

mare e si pose a bagnare la tempia del suo povero compagno di scuola. E intanto piangendo dirottamente e disperandosi, lo chiamava per nome e gli diceva:

– Eugenio!. . . povero Eugenio mio! . . . apri gli occhi, e guardami! . . . Perché non mi rispondi? Non sono stato io, sai, che ti ho fatto tanto male! Credilo, non sono stato io! . . . Apri gli occhi, Eugenio . . . Se tieni gli occhi chiusi, mi farai morire anche me . . . O Dio mio! come farò ora a tornare a casa? . . . Con che coraggio potrò presentarmi alla mia buona mamma? Che sarà di me? . . . Dove fuggirò? . . . Dove anderò a nascondermi? . . . Oh! quant'era meglio, mille volte meglio che fossi andato a scuola! . . . Perché ho dato retta a questi compagni, che sono la mia dannazione? . . . E il maestro me l'aveva detto! . . . e la mia mamma me l'aveva ripetuto: – Guardati dai cattivi compagni! – Ma io sono un testardo . . . un caparbiaccio . . . lascio dir tutti, e poi fo sempre a modo mio! E dopo mi tocca a scontarle . . . E così, da che sono al mondo, non ho mai avuto un quarto d'ora di bene. Dio mio! Che sarà di me, che sarà di me, che sarà di me? –

E Pinocchio continuava a piangere, a berciare, a darsi dei pugni nel capo e a chiamar per nome il povero Eugenio, quando sentì a un tratto un rumore sordo di passi che si avvicinavano.

Si voltò: erano due carabinieri.

– Che cosa fai costì sdraiato per terra? – domandarono a Pinocchio.

– Assisto questo mio compagno di scuola.

– Che gli è venuto male?

– Par di sì! . . .

– Altro che male! – disse uno dei carabinieri, chinandosi e osservando Eugenio da vicino. – Questo ragazzo è stato ferito in una tempia: chi è che l'ha ferito?

– Io no! – balbettò il burattino che non aveva più fiato in corpo.

bathe his poor schoolmate's temples. All the while, crying uncontrollably and wailing, he called him by name and said:

"Eugene! Poor Eugene! . . . Open your eyes and look at me! . . . Why don't you answer? It wasn't me who hurt you like that, really! Believe me, it wasn't me! . . . Open your eyes, Eugene! If you keep your eyes closed, you'll make me die too . . . Oh, my God, how can I go back home now? How can I dare face my good mother? . . .What will become of me? Where can I run away to? Where can I go to hide? . . . Oh, how much better, a thousand times better, it would have been if I had gone to school! Why did I listen to my comrades, who are my ruination? And the teacher had warned me! And my mother had repeated it to me: 'Beware of bad company!' But I'm a stubborn and pig-headed fool. I let them all talk, and then I do as I please! And afterward I have to pay for it . . . That's why ever since I was born I've never had fifteen minutes of peace. My God, what's to become of me, what's to become of me, what's to become of me?"

And Pinocchio continued to cry, howl, beat at his head, and call poor Eugene by name when all of a sudden he heard a muffled sound of approaching footsteps.

He turned around; and there were two carabinieri.

"What are you doing stretched out on the ground there?" they asked Pinocchio.

"I'm helping this schoolmate of mine."

"Has he been taken ill?"

"I think so . . ."

"I'll say he's ill!" said one of the carabinieri, stooping down and looking closely at Eugene. "This boy has been wounded in the temple. Who was it that struck him?"

"Not me," stammered the puppet, who was breathless.

– Se non sei stato tu, chi è stato dunque che l'ha ferito?

– Io no! – ripeté Pinocchio.

– E con che cosa è stato ferito?

– Con questo libro. – E il burattino raccattò di terra il *Trattato di Aritmetica*, rilegato in cartone e cartapecora, per mostrarlo al carabiniere.

– E questo libro di chi è?

– Mio.

– Basta così: non occorre altro. Rizzati subito, e vien via con noi.

– Ma io . . .

– Via con noi! . . .

– Ma io sono innocente . . .

– Via con noi! –

Prima di partire, i carabinieri chiamarono alcuni pescatori, che in quel momento passavano per l'appunto colla loro barca vicino alla spiaggia, e dissero loro:

– Vi affidiamo questo ragazzetto ferito nel capo. Portatelo a casa vostra e assistetelo. Domani torneremo a vederlo. –

Quindi si volsero a Pinocchio e dopo averlo messo in

"If it wasn't you, then who was it that struck him?"

"Not me," repeated Pinocchio.

"What was he struck with?"

"With this book." And the puppet picked up the *Manual of Arithmetic*, bound in cardboard and parchment, to show it to the carabiniere.

"And whose book is this?"

"Mine."

"Enough. That's all we need to know. Get up right away and come along with us."

"But I—"

"Come along with us!"

"But I'm innocent—"

"Come along with us!"

Before setting off, the carabinieri called out to some fishermen who just then happened to be going by in their boat close to shore, and said to them:

"We're leaving this boy who's been wounded in the head in your care. Take him home with you and look after him. We'll be back tomorrow to see him."

Then they turned to Pinocchio and, having placed

mezzo a loro due, gl'intimarono con accento soldatesco:

– Avanti! e cammina spedito! se no, peggio per te! –

Senza farselo ripetere, il burattino cominciò a camminare per quella viottola, che conduceva al paese. Ma il povero diavolo non sapeva più nemmeno lui in che mondo si fosse. Gli pareva di sognare, e che brutto sogno! Era fuori di sé. I suoi occhi vedevano tutto doppio: le gambe gli tremavano: la lingua gli era rimasta attaccata al palato e non poteva più spicciare una sola parola. Eppure, in mezzo a quella specie di stupidità e di rintontimento, una spina acutissima gli bucava il cuore: il pensiero, cioè, di dover passare sotto le finestre di casa della sua buona Fata, in mezzo ai carabinieri. Avrebbe preferito piuttosto di morire.

Erano già arrivati e stavano per entrare in paese, quando una folata di vento strapazzone levò di testa a Pinocchio il berretto, portandoglielo lontano una diecina di passi.

– Si contentano – disse il burattino ai carabinieri – che vada a riprendere il mio berretto?

– Vai pure; ma facciamo una cosa lesta. –

Il burattino andò, raccattò il berretto . . . ma invece di metterselo in capo, se lo mise in bocca fra i denti, e

him between them, in a curt, military tone they commanded:

"March! and move fast! if not, so much the worse for
you!"

Without waiting to have it repeated, the puppet began moving down the path that led to town. But the
poor devil no longer knew what in the world was going
on. He thought he was dreaming; and what a horrible
dream! He was beside himself. His eyes saw everything
double, his legs were shaking, his tongue stuck to the
roof of his mouth, and he couldn't utter a single word.
And yet, in the midst of that stupor and bewilderment
of his, there was one sharp thorn that pierced his heart:
the thought, that is, of having to pass beneath the window of his good Fairy's house, walking between two
carabinieri. He would rather have died.

They had already reached the town and were about
to enter when a strong gust of wind blew Pinocchio's
cap off, carrying it some ten yards or so away.

"Is it all right if I go and retrieve my cap?" the puppet
asked the carabinieri.

"Go ahead, but let's make it quick."

The puppet went and picked up his cap, but instead
of putting it on his head, he put it in his mouth, between

poi cominciò a correre di gran carriera verso la spiaggia del mare. Andava via come una palla di fucile.

I carabinieri, giudicando che fosse difficile raggiungerlo, gli aizzarono dietro un grosso cane mastino, che aveva guadagnato il primo premio a tutte le corse dei cani. Pinocchio correva, e il cane correva più di lui: per cui tutta la gente si affacciava alle finestre e si affollava in mezzo alla strada, ansiosa di veder la fine di un palio così inferocito. Ma non poté levarsi questa voglia, perché fra il can mastino e Pinocchio sollevarono lungo la strada un tal polverone, che dopo pochi minuti non era possibile di veder più nulla.

his teeth, and began to run as fast as he could toward the seashore. He sped like a rifle shot.

Deciding that it would be hard for them to catch up with him, the carabinieri set a huge mastiff after him, one that had won first prize in all the dog races. Pinocchio ran, but the dog ran even faster, so that all the people looked out the windows and flocked into the middle of the street, eager to see the conclusion of that fierce chase. But they were unable to satisfy their curiosity, because, between them, the mastiff and Pinocchio raised such a cloud of dust along the street that in a few moments it wasn't possible to see anything more.

CAPITOLO XXVIII

Pinocchio corre pericolo
di esser fritto in padella, come un pesce.

Durante quella corsa disperata, vi fu un momento terribile, un momento in cui Pinocchio si credé perduto: perché bisogna sapere che Alidoro (era questo il nome del can mastino) a furia di correre e correre, l'aveva quasi raggiunto.

Basti dire che il burattino sentiva dietro di sé, alla distanza d'un palmo, l'ansare affannoso di quella bestiaccia, e ne sentiva perfino la vampa calda delle fiatate.

Per buona fortuna la spiaggia era oramai vicina e il mare si vedeva lì a pochi passi.

Appena fu sulla spiaggia, il burattino spiccò un bellissimo salto, come avrebbe potuto fare un ranocchio, e andò a cascare in mezzo all'acqua. Alidoro invece voleva fermarsi; ma trasportato dall'impeto della corsa, entrò nell'acqua anche lui. E quel disgraziato non sapeva nuotare; per cui cominciò subito ad annaspare colle zampe per reggersi a galla: ma più annaspava e più andava col capo sott'acqua.

Quando tornò a rimettere il capo fuori, il povero cane aveva gli occhi impauriti e stralunati, e, abbaiando, gridava:

– Affogo! affogo!

– Crepa! – gli rispose Pinocchio da lontano, il quale si vedeva oramai sicuro da ogni pericolo.

– Aiutami, Pinocchio mio! . . . salvami dalla morte! . . . –

A quelle grida strazianti il burattino, che in fondo aveva un cuore eccellente, si mosse a compassione, e voltosi al cane gli disse:

CHAPTER XXVIII

Pinocchio runs the risk
of being fried in a pan like a fish.

During that frantic chase, there was a terrible moment when Pinocchio felt he was lost, because, you see, Alidoro—that was the mastiff's name—kept on running and running until he had almost caught up with him.

Suffice it to say that the puppet heard the heavy panting of that awful beast a hand's breadth away and that he even felt the hot puffs of his breathing.

Fortunately, the shore was now nearby and the sea was in sight only a few steps away.

As soon as he got to the shore, the puppet took a splendid leap, just as a frog might have done, and landed in the middle of the water. Instead, Alidoro tried to stop, but carried forward by the impetus of the chase, he went into the water too. Now, the poor wretch didn't know how to swim, so right away he began thrashing with his paws, trying to keep afloat. But the more he struggled, the more his head went under.

When he managed to get his head above water again, the poor dog's eyes were wild with terror, and he barked out:

"I'm drowning! I'm drowning!"

"Croak!" Pinocchio answered from afar, seeing himself safe from all danger now.

"Help me, dear Pinocchio! . . . save me from death!"

At those anguished cries, the puppet, who really had a very good heart, was moved to pity; and turning to the dog, he said:

– Ma se io ti aiuto a salvarti, mi prometti di non darmi più noia e di non corrermi dietro?

– Te lo prometto! te lo prometto! Spicciati per carità, perché se indugi un altro mezzo minuto, son bell'e morto. –

Pinocchio esitò un poco: ma poi ricordandosi che il suo babbo gli aveva detto tante volte che a fare una buona azione non ci si scapita mai, andò nuotando a raggiungere Alidoro, e, presolo per la coda con tutte e due le mani, lo portò sano e salvo sulla rena asciutta del lido.

Il povero cane non si reggeva più in piedi. Aveva bevuto, senza volerlo, tant'acqua salata, che era gonfiato come un pallone. Per altro il burattino, non volendo fare a fidarsi troppo, stimò cosa prudente di gettarsi novamente in mare; e allontanandosi dalla spiaggia, gridò all'amico salvato:

– Addio, Alidoro; fa' buon viaggio e tanti saluti a casa.

– Addio, Pinocchio – rispose il cane; – mille grazie di avermi liberato dalla morte. Tu m'hai fatto un gran servizio: e in questo mondo quel che è fatto è reso. Se capita l'occasione, ci riparleremo . . . –

Pinocchio seguitò a nuotare, tenendosi sempre vicino alla terra. Finalmente gli parve di esser giunto in un luogo sicuro; e dando un'occhiata alla spiaggia, vide sugli scogli una specie di grotta, dalla quale usciva un lunghissimo pennacchio di fumo.

– In quella grotta – disse allora fra sé – ci deve essere del fuoco. Tanto meglio! Anderò a rasciugarmi e a riscaldarmi, e poi? . . . e poi sarà quel che sarà. –

Presa questa risoluzione, si avvicinò alla scogliera; ma quando fu lì per arrampicarsi, sentì qualche cosa sotto l'acqua che saliva, saliva, saliva e lo portava per aria. Tentò subito di fuggire, ma oramai era tardi, perché con sua grandissima maraviglia si trovò rin-

"But if I do save you, will you promise not to bother me anymore and not to chase me?"

"I promise! I promise! Hurry, for mercy's sake, because if you wait even another half-minute I'll be dead and gone!"

Pinocchio hesitated a little; but then, recalling that his father had often told him that a good deed never goes for naught, he swam hard to reach Alidoro, and taking hold of him by the tail with both hands he brought him safe and sound onto the dry sand of the beach.

The poor dog couldn't even stand up. In spite of himself, he had drunk so much saltwater that he was swollen like a balloon. Even so, the puppet, not daring to be too trustful, thought it wiser to jump back into the sea; and as he struck out from shore, he called back to the friend he had rescued:

"Farewell, Alidoro; bon voyage, and best wishes to the folks at home."

"Farewell, Pinocchio," answered the dog; "a thousand thanks for having saved me from death. You've done me a great service, and in this world one good turn deserves another. If the chance ever arises, I won't forget it."

Pinocchio went on swimming, always keeping close to land. At last he felt he had reached a safe place, and giving a look toward the shore he saw a sort of cave among the rocks, with a long column of smoke rising from it.

"In that cave," he said to himself then, "there must be a fire. That's all to the good. I'll go dry myself and warm up, and then . . . And then let happen what may."

Having made up his mind, he swam toward the rocks; but just as he was about to scramble up them he felt something under the water that kept rising, rising, rising and that lifted him up right into the air. He tried to escape, but it was too late now, because to his great

chiuso dentro una grossa rete in mezzo a un brulichìo di pesci d'ogni forma e grandezza, che scodinzolavano e si dibattevano come tante anime disperate.

E nel tempo stesso vide uscire dalla grotta un pescatore così brutto, ma tanto brutto, che pareva un mostro marino. Invece di capelli aveva sulla testa un cespuglio foltissimo di erba verde; verde era la pelle del suo corpo, verdi gli occhi, verde la barba lunghissima, che gli scendeva fin quaggiù. Pareva un grosso ramarro ritto sui piedi di dietro.

Quando il pescatore ebbe tirata fuori la rete dal mare, gridò tutto contento:

– Provvidenza benedetta! Anch'oggi potrò fare una bella scorpacciata di pesce!

– Manco male, che io non sono un pesce! – disse Pinocchio dentro di sé, ripigliando un po' di coraggio.

La rete piena di pesci fu portata dentro la grotta, una grotta buia e affumicata, in mezzo alla quale friggeva

astonishment he found himself trapped in a large net, amid a swarming mass of fish of all shapes and sizes that were wriggling and writhing like so many souls in torment.

At the same time, he saw such an ugly fisherman come out of the cave, but really so ugly that he looked like a monster from the deep. Instead of hair, he had a very thick clump of green weeds on his head; green was the skin of his body; green his eyes; and green his long beard that reached all the way down to the ground. He looked like a huge green lizard standing upright on its hind legs.

When the fisherman had drawn in the net from the sea, he exclaimed with joy:

"The Lord be praised! Today, too, I'll be able to have a bellyful of fish!"

"It's a good thing I'm not a fish!" said Pinocchio to himself, cheering up.

The net full of fish was brought into the cave; a dark smoke-blackened cave in the middle of which was a

una gran padella d'olio, che mandava un odorino di moccolaia, da mozzare il respiro.

– Ora vediamo un po' che pesci abbiamo presi! – disse il pescatore verde; e ficcando nella rete una manona così spropositata, che pareva una pala da fornai, tirò fuori una manciata di triglie.

– Buone queste triglie! – disse, guardandole e annusandole con compiacenza. E dopo averle annusate, le scaraventò in una conca senz'acqua.

Poi ripeté più volte la solita operazione; e via via che cavava fuori gli altri pesci, sentiva venirsi l'acquolina in bocca e gongolando diceva:

– Buoni questi naselli! . . .

– Squisiti questi muggini! . . .

– Deliziose queste sogliole! . . .

– Prelibati questi ragnotti! . . .

– Carine queste acciughe col capo! . . . –

Come potete immaginarvelo, i naselli, i muggini, le sogliole, i ragnotti e l'acciughe, andarono tutti alla rinfusa nella conca, a tener compagnia alle triglie.

L'ultimo che restò nella rete fu Pinocchio.

Appena il pescatore l'ebbe cavato fuori, sgranò dalla maraviglia i suoi occhioni verdi, gridando quasi impaurito:

– Che razza di pesce è questo? Dei pesci fatti a questo modo non mi ricordo di averne mangiati mai! –

E tornò a guardarlo attentamente, e dopo averlo guardato ben bene per ogni verso, finì col dire:

– Ho capito: dev'essere un granchio di mare. –

Allora Pinocchio, mortificato di sentirsi scambiare per un granchio, disse con accento risentito:

– Ma che granchio e non granchio? Guardi come lei mi tratta! Io per sua regola sono un burattino.

– Un burattino? – replicò il pescatore. – Dico la veri-

large frying pan with sizzling oil that sent up a delicious smell like candlesnuff such as to cut your breath short.

"Now, let's see what kind of fish we've caught," said the green fisherman; and sticking his hand, which was so huge that it looked like a baker's peel, into the net, he pulled out a handful of red mullet.

"Very nice, these red mullet!" he said, looking at them and sniffing them with satisfaction. And after sniffing them, he flung them into a large earthen pot without any water in it.

Then he repeated the same operation several times; and as he drew out the other fish, his mouth watered and he gloated:

"Very nice, these hake!"

"Exquisite, these gray mullet!"

"Delicious, these sole!"

"Choice, these sea bass!"

"Pretty, these anchovies with their heads on!"[54]

As you can imagine, the hake, the gray mullet, the sole, the bass, and the anchovies all went together pell mell into the earthen pot to keep the red mullet company.

The last to remain in the net was Pinocchio.

As soon as the fisherman had pulled him out, he opened his enormous green eyes wide in amazement and cried out half-frightened:

"What sort of fish is this? I don't recall ever having eaten fish of this shape or form!"

He looked at him again, carefully; and after looking him all over closely, he finally said:

"I know; it must be a sea crab."

Then Pinocchio, mortified at hearing himself taken for a crab, said crossly:

"What do you mean, a crab? Be careful how you treat me! For your information, I'm a puppet."

"A puppet?" replied the fisherman. "To tell the truth,

tà, il pesce burattino è per me un pesce nuovo! Meglio
così! ti mangerò più volentieri.

– Mangiarmi? ma la vuol capire che io non sono un
pesce? O non sente che parlo, e ragiono come lei?

– È verissimo – soggiunse il pescatore – e siccome
vedo che sei un pesce, che hai la fortuna di parlare e di
ragionare, come me, così voglio usarti anch'io i dovuti
riguardi.

– E questi riguardi sarebbero? . . .

– In segno di amicizia e di stima particolare, lascerò a
te la scelta del come vuoi esser cucinato. Desideri esser
fritto in padella, oppure preferisci di esser cotto nel te-
game con la salsa di pomidoro?

– A dir la verità – rispose Pinocchio – se io debbo
scegliere, preferisco piuttosto di esser lasciato libero,
per potermene tornare a casa mia.

– Tu scherzi! Ti pare che io voglia perdere l'occasione
di assaggiare un pesce così raro? Non capita mica tutti i
giorni un pesce burattino in questi mari. Lascia fare a
me: ti friggerò in padella assieme a tutti gli altri pesci, e

a puppet-fish is a new fish to me.[55] So much the better;
I'll eat you with all the more relish."

"Eat me? But won't you understand that I'm not a
fish? Can't you hear that I talk and reason the way you
do?"

"That's quite true," the fisherman continued, "and
since I see that you're a fish that has the good fortune to
talk and reason like me, I intend to treat you with all due
respect."

"And what does this respect consist of?"

"As a token of my friendship and high esteem, I'll let
you choose the way you want to be cooked. Do you
want to be fried in a skillet, or do you prefer to be
cooked in a pan with tomato sauce?"

"To tell the truth," replied Pinocchio, "if I'm to
choose, I prefer rather to be set free, so I can go back
home."

"You're joking! Do you think I want to lose the
chance of tasting so rare a fish? It isn't every day that a
puppet-fish comes along in these waters. I know what
I'll do; I'll fry you in a skillet with the other fish, and

te ne troverai contento. L'esser fritto in compagnia è sempre una consolazione. –

L'infelice Pinocchio, a quest'antifona, cominciò a piangere, a strillare, a raccomandarsi: e piangendo diceva: – Quant'era meglio, che fossi andato a scuola! . . . Ho voluto dar retta ai compagni, e ora la pago! Ih! . . . Ih! . . . Ih! . . . –

E perché si divincolava come un'anguilla e faceva sforzi incredibili, per isgusciare dalle grinfie del pescatore verde, questi prese una bella buccia di giunco, e dopo averlo legato per le mani e per i piedi, come un salame, lo gettò in fondo alla conca cogli altri.

Poi, tirato fuori un vassoiaccio di legno, pieno di farina, si dètte a infarinare tutti quei pesci: e man mano che li aveva infarinati, li buttava a friggere dentro la padella.

I primi a ballare nell'olio bollente furono i poveri naselli: poi toccò ai ragnotti, poi ai muggini, poi alle sogliole e alle acciughe, e poi venne la volta di Pinocchio. Il quale, a vedersi così vicino alla morte (e che brutta morte!) fu preso da tanto tremito e da tanto spavento, che non aveva più né voce né fiato per raccomandarsi.

Il povero figliuolo si raccomandava cogli occhi! Ma il pescatore verde, senza badarlo neppure, lo avvoltolò cinque o sei volte nella farina, infarinandolo così bene dal capo ai piedi, che pareva diventato un burattino di gesso.

Poi lo prese per il capo, e . . .

you'll be glad of it. There's always some comfort in being fried in company with others."

At this tune, the wretched Pinocchio began to cry, to scream, to plead; and as he wept, he said:

"How much better it would have been if I had gone to school! . . . I preferred to listen to my comrades, and now I'm paying for it. Boo-hoo-hoo!"

And because he squirmed like an eel and made such frantic efforts to slip out of the clutches of the green fisherman, the latter took a nice length of reed, and after tying the puppet's hands and feet like a salami, he threw him into the bottom of the pot with the others.

Then, getting a large old wooden platter that was full of flour, he busied himself with rolling all those fish in it; and as he covered them with flour, he threw them one by one to be fried in the skillet.

The first to dance in the boiling oil were the poor hake; then it fell to the bass, then to the gray mullet, then to the sole and the anchovies; and finally it was Pinocchio's turn. Seeing himself so near death (and what a terrible death!) he was seized by such trembling and by such terror that he could no longer find voice or breath to beg for mercy.

The poor boy pleaded with his eyes! But without even paying any attention to him, the green fisherman rolled him in the flour five or six times, covering him so well from head to foot that he seemed to have turned into a plaster puppet.

Then he took him by the head, and . . .

CAPITOLO XXIX

Ritorna a casa della Fata, la quale
gli promette che il giorno dopo non sarà più
un burattino, ma diventerà un ragazzo.
Gran colazione di caffè-e-latte
per festeggiare questo grande avvenimento.

Mentre il pescatore era proprio sul punto di buttar Pinocchio nella padella, entrò nella grotta un grosso cane condotto là dall'odore acutissimo e ghiotto della frittura.

– Passa via! – gli gridò il pescatore minacciandolo e tenendo sempre in mano il burattino infarinato.

Ma il povero cane aveva una fame per quattro, e mugolando e dimenando la coda, pareva che dicesse:

– Dammi un boccone di frittura e ti lascio in pace.

– Passa via, ti dico! – gli ripeté il pescatore; e allungò la gamba per tirargli una pedata.

Allora il cane che, quando aveva fame davvero, non era avvezzo a lasciarsi posar mosche sul naso, si rivoltò ringhioso al pescatore, mostrandogli le sue terribili zanne.

In quel mentre si udì nella grotta una vocina fioca fioca che disse:

– Salvami, Alidoro! Se non mi salvi, son fritto!... –

Il cane riconobbe subito la voce di Pinocchio, e si accòrse con sua grandissima maraviglia che la vocina era uscita da quel fagotto infarinato che il pescatore teneva in mano.

Allora che cosa fa? Spicca un gran lancio da terra, abbocca quel fagotto infarinato e tenendolo leggermente coi denti, esce correndo dalla grotta, e via come un baleno!

CHAPTER XXIX

He returns to the Fairy's house,
and she promises him that the next day he will
no longer be a puppet but will become a boy.
Grand breakfast of caffè-e-latte
to celebrate this great event.

Just as the fisherman was about to throw Pinocchio into the skillet, a huge dog came into the cave, drawn there by the pungent, enticing smell of the frying fish.

"Go away," hollered the fisherman, threatening him and still holding the flour-coated puppet in his hand.

But the poor dog was absolutely famished; and yelping and wagging his tail, he seemed to say:

"Give me a bit of fried fish and I'll leave you alone."

"Go away, I said!" repeated the fisherman; and he raised his leg to give him a kick.

Then the dog, who didn't take any sass when he was really hungry, turned and snarled at the fisherman, baring his horrible fangs.

Just then a small voice, ever so faint, was heard in the cave saying:

"Save me, Alidoro! If you don't save me, I'm done!"

The dog recognized Pinocchio's voice at once, and to his great astonishment he noticed that the faint voice had come from the flour-coated bundle that the fisherman was holding in his hand.

And what does he do then? He takes a great leap from the ground, snaps up the flour-coated bundle in his mouth, and holding it gingerly between his teeth, runs out of the cave and is off like a flash.

Il pescatore, arrabbiatissimo di vedersi strappar di mano un pesce, che egli avrebbe mangiato tanto volentieri, si provò a rincorrere il cane; ma fatti pochi passi, gli venne un nodo di tosse e dové tornarsene indietro.

Intanto Alidoro, ritrovata che ebbe la viottola che conduceva al paese, si fermò e posò delicatamente in terra l'amico Pinocchio.

– Quanto ti debbo ringraziare! – disse il burattino.

– Non c'è bisogno – replicò il cane – tu salvasti me, e quel che è fatto è reso. Si sa: in questo mondo bisogna tutti aiutarsi l'uno coll'altro.

– Ma come mai sei capitato in quella grotta?

– Ero sempre qui disteso sulla spiaggia più morto che vivo, quando il vento mi ha portato da lontano un odorino di frittura. Quell'odorino mi ha stuzzicato l'appetito, e io gli sono andato dietro. Se arrivavo un minuto più tardi! . . .

– Non me lo dire! – urlò Pinocchio che tremava ancora dalla paura – Non me lo dire! Se tu arrivavi un minuto più tardi, a quest'ora io ero bell'e fritto, mangiato e digerito. Brrr! mi vengono i brividi soltanto a pensarvi! . . . –

Alidoro, ridendo, stese la zampa destra verso il burattino, il quale gliela strinse forte forte in segno di grande amicizia: e dopo si lasciarono.

Enraged at seeing a fish he was so anxious to eat snatched from his hand, the fisherman started to run after the dog; but after going a few steps he was seized with a fit of coughing and had to go back.

Meanwhile, when Alidoro got to the path leading to the town, he stopped and gently put his friend Pinocchio down on the ground.

"How thankful I am to you!" said the puppet.

"There's no need to thank me," replied the dog. "You saved me first, and one good turn deserves another. It's a fact; in this world we must help one another."

"But how did you ever happen to come to that cave?"

"I was still lying there on the beach more dead than alive when the wind brought me the delicious smell of something frying at a distance. That delicious smell whetted my appetite, and I followed it. If I had arrived a minute later! . . ."

"Don't say it!" shouted Pinocchio, who was still trembling with fear. "Don't say it! If you had arrived a minute later, by now I would have already been fried, eaten, and digested. Brrr! . . . I get the shivers just thinking of it!"

Laughing, Alidoro stretched his right paw out to the puppet, who clasped it fervently as a token of deep friendship. And then they parted.

Il cane riprese la strada di casa: e Pinocchio, rimasto solo, andò a una capanna lì poco distante, e domandò a un vecchietto che stava sulla porta a scaldarsi al sole:

– Dite, galantuomo, sapete nulla di un povero ragazzo ferito nel capo e che si chiamava Eugenio?

– Il ragazzo è stato portato da alcuni pescatori in questa capanna, e ora . . .

– Ora sarà morto! . . . – interruppe Pinocchio, con gran dolore.

– No: ora è vivo, ed è già ritornato a casa sua.

– Davvero? . . . davvero? . . . – gridò il burattino, saltando dall'allegrezza – Dunque la ferita non era grave? . . .

– Ma poteva riuscire gravissima e anche mortale, – rispose il vecchietto – perché gli tirarono nel capo un grosso libro rilegato in cartone.

– E chi glielo tirò?

– Un suo compagno di scuola: un certo Pinocchio . . .

– E chi è questo Pinocchio? – domandò il burattino facendo lo gnorri.

– Dicono che sia un ragazzaccio, un vagabondo, un vero rompicollo . . .

– Calunnie! Tutte calunnie!

– Lo conosci tu questo Pinocchio?

– Di vista! – rispose il burattino.

– E tu che concetto ne hai? – gli chiese il vecchietto.

– A me mi pare un gran buon figliuolo, pieno di voglia di studiare, ubbidiente, affezionato al suo babbo e alla sua famiglia . . . –

Mentre il burattino sfilava a faccia fresca tutte queste bugie, si toccò il naso e si accòrse che il naso gli era allungato più d'un palmo. Allora tutto impaurito cominciò a gridare:

– Non date retta, galantuomo, a tutto il bene che ve ne ho detto; perché conosco benissimo Pinocchio e

The dog went homeward; and Pinocchio, left alone, went to a hut nearby and spoke to an old man who was sunning himself in front of the door.

"Tell me, good sir, do you know anything about a poor boy named Eugene who was hurt in the head?"

"The boy was brought to this hut by some fishermen, and now—"

"He's probably dead now! . . ." interjected Pinocchio, with great anguish.

"No, he's alive now and has already returned home."

"Really, really?" cried the puppet, jumping for joy. "Then the wound wasn't serious?"

"But it could have been quite serious, and even fatal," answered the old man, "because somebody threw a big, cardboard-bound book at his head."

"Who threw it at him?"

"A schoolmate of his, a certain Pinocchio."

"And who is this Pinocchio?" the puppet asked, playing dumb.

"They say that he's a young rowdy, a vagabond, a real madcap of a boy."

"Lies, all lies!"

"Do you know this Pinocchio?"

"By sight," answered the puppet.

"And what's your opinion of him?" the old man asked him.

"I think he's a splendid fellow, fond of school, obedient, and very attached to his father and his family . . ."

While he was reeling off all these lies with a straight face, the puppet happened to touch his nose and noticed that it had grown by a palm's length. Then, all in a fright he began to exclaim:

"Don't believe all the nice things I've told you about him, good sir; because I know Pinocchio very well, and

posso assicurarvi anch'io che è davvero un ragazzaccio, un disubbidiente e uno svogliato, che invece di andare a scuola, va coi compagni a fare lo sbarazzino! –

Appena ebbe pronunziate queste parole, il suo naso raccorcì e tornò della grandezza naturale, come era prima.

– E perché sei tutto bianco a codesto modo? – gli domandò a un tratto il vecchietto.

– Vi dirò . . . senza avvedermene, mi sono strofinato a un muro, che era imbiancato di fresco – rispose il burattino, vergognandosi a raccontare che lo avevano infarinato come un pesce, per poi friggerlo in padella.

– O della tua giacchetta, de' tuoi calzoncini e del tuo berretto, che cosa ne hai fatto?

– Ho incontrato i ladri e mi hanno spogliato. Dite, buon vecchio, non avreste per caso da darmi un po' di vestituccio, tanto perché io possa ritornare a casa?

– Ragazzo mio; in quanto a vestiti, io non ho che un piccolo sacchetto, dove ci tengo i lupini. Se lo vuoi, pigliálo: eccolo là. –

E Pinocchio non se lo fece dire due volte: prese subito il sacchetto dei lupini che era vuoto, e dopo averci fatto colle forbici una piccola buca nel fondo e due buche dalle parti, se lo infilò a uso camicia. E vestito leggerino a quel modo, si avviò verso il paese.

Ma, lungo la strada, non si sentiva punto tranquillo; tant'è vero che faceva un passo avanti e uno indietro e, discorrendo da sé solo, andava dicendo:

– Come farò a presentarmi alla mia buona Fatina? Che dirà quando mi vedrà? . . . Vorrà perdonarmi questa seconda birichinata? . . . Scommetto che non me la perdona! . . . oh! non me la perdona di certo . . . E mi sta il dovere: perché io sono un monello che prometto sempre di correggermi, e non mantengo mai! . . . –

Arrivò al paese che era già notte buia; e perché faceva

I too can assure you that he really is a rowdy. He's disobedient and he's a loafer who instead of going to school goes around with his comrades to make trouble."

As soon as he had uttered these words, his nose shortened and returned to its natural length, as it was before.

"Why are you all white like that?" the old man asked him suddenly.

"Well, you see . . . without noticing it, I rubbed against a wall that had just been whitewashed," replied the puppet, ashamed to confess that he had been rolled in flour like a fish meant to be fried in a skillet.

"And what about your jacket, your trousers, and your cap? What have you done with them?"

"I ran into thieves, and they stripped me. Tell me, good old man, would you happen to have some old clothes to give me, just so I can go home?"

"As for clothes, my boy, all I have is a small sack in which I keep lupine seeds. Take it, if you like; it's right there."

And Pinocchio didn't wait to be told a second time. He quickly took the lupine sack, which was empty, made a little hole at the bottom with scissors, and a hole on each side, and slipped it on like a shirt. And scantily dressed like that, he set off for town.

But along the way he didn't feel at all at ease, so that he would take one step forward and then one backward; and talking to himself, he kept repeating:

"How can I face my dear good Fairy? What will she say when she sees me? . . . Will she forgive me for this second escapade? . . . I bet she won't forgive me. Oh, she certainly won't forgive me! And it serves me right, because I'm a brat, always promising to reform and never keeping my word."

When he reached the town it was already late at night;

tempaccio e l'acqua veniva giù a catinelle, andò diritto diritto alla casa della Fata coll'animo risoluto di bussare alla porta e di farsi aprire.

Ma, quando fu lì, sentì mancarsi il coraggio, e invece di bussare, si allontanò, correndo, una ventina di passi. Poi tornò una seconda volta alla porta, e non concluse nulla: poi si avvicinò una terza volta, e nulla: la quarta volta prese, tremando, il battente di ferro in mano e bussò un piccolo colpettino.

Aspetta, aspetta, finalmente dopo mezz'ora si aprì una finestra dell'ultimo piano (la casa era di quattro piani) e Pinocchio vide affacciarsi una grossa lumaca, che aveva un lumicino acceso sul capo, la quale disse:

and because it was horrid weather, with the rain coming down in bucketfuls, he went straight to the Fairy's house determined to knock at the door and make his way in.

But when he got there, he felt his courage fail, and instead of knocking he ran back away from it some twenty steps or so. Then he went up to the door a second time, but nothing came of it. Then he approached a third time, and again nothing. The fourth time, he took the iron knocker tremblingly in his hand and gave a faint little knock.

He waited and waited, until finally after half an hour a window opened on the top floor—the house had four floors—and Pinocchio saw a large Snail with a little lighted lamp on her head look out. She said:

– Chi è a quest'ora?

– La Fata è in casa? – domandò il burattino.

– La Fata dorme e non vuol essere svegliata: ma tu chi sei?

– Sono io!

– Chi io?

– Pinocchio.

– Chi Pinocchio?

– Il burattino, quello che sta in casa colla Fata.

– Ah! ho capito; – disse la Lumaca – aspettami costì, ché ora scendo giù e ti apro subito.

– Spicciatevi, per carità, perché io muoio dal freddo.

– Ragazzo mio, io sono una lumaca, e le lumache non hanno mai fretta. –

Intanto passò un'ora, ne passarono due, e la porta non si apriva: per cui Pinocchio, che tremava dal freddo, dalla paura e dall'acqua che aveva addosso, si fece cuore e bussò una seconda volta, e bussò più forte.

A quel secondo colpo si aprì una finestra del piano di sotto e si affacciò la solita lumaca.

– Lumachina bella – gridò Pinocchio dalla strada – sono due ore che aspetto! E due ore, a questa serataccia, diventano più lunghe di due anni. Spicciatevi, per carità.

– Ragazzo mio, – gli rispose dalla finestra quella bestiòla tutta pace e tutta flemma – ragazzo mio, io sono una lumaca, e le lumache non hanno mai fretta. –

E la finestra si richiuse.

Di lì a poco sonò la mezzanotte: poi il tocco, poi le due dopo mezzanotte, e la porta era sempre chiusa.

Allora Pinocchio, perduta la pazienza, afferrò con rabbia il battente della porta per bussare un colpo da far rintronare tutto il casamento: ma il battente che era di ferro, diventò a un tratto un'anguilla viva, che sguscian-

"Who is it at this hour?"

"Is the Fairy at home?" the puppet asked.

"The Fairy is sleeping and does not want to be awakened. Who are you, anyway?"

"It's me."

" 'Me' who?"

"Pinocchio."

"Pinocchio who?"

"The puppet; the one who lives with the Fairy."

"Ah, I see," said the Snail. "Wait for me there; I'll come down and open the door for you right away."

"Hurry, for pity's sake, because I'm freezing to death."

"My boy, I am a snail, and snails are never in a hurry."

Meanwhile an hour passed; and then two hours passed, but the door didn't open. So Pinocchio, who was shivering on account of the cold, the fear, and the drenching he was getting, plucked up his courage and knocked a second time; and he knocked harder.

At this second knock a window opened on the next floor down, and the same Snail looked out.

"Dear little Snail," called Pinocchio from the street, "I've been waiting for two hours! And two hours in such a wretched night as this seem longer than two years. Hurry, for pity's sake."

"My boy," answered that little creature from the window, quite calm and unperturbed, "my boy, I am a snail, and snails are never in a hurry."

And the window closed again.

A short while later midnight struck; then one o'clock, then two o'clock; but the door was still shut.

So Pinocchio, losing all patience, grasped the door knocker angrily, intending to give a bang that would deafen everyone in the building; but the knocker, which was made of iron, suddenly became a live eel that wrig-

dogli dalle mani sparì in un rigagnolo d'acqua che scorreva in mezzo alla strada.

– Ah! sì? – gridò Pinocchio sempre più accecato dalla collera. – Se il battente è sparito, io seguiterò a bussare a furia di calci. –

E tiratosi un poco indietro, lasciò andare una solennissima pedata nell'uscio della casa. Il colpo fu così forte, che il piede penetrò nel legno fino a mezzo: e quando il burattino si provò a ricavarlo fuori, fu tutta fatica inutile: perché il piede c'era rimasto conficcato dentro, come un chiodo ribadito.

Figuratevi il povero Pinocchio! Dové passare tutto il resto della notte con un piede in terra e con quell'altro per aria.

La mattina, sul far del giorno, finalmente la porta si

gled out of his hands and disappeared into the small stream of water going down the middle of the street.

"Oh, is that so?" shouted Pinocchio, blinder than ever with rage. "If the knocker has disappeared, I'll just go on knocking by kicking."

And backing up a little, he let go a whopping kick at the door, so hard that his foot went halfway through; and when the puppet tried to pull it back out, it proved to be a hopeless effort because his foot was stuck tight there like a riveted nail.

Imagine poor Pinocchio! He had to spend the rest of the night with one foot on the ground, and the other up in the air.

In the morning, at dawn, the door finally opened. To

aprì. Quella brava bestiòla della Lumaca, a scendere dal quarto piano fino all'uscio di strada, ci aveva messo solamente nove ore. Bisogna proprio dire che avesse fatto una sudata.

– Che cosa fate con codesto piede conficcato nell'uscio? – domandò ridendo al burattino.

– È stata una disgrazia. Vedete un po', Lumachina bella, se vi riesce di liberarmi da questo supplizio.

– Ragazzo mio, costì ci vuole un legnaiolo, e io non ho fatto mai la legnaiola.

– Pregate la Fata da parte mia! . . .

– La Fata dorme e non vuol essere svegliata.

– Ma che cosa volete che io faccia inchiodato tutto il giorno a questa porta?

– Divertiti a contare le formicole che passano per la strada.

– Portatemi almeno qualche cosa da mangiare, perché mi sento rifinito.

– Subito! – disse la Lumaca.

Difatti dopo tre ore e mezzo, Pinocchio la vide tornare con un vassoio d'argento in capo. Nel vassoio c'era un pane, un pollastro arrosto e quattro albicocche mature.

– Ecco la colazione che vi manda la Fata – disse la Lumaca.

Alla vista di quella grazia di Dio, il burattino sentì consolarsi tutto. Ma quale fu il suo disinganno, quando incominciando a mangiare, si dové accorgere che il pane era di gesso, il pollastro di cartone e le quattro albicocche di alabastro, colorite, come se fossero vere.

Voleva piangere, voleva darsi alla disperazione, voleva buttar via il vassoio e quel che c'era dentro; ma invece, o fosse il gran dolore o la gran languidezza di stomaco, fatto sta che cadde svenuto.

Quando si riebbe, si trovò disteso sopra un sofà, e la Fata era accanto a lui.

come down from the fourth floor to the front door, that clever little creature, the Snail, had taken but nine hours. You really have to say that she had worked up quite a sweat.

"What are you doing with that foot of yours stuck in the door?" she asked, laughing at the puppet.

"It was an accident. Dear little Snail, try to see if you can free me from this torture."

"My boy, it takes a carpenter for that job, and I have never been a carpenter."

"Beg the Fairy for me!"

"The Fairy is sleeping and does not want to be awakened."

"But what do you expect me to do, nailed all day to this door?"

"Amuse yourself by counting the ants that go by."

"At least bring me something to eat, because I feel faint."

"Right away!" said the Snail.

In fact, after three and a half hours, Pinocchio saw her returning with a silver tray on her head. On the tray there was bread, a roast chicken, and four ripe apricots.

"Here is the breakfast sent to you by the Fairy," said the Snail.

At the sight of all those good things, the puppet's spirits were raised. But how great was his disappointment when, on beginning to eat, he was forced to acknowledge that the bread was of chalk, the chicken of cardboard, and the four apricots of alabaster, painted to look real.

He wanted to cry, to give up in despair, to throw away the tray and everything on it; but instead, either because of his grief or because of the empty feeling in his stomach, the fact is that he fainted.

When he came to, he found himself stretched out on a sofa, with the Fairy by his side.

– Anche per questa volta ti perdono – gli disse la Fata – ma guai a te, se me ne fai un'altra delle tue! . . . –

Pinocchio promise e giurò che avrebbe studiato, e che si sarebbe condotto sempre bene. E mantenne la parola per tutto il resto dell'anno. Difatti agli esami delle vacanze, ebbe l'onore di essere il più bravo della scuola; e i suoi portamenti, in generale, furono giudicati così lodevoli e soddisfacenti, che la Fata, tutta contenta, gli disse:

– Domani finalmente il tuo desiderio sarà appagato!

– Cioè?

– Domani finirai di essere un burattino di legno, e diventerai un ragazzo perbene. –

Chi non ha veduto la gioia di Pinocchio, a questa notizia tanto sospirata, non potrà mai figurarsela. Tutti i suoi amici e compagni di scuola dovevano essere invitati per il giorno dopo a una gran colazione in casa della Fata, per festeggiare insieme il grande avvenimento: e la Fata aveva fatto preparare dugento tazze di caffè-e-latte e quattrocento panini imburrati di dentro e di fuori. Quella giornata prometteva di riuscire molto bella e molto allegra: ma . . .

Disgraziatamente, nella vita dei burattini, c'è sempre un *ma*, che sciupa ogni cosa.

"I will forgive you this time too," the Fairy said to him, "but it will be too bad for you if you play me another of your pranks."

Pinocchio promised and swore that he would study and that he would always behave himself. And he kept his word throughout the rest of the school year. Indeed, at the exams before vacation time he had the honor of being the best student in school; and his general conduct was considered so satisfactory and so praiseworthy that the Fairy said to him:

"Tomorrow at last your wish will be granted."

"That is?"

"Tomorrow you are to stop being a wooden puppet, and you will become a proper boy."

Anyone who didn't see Pinocchio's joy at this longed-for news can never imagine what it was like. All his friends and schoolmates were to be invited the next day to a grand breakfast in the Fairy's house to celebrate together the great event; and the Fairy made preparations for two hundred cups of *caffè-e-latte* and four hundred buns buttered on the inside and on the outside.[56] It promised to be a great and joyous day, but . . .

Unfortunately, in the lives of puppets, there is always a "but" that spoils everything.

CAPITOLO XXX

*Pinocchio, invece di diventare un ragazzo,
parte di nascosto col suo amico Lucignolo
per il «Paese dei balocchi».*

Com'è naturale, Pinocchio chiese subito alla Fata il permesso di andare in giro per la città a fare gl'inviti: e la Fata gli disse:

– Va' pure a invitare i tuoi compagni per la colazione di domani: ma ricordati di tornare a casa prima che faccia notte. Hai capito?

– Fra un'ora prometto di esser bell'e ritornato – replicò il burattino.

– Bada, Pinocchio! I ragazzi fanno presto a promettere, ma il più delle volte, fanno tardi a mantenere.

– Ma io non sono come gli altri: io, quando dico una cosa, la mantengo.

– Vedremo. Caso poi tu disubbidissi, tanto peggio per te.

– Perché?

– Perché i ragazzi che non dànno retta ai consigli di chi ne sa più di loro, vanno sempre incontro a qualche disgrazia.

– E io l'ho provato! – disse Pinocchio. – Ma ora non ci ricasco più!

– Vedremo se dici il vero. –

Senza aggiungere altre parole, il burattino salutò la sua buona Fata, che era per lui una specie di mamma, e cantando e ballando uscì fuori dalla porta di casa.

In poco più d'un'ora, tutti i suoi amici furono invitati. Alcuni accettarono subito e di gran cuore: altri, da principio, si fecero un po' pregare: ma quando seppero che i panini da inzuppare nel caffè-e-latte sarebbero stati

CHAPTER XXX

Instead of becoming a boy,
Pinocchio goes off secretly
with his friend Lampwick to Funland.

As is only natural, Pinocchio immediately asked the Fairy for permission to go around the town to extend the invitations, and the Fairy said:

"Go right ahead and invite your comrades to tomorrow's breakfast, but remember to return home before it gets dark. Do you understand?"

"I promise to be back in an hour," replied the puppet.

"Take care, Pinocchio! Children are quick to make promises, but most of the time they are slow in keeping them."

"But I'm not like the others; when I say something, I mean it."

"We shall see. If you should disobey, though, it will be much the worse for you."

"Why?"

"Because children who don't heed the advice of those who know better than they do always end up in some kind of trouble."

"And I know that from experience!" exclaimed Pinocchio. "But I won't fall into the same trap again."

"We shall see if you are telling the truth."

Without adding another word, the puppet said good-bye to his good Fairy, who was like a mother to him, and went out the front door, singing and dancing.

In just about an hour all his friends had been invited. Some of them accepted at once and eagerly; others waited to be coaxed at first, but when they learned that the buns to be dunked in the *caffè-e-latte* would even be

imburrati anche dalla parte di fuori, finirono tutti col dire: – «Verremo anche noi, per farti piacere.»

Ora bisogna sapere che Pinocchio, fra i suoi amici e compagni di scuola, ne aveva uno prediletto e carissimo, il quale si chiamava di nome Romeo: ma tutti lo chiamavano col soprannome di *Lucignolo*, per via del suo personalino asciutto, secco e allampanato, tale e quale come il lucignolo nuovo di un lumino da notte.

Lucignolo era il ragazzo più svogliato e più birichino di tutta la scuola: ma Pinocchio gli voleva un gran bene. Difatti andò subito a cercarlo a casa, per invitarlo alla colazione, e non lo trovò: tornò una seconda volta, e Lucignolo non c'era: tornò una terza volta, e fece la strada invano.

Dove poterlo ripescare? Cerca di qua, cerca di là, finalmente lo vide nascosto sotto il portico di una casa di contadini.

– Che cosa fai costì? – gli domandò Pinocchio, avvicinandosi.

– Aspetto [di] partire . . .

– Dove vai?

– Lontano, lontano, lontano!

– E io che son venuto a cercarti a casa tre volte! . . .

– Che cosa volevi da me?

– Non sai il grande avvenimento? Non sai la fortuna che mi è toccata?

– Quale?

– Domani finisco di essere un burattino e divento un ragazzo come te, e come tutti gli altri.

– Buon pro ti faccia.

– Domani, dunque, ti aspetto a colazione a casa mia.

– Ma se ti dico che parto questa sera.

– A che ora?

buttered on the outside, they all ended by saying: "We'll come too, as a favor to you."

Now you should know that among his schoolmates, Pinocchio had one who was his favorite, who was very dear to him, and whose name was Romeo; but everybody called him by his nickname Lampwick because of his scrawny little frame, just like the new wick of a night-lamp.[57]

Lampwick was the laziest and the most roguish boy in the whole school, but Pinocchio was extremely fond of him. In fact, he went right away to look for him at his house so as to invite him to the breakfast, but he didn't find him. He went back a second time, but Lampwick wasn't there. He went back a third time, but to no avail.

Where could he dig him up? He looked high and low for him, and finally saw him hiding under the portico of a peasant's house.

"What are you doing there?" asked Pinocchio, going up to him.

"I'm waiting [for midnight], so I can run away."[58]

"Where are you going?"

"Far, far, far away!"

"And I went to your house three times to look for you!"

"What did you want me for?"

"Don't you know about the great event? Don't you know about my good luck?"

"What is it?"

"Tomorrow I stop being a puppet and I become a boy like you and all the others."

"A lot of good may it do you."

"So I expect you for breakfast tomorrow, at my house."

"But I've just told you that I'm leaving tonight."

"At what time?"

– Fra poco.

– E dove vai?

– Vado ad abitare in un paese . . . che è il più bel paese di questo mondo: una vera cuccagna! . . .

– E come si chiama?

– Si chiama il «Paese dei balocchi». Perché non vieni anche tu?

– Io? no davvero!

– Hai torto, Pinocchio! Credilo a me che, se non vieni, te ne pentirai. Dove vuoi trovare un paese più sano per noialtri ragazzi? Lì non vi sono scuole: lì non vi sono maestri: lì non vi sono libri. In quel paese benedetto non si studia mai. Il giovedì non si fa scuola: e ogni settimana è composta di sei giovedì e di una domenica.

Figurati che le vacanze dell'autunno cominciano col primo di gennaio e finiscono coll'ultimo di dicembre. Ecco un paese, come piace veramente a me! Ecco come dovrebbero essere tutti i paesi civili! . . .

– Ma come si passano le giornate nel «Paese dei balocchi»?

– Si passano baloccandosi e divertendosi dalla mattina alla sera. La sera poi si va a letto, e la mattina dopo si ricomincia daccapo. Che te ne pare?

"In a little while."

"But where are you going?"

"I'm going to live in a land that's the most beautiful land in the world: really easy living and merriment."

"What is it called?"

"It's called Funland. Why don't you come too?"

"Me? Certainly not!"

"You're making a mistake, Pinocchio! Believe me, if you don't come you'll regret it. Where do you expect to find a more wholesome place for us kids? There are no schools there; there are no teachers there; there are no books there. They never study in that blessed land. There's no school on Thursday, and every week is made

up of six Thursdays and a Sunday.[59] Just think that vacation begins on the first of January and ends on the last day of December. Now that's the sort of place that appeals to me! That's how all civilized countries should be!"

"But how do they pass the days there in Funland?"

"The days go by in play and good times from morning till night. Then at night you go to bed, and the next morning you begin all over again. What do you think of that?"

– Uhm! . . . – fece Pinocchio; e tentennò leggermente il capo, come dire: – «È una vita che la farei volentieri anch'io!»

– Dunque, vuoi partire con me? Sì o no? Risolviti.

– No, no, no e poi no. Oramai ho promesso alla mia
buona Fata di diventare un ragazzo per bene, e voglio
mantenere la promessa. Anzi, siccome vedo che il sole
va sotto, così ti lascio subito e scappo via. Dunque addio, e buon viaggio.

– Dove corri con tanta furia?

– A casa. La mia buona Fata vuole che ritorni prima
di notte.

– Aspetta altri due minuti.

– Faccio troppo tardi.

– Due minuti soli.

– E se poi la Fata mi grida?

– Lasciala gridare. Quando avrà gridato ben bene, si
cheterà – disse quella birba di Lucignolo.

– E come fai? Parti solo o in compagnia?

– Solo? Saremo più di cento ragazzi.

– E il viaggio lo fate a piedi?

– Fra poco passerà di qui il carro che mi deve prendere e condurre fin dentro ai confini di quel fortunatissimo paese.

– Che cosa pagherei che il carro passasse ora! . . .

– Perché?

– Per vedervi partire tutti insieme.

– Rimani qui un altro poco e ci vedrai.

– No, no: voglio ritornare a casa.

– Aspetta altri due minuti.

– Ho indugiato anche troppo. La Fata starà in pensiero per me.

– Povera Fata! Che ha paura forse che ti mangino i
pipistrelli?

– Ma dunque – soggiunse Pinocchio – tu sei vera-

"Hmm!" went Pinocchio, and he nodded his head slightly, as though to say: "It's a life that I too would gladly lead!"

"So then, do you want to leave with me? Yes or no? Make up your mind."

"No, no, a thousand times no. I've promised my good Fairy to become a good boy now, and I intend to keep my word. In fact, now that I see the sun is going down, I have to leave you and run. Good-bye, then; and bon voyage."

"Where are you rushing off to?"

"Home. My good Fairy wants me to be back before dark."

"Wait another two minutes."

"Then I'll be too late."

"Just two minutes."

"And what if the Fairy yells at me?"

"Let her yell. When she's tired of yelling, she'll calm down," said that scapegrace of a Lampwick.

"But how will you manage? Are you going alone or with others?"

"Alone? There'll be more than a hundred of us kids."

"And are you making the trip by foot?"

"In a little while the wagon's coming by to pick me up and take me all the way, within the boundaries of that happy land."

"I'd give anything to have the wagon pass by now!"

"Why?"

"To see all of you going off together."

"Wait here a little longer and you will see us."

"No, no; I want to go back home."

"Wait another two minutes."

"I've already waited too long. The Fairy must be worrying about me."

"Poor Fairy! Is she afraid that the bats will eat you?"

"But then," continued Pinocchio, "you're really

351

mente sicuro che in quel paese non ci sono punte scuole? . . .

– Neanche l'ombra.

– E nemmeno i maestri?

– Nemmen uno.

– E non c'è mai l'obbligo di studiare?

– Mai, mai, mai!

– Che bel paese! – disse Pinocchio, sentendo venirsi l'acquolina in bocca. – Che bel paese! Io non ci sono stato mai, ma me lo figuro! . . .

– Perché non vieni anche tu?

– È inutile che tu mi tenti! Oramai ho promesso alla mia buona Fata di diventare un ragazzo di giudizio, e non voglio mancare alla parola.

– Dunque addio, e salutami tanto le scuole ginnasiali! . . . e anche quelle liceali, se le incontri per la strada.

– Addio, Lucignolo: fa' buon viaggio, divertiti e rammentati qualche volta degli amici. –

Ciò detto, il burattino fece due passi in atto di andarsene: ma poi, fermandosi e voltandosi all'amico, gli domandò:

– Ma sei proprio sicuro che in quel paese tutte le settimane sieno composte di sei giovedì e di una domenica?

– Sicurissimo.

– Ma lo sai di certo che le vacanze abbiano principio col primo di gennaio e finiscano coll'ultimo di dicembre?

– Di certissimo!

– Che bel paese! – ripeté Pinocchio, sputando dalla soverchia consolazione. Poi, fatto un animo risoluto, soggiunse in fretta e furia:

– Dunque, addio davvero: e buon viaggio.

– Addio.

– Fra quanto partirete?

– Fra poco!

sure that there are absolutely no schools in that land?"

"Not even the ghost of one."

"And not even schoolteachers?"

"Not a single one."

"And nobody ever has to study?"

"Never, never, never!"

"What a wonderful land!" said Pinocchio, his mouth watering. "What a wonderful land! I've never been there, but I can just imagine it."

"Why don't you come too?"

"It's no use for you to tempt me! I've promised my good Fairy to be a sensible boy now, and I don't want to go back on my word."

"Well, farewell then, and give my best regards to the grammar schools . . . and the high schools too, if you meet them on the way."

"Farewell, Lampwick; have a good journey, have fun and remember your friends sometimes."

Having said this, the puppet took a few steps as if to leave; but then, stopping and turning to his friend, he asked him:

"But are you really sure that in that land all the weeks are made up of six Thursdays and a Sunday?"

"Quite sure!"

"But are you positive that vacation time begins on the first of January and ends on the last day of December?"

"Quite positive!"

"What a wonderful land!" repeated Pinocchio, spitting out of sheer delight. Then, taking a resolute stance, he quickly added:

"Well, goodbye for real, and bon voyage."

"Good-bye."

"How soon will you be leaving?"

"In a little while!"

– Sarei quasi quasi capace di aspettare.

– E la Fata? . . .

– Oramai ho fatto tardi! . . . e tornare a casa un'ora prima o un'ora dopo, è lo stesso.

– Povero Pinocchio! E se la Fata ti grida?

– Pazienza! La lascerò gridare. Quando avrà gridato ben bene, si cheterà. –

Intanto si era già fatta notte e notte buia: quando a un tratto videro muoversi in lontananza un lumicino . . . e sentirono un suono di bubboli e uno squillo di trombetta, così piccolino e soffocato, che pareva il sibilo di una zanzara!

– Eccolo! – gridò Lucignolo, rizzandosi in piedi.

– Chi è? – domandò sottovoce Pinocchio.

– È il carro che viene a prendermi. Dunque, vuoi venire, sì o no?

– Ma è proprio vero – domandò il burattino – che in quel paese i ragazzi non hanno mai l'obbligo di studiare?

– Mai, mai, mai!

– Che bel paese! . . . che bel paese! . . . che bel paese! . . . –

["That's too bad! If it were only an hour before you leave,] I might almost wait."[60]

"And the Fairy? . . ."

"I'm already late anyway, and to go home an hour sooner or an hour later doesn't matter."

"Poor Pinocchio! And what if the Fairy yells at you?"

"So what! I'll let her yell. When she's tired of yelling, she'll calm down."

Meanwhile night had fallen and it was quite dark, when all of a sudden they saw a dim light moving in the distance; and they heard a sound of harness bells and the blare of a trumpet, but so faint and muffled that it seemed like the buzzing of a mosquito.

"There it is!" shouted Lampwick, getting to his feet.

"Who is it?" asked Pinocchio in a low voice.

"It's the wagon that's coming to pick me up. Well, are you coming, yes or no?"

"But is it really true," the puppet asked, "that in that land kids never have to study?"

"Never, never, never!"

"What a wonderful land, what a wonderful land, what a wonderful land!"

CAPITOLO XXXI

Dopo cinque mesi di cuccagna,
Pinocchio con sua gran maraviglia,
sente spuntarsi un bel pajo d'orecchie asinine,
e diventa un ciuchino, con la coda e tutto.

Finalmente il carro arrivò: e arrivò senza fare il più piccolo rumore, perché le sue ruote erano fasciate di stoppa e di cenci.

Lo tiravano dodici pariglie di ciuchini, tutti della medesima grandezza, ma di diverso pelame.

Alcuni erano bigi, altri bianchi, altri brizzolati a uso pepe e sale, e altri rigati da grandi strisce gialle e turchine.

Ma la cosa più singolare era questa: che quelle dodici pariglie, ossia quei ventiquattro ciuchini, invece di esser ferrati come tutte le altre bestie da tiro o da soma, avevano in piedi degli stivaletti da uomo fatti di pelle bianca.

E il conduttore del carro? . . .

CHAPTER XXXI

After five months of fun and easy living,
Pinocchio, to his great surprise,
feels a fine pair of donkey ears sprout from his head,
and he becomes a donkey, tail and all.

At last the wagon arrived; and it arrived without making the slightest noise, because its wheels were swathed
in rags and tow.

It was drawn by twelve pairs of donkeys, all of the
same size, but with different colored coats.

Some were ashen gray, some white, others were
speckled in the manner of pepper-and-salt, and others
had wide stripes of yellow and blue.

But the most curious thing of all was this: those
twelve pairs, that is, those twenty-four donkeys, instead of being shod like all other draft animals or beasts
of burden, had men's high-shoes of white leather on
their feet.[61]

And the driver of the wagon?

Figuratevi un omino più largo che lungo, tenero e untuoso come una palla di burro, con un visino di melarosa, una bocchina che rideva sempre e una voce sottile e carezzevole, come quella d'un gatto, che si raccomanda al buon cuore della padrona di casa.

Tutti i ragazzi, appena lo vedevano, ne restavano innamorati e facevano a gara nel montare sul suo carro, per esser condotti da lui in quella vera cuccagna conosciuta nella carta geografica col seducente nome di «Paese de' balocchi».

Difatti il carro era già tutto pieno di ragazzetti fra gli otto e i dodici anni, ammonticchiati gli uni sugli altri come tante acciughe nella salamoia. Stavano male, stavano pigiati, non potevano quasi respirare: ma nessuno diceva *ohi!* nessuno si lamentava. La consolazione di sapere che fra poche ore sarebbero giunti in un paese, dove non c'erano né libri, né scuole, né maestri, li rendeva così contenti e rassegnati, che non sentivano né i disagi, né gli strapazzi, né la fame, né la sete, né il sonno.

Appena che il carro si fu fermato, l'Omino si volse a Lucignolo, e con mille smorfie e mille manierine, gli domandò sorridendo:

– Dimmi, mio bel ragazzo, vuoi venire anche tu in quel fortunato paese?

– Sicuro che ci voglio venire.

– Ma ti avverto, carino mio, che nel carro non c'è più posto. Come vedi, è tutto pieno! . . .

– Pazienza! – replicò Lucignolo – se non c'è posto dentro, mi adatterò a star seduto sulle stanghe del carro. –

E spiccato un salto, montò a cavalcioni sulle stanghe.

– E tu, amor mio – disse l'Omino volgendosi tutto complimentoso a Pinocchio – che intendi fare? Vieni con noi, o rimani? . . .

– Io rimango – rispose Pinocchio. – Io voglio tornar-

Picture a little man more wide than tall, soft and oily like a lump of butter, with a small face like a rosy apple, a little mouth that was always smiling, and a thin wheedling voice like that of a cat appealing to the tender heart of the mistress of the house.

All boys were charmed by him as soon as they saw him and fought with one another in getting up into his wagon so as to be taken by him to that true land of heart's desire known on the geographical map by the seductive name of Funland.

In fact the wagon was already full of young boys between eight and twelve years old, piled one on top of the other like anchovies in brine. They were uncomfortable, they were squeezed together, and they could hardly breathe; but nobody said ow! nobody complained. The consolation of knowing that in a few hours they would reach a land where there were no books, no schools, no teachers made them so pleased and so patient that they didn't feel any discomfort, or hardship, or hunger, or thirst, or sleepiness.

As soon as the wagon had stopped, the little man turned to Lampwick, and with a thousand mincing ways and words he asked him, smiling:

"Tell me, my handsome lad, do you want to come to that happy land too?"

"You bet I want to come."

"But I warn you, my dear, there's no more room in the wagon. As you see, it's quite full."

"That's all right!" replied Lampwick, "if there's no room inside, I'll put up with sitting on the shafts of the wagon."

And with a jump he mounted astride the shafts.

"And you, my love," said the little man, turning ceremoniously to Pinocchio, "what do you intend to do? Are you coming with us or staying?"

"I'm staying," answered Pinocchio. "I want to go

359

mene a casa mia: voglio studiare e voglio farmi onore alla scuola, come fanno tutti i ragazzi perbene.

– Buon pro ti faccia!

– Pinocchio! – disse allora Lucignolo. – Da' retta a me: vieni con noi, e staremo allegri.

– No, no, no!

– Vieni con noi e staremo allegri – gridarono altre quattro voci di dentro al carro.

– Vieni con noi e staremo allegri – urlarono tutte insieme un centinaio di voci.

– E se vengo con voi, che cosa dirà la mia buona Fata? – disse il burattino che cominciava a intenerirsi e a ciurlar nel manico.

– Non ti fasciare il capo con tante malinconie. Pensa che andiamo in un paese dove saremo padroni di fare il chiasso dalla mattina alla sera! –

Pinocchio non rispose, ma fece un sospiro: poi fece un altro sospiro: poi un terzo sospiro: finalmente disse:

– Fatemi un po' di posto: voglio venire anch'io! . . .

– I posti son tutti pieni – replicò l'Omino – ma per mostrarti quanto sei gradito, posso cederti il mio posto a cassetta . . .

– E voi? . . .

– E io farò la strada a piedi.

– No davvero, che non lo permetto. Preferisco piuttosto di salire in groppa a qualcuno di questi ciuchini! – gridò Pinocchio.

Detto fatto, si avvicinò al ciuchino manritto della prima pariglia, e fece l'atto di volerlo cavalcare: ma la bestiòla, voltandosi a secco, gli dètte una gran musata nello stomaco e lo gettò a gambe all'aria.

Figuratevi la risatona impertinente e sgangherata di tutti quei ragazzi presenti alla scena.

Ma l'Omino non rise. Si accostò pieno di amorevo-

back home. I want to study and do well at school, the way all good boys do."

"A lot of good may it do you!"

"Pinocchio!" said Lampwick then. "Listen to me; come away with us, and we'll have a wonderful time."

"No, no, no!"

"Come away with us, and we'll have a wonderful time," shouted four other voices from within the wagon.

"Come away with us, and we'll have a wonderful time," yelled a hundred or so voices all together from within the wagon.

"But if I come with you, what will my good Fairy say?" said the puppet, who was beginning to soften and waver.

"Don't wrap your head in such gloomy thoughts. Just think that we're going to a place where we'll be free to make a hullabaloo from morning to night."

Pinocchio didn't answer, but he heaved a sigh. Then he heaved another sigh; and then a third sigh. Finally, he said:

"Make some room for me. I want to come too."

"The places are all taken," replied the little man, "but to show you how welcome you are, I can give you my place on the box."

"And you?"

"And I'll go along on foot."

"No, really; I won't let you do that. I'd rather get up on the back of one of these donkeys," cried Pinocchio.

So saying, he went up to the right-hand donkey of the first pair[62] and made as if to mount him. But the creature, swerving around unexpectedly, butted him hard in the stomach and sent him sprawling with his legs in the air.

Just imagine the hoots and howls of laughter of all those boys who were looking on.

But the little man didn't laugh. He went up ever so

lezza al ciuchino ribelle, e, facendo finta di dargli un bacio, gli staccò con un morso la metà dell'orecchio de-
stro.

Intanto Pinocchio, rizzatosi da terra tutto infuriato,
schizzò con un salto sulla groppa di quel povero animale. E il salto fu così bello, che i ragazzi, smesso di
ridere, cominciarono a urlare: *viva Pinocchio!* e a fare una
smanacciata di applausi, che non finivano più.

Quand'ecco che all'improvviso il ciuchino alzò tutte
e due le gambe di dietro, e dando una fortissima sgrop-
ponata, scaraventò il povero burattino in mezzo alla
strada, sopra un monte di ghiaia.

Allora grandi risate daccapo: ma l'Omino, invece di
ridere, si sentì preso da tanto amore per quell'irrequieto
asinello che, con un bacio, gli portò via di netto la metà
di quell'altro orecchio. Poi disse al burattino:

– Rimonta pure a cavallo, e non aver paura. Quel ciuchino aveva qualche grillo per il capo: ma io gli ho detto
due paroline negli orecchi, e spero di averlo reso man-
sueto e ragionevole. –

lovingly to the rebellious donkey, and while making as though to give him a kiss bit off half of his right ear.

Meanwhile, Pinocchio got up from the ground in a rage and with one leap sprang onto the poor animal's back. And it was such a magnificent leap that the boys stopped their laughter and began to shout: "Hurrah for Pinocchio!" clapping wildly as if they would never stop.

But all of a sudden the donkey kicked up both his hind legs, bucking so violently that he threw the poor puppet onto a heap of gravel in the middle of the road.

At that, there were renewed howls of laughter. But the little man, instead of laughing, was overcome by so much tenderness for that cute, fretful donkey, that with a kiss he took half of his other ear clean off. Then he said to the puppet:

"Get back up on him, and don't be afraid. That donkey had some whim[63] or other in his head; but I've whispered a few sweet words in his ear, and I think I've got him to be gentle and sensible."

Pinocchio montò: e il carro cominciò a muoversi: ma nel tempo che i ciuchini galoppavano e che il carro correva sui ciottoli della via maestra, gli parve al burattino di sentire una voce sommessa e appena intelligibile, che gli disse:

– Povero gonzo! Hai voluto fare a modo tuo, ma te ne pentirai! –

Pinocchio, quasi impaurito, guardò di qua e di là, per conoscere da qual parte venissero queste parole; ma non vide nessuno: i ciuchini galoppavano, il carro correva, i ragazzi dentro al carro dormivano, Lucignolo russava come un ghiro e l'Omino seduto a cassetta, canterellava fra i denti:

> Tutti la notte dormono
> E io non dormo mai . . .

Fatto un altro mezzo chilometro, Pinocchio sentì la solita vocina fioca che gli disse:

– Tienlo a mente, grullerello! I ragazzi che smettono di studiare e voltano le spalle ai libri, alle scuole e ai maestri, per darsi interamente ai balocchi e ai divertimenti, non possono far altro che una fine disgraziata! . . . Io lo so per prova! . . . e te lo posso dire! Verrà un giorno che piangerai anche tu, come oggi piango io . . . ma allora sarà tardi! . . . –

A queste parole bisbigliate sommessamente, il burattino, spaventato più che mai, saltò giù dalla groppa della cavalcatura, e andò a prendere il suo ciuchino per il muso.

E immaginatevi come restò, quando s'accòrse che il suo ciuchino piangeva . . . e piangeva proprio come un ragazzo!

– Ehi, signor Omino, – gridò allora Pinocchio al padrone del carro – sapete che cosa c'è di nuovo? Questo ciuchino piange.

– Lascialo piangere: riderà quando sarà sposo.

Pinocchio got on, and the wagon started off. But while the donkeys were galloping along and the wagon was rolling over the cobblestones of the highway, the puppet thought he heard a low, barely audible voice that said to him:

"Poor simpleton; you wanted your own way, but you'll regret it."

Somewhat frightened, Pinocchio looked all around to find out where the words came from, but he didn't see anyone: the donkeys were galloping, the wagon was rolling along, the boys inside the wagon were sleeping, Lampwick was snoring like a dormouse, and the little man, sitting on the driver's box, was singing to himself in a low voice between his teeth:

> Everybody sleeps at night,
> But never asleep am I . . .

After another half mile, Pinocchio heard the same faint voice say to him:

"Remember this, you silly fool! Boys who give up studying and turn their backs on books, schools, and teachers to do nothing but play games and have fun are bound to come to a bad end. I know from experience, and so I can tell you. A day will come when you'll cry too, just as I'm crying now; but it will be too late then."

At these words, which were whispered in a low tone, the puppet, more frightened than ever, jumped down from his mount and went to take hold of the donkey by the muzzle.

But imagine his surprise when he found that the donkey was crying—and crying just like a boy!

"Hey, Mister little man," shouted Pinocchio to the wagon owner, "do you know what? This donkey is crying."

"Let him cry; he'll laugh on his wedding day."[64]

365

– Ma che forse gli avete insegnato anche a parlare?

– No: ha imparato da sé a borbottare qualche parola, essendo stato tre anni in una compagnia di cani ammaestrati.

– Povera bestia! . . .

– Via, via – disse l'Omino – non perdiamo il nostro tempo a veder piangere un ciuco. Rimonta a cavallo, e andiamo: la nottata è fresca e la strada è lunga. –

Pinocchio obbedì senza rifiatare. Il carro riprese la sua corsa: e la mattina, sul far dell'alba, arrivarono felicemente nel «Paese dei balocchi».

Questo paese non somigliava a nessun altro paese del mondo. La sua popolazione era tutta composta di ragazzi. I più vecchi avevano 14 anni: i più giovani ne avevano 8 appena. Nelle strade, un'allegria, un chiasso, uno strillìo da levar di cervello! Branchi di monelli da per tutto: chi giocava alle noci, chi alle piastrelle, chi alla palla, chi andava in velocipede, chi sopra un cavallino di legno: questi facevano a mosca-cieca, quegli altri si rincorrevano: altri, vestiti da pagliacci, mangiavano la stoppa accesa: chi recitava, chi cantava, chi faceva i salti mortali, chi si divertiva a camminare colle mani in terra e colle gambe in aria: chi mandava il cerchio, chi passeggiava vestito da generale coll'elmo di foglio e lo squadrone di cartapesta: chi rideva, chi urlava, chi chiamava, chi batteva le mani, chi fischiava, chi rifaceva il verso alla gallina quando ha fatto l'ovo: insomma un tal pandemonio, un tal passeraio, un tal baccano indiavolato, da doversi mettere il cotone negli orecchi per non rimanere assorditi. Su tutte le piazze si vedevano teatrini di tela, affollati di ragazzi dalla mattina alla sera, e su tutti i muri delle case si leggevano scritte col carbone delle bellissime cose come queste: *viva i balocci!* (invece di *ba-*

"Did you by any chance teach him how to talk?"

"No; he learned how to mumble a few words on his own during the three years he lived with a company of performing dogs."

"Poor beast!"

"Come, come," said the little man, "let's not waste time watching a donkey cry. Get back on, and let's get going. It's a cold night, and it's a long way."

Pinocchio obeyed without breathing another word. The wagon rolled on again, and the next morning at daybreak they arrived safely in Funland.

This land didn't resemble any other place in the world. Its population was made up entirely of boys. The oldest were fourteen, the youngest barely eight years old. In the streets there was such gaiety, such a din, such wild shouting as to take your head off! Groups of urchins were everywhere. Some were playing at walnuts,[65] some at quoits, some at ball. Some were riding bicycles, some were on wooden horses. Here a group played blindman's buff; there a group played tag; others, dressed as clowns, played at swallowing burning tow; some were acting, some were singing, some were turning somersaults, some were having fun walking on their hands with their feet in the air; some rolled hoops, some strutted about dressed as generals with paper helmets and cardboard sabres; some laughed, some yelled, some called to others, some clapped their hands, some whistled, some imitated hens cackling after laying eggs. In short, such pandemonium, such screeching, such a wild tumult, that you needed cotton wool in your ears to keep from going deaf. In every square you could see canvas puppet theaters crowded with boys from morning till night; and on all the walls of the houses you could read, written in charcoal, such choice sayings as these: "Hurray for phun and gams!" (instead of "fun and

locchi): *non vogliamo più schole* (invece di *non vogliamo più scuole*): *abbasso Larin Metica* (invece di *l'aritmetica*) e altri fiori consimili.

Pinocchio, Lucignolo e tutti gli altri ragazzi, che avevano fatto il viaggio coll'Omino, appena ebbero messo il piede dentro la città, si ficcarono subito in mezzo alla gran baraonda, e in pochi minuti, com'è facile immaginarselo, diventarono gli amici di tutti. Chi più felice, chi più contento di loro?

In mezzo ai continui spassi e agli svariati divertimenti, le ore, i giorni, le settimane passavano come tanti baleni.

– Oh! che bella vita! – diceva Pinocchio tutte le volte che per caso s'imbatteva in Lucignolo.

– Vedi, dunque, se avevo ragione? – ripigliava quest'ultimo. – E dire che tu non volevi partire! E pensare che t'eri messo in capo di tornartene a casa dalla tua Fata, per perdere il tempo a studiare! . . . Se oggi ti sei liberato dalla noia dei libri e delle scuole, lo devi a me, ai miei consigli, alle mie premure, ne convieni? Non vi sono che i veri amici che sappiano rendere di questi grandi favori.

– È vero, Lucignolo! Se oggi io sono un ragazzo veramente contento, è tutto merito tuo. E il maestro, invece, sai che cosa mi diceva, parlando di te? Mi diceva sempre: – Non praticare quella birba di Lucignolo, perché Lucignolo è un cattivo compagno e non può consigliarti altro che a far del male! . . .

– Povero maestro! – replicò l'altro tentennando il capo. – Lo so pur troppo che mi aveva a noia, e che si divertiva sempre a calunniarmi; ma io sono generoso e gli perdono!

– Anima grande! – disse Pinocchio, abbracciando affettuosamente l'amico e dandogli un bacio in mezzo agli occhi.

games"), "We don't want no more skools!" (instead of "We don't want any more schools"), "Down with Uhrit Matik!" (instead of "arithmetic"), and other such gems.

Pinocchio, Lampwick, and all the other boys who had made the trip with the little man had no sooner set foot in this town than they plunged into the midst of the hullabaloo, and in a few minutes, as you can readily imagine, they became friends with everyone. Could anyone be happier, could anyone be more satisfied than they?

In the midst of continual amusements and games of all sorts, the hours, the days, the weeks passed like lightning.

"Oh, what a beautiful life!" Pinocchio would say, whenever he happened to run into Lampwick.

"Do you see now that I was right?" the latter would retort. "And to think that you didn't want to leave! To think that you had taken it into your head to go back home to your Fairy and waste your time studying! . . . If you've escaped from the nuisance of books and schools now, you owe it to me, to my advice and concern. Don't you agree? It's only true friends who can do such big favors."

"That's true, Lampwick. If I'm really a happy boy today, the credit is all yours. And yet, do you know what our teacher used to say: 'Don't go around with that rogue of a Lampwick, because Lampwick is bad company and his advice can only lead you astray.' "

"Poor teacher!" replied the other, shaking his head. "I know only too well that he couldn't stand me and that he always enjoyed maligning me; but I'm noble-minded and so I forgive him!"

"Magnanimous soul!" said Pinocchio, embracing his friend warmly and kissing him between the eyes.

Intanto era già da cinque mesi che durava questa bella cuccagna di baloccarsi e di divertirsi le giornate intere, senza mai vedere in faccia né un libro, né una scuola; quando una mattina Pinocchio, svegliandosi, ebbe, come si suol dire, una gran brutta sorpresa, che lo messe proprio di malumore.

And so five months had already gone by in this wonderful life of ease passed in fun and games all day long without ever coming face to face with a book or a school, when Pinocchio, on waking up one morning, had, as we are wont to say, a rather disagreeable surprise that really put him in a bad mood.

CAPITOLO XXXII

A Pinocchio gli vengono gli orecchi di ciuco,
e poi diventa un ciuchino vero e comincia a ragliare.

— E questa sorpresa quale fu?

– Ve lo dirò io, miei cari e piccoli lettori: la sorpresa
fu che a Pinocchio, svegliandosi, gli venne fatto naturalmente di grattarsi il capo; e nel grattarsi il capo si accòrse . . .

Indovinate un po' di che cosa si accòrse?

Si accòrse con suo grandissimo stupore, che gli orecchi gli erano cresciuti più d'un palmo.

Voi sapete che il burattino, fin dalla nascita, aveva gli
orecchi piccini piccini: tanto piccini che, a occhio nudo,
non si vedevano neppure! Immaginatevi dunque come
restò, quando dové toccar con mano che i suoi orecchi,
durante la notte, erano così allungati, che parevano due
spazzole di padule.

Andò subito in cerca di uno specchio, per potersi vedere: ma non trovando uno specchio, empì d'acqua la
catinella del lavamano, e specchiandovisi dentro, vide
quel che non avrebbe mai voluto vedere: vide, cioè, la
sua immagine abbellita di un magnifico paio di orecchi
asinini.

Lascio pensare a voi il dolore, la vergogna, e la disperazione del povero Pinocchio!

Cominciò a piangere, a strillare, a battere la testa nel
muro: ma quanto più si disperava, e più i suoi orecchi
crescevano, crescevano, crescevano e diventavano pe-
losi verso la cima.

Al rumore di quelle grida acutissime, entrò nella
stanza una bella Marmottina, che abitava il piano di sopra: la quale, vedendo il burattino in così grandi smanie,
gli domandò premurosamente:

CHAPTER XXXII

*Pinocchio gets donkey ears, and then
turns into a real donkey and begins to bray.*

And what was the surprise?

I'll tell you, my dear little readers: the surprise was that Pinocchio, on waking up, quite naturally happened to scratch his head; and in scratching his head he noticed . . .

Can you possibly guess what he noticed?

To his great amazement, he noticed that his ears had grown more than a palm's width.

You remember that ever since his birth the puppet had tiny, tiny ears, so tiny that they couldn't even be seen with the naked eye. Now just imagine how he felt when he realized that during the night his ears had grown so long that they looked like two dusters made of sedge.

Right away he looked for a mirror so he could see himself; but not finding a mirror, he filled the wash-stand basin with water, and reflecting himself in it, saw what he would never have wanted to see: that is, he saw his image adorned with a magnificent pair of asinine ears.[66]

I leave you to think of poor Pinocchio's anguish, shame, and despair.

He began to cry, to scream, to beat his head against the wall; but the more he carried on, the more his ears grew and grew and grew, becoming hairy toward the top.

At the sound of those piercing shrieks a pretty little Marmot, who lived on the floor above, came into the room; and seeing the puppet in such a frenzy, she asked him anxiously:

– Che cos'hai, mio caro casigliano?

– Sono malato, Marmottina mia, molto malato . . .
e malato d'una malattia che mi fa paura! Te ne intendi tu
del polso?

– Un pochino.

– Senti dunque se per caso avessi la febbre. –
La Marmottina alzò la zampa destra davanti: e dopo
aver tastato il polso a Pinocchio, gli disse sospirando:

– Amico mio, mi dispiace doverti dare una cattiva
notizia! . . .

– Cioè?

– Tu hai una gran brutta febbre!

– E che febbre sarebbe?

– È la febbre del somaro.

– Non la capisco questa febbre! – rispose il burattino,
che l'aveva pur troppo capita.

– Allora te la spiegherò io – soggiunse la Marmottina.
– Sappi dunque che fra due o tre ore tu non sarai più né
un burattino, né un ragazzo . . .

– E che cosa sarò?

– Fra due o tre ore, tu diventerai un ciuchino vero e

"What's wrong, my dear fellow-lodger?"

"I'm sick, dear Marmot, very sick . . . and sick with a disease that scares me. Do you know how to take a pulse?"

"A little."

"Feel mine then and see if by chance I have a fever."

The Marmot raised her right forepaw, and after having felt Pinocchio's pulse, said to him with a sigh:

"My friend, I'm sorry to have to give you some bad news."

"What is it?"

"You've got a terrible fever."

"But what kind of fever is it?"

"It's jackass fever."[67]

"I don't understand what that sort of fever is," answered the puppet, who, alas, understood it only too well.

"Then I'll explain it to you," the Marmot went on. "I must tell you that in two or three hours you'll be neither a puppet nor a boy anymore."

"What'll I be then?"

"In two or three hours you'll become an actual don-

proprio, come quelli che tirano il carretto e che portano i cavoli e l'insalata al mercato.

– Oh! povero me! povero me! – gridò Pinocchio pigliandosi con le mani tutt'e due gli orecchi, e tirandoli e strapazzandoli rabbiosamente, come se fossero gli orecchi di un altro.

– Caro mio, – replicò la Marmottina per consolarlo – che cosa ci vuoi tu fare? Oramai è destino. Oramai è scritto nei decreti della sapienza, che tutti quei ragazzi svogliati che, pigliando a noia i libri, le scuole e i maestri, passano le loro giornate in balocchi, in giochi e in divertimenti, debbano finire prima o poi col trasformarsi in tanti piccoli somari.

– Ma davvero è proprio così? – domandò singhiozzando il burattino.

– Pur troppo è così! E ora i pianti sono inutili. Bisognava pensarci prima!

– Ma la colpa non è mia: la colpa, credilo, Marmottina, è tutta di Lucignolo! . . .

– E chi è questo Lucignolo?

– Un mio compagno di scuola. Io volevo tornare a casa: io volevo essere ubbidiente: io volevo seguitare a studiare e a farmi onore . . . ma Lucignolo mi disse: – «Perché vuoi tu annoiarti a studiare? perché vuoi andare alla scuola? . . . Vieni piuttosto con me, nel Paese dei balocchi: lì non studieremo più; lì ci divertiremo dalla mattina alla sera e staremo sempre allegri.»

– E perché seguisti il consiglio di quel falso amico? di quel cattivo compagno?

– Perché? . . . perché, Marmottina mia, io sono un burattino senza giudizio . . . e senza cuore. Oh! se avessi avuto un zinzino di cuore, non avrei mai abbandonata quella buona Fata, che mi voleva bene come una mamma e che aveva fatto tanto per me! . . . e a quest'ora non sarei più un burattino . . . ma sarei invece un ragazzino ammodo, come ce n'è tanti! Oh! . . . ma se incon-

key, just like the ones that pull carts and carry cabbage and lettuce to the market."

"Oh poor me! Poor me!" cried Pinocchio, seizing both his ears with his hands, and pulling and mauling them furiously as though they were somebody else's ears.

"My dear boy," continued the Marmot, to comfort him, "what can you do about it? That's the way it is. It's written in the Decrees of Wisdom[68] that all lazy boys who hate books, schools, and teachers, and who spend their days in play and games and amusements, must end up sooner or later by turning into little jackasses."

"But is that really true?" asked the puppet, sobbing.

"Alas, that's the way it is. And crying doesn't do any good now. You should have thought of it before!"

"But it's not my fault; believe me, dear Marmot, it's all Lampwick's fault."

"And who is this Lampwick?"

"A schoolmate of mine. I wanted to go back home; I wanted to be obedient; I wanted to continue studying and do well . . . but Lampwick said to me: 'Why do you want to be bothered studying? Why do you want to go to school? Come with me to Funland instead; we'll never study there, we'll have fun from morning to night and always have a wonderful time.'"

"And why did you follow the advice of a false friend? of such a bad companion?"

"Why? . . . because, dear Marmot, I'm a puppet without any sense . . . and without a heart. Oh, if I had had even the tiniest bit of heart I would never have deserted that good Fairy who loved me like a mother and who had done so much for me! . . . and by this time I wouldn't be a puppet anymore, but instead I'd be a fine boy like so many others. Oh, . . . but if I meet Lamp-

tro Lucignolo, guai a lui! Gliene voglio dire un sacco e una sporta! . . . –

E fece l'atto di volere uscire. Ma quando fu sulla porta, si ricordò che aveva gli orecchi d'asino, e vergognandosi di mostrarli in pubblico, che cosa inventò? Prese un gran berretto di cotone, e, ficcatoselo in testa, se lo ingozzò fin sotto la punta del naso.

Poi uscì: e si dètte a cercare Lucignolo da per tutto. Lo cercò nelle strade, nelle piazze, nei teatrini, in ogni luogo: ma non lo trovò. Ne chiese notizia a quanti incontrò per la via, ma nessuno l'aveva veduto.

Allora andò a cercarlo a casa: e arrivato alla porta, bussò.

– Chi è? – domandò Lucignolo di dentro.

– Sono io! – rispose il burattino.

– Aspetta un poco, e ti aprirò. –

Dopo mezz'ora la porta si aprì: e figuratevi come restò Pinocchio quando, entrando nella stanza, vide il suo amico Lucignolo con un gran berretto di cotone in testa, che gli scendeva fin sotto il naso.

Alla vista di quel berretto, Pinocchio sentì quasi consolarsi e pensò subito dentro di sé:

– Che l'amico sia malato della mia medesima malattia? Che abbia anche lui la febbre del ciuchino? . . . –

wick, it'll be too bad for him! I'll give him a piece of my mind!"

Then he made as if to go out, but when he reached the door he remembered that he had donkey's ears, and being ashamed to show them in public, what did he think of? He took a large cotton cap, stuck it on his head, and pulled it all the way down over the tip of his nose.

Then he went out and started looking everywhere for Lampwick. He looked for him in the streets, in the squares, in the little puppet shows, every place; but he didn't find him. He asked everyone he met along the way about him, but no one had seen him.

So then he went to look for him at his home, and when he got to the door he knocked.

"Who is it?" asked Lampwick from within.

"It's me," answered the puppet.

"Wait a moment, and I'll open for you."

After half an hour the door opened; and just imagine how surprised Pinocchio was when, on going into the room, he saw his friend Lampwick with a large cotton cap on his head that came down over his nose.

At the sight of that cap, Pinocchio almost felt relieved, and at once he thought to himself: "Can my friend be suffering from the same illness that I have? I wonder if he has jackass fever too?"

E facendo finta di non essersi accorto di nulla, gli domandò sorridendo:

– Come stai, mio caro Lucignolo?

– Benissimo: come un topo in una forma di cacio parmigiano.

– Lo dici proprio sul serio?

– E perché dovrei dirti una bugia?

– Scusami, amico: e allora perché tieni in capo codesto berretto di cotone che ti cuopre tutti gli orecchi?

– Me l'ha ordinato il medico, perché mi son fatto male a un ginocchio. E tu, caro Pinocchio, perché porti codesto berretto di cotone ingozzato fin sotto il naso?

– Me l'ha ordinato il medico, perché mi sono sbucciato un piede.

– Oh! povero Pinocchio! . . .

– Oh! povero Lucignolo! . . . –

A queste parole tenne dietro un lunghissimo silenzio, durante il quale i due amici non fecero altro che guardarsi fra loro in atto di canzonatura.

Finalmente il burattino, con una vocina melliflua e flautata, disse al suo compagno:

But pretending not to notice anything, he smiled and asked:

"How are you, my dear Lampwick?"

"Fine! Like a mouse in a wheel of Parmesan cheese."

"Do you really mean it?"

"Why should I lie to you?"

"Excuse me, my friend; but then why do you have that cotton cap on your head, covering your ears?"

"The doctor ordered it because I hurt myself in the knee. And you, dear Pinocchio, why are you wearing that cotton cap pulled all the way down over your nose?"

"The doctor ordered it because I scraped my foot."

"Oh, poor Pinocchio!"

"Oh, poor Lampwick!"

Following these words there was a long, long silence during which the two friends just looked at each other mockingly.

At last the puppet, in a honey-sweet, flutelike tone, said to his comrade:

– Levami una curiosità, mio caro Lucignolo: hai mai sofferto di malattia agli orecchi?

– Mai! . . . E tu?

– Mai! Per altro da questa mattina in poi ho un orecchio che mi fa spasimare.

– Ho lo stesso male anch'io.

– Anche tu? . . . E qual è l'orecchio che ti duole?

– Tutti e due. E tu?

– Tutti e due. Che sia la medesima malattia?

– Ho paura di sì.

– Vuoi farmi un piacere, Lucignolo?

– Volentieri! Con tutto il cuore.

– Mi fai vedere i tuoi orecchi?

– Perché no? Ma prima voglio vedere i tuoi, caro Pinocchio.

– No: il primo devi essere tu.

– No, carino! Prima tu, e dopo io!

– Ebbene, – disse allora il burattino – facciamo un patto da buoni amici.

– Sentiamo il patto.

– Leviamoci tutti e due il berretto nello stesso tempo: accetti?

– Accetto.

– Dunque attenti!

E Pinocchio cominciò a contare a voce alta:

– Uno! Due! Tre! –

Alla parola *tre!* i due ragazzi presero i loro berretti di capo e li gettarono in aria.

E allora avvenne una scena, che parrebbe incredibile, se non fosse vera. Avvenne, cioè, che Pinocchio e Lucignolo, quando si videro colpiti tutti e due dalla medesima disgrazia, invece di restar mortificati e dolenti, cominciarono ad ammiccarsi i loro orecchi smisuratamente cresciuti, e dopo mille sguaiataggini finirono col dare in una bella risata.

E risero, risero, risero da doversi reggere il corpo: se

"Just out of curiosity, my dear Lampwick, have you ever had anything wrong with your ears?"

"Never! . . . How about you?"

"Never! Except that since this morning one of my ears has been killing me."

"I have the same trouble."

"You too? . . . Which ear is it that hurts you?"

"Both of them. And you?"

"Both of them. Could it be the same illness?"

"I'm afraid so."

"Will you do me a favor, Lampwick?"

"Gladly! With all my heart!"

"Will you let me see your ears?"

"Why not? But first I want to see yours, dear Pinocchio."

"No, you have to be first."

"No, my dear fellow! You first, and then me."

"Well," the puppet said then, "let's make a gentleman's agreement."

"Let's hear the agreement."

"Let's take off our caps at the same time; do you agree?"

"I agree."

"All right, then, ready!" And Pinocchio began to count out loud: "one! two! three!"

At the word *three* the two boys took their caps off and threw them into the air.

And then a scene took place that would seem unbelievable if it weren't true. What happened was that when they saw they were both afflicted with the same misfortune, Pinocchio and Lampwick, instead of feeling ashamed and distressed, began to poke fun at each other's preposterously overgrown ears; and after a thousand coarse antics they ended by breaking into a good long laugh.

And they laughed and laughed and laughed so that

383

non che, sul più bello del ridere, Lucignolo tutt'a un tratto si chetò, e barcollando e cambiando di colore, disse all'amico:

– Aiuto, aiuto, Pinocchio!

– Che cos'hai?

– Ohimè! non mi riesce più di star ritto sulle gambe.

– Non mi riesce più neanche a me – gridò Pinocchio, piangendo e traballando.

E mentre dicevano così, si piegarono tutti e due carponi a terra e, camminando con le mani e coi piedi, cominciarono a girare e a correre per la stanza. E intanto che correvano, i loro bracci diventarono zampe, i loro visi si allungarono e diventarono musi, e le loro schiene si coprirono di un pelame grigiolino chiaro brizzolato di nero.

Ma il momento più brutto per que' due sciagurati sapete quando fu? Il momento più brutto e più umiliante fu quello quando sentirono spuntarsi di dietro la coda. Vinti allora dalla vergogna e dal dolore, si provarono a piangere e a lamentarsi del loro destino.

Non l'avessero mai fatto! Invece di gemiti e di lamenti, mandavano fuori dei ragli asinini; e ragliando sonoramente, facevano tutti e due in coro: *j-a, j-a, j-a.*

In quel frattempo fu bussato alla porta, e una voce di fuori disse:

– Aprite! Sono l'Omino, sono il conduttore del carro che vi portò in questo paese. Aprite subito, o guai a voi! –

they had to hold their sides; but at the height of their laughter Lampwick suddenly became silent, then, reeling about and changing color, he said to his friend:

"Help, Pinocchio, help!"

"What's wrong with you?"

"Oh, dear me! I can't stand up straight anymore."

"I can't either," exclaimed Pinocchio, crying and staggering.

And while they were talking like this, the two of them bent over on all fours and began running around the room on their hands and feet. And while they were running, their arms turned into legs with hoofs, their faces grew longer and turned into muzzles, and their backs became covered with a light-gray coat speckled with black.

But do you know what was the worst moment for those two wretches? The worst and most humiliating moment was when they felt a tail growing behind. Overcome with shame and grief then, they tried to cry and complain about their fate.

Would that they had never done so! Instead of moans and lamentations, they let out asinine brays; and braying loud and long, the two of them went in chorus:

"Hee-haw! Hee-haw! Hee-haw!"

Just then there was a knocking at the door, and a voice from outside said:

"Open up! It's me, the little man, the driver of the wagon that brought you to this place. Open at once, or it'll be too bad for you!"

CAPITOLO XXXIII

Diventato un ciuchino vero,
è portato a vendere, e lo compra il Direttore
di una compagnia di pagliacci,
per insegnargli a ballare e a saltare i cerchi:
ma una sera azzoppisce e allora lo ricompra un altro,
per far con la sua pelle un tamburo.

Vedendo che la porta non si apriva, l'Omino la spalancò con un violentissimo calcio: ed entrato nella stanza, disse col suo solito risolino a Pinocchio e a Lucignolo:

– Bravi ragazzi! Avete ragliato bene, e io vi ho subito riconosciuti alla voce. E per questo eccomi qui. –

A tali parole, i due ciuchini rimasero mogi mogi, colla testa giù, con gli orecchi bassi e con la coda fra le gambe.

Da principio l'Omino li lisciò, li accarezzò, li palpeggiò: poi, tirata fuori la striglia, cominciò a strigliarli per bene. E quando a furia di strigliarli, li ebbe fatti lustri come due specchi, allora messe loro la cavezza e li con-

CHAPTER XXXIII

*Having become a real donkey, he is led
to market and bought by a circus Manager
who wants to teach him how to dance and jump
through hoops. But one evening he goes lame,
and then he is bought by someone
who wants to use his hide to make a drum.*

Seeing that the door didn't open, the little man burst it open with a violent kick; and when he had entered the room, he spoke to Pinocchio and Lampwick with his usual snigger:

"Well done, boys! You brayed beautifully, and I recognized you by your voices right away. And so, here I am."

At these words the two donkeys became silent and crestfallen, with their heads lowered, their ears turned down and their tails between their legs.

First the little man patted them, stroked them, felt them all over; then, taking out a currycomb, he set about grooming them carefully. And when by dint of combing he had made them as shiny as two mirrors, he

dusse sulla piazza del mercato, con la speranza di venderli e di beccarsi un discreto guadagno.

E i compratori, difatti, non si fecero aspettare.

Lucignolo fu comprato da un contadino, a cui era morto il somaro il giorno avanti, e Pinocchio fu venduto al Direttore di una compagnia di pagliacci e di saltatori di corda, il quale lo comprò per ammaestrarlo e per farlo poi saltare e ballare insieme con le altre bestie della compagnia.

E ora avete capito, miei piccoli lettori, qual era il bel mestiere che faceva l'Omino? Questo brutto mostriciattolo, che aveva la fisonomia tutta di latte e miele, andava di tanto in tanto con un carro a girare per il mondo: strada facendo raccoglieva con promesse e con moine tutti i ragazzi svogliati, che avevano a noia i libri e le scuole: e dopo averli caricati sul suo carro, li conduceva nel «Paese dei balocchi» perché passassero tutto il loro tempo in giochi, in chiassate e in divertimenti. Quando poi quei poveri ragazzi illusi, a furia di baloccarsi sempre e di non studiar mai, diventavano tanti ciuchini, allora tutto allegro e contento s'impadroniva di loro e li portava a vendere sulle fiere e su i mercati. E così in pochi anni aveva fatto fior di quattrini ed era diventato milionario.

Quel che accadesse di Lucignolo, non lo so: so, per altro, che Pinocchio andò incontro fin dai primi giorni a una vita durissima e strapazzata.

Quando fu condotto nella stalla, il nuovo padrone gli empì la greppia di paglia: ma Pinocchio, dopo averne assaggiata una boccata, la risputò.

Allora il padrone, brontolando, gli empì la greppia di fieno: ma neppure il fieno gli piacque.

– Ah! non ti piace neppure il fieno? – gridò il padrone imbizzito. – Lascia fare, ciuchino bello, che se hai dei capricci per il capo, penserò io a levarteli! . . . –

E a titolo di correzione, gli affibbiò subito una frustata nelle gambe.

put halters on them and led them to market in the hope of selling them and making a nice profit for himself.

And in fact it wasn't long before buyers showed up.

Lampwick was bought by a peasant whose jackass had died the day before; and Pinocchio was sold to the Manager of a circus troupe of clowns and tightrope artists, who bought him in order to train him to jump and dance with the other animals in his company.

And now, my little readers, do you understand what the fine trade carried on by the little man was? From time to time this revolting little monster whose face was all milk and honey would go traveling far and wide with his wagon. Along the way, by means of promises and blandishments he picked up all the lazy boys who didn't like school and books; and after loading them into his wagon, he would drive them to Funland so that they could spend all their time in games, rumpuses, and amusements. When, by virtue of playing all the time and never studying, those poor gullible boys turned into so many donkeys, then all happy and content he would seize them and take them to be sold at fairs and markets. And in this way, within a few years he had made piles of money and had become a millionaire.

What befell Lampwick, I don't know. But I do know that Pinocchio, from the very start, fell into a life of extremely harsh and abusive treatment.

After he was led to the stable, his new master filled his manger with straw; but after tasting a mouthful of it, Pinocchio spat it out.

Then the master, grumbling, filled the manger with hay; but he didn't like the hay either.

"Ah, so you don't care for hay either?" the master shouted, flying into a rage. "Leave it to me, my pretty donkey; if you've got fancies in your head, I know how to get rid of them."

And to teach him a lesson, he cracked the whip against the donkey's legs.

Pinocchio, dal gran dolore, cominciò a piangere e a ragliare, e ragliando disse:

– J-a, j-a, la paglia non la posso digerire! . . .

– Allora mangia il fieno! – replicò il padrone, che intendeva benissimo il dialetto asinino.

– J-a, j-a, il fieno mi fa dolere il corpo! . . .

– Pretenderesti, dunque, che un somaro, par tuo, lo dovessi mantenere a petti di pollo e cappone in galantina? – soggiunse il padrone arrabbiandosi sempre più, e affibbiandogli una seconda frustata.

A quella seconda frustata Pinocchio, per prudenza, si chetò subito e non disse altro.

Intanto la stalla fu chiusa e Pinocchio rimase solo: e perché erano molte ore che non aveva mangiato, cominciò a sbadigliare dal grande appetito. E, sbadigliando, spalancava una bocca che pareva un forno.

Alla fine, non trovando altro nella greppia, si rassegnò a masticare un po' di fieno: e dopo averlo masticato ben bene, chiuse gli occhi e lo tirò giù.

– Questo fieno non è cattivo – poi disse dentro di sé – ma quanto sarebbe stato meglio che avessi continuato a studiare! . . . A quest'ora, invece di fieno, potrei mangiare un cantuccio di pan fresco e una bella fetta di salame! Pazienza! . . . –

La mattina dopo, svegliandosi, cercò subito nella greppia un altro po' di fieno; ma non lo trovò, perché l'aveva mangiato tutto nella notte.

Allora prese una boccata di paglia tritata; e in quel mentre che la stava masticando, si dové persuadere che il sapore della paglia tritata non somigliava punto né al risotto alla milanese né ai maccheroni alla napoletana.

– Pazienza! – ripeté, continuando a masticare. – Che almeno la mia disgrazia possa servire di lezione a tutti i ragazzi disobbedienti e che non hanno voglia di studiare. Pazienza! . . . pazienza! . . .

– Pazienza un corno! – urlò il padrone, entrando in

Pinocchio began to cry and bray with pain; and braying, he said:

"Hee-haw! Hee-haw! I can't digest straw!"

"Then eat the hay," retorted his owner, who understood the Asinine dialect quite well.[69]

"Hee-haw! Hee-haw! hay gives me a bellyache."

"Do you expect me to feed a jackass like you breast of chicken and capon in aspic?" added his master, growing angrier all the time and giving him a second lash with the whip.

After this second lash, Pinocchio, out of prudence, immediately became silent and said no more.

Then the stable door was closed, and Pinocchio was left alone. But because he hadn't eaten for many hours, he began to yawn with hunger. And in yawning he opened his mouth so wide that it looked like an oven.

Not finding anything else in the manger, he finally resigned himself to chewing some hay; and after chewing it long and well, he shut his eyes and swallowed it.

"This hay isn't bad," he said then to himself, "but how much better it would have been if I had gone on studying! . . . Instead of hay, now I could be eating a piece of fresh bread and a nice slice of salami. Well, it can't be helped now!"

On waking up the next morning, he immediately looked in the manger for some more hay; but he didn't find any, because he had eaten it all up during the night.

So then he took a mouthful of chopped straw; but while he chewed away at it, he was forced to admit that the taste of chopped straw wasn't at all like that of *risotto alla milanese* or *maccheroni alla napoletana*.

"Well, it can't be helped now!" he said again, continuing to chew. "But at least let my misfortune serve as a lesson to all disobedient children and to those who don't want to study. So be it! . . . So be it! . . ."

"So be it, my foot!" bellowed the master, coming

quel momento nella stalla. – Credi forse, mio bel ciuchino, ch'io ti abbia comprato unicamente per darti da
bere e da mangiare? Io ti ho comprato perché tu lavori e
perché tu mi faccia guadagnare molti quattrini. Su, dunque, da bravo! Vieni con me nel Circo e là ti insegnerò
a saltare i cerchi, a rompere col capo le botti di foglio e
a ballare il valzer e la polca, stando ritto sulle gambe di
dietro. –

Il povero Pinocchio, o per amore o per forza, dové
imparare tutte queste bellissime cose; ma, per imparar-
le, gli ci vollero tre mesi di lezioni, e molte frustate da
levare il pelo.

Venne finalmente il giorno, in cui il suo padrone poté
annunziare uno spettacolo veramente straordinario. I
cartelloni di vario colore, attaccati alle cantonate delle
strade, dicevano così:

GRANDE SPETTACOLO DI GALA

Per questa sera

AVRANNO LUOGO I SOLITI SALTI
ED ESERCIZI SORPRENDENTI
ESEGUITI DA TUTTI GLI ARTISTI
e da tutti i cavalli d'ambo i sessi della compagnia

e più

sarà presentato per la prima volta
il famoso

CIUCHINO PINOCCHIO
detto

LA STELLA DELLA DANZA

Il teatro sarà illuminato a giorno.

into the stable at that moment. "Do you by any chance think, my pretty little donkey, that I bought you just to give you food and drink? I bought you so you'd work and help me make a lot of money. So come on, then; there's a good fellow! Come into the ring with me, and I'll teach you how to jump through hoops, burst head-first through paper barrels, and dance the waltz and polka standing on your hind legs."

Whether he liked it or not, poor Pinocchio had to learn all these fine tricks; but in order to learn them it took him three months of training and a lot of whippings that almost took the hair off his hide.

Finally, the day came when his master was able to announce a truly exceptional event. Posters of various colors, pasted at street corners, read like this:

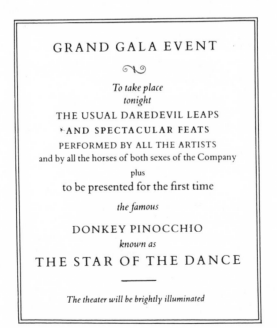

GRAND GALA EVENT

To take place
tonight
THE USUAL DAREDEVIL LEAPS
AND SPECTACULAR FEATS
PERFORMED BY ALL THE ARTISTS
and by all the horses of both sexes of the Company
plus
to be presented for the first time

the famous

DONKEY PINOCCHIO
known as
THE STAR OF THE DANCE

———

The theater will be brightly illuminated

Quella sera, come potete figurarvelo, un'ora prima che cominciasse lo spettacolo, il teatro era pieno stipato.

Non si trovava più né una poltrona, né un posto distinto, né un palco, nemmeno a pagarlo a peso d'oro.

Le gradinate del Circo formicolavano di bambini, di bambine e di ragazzi di tutte le età, che avevano la febbre addosso per la smania di veder ballare il famoso ciuchino Pinocchio.

Finita la prima parte dello spettacolo, il Direttore della compagnia, vestito in giubba nera, calzoni bianchi a coscia e stivaloni di pelle fin sopra ai ginocchi, si presentò all'affollatissimo pubblico e, fatto un grande inchino, recitò con molta solennità il seguente spropositato discorso:

«Rispettabile pubblico, cavalieri e dame!

«L'umile sottoscritto essendo di passaggio per questa illustre metropolitana, ho voluto procrearmi l'onore nonché il piacere di presentare a questo intelligente e cospicuo uditorio un celebre ciuchino, che ebbe già l'onore di ballare al cospetto di Sua Maestà l'imperatore di tutte le principali Corti d'Europa.

«E col ringraziandoli, aiutateci della vostra animatrice presenza e compatiteci!»

Questo discorso fu accolto da molte risate e da molti applausi; ma gli applausi raddoppiarono e diventarono una specie di uragano alla comparsa del ciuchino Pinocchio in mezzo al Circo. Egli era tutto agghindato a festa. Aveva una briglia nuova di pelle lustra, con fibbie e borchie d'ottone; due camelie bianche agli orecchi: la criniera divisa in tanti riccioli legati con fiocchettini di seta rossa: una gran fascia d'oro e d'argento attraverso alla vita, e la coda tutta intrecciata con nastri di velluto paonazzo e celeste. Era insomma un ciuchino da innamorare!

That evening, as you may well imagine, the house was crammed full an hour before the show was to begin.

There wasn't an orchestra seat left to be had, nor a place in the loges, nor a box; not even by paying its weight in gold.

The gallery tiers were swarming with children, with girls and boys of all ages who were in a fever of excitement waiting to see the famous donkey Pinocchio dance.

When the first part of the show was over, the circus Manager, dressed in a black tailcoat, white tights, and high leather boots extending above the knee, came before the packed audience; and after making a deep bow, he very solemnly declaimed the following ludicrous speech:

"Honorable public, cavalieres and noble ladies! Your humble undersigned passing through this illustrious metropolitan,[70] I determined to procreate myself the honor not to mention the pleasure of presenting to this intelligent and conspicuous audience a celebrated donkey who formerly had the honor of dancing in the presence of His Majesty the Emperor of all the principal Courts of Europe.

"And by way to thank you, assist us with your animating presence and bear with us."

This speech was received with a great deal of laughter and much applause; but the applause redoubled and became a virtual storm at the appearance of the donkey Pinocchio in the middle of the ring. He was all primped up smartly. He had a new bridle of patent leather with brass studs and buckles, two white camellias at his ears, his mane divided into a lot of ringlets tied with pretty red silk tassels, a broad gold-and-silver sash around his middle and his tail braided with purple and sky-blue velvet ribbons. In short, he was a donkey to steal your heart away.

Il Direttore, nel presentarlo al pubblico, aggiunse queste parole:

«Miei rispettabili auditori! Non starò qui a farvi menzogna delle grandi difficoltà da me soppressate per comprendere e soggiogare questo mammifero, mentre pascolava liberamente di montagna in montagna nelle pianure della zona torrida. Osservate, vi prego, quanta selvaggina trasudi da' suoi occhi, conciossiaché essendo riusciti vanitosi tutti i mezzi per addomesticarlo al vivere dei quadrupedi civili, ho dovuto più volte ricorrere all'affabile dialetto della frusta. Ma ogni mia gentilezza, invece di farmi da lui benvolere, me ne ha maggiormente cattivato l'animo. Io però, seguendo il sistema di Galles, trovai nel suo cranio una piccola cartagine ossea, che la stessa Facoltà medicea di Parigi riconobbe esser quello il bulbo rigeneratore dei capelli e della danza pirrica. E per questo io lo volli ammaestrare nel ballo, nonché nei relativi salti dei cerchi e delle botti foderate di foglio. Ammiratelo! e poi giudicatelo! Prima però di prendere cognato da voi, permettete, o signori, che io vi inviti al diurno spettacolo di domani sera: ma nell'apoteosi che il tempo piovoso minacciasse acqua, allora lo spettacolo, invece di domani sera, sarà posticipato a domattina, alle ore 11 antimeridiane del pomeriggio.»

E qui il Direttore fece un'altra profondissima riverenza: quindi volgendosi a Pinocchio, gli disse:

– Animo, Pinocchio! Avanti di dar principio ai vostri esercizi, salutate questo rispettabile pubblico, cavalieri, dame e ragazzi! –

Pinocchio, ubbidiente, piegò subito i due ginocchi davanti, e rimase inginocchiato fino a tanto che il Direttore, schioccando la frusta, non gli gridò:

– Al passo! –

Allora il ciuchino si rizzò sulle quattro gambe, e co-

In introducing him to the public, the Manager added these [few] words:

"My worthy auditors! I will not here make mention of the mendacious difficulties suppressated[71] by me in order to reprehend and subjugate this mammal while he was grazing freely from mountain to mountain in the plains of the torrid zone. Observe, I beg you, how much wild game transudes from his eyes, for inasmuch and insofar as all means of taming him to the life of civilized quadrupeds having proved vainglorious, I was obliged several times to resort to the amiable language of the whip. But every kindness of mine, instead of endearing me to him, has only won him over to me. I, however, following the system of Wales,[72] found a small bony Carthage in his cranium, which the Medicean Faculty of Paris itself declared to be the bulb that regenerates hair and the pyrrhic dance. And for this reason I decided to train him in dancing, let alone the relative jumps through hoops and paper-sheathed barrels. Esteem him! And then judge him! However, before taking my lease[73] from you, allow me, ladies and gentlemen, to invite you to tomorrow night's matinee. But in the apotheosis that the rain should threaten wet weather, then the show, instead of tomorrow night, will be postponed until tomorrow morning, at 11 A.M. in the afternoon."

And here the Manager made another very deep bow; then, turning to Pinocchio, he said:

"Come now, Pinocchio! Before beginning your feats, hail this worthy audience—cavalieres, noble ladies, and children!"

In obedience, Pinocchio quickly bent his two front knees to the ground and remained kneeling until the Manager, cracking his whip, cried out to him:

"Walk!"

Then the donkey got up on his four legs and began

minciò a girare intorno al Circo, camminando sempre di passo.

Dopo un poco il Direttore gridò:

– Al trotto! – e Pinocchio, ubbidiente al comando, cambiò il passo in trotto.

– Al galoppo! – e Pinocchio staccò il galoppo.

– Alla carriera! – e Pinocchio si dètte a correre di gran carriera. Ma in quella che correva come un barbero, il Direttore, alzando il braccio in aria, scaricò un colpo di pistola.

A quel colpo il ciuchino, fingendosi ferito, cadde disteso nel Circo, come se fosse moribondo davvero.

Rizzatosi da terra in mezzo a uno scoppio di applausi, d'urli e di battimani, che andavano alle stelle, gli venne fatto naturalmente di alzare la testa e di guardare in su . . . e guardando, vide in un palco una bella signora, che aveva al collo una grossa collana d'oro dalla quale pendeva un medaglione. Nel medaglione c'era dipinto il ritratto d'un burattino.

to go around the ring, walking steadily at a slow pace.

After a while the Manager cried:

"Trot!" And Pinocchio, in obedience to the command, shifted his pace into a trot.

"Gallop!" And Pinocchio went into a gallop.

"Charge!" And Pinocchio started to charge at full speed. But while he was speeding like a racehorse, the Manager raised his arm in the air and fired off a pistol.

At that shot, the donkey, pretending to be wounded, fell full-length in the ring as though he were really dying.

After he had raised himself from the ground amid an explosion of cheers, shouts, and clapping that rose to the stars, he instinctively lifted his head to look up . . . and as he looked, he saw in one of the boxes a beautiful lady who had around her neck a thick gold chain from which hung a medallion. On the medallion was the portrait of a puppet.

– Quel ritratto è il mio! . . . quella signora è la Fata! – disse dentro di sé Pinocchio, riconoscendola subito: e lasciandosi vincere dalla gran contentezza, si provò a gridare:

– Oh Fatina mia! oh Fatina mia! . . . –

Ma invece di queste parole, gli uscì dalla gola un raglio così sonoro e prolungato, che fece ridere tutti gli spettatori, e segnatamente tutti i ragazzi che erano in teatro.

Allora il Direttore, per insegnargli e per fargli intendere che non è buona creanza di mettersi a ragliare in faccia al pubblico, gli diè col manico della frusta una bacchettata sul naso.

Il povero ciuchino, tirato fuori un palmo di lingua, durò a leccarsi il naso almeno cinque minuti, credendo forse così di rasciugarsi il dolore che aveva sentito.

Ma quale fu la sua disperazione quando, voltandosi in su una seconda volta, vide che il palco era vuoto e che la Fata era sparita! . . .

Si sentì come morire: gli occhi gli si empirono di lacrime e cominciò a piangere dirottamente. Nessuno però se ne accòrse, e, meno degli altri, il Direttore, il quale, anzi, schioccando la frusta, gridò:

– Da bravo, Pinocchio! Ora farete vedere a questi signori con quanta grazia sapete saltare i cerchi. –

Pinocchio si provò due o tre volte: ma ogni volta che arrivava davanti al cerchio, invece di attraversarlo, ci passava più comodamente di sotto. Alla fine spiccò un salto e l'attraversò: ma le gambe di dietro gli rimasero disgraziatamente impigliate nel cerchio: motivo per cui ricadde in terra dall'altra parte tutto in un fascio.

Quando si rizzò, era azzoppito, e a malapena poté ritornare alla scuderia.

– Fuori Pinocchio! Vogliamo il ciuchino! Fuori il ciu-

"That's my portrait! . . . that lady is the Fairy!" said Pinocchio to himself, recognizing her at once; and allowing himself to be overcome with great joy, he tried to cry out:

"Oh, my dear Fairy; oh, my dear Fairy!"

But instead of these words, out of his throat came a bray so loud and so long that it made all the spectators laugh, especially all the children who were in the theater.

Then the Manager, in order to teach him a lesson and make him understand that it's not good manners to go around braying in the public's face, gave him a rap on the nose with the handle of his whip.

The poor little donkey stuck his tongue way out and licked his nose for at least five minutes, thinking perhaps that in this way he could wipe away the pain he felt.

But how great was his despair when, turning his gaze upward a second time, he saw that the box was empty and that the Fairy had vanished!

He felt as though he would die; his eyes filled with tears and he began to weep bitterly. However, nobody noticed it, least of all the Manager who, on the contrary, cracked his whip and cried out:

"There's a good fellow, Pinocchio! Now you'll show these ladies and gentlemen how gracefully you can jump through the hoops."

Pinocchio made two or three attempts, but whenever he came up to the hoop, instead of going through it he found it more convenient to duck under it. Finally, he made a leap and went through it, but unluckily his hind legs got caught in the hoop, so that he fell to the ground in a heap on the other side.

When he got up again, he was lame and could hardly make it back to the stable.

"Bring out Pinocchio! We want the donkey! Bring

chino! – gridavano i ragazzi dalla platea, impietositi e commossi al tristissimo caso.

Ma il ciuchino per quella sera non si fece più rivedere.

La mattina dopo il veterinario, ossia il medico delle bestie, quando l'ebbe visitato, dichiarò che sarebbe rimasto zoppo per tutta la vita.

Allora il Direttore disse al suo garzone di stalla:

– Che vuoi tu che mi faccia d'un somaro zoppo? Sarebbe un mangiapane a ufo. Portalo dunque in piazza e rivendilo. –

Arrivati in piazza, trovarono subito il compratore, il quale domandò al garzone di stalla:

– Quanto vuoi di codesto ciuchino zoppo?

– Venti lire.

– Io ti do venti soldi. Non credere che io lo compri per servirmene: lo compro unicamente per la sua pelle. Vedo che ha la pelle molto dura, e con la sua pelle voglio fare un tamburo per la banda musicale del mio paese. –

Lascio pensare a voi, ragazzi, il bel piacere che fu per

out the donkey!'' shouted the children from the orchestra floor, moved and much distressed by that pitiful accident.

But the donkey wasn't seen anymore that evening.

The following morning, after the veterinary—that is, the animal doctor—had examined him, he declared that he would be lame for life.

So the Manager said to his stable-boy:

"What do you expect me to do with a lame jackass? He'd be a useless sponger eating for nothing. So take him to the square and sell him."

When they reached the square, right away they found a buyer who asked the stable-boy:

"How much do you want for that lame donkey of yours?"

"Twenty dollars."

"I'll give you twenty pennies. Don't think I'm buying him to have him work for me; I'm buying him only for his hide. I see he has a tough hide, and I want to make a drum with it, for my village band."

I leave it to you, children, to imagine what a great

il povero Pinocchio, quando sentì che era destinato a diventare un tamburo!

Fatto sta che il compratore, appena pagati i venti soldi, condusse il ciuchino sulla riva del mare; e messogli un sasso al collo e legatolo per una zampa con una fune che teneva in mano, gli diè improvvisamente uno spintone e lo gettò nell'acqua.

Pinocchio, con quel macigno al collo, andò subito a fondo: e il compratore, tenendo sempre stretta in mano la fune, si pose a sedere sopra uno scoglio, aspettando che il ciuchino avesse tutto il tempo di morire affogato, per poi scorticarlo e levargli la pelle.

pleasure it was for poor Pinocchio when he heard that he was destined to become a drum.

So it was that as soon as the buyer had paid the twenty pennies, he led the donkey to the seashore; and after putting a stone around his neck and tying one of his legs with a rope that he held onto with his hand, he suddenly gave him a shove and threw him into the water.

With that stone around his neck, Pinocchio quickly sank to the bottom; and the buyer, holding the rope tightly in his hand, sat down on a rock, giving the donkey all the time he needed to drown to death so that he could then skin him and remove his hide.

CAPITOLO XXXIV

Pinocchio, gettato in mare, è mangiato dai pesci
e ritorna ad essere un burattino come prima:
ma mentre nuota per salvarsi,
è ingojato dal terribile Pesce-cane.

Dopo cinquanta minuti che il ciuchino era sott'acqua, il compratore disse, discorrendo da sé solo:

– A quest'ora il mio povero ciuchino zoppo deve essere bell'e affogato. Ritiriamolo dunque su, e facciamo con la sua pelle questo bel tamburo. –

E cominciò a tirare la fune, con la quale lo aveva legato per una gamba: e tira, tira, tira, alla fine vide apparire a fior d'acqua . . . indovinate? Invece di un ciuchino morto, vide apparire a fior d'acqua un burattino vivo, che scodinzolava come un'anguilla.

Vedendo quel burattino di legno, il pover'uomo credé di sognare e rimase lì intontito, a bocca aperta e con gli occhi fuori della testa.

CHAPTER XXXIV

*Thrown into the sea, Pinocchio is eaten
by fish and becomes a puppet as before;
but while he is swimming to safety,
he is swallowed by the terrible Shark.*

After the donkey had been under water for fifty minutes, the buyer said to himself:

"By this time my poor lame donkey must be good
and drowned. Let's drag him back up and make that fine
drum with his hide."

So he began pulling up the rope that he had tied to
the donkey's leg; and he pulled and pulled and pulled
until at last he saw appearing on the surface of the water
. . . can you guess what? Instead of a dead donkey, he
saw come to the surface a live puppet who was wriggling like an eel.

Seeing that wooden puppet, the poor man thought
he was dreaming and stood there dumbfounded, with
his mouth wide open and his eyes popping out of his
head.

Riavutosi un poco dal suo primo stupore, disse piangendo e balbettando:

– E il ciuchino che ho gettato in mare dov'è? . . .

– Quel ciuchino son io! – rispose il burattino, ridendo.

– Tu?

– Io.

– Ah! mariuolo! Pretenderesti forse di burlarti di me?

– Burlarmi di voi? Tutt'altro, caro padrone: io vi parlo sul serio.

– Ma come mai tu, che poco fa eri un ciuchino, ora stando nell'acqua, sei diventato un burattino di legno? . . .

– Sarà effetto dell'acqua del mare. Il mare ne fa di questi scherzi.

– Bada burattino, bada! . . . Non credere di divertirti alle mie spalle! Guai a te, se mi scappa la pazienza!

– Ebbene, padrone; volete sapere tutta la vera storia? Scioglietemi questa gamba e io ve la racconterò. –

Quel buon pasticcione del compratore, curioso di conoscere la vera storia, gli sciolse subito il nodo della fune, che lo teneva legato: e allora Pinocchio, trovandosi libero come un uccello nell'aria, prese a dirgli così:

– Sappiate dunque che io ero un burattino di legno, come sono oggi: ma mi trovavo a tocco e non tocco di diventare un ragazzo, come in questo mondo ce n'è tanti: se non che per la mia poca voglia di studiare e per dar retta ai cattivi compagni, scappai di casa . . . e un bel giorno, svegliandomi, mi trovai cambiato in un somaro con tanto d'orecchi . . . e con tanto di coda! . . . Che vergogna fu quella per me! . . . Una vergogna, caro padrone, che Sant'Antonio benedetto non la faccia provare neppure a voi! Portato a vendere sul mercato degli asini, fui comprato dal Direttore di una compagnia equestre, il quale si messe in capo di far di me un gran

When he had recovered a little from his initial shock, amid his crying and stammering he said:

"But where's the donkey I threw into the sea?"

"I'm that donkey," answered the puppet, laughing.

"You?"

"Me!"

"Ah, you cheat! Are you trying to make a fool of me?"

"Make a fool of you? By no means, dear master; I really mean what I'm saying."

"But how is it possible that you who were a donkey a short while ago have now turned into a wooden puppet just by being in the water?"

"It must be the effect of the seawater. The sea plays tricks like that."

"Watch out, puppet, watch out! . . . Don't think you can amuse yourself at my expense. It'll be too bad for you if I lose my temper!"

"Well then, master; do you want to know the whole story? Untie this leg for me, and I'll tell you."

That fine oaf of a buyer, being curious to know the true story, quickly undid the knot in the rope that kept the puppet bound; and then Pinocchio, finding himself as free as a bird in the air, went on to say as follows:

"Well, the fact is that I was a wooden puppet, just as I am now, but I was on the verge of becoming a boy like any other boy in the world; however, because of my dislike for school and because I listened to bad companions, I ran away from home . . . and then one fine day, when I woke up, I found myself changed into a jackass with enormous ears . . . and a long, long tail. What a humiliation that was for me! . . . Such a humiliation, dear master, that I pray blessed Saint Anthony may never let even you experience it.[74] Taken to the donkey fair to be sold, I was bought by the Manager of a company of performing horses who took it into his head to

ballerino e un gran saltatore di cerchi: ma una sera, durante lo spettacolo, feci in teatro una brutta cascata e rimasi zoppo da tutt'e due le gambe. Allora il Direttore, non sapendo che cosa farsi d'un asino zoppo, mi mandò a rivendere, e voi mi avete comprato! . . .

– Pur troppo! E ti ho pagato venti soldi. E ora chi mi rende i miei poveri venti soldi?

– E perché mi avete comprato? Voi mi avete comprato per fare con la mia pelle un tamburo! . . . un tamburo! . . .

– Pur troppo! E ora dove troverò un'altra pelle? . . .

– Non vi date alla disperazione, padrone. Dei ciuchini ce n'è tanti in questo mondo!

– Dimmi, monello impertinente; e la tua storia finisce qui?

– No – rispose il burattino – ci sono altre due parole, e poi è finita. Dopo avermi comprato, mi avete condotto in questo luogo per uccidermi, ma poi, cedendo a un sentimento pietoso d'umanità, avete preferito di legarmi un sasso al collo e di gettarmi in fondo al mare. Questo sentimento di delicatezza vi onora moltissimo e io ve ne serberò eterna riconoscenza. Per altro, caro padrone, questa volta avete fatto i vostri conti senza la Fata . . .

– E chi è questa Fata?

– È la mia mamma, la quale somiglia a tutte quelle buone mamme, che vogliono un gran bene ai loro ragazzi, e non li perdono mai d'occhio, e li assistono amorosamente in ogni disgrazia, anche quando questi ragazzi, per le loro scapataggini e per i loro cattivi portamenti, meriterebbero di esser abbandonati e lasciati in balìa a sé stessi. Dicevo, dunque, che la buona Fata, appena mi vide in pericolo di affogare, mandò subito intorno a me un branco infinito di pesci, i quali credendomi davvero un ciuchino bell'e morto, cominciarono a mangiarmi! E che bocconi che facevaṅo! Non avrei

make a great dancer and a great hoop-jumper of me; but one night, during the performance, I had a nasty fall and remained lame in both legs. Then the Manager, not knowing what to do with a lame donkey, sent me to be sold again, and you bought me."

"Unfortunately! And I paid twenty pennies for you. And now who's going to give me back my poor twenty pennies?"

"And why did you buy me? You bought me to make a drum out of my hide! . . . a drum!"

"Unfortunately! And now where can I find another hide?"

"Don't give up all hope, master. There are plenty of donkeys in this world!"

"Tell me, you impudent brat, is that the end of your story?"

"No," replied the puppet, "another word or two, and then it'll be over. After buying me, you led me to this place to kill me; but then, yielding to a humane feeling of compassion, you preferred to tie a stone around my neck and throw me into the sea. Such an exquisite sentiment does you great honor, and I will be forever grateful to you for it. However, my dear master, you reckoned without the Fairy this time."

"And who is this Fairy?"

"She's my mother, and she's like all those good mothers who love their children deeply and never lose sight of them and who help them lovingly in all their troubles, even when these children, because of their recklessness and bad ways, would fully deserve to be abandoned and left to shift for themselves. As I was saying, then, as soon as my good Fairy saw me in danger of drowning, she quickly sent an immense shoal of fish around me; and they, taking me truly for a dead donkey, began to eat me up. And what huge bites they took! I

mai creduto che i pesci fossero più ghiotti anche dei ragazzi! . . . Chi mi mangiò gli orecchi, chi mi mangiò il muso, chi il collo e la criniera, chi la pelle delle zampe, chi la pelliccia della schiena . . . e, fra gli altri, vi fu un pesciolino così garbato, che si degnò perfino di mangiarmi la coda.

– Da oggi in poi – disse il compratore inorridito – faccio giuro di non assaggiar più carne di pesce. Mi dispiacerebbe troppo di aprire una triglia o un nasello fritto e di trovargli in corpo una coda di ciuco!

– Io la penso come voi – replicò il burattino, ridendo. – Del resto, dovete sapere che quando i pesci ebbero finito di mangiarmi tutta quella buccia asinina, che mi copriva dalla testa ai piedi, arrivarono, com'è naturale, all'osso . . . o per dir meglio, arrivarono al legno, perché, come vedete, io son fatto di legno durissimo.

would never have thought that fish were greedier than boys. Some ate my ears, some ate my muzzle, some my neck and mane, some the skin of my legs, some the coat of my back; and among them there was one little fish who was so amiable that he even went so far as to eat my tail."

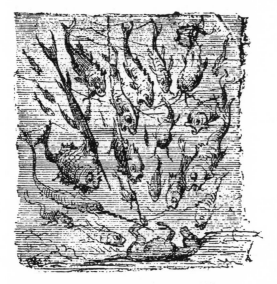

"From now on," said the horrified buyer, "I swear I'll never taste fish again. I wouldn't be exactly pleased to open a red mullet or a fried hake and find a donkey tail inside."

"I'm of the same opinion," replied the puppet, laughing. "Anyway, the fact is that when the fish had finished eating all that donkey bark that covered me from head to foot, they naturally came to the bone, or rather to the wood; because, as you can see, I'm made of especially hard wood. But after taking just a few

413

Ma dopo dati i primi morsi, quei pesci ghiottoni si accòrsero subito che il legno non era ciccia per i loro denti, e nauseati da questo cibo indigesto se ne andarono chi in qua, chi in là, senza voltarsi nemmeno a dirmi grazie. Ed eccovi raccontato come qualmente voi, tirando su la fune, avete trovato un burattino vivo, invece d'un ciuchino morto.

– Io mi rido della tua storia – gridò il compratore imbestialito. – Io so che ho speso venti soldi per comprarti, e rivoglio i miei quattrini. Sai che cosa farò? Ti porterò daccapo al mercato, e ti rivenderò a peso di legno stagionato per accendere il fuoco nel caminetto.

– Rivendetemi pure: io sono contento – disse Pinocchio.

Ma nel dir così, fece un bel salto e schizzò in mezzo all'acqua. E nuotando allegramente e allontanandosi dalla spiaggia, gridava al povero compratore:

– Addio, padrone; se avete bisogno di una pelle per fare un tamburo, ricordatevi di me. –

E poi rideva e seguitava a nuotare: e dopo un poco, rivoltandosi indietro, urlava più forte:

– Addio, padrone; se avete bisogno di un po' di legno stagionato per accendere il caminetto, ricordatevi di me. –

Fatto sta che in un batter d'occhio si era tanto allontanato, che non si vedeva quasi più; ossia, si vedeva solamente sulla superficie del mare un puntolino nero, che di tanto in tanto rizzava le gambe fuori dell'acqua e faceva capriòle e salti, come un delfino in vena di buon umore.

Intanto che Pinocchio nuotava alla ventura, vide in mezzo al mare uno scoglio che pareva di marmo bianco, e su in cima allo scoglio, una bella caprettina che belava amorosamente e gli faceva segno di avvicinarsi.

bites, those greedy fish soon discovered that wood wasn't meat for their teeth, and disgusted by such indigestible food they went off, some one way, some another way, without even looking back to thank me. And there you have the explanation of how it was that when you pulled in the rope you found a live puppet instead of a dead donkey."

"I don't give a fig for your story," shouted the buyer, flying into a rage. "I know that I spent twenty pennies to buy you, and I want my money back. Do you know what I'll do? I'll take you back to the market and resell you for your weight in seasoned wood, good for kindling a fire in the hearth."

"Go ahead and resell me; it's all right with me," said Pinocchio.

But as he said this, he took a great leap and splashed into the middle of the water; and as he swam merrily farther and farther away from shore, he shouted to the poor buyer:

"Farewell, master! If you ever need a skin to make a drum, think of me."

And he laughed and went on swimming. And after a little while, turning around he shouted still louder:

"Farewell, master! If you ever need some seasoned wood to kindle a fire in the hearth, think of me."

So it was that in the twinkling of an eye he had gone so far that he could hardly be seen anymore; or rather, all that could be seen on the surface of the sea was a small black speck which every once in a while raised its legs out of the water and cut capers like a dolphin in a sportive mood.

While he was swimming along aimlessly, Pinocchio saw a rock that seemed made of white marble there in the middle of the sea, and on top of the rock a pretty little She-Goat who was bleating tenderly and beckoning him to come near.

415

La cosa più singolare era questa: che la lana della caprettina, invece di esser bianca, o nera, o pallata di più colori, come quella delle altre capre, era invece tutta turchina, ma d'un turchino così sfolgorante, che rammentava moltissimo i capelli della bella Bambina.

Lascio pensare a voi se il cuore del povero Pinocchio cominciò a battere più forte! Raddoppiando di forza e di energia si diè a nuotare verso lo scoglio bianco: ed era già a mezza strada, quand'ecco uscir fuori dell'acqua e venirgli incontro un'orribile testa di mostro marino, con la bocca spalancata come una voragine, e tre filari di zanne, che avrebbero fatto paura anche a vederle dipinte.

E sapete chi era quel mostro marino?

Quel mostro marino era né più né meno quel gigantesco Pesce-cane ricordato più volte in questa storia, e che per le sue stragi e per la sua insaziabile voracità, veniva soprannominato «l'Attila dei pesci e dei pescatori».

Immaginatevi lo spavento del povero Pinocchio, alla vista del mostro. Cercò di scansarlo, di cambiare strada: cercò di fuggire: ma quella immensa bocca spalancata gli veniva sempre incontro con la velocità di una saetta.

– Affrettati, Pinocchio, per carità! – gridava belando la bella caprettina.

E Pinocchio nuotava disperatamente con le braccia, col petto, con le gambe e coi piedi.

– Corri, Pinocchio, perché il mostro si avvicina! . . . –

E Pinocchio, raccogliendo tutte le sue forze, raddoppiava di lena nella corsa.

– Bada, Pinocchio! . . . il mostro ti raggiunge! . . . Eccolo! . . . Eccolo! . . . Affrettati per carità, o sei perduto! . . . –

E Pinocchio a nuotare più lesto che mai, e via, e via, e via, come anderebbe una palla di fucile. E già si acco-

The most curious thing of all was that the pretty Goat's hair, instead of being white or black, or spotted with the two colors, like that of other goats, was all blue—but such a radiant blue that it very much recalled the hair of the beautiful Little Girl.

I'll leave it to you to guess whether poor Pinocchio's heart began to beat faster. Redoubling his efforts he began swimming toward the white rock; and he was already halfway there when suddenly there rose from the water the horrible head of a sea monster that came at him with its mouth yawning like a chasm, and three rows of long sharp teeth that, even in a picture, would have been terrifying to see.

And do you know who that sea monster was?

The sea monster was neither more nor less than the gigantic Shark referred to several times in this story and who, because of his insatiable appetite and the havoc he wreaked, had come to be nicknamed "the Attila of Fish and Fishermen."

Just imagine poor Pinocchio's terror at the sight of that monster. He tried to avoid him, to change his course, to get away. But that enormous, gaping mouth kept coming at him with the speed of lightning.

"Hurry, Pinocchio, for mercy's sake!" the pretty little Goat bleated loudly.

And Pinocchio swam desperately with his arms, with his chest, with his legs and feet.

"Be quick, Pinocchio, for the monster's getting closer!"

And gathering all his strength, Pinocchio strained twice as hard in the chase.

"Look out, Pinocchio! . . . The monster's catching up with you! . . . There he is! . . . there he is! . . . Hurry, for mercy's sake, or you're lost!"

And Pinocchio swam faster than ever, on and on and on, like a rifle shot. And already he was near the rock,

stava allo scoglio, e già la caprettina, spenzolandosi tutta sul mare, gli porgeva le sue zampine davanti per aiutarlo a uscir fuori dell'acqua . . . Ma! . . .

Ma oramai era tardi! Il mostro lo aveva raggiunto. Il mostro, tirando il fiato a sé, si bevve il povero burattino, come avrebbe bevuto un uovo di gallina, e lo inghiottì con tanta violenza e con tanta avidità, che Pinocchio,

cascando giù in corpo al Pesce-cane, batté un colpo così screanzato da restarne sbalordito per un quarto d'ora.

Quando ritornò in sé da quello sbigottimento, non sapeva raccapezzarsi, nemmeno lui, in che mondo si fosse. Intorno a sé c'era da ogni parte un gran buio: ma un buio così nero e profondo, che gli pareva di essere entrato col capo in un calamaio pieno d'inchiostro. Stette in ascolto e non sentì nessun rumore: solamente di tanto in tanto sentiva battersi nel viso alcune grandi buffate di vento. Da principio non sapeva intendere da dove quel vento uscisse: ma poi capì che usciva dai polmoni del mostro. Perché bisogna sapere che il Pesce-cane soffriva moltissimo d'asma, e quando respirava, pareva proprio che soffiasse la tramontana.

and now the little Goat, hanging as far as she could over the water, was holding out her little hoofs to help him out of the sea . . . But! . . .

But by then it was too late! The monster had caught up with him. Drawing his breath in, the monster sucked in the poor puppet as easily as he would have sucked a hen's egg. And he swallowed him with such vehemence

and with such greed that Pinocchio, falling into the belly of the Shark, landed with so rude a jolt that he lay dazed for a quarter of an hour.

When he came to after the shock, he couldn't figure out where in the world he was. All around him there was total darkness, so deep and black a darkness that he felt as if he had gone headfirst into a full inkwell. He listened carefully, but he didn't hear a sound. However, from time to time he felt strong gusts of wind smacking against his face. At first he couldn't understand where the wind came from, but then he realized that it came from the monster's lungs. Because, you see, the Shark suffered badly from asthma; and when he breathed, it was just as if the north wind were blowing.

Pinocchio, sulle prime, s'ingegnò di farsi un po' di coraggio: ma quand'ebbe la prova e la riprova di trovarsi chiuso in corpo al mostro marino, allora cominciò a piangere e a strillare; e piangendo diceva:

– Aiuto! aiuto! Oh povero me! Non c'è nessuno che venga a salvarmi?

– Chi vuoi che ti salvi, disgraziato? . . . – disse in quel buio una vociaccia fessa di chitarra scordata.

– Chi è che parla così? – domandò Pinocchio, sentendosi gelare dallo spavento.

– Sono io! sono un povero Tonno, inghiottito dal Pesce-cane insieme con te. E tu che pesce sei?

– Io non ho che veder nulla coi pesci. Io sono un burattino.

– E allora, se non sei un pesce, perché ti sei fatto inghiottire dal mostro?

– Non son io, che mi son fatto inghiottire: gli è lui che mi ha inghiottito! Ed ora che cosa dobbiamo fare qui al buio? . . .

– Rassegnarsi e aspettare che il Pesce-cane ci abbia digeriti tutti e due! . . .

– Ma io non voglio esser digerito! – urlò Pinocchio, ricominciando a piangere.

– Neppure io vorrei esser digerito – soggiunse il Tonno – ma io sono abbastanza filosofo e mi consolo pensando che, quando si nasce Tonni, c'è più dignità a morir sott'acqua che sott'olio! . . .

– Scioccherie! – gridò Pinocchio.

– La mia è un'opinione – replicò il Tonno – e le opinioni, come dicono i Tonni politici, vanno rispettate!

– Insomma . . . io voglio andarmene di qui . . . io voglio fuggire . . .

– Fuggi, se ti riesce! . . .

– È molto grosso questo Pesce-cane che ci ha inghiottiti? – domandò il burattino.

At first Pinocchio did his best to keep his courage up, but when he knew for a fact beyond all doubt that he was trapped in the belly of the sea monster, he began to bawl and scream:

"Help! Help! Oh, poor me! Won't anybody come to my rescue?"

"Whom do you expect to rescue you, unlucky fellow?" said a cracked, harsh voice in the darkness, sounding like an untuned guitar.

"Who's that speaking?" asked Pinocchio, frozen with terror.

"It is I! I am a poor Tuna, swallowed by the Shark along with you. And what kind of fish are you?"

"I don't have anything to do with fish. I'm a puppet."

"Well then, if you're not a fish, why did you let yourself get swallowed by the monster?"

"I didn't let myself be swallowed; *he* just went and swallowed me! And now what are we going to do here in the dark?"

"Accept the situation, and wait for the Shark to digest us both."

"But I don't want to be digested!" bellowed Pinocchio, beginning to cry again.

"I'd rather not be digested, either," continued the Tuna, "but I'm enough of a philosopher to console myself with the thought that when one is born a Tuna there's more dignity in dying under water than under oil."

"That's ridiculous!" shouted Pinocchio.

"That's my opinion," replied the Tuna, "and opinions, as all Tuna politicians say, are to be respected."

"Well, I want to get out of here; I want to escape."

"Escape, if you can."

"Is this Shark that has swallowed us very big?" asked the puppet.

– Figurati che il suo corpo è più lungo di un chilometro senza contare la coda. –

Nel tempo che facevano questa conversazione al buio, parve a Pinocchio di veder lontan lontano una specie di chiarore.

– Che cosa sarà mai quel lumicino lontano lontano? – disse Pinocchio.

– Sarà qualche nostro compagno di sventura, che aspetterà come noi il momento di esser digerito! . . .

– Voglio andare a trovarlo. Non potrebbe darsi il caso che fosse qualche vecchio pesce capace d'insegnarmi la strada per fuggire?

– Io te l'auguro di cuore, caro burattino.

– Addio, Tonno.

– Addio, burattino: e buona fortuna.

– Dove ci rivedremo? . . .

– Chi lo sa? . . . È meglio non pensarci neppure! –

"Just figure that his body is more than a mile long, without counting his tail."

While they were carrying on this conversation in the dark, Pinocchio saw what he thought was a glimmer of light far, far away.

"What can that little light far, far away there be?" said Pinocchio.

"It's probably one of our companions in distress, waiting his turn like us to be digested."

"I want to go and see him. Who knows? It might be some old fish able to tell me the way to escape."

"I hope so for your sake, with all my heart, dear puppet."

"Good-bye, Tuna."

"Good-bye, puppet, and good luck."

"Where shall we meet again?"

"Who knows? . . . It's better not even to think about it!"

CAPITOLO XXXV

Pinocchio ritrova in corpo al Pesce-cane . . .
chi ritrova? Leggete questo capitolo
e lo saprete.

Pinocchio, appena che ebbe detto addio al suo buon amico Tonno, si mosse brancolando in mezzo a quel bujo, e camminando a tastoni dentro il corpo del Pesce-cane, si avviò un passo dietro l'altro verso quel piccolo chiarore che vedeva baluginare lontano lontano.

E nel camminare sentì che i suoi piedi sguazzavano in una pozzanghera d'acqua grassa e sdrucciolona, e quell'acqua sapeva di un odore così acuto di pesce fritto, che gli pareva d'essere a mezza quaresima.

E più andava avanti, e più il chiarore si faceva rilucente e distinto: finché, cammina cammina, alla fine arrivò: e quando fu arrivato . . . che cosa trovò? Ve lo do a indovinare in mille: trovò una piccola tavola apparecchiata, con sopra una candela accesa infilata in una bottiglia di cristallo verde, e seduto a tavola un vecchiettino tutto bianco, come se fosse di neve o di panna montata, il quale se ne stava lì biascicando alcuni pesciolini vivi, ma tanto vivi, che alle volte mentre li mangiava, gli scappavano perfino di bocca.

A quella vista il povero Pinocchio ebbe un'allegrezza così grande e così inaspettata, che ci mancò un ette non cadesse in delirio. Voleva ridere, voleva piangere, voleva dire un monte di cose; e invece mugolava confusamente e balbettava delle parole tronche e sconclusionate. Finalmente gli riuscì di cacciar fuori un grido di gioja, e spalancando le braccia e gettandosi al collo del vecchietto, cominciò a urlare:

CHAPTER XXXV

In the Shark's belly Pinocchio finds . . .
whom does he find? Read this chapter
and you will know.

Right after he had bidden adieu to his good friend Tuna, Pinocchio set out gropingly in the midst of that darkness, and feeling his way along the inside of the Shark, he advanced one step at a time toward the faint light that he saw glimmering far, far off.

And as he walked, he felt his feet splashing in a pool of greasy, slippery water which gave off such an acrid smell of fried fish that he thought it was mid-Lent.[75]

And the farther he advanced, the brighter and more distinct the glimmer of light became, until after walking and walking, he finally got to it; and when he did get to it . . . what did he find? I'll give you a thousand guesses: he found a small table laid for a meal, with a burning candle stuck in a green glass bottle on it; and sitting at the table was a little old man, all white as though he were made of snow or whipped cream, who was chewing with difficulty on some small live fishes so very alive that even while he was eating them, they would sometimes leap right out of his mouth.

At that sight poor Pinocchio was seized by such a great and unexpected joy that he practically became delirious.[76] He wanted to laugh, he wanted to cry, he wanted to say so many many things; but instead he mumbled indistinctly and stammered a few broken incoherent words. Finally, he succeeded in letting out a shout of joy; and opening his arms wide, he threw himself around the old man's neck and began to exclaim:

– Oh! babbino mio! finalmente vi ho ritrovato! Ora poi non vi lascio più, mai più, mai più!

– Dunque gli occhi mi dicono il vero? – replicò il vecchietto, stropicciandosi gli occhi – Dunque tu se' proprio il mi' caro Pinocchio?

– Sì, sì, sono io, proprio io! E voi mi avete digià perdonato, non è vero? Oh! babbino mio, come siete buono! . . . e pensare che io, invece . . . Oh! ma se sapeste quante disgrazie mi son piovute sul capo e quante cose mi sono andate a traverso! Figuratevi che il giorno che voi, povero babbino, col vendere la vostra casacca, mi compraste l'Abbecedario per andare a scuola, io scappai a vedere i burattini, e il burattinajo mi voleva mettere sul fuoco perché gli cocessi il montone arrosto, che fu quello poi che mi dètte cinque monete d'oro, perché le portassi a voi, ma io trovai la Volpe e il Gatto, che mi condussero all'Osteria del Gambero Rosso, dove man-

"Oh, dear, dear father! At last I've found you again! Now I'll never leave you again, never, never again!"

"Then my eyes do not deceive me?" replied the old man, rubbing his eyes. "Then you're really my own dear Pinocchio?"

"Yes, yes, it's me, really me! And you've already forgiven me, haven't you? Oh, dear Father, how good you are! And to think that instead I . . . Oh, but if you only knew how many misfortunes have fallen on my head and how many things have gone wrong for me! Just think that on the day you sold your jacket, poor dear Father, and bought me the spelling-book so that I could go to school, I ran away to see the puppets, and the puppeteer wanted to put me into the fire to roast his mutton, he was the one that gave me five gold coins to bring to you, but I came across the Fox and the Cat who took me to the Red Crawfish Inn where they ate like wolves, and

giarono come lupi, e partito solo di notte incontrai gli assassini che si messero a corrermi dietro, e io via, e loro dietro, e io via, e loro sempre dietro, e io via, finché m'impiccarono a un ramo della Quercia Grande, dovecché la bella Bambina dai capelli turchini mi mandò a prendere con una carrozzina, e i medici, quando m'ebbero visitato, dissero subito: – «Se non è morto, è segno che è sempre vivo» – e allora mi scappò detta una bugia, e il naso cominciò a crescermi e non mi passava più dalla porta di camera, motivo per cui andai con la Volpe e col Gatto a sotterrare le quattro monete d'oro, che una l'avevo spesa all'Osteria, e il pappagallo si messe a ridere, e viceversa di duemila monete non trovai più nulla, la quale il Giudice quando seppe che ero stato derubato, mi fece subito mettere in prigione, per dare una soddisfazione ai ladri, di dove, col venir via, vidi un bel grappolo d'uva in un campo, che rimasi preso alla tagliola e il contadino di santa ragione mi messe il collare da cane perché facessi la guardia al pollajo, che riconobbe la mia innocenza e mi lasciò andare, e il Serpente, colla coda che gli fumava, cominciò a ridere e gli si strappò una vena sul petto, e così ritornai alla casa della bella Bambina, che era morta, e il Colombo vedendo che piangevo mi disse: – «Ho visto il tu' babbo che si fabbricava una barchettina per venirti a cercare» – e io gli dissi – «Oh! se avessi l'ali anch'io» – e lui mi disse – «Vuoi venire dal tuo babbo?» – e io gli dissi – «Magari! ma chi mi ci porta?» – e lui mi disse – «Ti ci porto io» – e io gli dissi – «Come?» – e lui mi disse – «Montami sulla groppa» – e così abbiamo volato tutta la notte, poi la mattina tutti i pescatori che guardavano verso il mare mi dissero – «C'è un pover'omo in una barchetta che sta per affogare» – e io da lontano vi riconobbi subito, perché me lo diceva il core, e vi feci segno di tornare alla spiaggia . . .

– Ti riconobbi anch'io – disse Geppetto – e sarei vo-

when I left alone at night I met the assassins who started to chase after me, and I ran away with them behind me, and I kept on running and they kept right behind me, and I kept running, until they hanged me from a branch of the Great Oak, which was where the beautiful Little Girl with blue hair sent a carriage to get me, and the doctors, after they had examined me, said right away: 'If he's not dead, it's an indication that he's still alive,' and then a lie slipped from me and my nose began to grow and couldn't pass through the bedroom door anymore, which is why I went with the Fox and the Cat to bury the four gold coins, since I had spent one at the Inn, and the Parrot began to laugh, and instead of two thousand coins I didn't find anything, which when the Judge found out that I had been robbed he had me put in jail right away to compensate the thieves, from where, when I came out, I saw a beautiful bunch of grapes in a field, but I got caught in an animal trap, and the peasant with all the right in the world put a dog collar on me so that I'd guard his chicken coop, but he recognized my innocence and let me go, and the Serpent, with his tail smoking, began to laugh and burst a vein in his chest, and so I went back to the house of the beautiful Little Girl, who was dead, and seeing me cry the Pigeon said to me: 'I saw your father building a little boat to go and look for you,' and I said: 'Oh, if I only had wings too!' and he said: 'Do you want to go to your father?' and I said: 'Oh, do I! But who'll take me there?' and he said: 'I'll take you to him,' and I said: 'How?' and he said: 'Climb on my back,' and so we flew all night, then in the morning all the fishermen who were looking out to sea said to me: 'There's a poor man in a boat who's drowning,' and from far away I recognized you immediately, because my heart told me it was you, and I signaled to you to come back to shore.''

"I recognized you, too," said Geppetto, "and I

429

lentieri tornato alla spiaggia: ma come fare? Il mare era grosso e un cavallone m'arrovesciò la barchetta. Allora un orribile Pesce-cane che era lì vicino, appena che m'ebbe visto nell'acqua corse subito verso di me, e tirata fuori la lingua, mi prese pari pari, e m'inghiottì come un tortellino di Bologna.

– E quant'è che siete chiuso qui dentro? – domandò Pinocchio.

– Da quel giorno in poi, saranno oramai due anni: due anni, Pinocchio mio, che mi son parsi due secoli!

– E come avete fatto a campare? E dove avete trovata la candela? E i fiammiferi per accenderla, chi ve li ha dati?

– Ora ti racconterò tutto. Devi dunque sapere che quella medesima burrasca, che rovesciò la mia barchetta, fece anche affondare un bastimento mercantile. I marinaj si salvarono tutti, ma il bastimento calò a fondo e il solito Pesce-cane che quel giorno aveva un appetito eccellente, dopo avere inghiottito me, inghiottì anche il bastimento . . .

– Come? Lo inghiottì tutto in un boccone? . . . – domandò Pinocchio maravigliato.

– Tutto in un boccone: e risputò solamente l'albero maestro, perché gli era rimasto fra i denti come una lisca. Per mia gran fortuna, quel bastimento era carico non solo di carne conservata in cassette di stagno, ma di biscotto, ossia di pane abbrostolito, di bottiglie di vino, d'uva secca, di cacio, di caffè, di zucchero, di candele steariche e di scatole di fiammiferi di cera. Con tutta questa grazia di Dio ho potuto campare due anni: ma oggi sono agli ultimi sgoccioli: oggi nella dispensa non c'è più nulla, e questa candela, che vedi accesa, è l'ultima candela che mi sia rimasta . . .

– E dopo? . . .

– E dopo, caro mio, rimarremo tutt'e due al bujo.

would have been glad to get back to shore, but what could I do? The sea was rough, and a big wave over-turned my boat. Then a horrible Shark who was nearby no sooner saw me in the water than he rushed toward me, stuck out his tongue, caught me up neatly, and swallowed me as if I were a Bolognese *tortellino*."[77]

"And how long have you been trapped in here?" asked Pinocchio.

"Ever since that day. It must be two years by now. Two years, my dear Pinocchio, that have seemed like two centuries to me."

"But how have you managed to survive? And where did you find the candle? And who gave you the matches to light it?"

"I'll tell you everything now. The fact is that the same storm that upset my boat also caused a merchant ship to sink. All the sailors were saved, but the ship sank to the bottom; and this same Shark, who had a splendid ap-petite that day, after swallowing me, also swallowed the ship."

"What? He swallowed it whole in one mouthful?" asked Pinocchio, astounded.

"All in one mouthful; and he spat out only the main-mast, because it had got stuck between his teeth like a fishbone. Quite fortunately for me, the ship was loaded not only with tins of preserved meat, but also with hardtack, that is, ship biscuits, bottles of wine, raisins, cheese, coffee, sugar, tallow candles, and boxes of wax matches. With all that bounty from Heaven, I've been able to survive for two years. But now I'm down to the end; now there's nothing left in the pantry, and this can-dle you see lit is the last one I have left."

"And then? . . ."

"And then, my dear boy, we'll both be left in the dark."

– Allora, babbino mio – disse Pinocchio – non c'è tempo da perdere. Bisogna pensar subito a fuggire . . .

– A fuggire? . . . e come?

– Scappando dalla bocca del Pesce-cane e gettandosi a nuoto in mare.

– Tu parli bene: ma io, caro Pinocchio, non so nuotare.

– E che importa? . . . Voi mi monterete a cavalluccio sulle spalle e io, che sono un buon nuotatore, vi porterò sano e salvo fino alla spiaggia.

– Illusioni, ragazzo mio! – replicò Geppetto, scotendo il capo e sorridendo malinconicamente. – Ti par egli possibile che un burattino, alto appena un metro, come sei tu, possa aver tanta forza da portarmi a nuoto sulle spalle?

– Provatevi e vedrete! A ogni modo se sarà scritto in cielo che dobbiamo morire, avremo almeno la gran consolazione di morire abbracciati insieme. –

E senza dir altro, Pinocchio prese in mano la candela, e andando avanti per far lume, disse al suo babbo:

– Venite dietro a me, e non abbiate paura. –

E così camminarono un bel pezzo, e traversarono tutto il corpo e tutto lo stomaco del Pesce-cane. Ma giunti al punto dove cominciava la spaziosa gola del mostro, pensarono bene di fermarsi per dare un'occhiata e cogliere il momento opportuno alla fuga.

Ora bisogna sapere che il Pesce-cane, essendo molto vecchio e soffrendo d'asma e di palpitazione di cuore, era costretto a dormire a bocca aperta: per cui Pinocchio, affacciandosi al principio della gola e guardando in su, poté vedere al di fuori di quell'enorme bocca spalancata un bel pezzo di cielo stellato e un bellissimo lume di luna.

"Then there's no time to lose, dear Father," said Pinocchio. "We have to think about getting away right now."

"Getting away? But how?"

"By escaping through the Shark's mouth, and throwing ourselves into the sea."

"That's easy for you to say, dear Pinocchio, but *I* don't know how to swim."

"What does that matter? You can get astride my shoulders, and since I'm a strong swimmer, I'll bring you safe and sound to the shore."

"You're dreaming, my boy!" replied Geppetto, shaking his head and smiling sadly. "Do you think it's possible that a puppet, barely three feet tall, as you are, can have enough strength to swim with me on his shoulders?"

"Give it a try, and you'll see! In any case, if it's written in Heaven that we must die, at least we'll have the great consolation of dying clasped together."

And without another word Pinocchio took the candle in his hand; and lighting the way as he went ahead, he said to his father:

"Follow me, and don't be afraid."

And thus they walked a long way, traversing the whole belly and the whole length of the Shark's body.[78] But when they reached the point where the monster's spacious throat began, they decided to stop and take a look so as to seize the right moment for their escape.

Now you should know that because the Shark was very old and suffered from asthma and palpitations of the heart, he was obliged to sleep with his mouth open, so that when Pinocchio came to where his throat began and looked up he could see on the outside of that enormous gaping mouth quite a bit of starry sky and very bright moonlight.

– Questo è il vero momento di scappare – bisbigliò allora voltandosi al suo babbo. – Il Pesce-cane dorme come un ghiro: il mare è tranquillo e ci si vede come di giorno. Venite dunque, babbino, dietro a me, e fra poco saremo salvi. –

Detto fatto, salirono su per la gola del mostro marino, e arrivati in quell'immensa bocca, cominciarono a camminare in punta di piedi sulla lingua; una lingua così larga e così lunga, che pareva il viottolone d'un giardino. E già stavano lì lì per fare il gran salto e per gettarsi a nuoto nel mare, quando, sul più bello, il Pesce-cane starnutì, e nello starnutire, dètte uno scossone così violento, che Pinocchio e Geppetto si trovarono rimbalzati all'indietro e scaraventati novamente in fondo allo stomaco del mostro.

Nel grand'urto della caduta la candela si spense, e padre e figliuolo rimasero al bujo.

– E ora?. . . – domandò Pinocchio facendosi serio.

– Ora, ragazzo mio, siamo bell'e perduti.

– Perché perduti? Datemi la mano, babbino, e badate di non sdrucciolare! . . .

– Dove mi conduci?

– Dobbiamo ritentare la fuga. Venite con me e non abbiate paura. –

Ciò detto, Pinocchio prese il suo babbo per la mano: e camminando sempre in punta di piedi, risalirono insieme su per la gola del mostro: poi traversarono tutta la lingua e scavalcarono i tre filari di denti. Prima però di fare il gran salto, il burattino disse al suo babbo:

– Montatemi a cavalluccio sulle spalle e abbracciatemi forte forte. Al resto ci penso io. –

Appena Geppetto si fu accomodato per bene sulle spalle del figliolo, il bravo Pinocchio, sicuro del fatto suo, si gettò nell'acqua e cominciò a nuotare. Il mare era tranquillo come un olio: la luna splendeva in tutto il suo

"This is the right moment to escape," he whispered then, turning to his father. "The Shark is sleeping like a dormouse, the sea is calm and it's as clear as day. So follow me, dear Father, and in a little while we'll be safe."

Without further ado they climbed up the sea monster's throat, and after arriving at the huge mouth they began to walk on tiptoe along his tongue—a tongue so wide and so long that it resembled a large garden lane. They were just on the point of taking the great leap into the sea to swim away, when, right then, the Shark sneezed, and in sneezing he gave such a violent jolt that Pinocchio and Geppetto were bounced back and catapulted once more into the pit of the monster's body.

In the heavy impact of the fall, the candle went out and father and son were left in the dark.

"And now?" asked Pinocchio, becoming somber.

"Now, my boy, we're really done for."

"Why are we done for? Give me your hand, dear Father, and be careful not to slip."

"Where are you taking me?"

"We must try again to escape. Come with me, and don't be afraid."

With these words Pinocchio took his father by the hand, and walking all the while on tiptoe, together they went up again through the monster's throat; then they traversed the length of his tongue and surmounted his three rows of teeth. Before taking the great leap, however, the puppet said to his father:

"Climb astride my shoulders and hold your arms around me very tight. I'll take care of the rest."

As soon as Geppetto had settled himself firmly on his son's shoulders, good Pinocchio fearlessly threw himself into the water and began swimming. The sea was as smooth as oil, the moon was shining in all its splen-

chiarore e il Pesce-cane seguitava a dormire di un sonno
così profondo, che non l'avrebbe svegliato nemmeno
una cannonata.

dor, and the Shark went on sleeping so soundly that not even a cannon shot would have awakened him.

CAPITOLO XXXVI

Finalmente Pinocchio cessa d'essere un burattino
e diventa un ragazzo.

Mentre Pinocchio nuotava alla svelta per raggiungere la spiaggia, si accòrse che il suo babbo, il quale gli stava a cavalluccio sulle spalle e aveva le gambe mezze nell'acqua, tremava fitto fitto, come se al pover'uomo gli battesse la febbre terzana.

Tremava di freddo o di paura? Chi lo sa? . . . Forse un po' dell'uno e un po' dell'altra. Ma Pinocchio, credendo che quel tremito fosse di paura, gli disse per confortarlo:

– Coraggio, babbo! Fra pochi minuti arriveremo a terra e saremo salvi.

– Ma dov'è questa spiaggia benedetta? – domandò il vecchietto, diventando sempre più inquieto, e appuntando gli occhi, come fanno i sarti quando infilano l'ago.
– Eccomi qui, che guardo da tutte le parti e non vedo altro che cielo e mare.

– Ma io vedo anche la spiaggia – disse il burattino. – Per vostra regola io sono come i gatti: ci vedo meglio di notte che di giorno. –

Il povero Pinocchio faceva finta di esser di buon umore: ma invece . . . invece cominciava a scoraggirsi: le forze gli scemavano, il suo respiro diventava grosso e affannoso . . . insomma non ne poteva più, e la spiaggia era sempre lontana.

Nuotò finché ebbe fiato: poi si voltò col capo verso Geppetto, e disse con parole interrotte:

– Babbo mio . . . ajutatevi . . . perché io muojo! . . . –

E padre e figliuolo erano oramai sul punto di affogare, quando udirono una voce di chitarra scordata che disse:

CHAPTER XXXVI

*At last Pinocchio ceases to be a puppet
and becomes a boy.*

While Pinocchio was swimming hurriedly to reach the shore he noticed that his father, who was astride his shoulders and had his legs half in the water, was shivering hard, as if the poor man were stricken with malaria.

Was he shivering with cold or with fear? Who knows? Perhaps a little of each. But Pinocchio thought that the trembling was from fear, and in order to comfort him he said:

"Take heart, Father! In a few minutes we'll reach land and be safe."

"But where is this blessed shore?" asked the old man, getting more and more worried and squinting just as tailors do when they thread a needle. "I've been looking all around, but all I see is sky and sea."

"But I see the shore, too," said the puppet. "Let me tell you, I'm like a cat; I see better by night than by day."

Poor Pinocchio was pretending to be in high spirits, but instead . . . instead he was beginning to lose heart. His strength was giving out, his breathing was becoming heavy and labored . . . in short, he was worn out and the shore was still far off.

He swam until he was out of breath; then he turned to Geppetto and spoke in a broken voice:

"Father . . . save yourself . . ."⁷⁹ for I'm dying!"

And father and son were now just about to drown when they heard a voice like an untuned guitar that said:

– Chi è che muore?

– Sono io e il mio povero babbo!

– Questa voce la riconosco! Tu sei Pinocchio! . . .

– Preciso: e tu?

– Io sono il Tonno, il tuo compagno di prigionia in corpo al Pesce-cane.

– E come hai fatto a scappare?

– Ho imitato il tuo esempio. Tu sei quello che mi hai insegnato la strada, e dopo te, sono fuggito anch'io.

– Tonno mio, tu capiti proprio a tempo! Ti prego per l'amore che porti ai Tonnini tuoi figliuoli: ajutaci, o siamo perduti.

– Volentieri e con tutto il cuore. Attaccatevi tutti e due alla mia coda, e lasciatevi guidare. In quattro minuti vi condurrò alla riva. –

Geppetto e Pinocchio, come potete immaginarvelo, accettarono subito l'invito: ma invece di attaccarsi alla coda, giudicarono più comodo di mettersi addirittura a sedere sulla groppa del Tonno.

– Siamo troppo pesi? – gli domandò Pinocchio.

– Pesi? Neanche per ombra; mi par di avere addosso due gusci di conchiglia – rispose il Tonno, il quale era di una corporatura così grossa e robusta, da parere un vitello di due anni.

Giunti alla riva, Pinocchio saltò a terra il primo, per ajutare il suo babbo a fare altrettanto: poi si voltò al Tonno, e con voce commossa gli disse: ·

– Amico mio, tu hai salvato il mio babbo! Dunque non ho parole per ringraziarti abbastanza! Permetti almeno che ti dia un bacio, in segno di riconoscenza eterna! . . . –

Il Tonno cacciò il muso fuori dell'acqua, e Pinocchio, piegandosi coi ginocchi a terra, gli posò un affettuosissimo bacio sulla bocca. A questo tratto di spontanea e vivissima tenerezza, il povero Tonno, che non c'era avvezzo, si sentì talmente commosso, che vergognandosi

"Who is it that's dying?"

"I am, and my poor father."

"I recognize that voice! You're Pinocchio!"

"Quite right, and you?"

"I'm the Tuna, your prison mate in the Shark's belly."

"But how did you manage to escape?"

"I followed your example. You're the one who taught me the way; and after you, I got away too."

"Dear Tuna, you've shown up just in time! I beg you by the love you bear your little tuna children, help us or we're lost."

"Willingly, and with all my heart. Hang onto my tail, both of you, and let me tow you. In four minutes I'll get you to shore."

As you can well imagine, Geppetto and Pinocchio accepted the offer at once, but instead of hanging onto his tail, they thought it would be more convenient if they got right on the Tuna's back.

"Are we too heavy?" Pinocchio asked him.

"Heavy? Not in the least; I feel as if I had a couple of empty seashells on me," answered the Tuna, who was so big and sturdy in build that he looked like a two-year-old bullock.

On arriving at the shore, Pinocchio was first to jump down, in order to help his father do the same. Then he turned to the Tuna and said to him in a voice full of emotion:

"My friend, you've saved my father! I can't find words to thank you enough. Allow me at least to give you a kiss as a sign of my eternal gratitude."

The Tuna stuck his snout out of the water, and Pinocchio, kneeling down to the ground, bestowed a most affectionate kiss on his mouth. At this show of spontaneous and most heartfelt tenderness, the Tuna, who wasn't used to that sort of thing, was so moved

441

a farsi veder piangere come un bambino, ricacciò il capo sott'acqua e sparì.

Intanto s'era fatto giorno.

Allora Pinocchio, offrendo il suo braccio a Geppetto, che aveva appena il fiato di reggersi in piedi, gli disse:

– Appoggiatevi pure al mio braccio, caro babbino, e andiamo. Cammineremo pian pianino come le formicole, e quando saremo stanchi, ci riposeremo lungo la via.

– E dove dobbiamo andare? – domandò Geppetto.

– In cerca di una casa o d'una capanna, dove ci diano per carità un boccon di pane e un po' di paglia che ci serva da letto. –

Non avevano ancora fatti cento passi, che videro seduti sul ciglione della strada due brutti ceffi, i quali stavano lì in atto di chiedere l'elemosina.

Erano il Gatto e la Volpe: ma non si riconoscevano più da quelli d'una volta. Figuratevi che il Gatto, a furia di fingersi cieco, aveva finito coll'accecare davvero: e la Volpe invecchiata, intignata e tutta perduta da una parte, non aveva più nemmeno la coda. Così è. Quella trista ladracchiola, caduta nella più squallida miseria, si trovò costretta un bel giorno a vendere perfino la sua bellissima coda a un merciajo ambulante, che la comprò per farsene uno scacciamosche.

– O Pinocchio – gridò la Volpe con voce di piagnisteo – fai un po' di carità a questi due poveri infermi.

– Infermi! – ripeté il Gatto.

– Addio, mascherine! – rispose il burattino. – Mi avete ingannato una volta, e ora non mi ripigliate più.

– Credilo, Pinocchio, che oggi siamo poveri e disgraziati davvero!

– Davvero! – ripeté il Gatto.

– Se siete poveri, ve lo meritate. Ricordatevi del proverbio che dice: «I quattrini rubati non fanno mai frutto.» Addio, mascherine!

that, lest he be seen crying like a baby, he ducked his head under the water again and disappeared.

Meanwhile, day had dawned.

Then Pinocchio, offering his arm to Geppetto, who barely had the strength to stand on his feet, said to him:

"Just lean on my arm, dear Father, and let's go on. We'll go little by little, just as ants do, and when we're tired we'll rest along the way."

"But where are we to go?" asked Geppetto.

"In search of a house or a hut, where out of charity somebody might give us a piece of bread and some straw to lie on."

They hadn't yet gone a hundred steps when they saw two ugly mugs sitting by the side of the road and begging for alms.

It was the Cat and the Fox, but they were no longer recognizable from before. Just imagine, the Cat, by having pretended for so long to be blind, had ended up really going blind; and the Fox, now old, mangy, and completely paralyzed on one side, didn't even have his tail anymore. So it is. The wretched swindler, having fallen into the most abject misery, finally was forced to sell even his magnificent tail to a peddler, who bought it to make himself a flywhisk.

"Oh, Pinocchio," cried the Fox in a whining voice, "give some alms to us two poor invalids."

"Invalids!" repeated the Cat.

"Farewell, pretty masqueraders!" the puppet answered. "You tricked me once, but you won't fool me again."

"Believe me, Pinocchio, now we're poor and miserable for real!"

"For real!" repeated the Cat.

"If you're poor, it serves you right. Remember the proverb that says: 'Stolen money brings no gain.' Farewell, pretty masqueraders!"

– Abbi compassione di noi! . . .

– Di noi!

– Addio, mascherine! Ricordatevi del proverbio che dice: «La farina del diavolo va tutta in crusca.»

– Non ci abbandonare! . . .

– . . . are! – ripeté il Gatto.

– Addio, mascherine! Ricordatevi del proverbio che dice: «Chi ruba il mantello al suo prossimo, per il solito muore senza camicia.» –

E così dicendo, Pinocchio e Geppetto seguitarono tranquillamente per la loro strada: finché, fatti altri cento passi, videro in fondo a una viottola, in mezzo ai campi, una bella capanna tutta di paglia, e col tetto coperto d'embrici e di mattoni.

– Quella capanna dev'essere abitata da qualcuno – disse Pinocchio. – Andiamo là, e bussiamo. –

Difatti andarono, e bussarono alla porta.

– Chi è? – disse una vocina di dentro.

– Siamo un povero babbo e un povero figliuolo, senza pane e senza tetto – rispose il burattino.

– Girate la chiave, e la porta si aprirà – disse la solita vocina.

Pinocchio girò la chiave, e la porta si aprì. Appena entrati dentro, guardarono di qua, guardarono di là, e non videro nessuno.

– O il padrone della capanna dov'è? – disse Pinocchio maravigliato.

– Eccomi quassù! –

Babbo e figliuolo si voltarono subito verso il soffitto, e videro sopra un travicello il Grillo-parlante.

– Oh! mio caro Grillino – disse Pinocchio salutandolo garbatamente.

– Ora mi chiami il «Tuo caro Grillino», non è vero? Ma ti rammenti di quando, per cacciarmi di casa tua, mi tirasti un manico di martello? . . .

"Have pity on us!"

"On us!"

"Farewell, pretty masqueraders! Remember the proverb that says: 'The devil's grain yields naught but chaff.'"

"Don't desert us!"

". . . sert us!" repeated the Cat.

"Farewell, pretty masqueraders! Remember the proverb that says: 'He who steals his neighbor's cloak is bound to die without a shirt.'"

And with that, Pinocchio and Geppetto continued calmly on their way until, after having gone another hundred steps, they saw at the end of a country lane in the middle of the fields a charming hut all made of straw, but with its roof covered with tile and bricks.[80]

"That hut must be inhabited by somebody," said Pinocchio. "Let's go there and knock."

In fact, they went and knocked at the door.

"Who is it?" said a little voice from within.

"It's a poor father and a poor son, without bread and without a roof over their heads," answered the puppet.

"Turn the key and the door will open," said the same little voice.

Pinocchio turned the key, and the door opened. As soon as they went in they looked all around, but they didn't see anybody.

"But where's the owner of this hut?" said an amazed Pinocchio.

"Here I am, up here!"

Father and son looked up quickly toward the ceiling, and there, on a joist, they saw the Talking Cricket.

"Oh, my dear little Cricket," said Pinocchio, greeting him politely.

"So I'm 'your dear little Cricket' now, am I? But do you remember when you threw a mallet[81] at me to chase me out of your house?"

– Hai ragione, Grillino! Scaccia anche me . . . tira anche a me un manico di martello: ma abbi pietà del mio povero babbo . . .

– Io avrò pietà del babbo e anche del figliuolo: ma ho voluto rammentarti il brutto garbo ricevuto, per insegnarti che in questo mondo, quando si può, bisogna mostrarsi cortesi con tutti, se vogliamo esser ricambiati con pari cortesia nei giorni del bisogno.

– Hai ragione, Grillino, hai ragione da vendere e io terrò a mente la lezione che mi hai data. Ma mi dici come hai fatto a comprarti questa bella capanna?

– Questa capanna mi è stata regalata jeri da una graziosa capra, che aveva la lana d'un bellissimo colore turchino.

– E la capra dov'è andata? – domandò Pinocchio, con vivissima curiosità.

– Non lo so.

– E quando ritornerà? . . .

– Non ritornerà mai. Ieri è partita tutta afflitta, e, belando, pareva che dicesse: – «Povero Pinocchio . . . oramai non lo rivedrò più . . . il Pesce-cane a quest'ora l'avrà bell'e divorato! . . .»

– Ha detto proprio così? . . . Dunque era lei! . . . era lei! . . . era la mia cara Fatina! . . . – cominciò a urlare Pinocchio, singhiozzando e piangendo dirottamente.

Quand'ebbe pianto ben bene, si rasciugò gli occhi e, preparato un buon lettino di paglia, vi distese sopra il vecchio Geppetto. Poi domandò al Grillo-parlante:

– Dimmi, Grillino: dove potrei trovare un bicchiere di latte per il mio povero babbo?

– Tre campi distante di qui c'è l'ortolano Giangio, che tiene le mucche. Va' da lui e troverai il latte che cerchi. –

Pinocchio andò di corsa a casa dell'ortolano Giangio: ma l'ortolano gli disse:

"You're right, dear Cricket! Chase me away now, . . . throw a mallet at me now, too; but have pity on my poor father."

"I'll have pity on the father and on the son, too; but I wanted to remind you of the nasty turn I received from you, so as to teach you that in this world we must be kind to everybody, whenever we can, if we want to be repaid with equal kindness in time of need."

"You're right, dear Cricket; you're more than right, and I'll remember the lesson you've given me. But will you tell me how you managed to buy this charming hut?"

"This hut was given to me as a gift yesterday by a pretty Goat whose hair was of a very beautiful blue color."

"And where has the Goat gone?" asked Pinocchio with burning curiosity.

"I don't know."

"But when will she come back?"

"She's never coming back. She went away yesterday, quite sad and bleating as if to say: 'Poor Pinocchio, I'll never see him again; by now the Shark must have eaten him all up.'"

"Did she really say that? Then it was her! It was her! . . . It was my dear little Fairy!" Pinocchio began to exclaim, sobbing and weeping bitterly.

When he had had a good cry, he dried his eyes, and having prepared a nice little bed of straw, he made old Geppetto lie on it. Then he asked the Talking Cricket:

"Tell me, dear Cricket, where can I find a glass of milk for my poor father?"

"Three fields away from here there's Giangio, a market gardener, who keeps cows. Go to him and you'll find all the milk you want."

Pinocchio went on the run to the house of Giangio the market gardener; but the market gardener said to him:

– Quanto ne vuoi del latte?

– Ne voglio un bicchiere pieno.

– Un bicchiere di latte costa un soldo. Comincia intanto dal darmi il soldo.

– Non ho nemmeno un centesimo – rispose Pinocchio tutto mortificato e dolente.

– Male, burattino mio – replicò l'ortolano. – Se tu non hai nemmeno un centesimo, io non ho nemmeno un dito di latte.

– Pazienza! – disse Pinocchio, e fece l'atto di andarsene.

– Aspetta un po' – disse Giangio. – Fra te e me ci possiamo accomodare. Vuoi adattarti a girare il *bindolo*?

– Che cos'è il bindolo?

– Gli è quell'ordigno di legno, che serve a tirar su l'acqua dalla cisterna per annaffiare gli ortaggi.

– Mi proverò . . .

– Dunque, tirami su cento secchie d'acqua, e io ti regalerò in compenso un bicchiere di latte.

– Sta bene. –

Giangio condusse il burattino nell'orto e gl'insegnò la maniera di girare il *bindolo*. Pinocchio si pose subito al lavoro; ma prima di aver tirato su le cento secchie d'ac-

"How much milk do you want?"

"I want a full glass."

"A glass of milk costs one penny. So start by giving me the penny."

"I don't have even half a penny," answered Pinocchio, quite humiliated and dejected.

"That's bad, my dear puppet," replied the gardener. "If you don't have even half a penny, I don't have even a drop of milk."

"Never mind!" said Pinocchio, as he turned to go.

"Wait a moment," said Giangio. "We can make a deal between us. Are you willing to turn a windlass?"

"What's a windlass?"

"It's that wooden device that's used for drawing up water from the cistern to water the vegetables."

"I'll give it a try."

"Then draw up a hundred buckets of water for me, and I'll give you a glass of milk in return."

"All right."

Giangio took the puppet into the vegetable garden and showed him how to turn the windlass. Pinocchio got to work right away; but before he had drawn the hundred buckets of water, he was dripping with sweat

qua, era tutto grondante di sudore dalla testa ai piedi.
Una fatica a quel modo non l'aveva durata mai.

– Finora questa fatica di girare il bindolo – disse l'ortolano – l'ho fatta fare al mio ciuchino: ma oggi quel
povero animale è in fin di vita.

– Mi menate a vederlo? – disse Pinocchio.

– Volentieri. –

Appena che Pinocchio fu entrato nella stalla vide un
bel ciuchino disteso sulla paglia, rifinito dalla fame e dal
troppo lavoro. Quando l'ebbe guardato fisso fisso, disse
dentro di sé, turbandosi:

– Eppure quel ciuchino lo conosco! Non mi è fisonomia nuova! –

E chinatosi fino a lui, gli domandò in dialetto asinino:
– Chi sei? –

A questa domanda, il ciuchino aprì gli occhi moribondi, e rispose balbettando nel medesimo dialetto:

– Sono Lu . . . ci . . . gno . . . lo . . . –

E dopo richiuse gli occhi e spirò.

– Oh! povero Lucignolo! – disse Pinocchio a mezza
voce: e presa una manciata di paglia, si rasciugò una lacrima che gli colava giù per il viso.

– Ti commuovi tanto per un asino che non ti costa
nulla? – disse l'ortolano. – Che cosa dovrei far io che lo
comprai a quattrini contanti?

– Vi dirò . . . era un mio amico! . . .

– Tuo amico?

– Un mio compagno di scuola! . . .

– Come?! – urlò Giangio dando in una gran risata. –
Come?! avevi dei somari per compagni di scuola? . . .
Figuriamoci i begli studi che devi aver fatto! . . . –

Il burattino, sentendosi mortificato da quelle parole,
non rispose: ma prese il suo bicchiere di latte quasi caldo,
e se ne tornò alla capanna.

from head to foot. Never before had he worked that hard.

"Until now, I've had my donkey do this job of turning the windlass," the market gardener said; "but today that poor creature is near death."

"Will you take me to see him?" said Pinocchio.

"Gladly."

As soon as Pinocchio went into the stable, he saw a fine little donkey stretched out on the straw, worn out from hunger and too much work. After he had looked long and hard at him, he became troubled and said to himself:

"Surely I know this little donkey! He looks familiar to me."

And bending down to him, he asked him in the Asinine dialect:

"Who are you?"

At this question the donkey opened his dying eyes and stammered in the same dialect:

"I'm La-amp-wi-ick."

Then he shut his eyes again and died.

"Oh, poor Lampwick!" said Pinocchio softly. And picking up a handful of straw, he wiped away a tear that was rolling down his cheek.

"You feel so sorry for a jackass that didn't cost you anything?" said the market gardener. "Then how should I feel, who paid hard cash for him?"

"Well, you see . . . he was a friend of mine."

"A friend of yours?"

"A schoolmate of mine."

"What?" howled Giangio, breaking into a loud guffaw. "What?! You had jackasses for classmates? . . . I can just imagine the fine education you must have gotten!"

Mortified by those words, the puppet made no reply; he just took his glass of milk, which was still warm, and went back to the hut.

E da quel giorno in poi, continuò più di cinque mesi a levarsi ogni mattina, prima dell'alba, per andare a girare il bindolo, e guadagnare così quel bicchiere di latte, che faceva tanto bene alla salute cagionosa del suo babbo. Né si contentò di questo: perché a tempo avanzato, imparò a fabbricare anche i canestri e i panieri di giunco: e coi quattrini che ne ricavava, provvedeva con moltissimo giudizio a tutte le spese giornaliere. Fra le altre cose, costruì da sé stesso un elegante carrettino per condurre a spasso il suo babbo nelle belle giornate, e per fargli prendere una boccata d'aria.

Nelle veglie poi della sera, si esercitava a leggere e a scrivere. Aveva comprato nel vicino paese per pochi centesimi un grosso libro, al quale mancavano il frontespizio e l'indice, e con quello faceva la sua lettura. Quanto allo scrivere, si serviva di un fuscello temperato a uso penna; e non avendo né calamajo né inchiostro, lo intingeva in una boccettina ripiena di sugo di more e di ciliege.

Fatto sta, che con la sua buona volontà d'ingegnarsi, di lavorare e di tirarsi avanti, non solo era riuscito a man-

And from that day on, for more than five months he got up faithfully every morning before dawn so as to turn the windlass and earn the glass of milk that did so much good for the delicate health of his father. But he didn't stop at this, for in his spare time he also learned how to weave all kinds of baskets from rushes; and with the money he gained he provided very sensibly for all their daily needs. Among other things, he built a fine little cart all by himself so as to take his father out on nice days and let him get a breath of fresh air.

And during the evening hours he practiced his reading and writing. In the nearby town, for a few cents he had bought a big book from which the title page and table of contents were missing; and from this he did his reading.[82] As for writing, he used a twig that he sharpened in the manner of a pen; and because he had neither ink nor inkwell, he would dip it into a small vial filled with blackberry-and-cherry juice.

So it was that by his readiness to use his wits, to work and to get ahead, he not only succeeded in keeping his

tenere quasi agiatamente il suo genitore sempre malaticcio, ma per di più aveva potuto mettere da parte anche quaranta soldi per comprarsi un vestitino nuovo.

Una mattina disse a suo padre:

– Vado qui al mercato vicino, a comprarmi una giacchettina, un berrettino e un pajo di scarpe. Quando tornerò a casa – soggiunse ridendo – sarò vestito così bene, che mi scambierete per un gran signore. –

E uscito di casa, cominciò a correre tutto allegro e contento. Quando a un tratto sentì chiamarsi per nome: e voltandosi, vide una bella lumaca che sbucava fuori dalla siepe.

– Non mi riconosci? – disse la Lumaca.

– Mi pare e non mi pare . . .

– Non ti ricordi di quella Lumaca, che stava per cameriera con la Fata dai capelli turchini? non ti rammenti di quella volta, quando scesi a farti lume e che tu rimanesti con un piede confitto nell'uscio di casa?

– Mi rammento di tutto – gridò Pinocchio. – Rispondimi subito, Lumachina bella: dove hai lasciato la mia buona Fata? che fa? mi ha perdonato? si ricorda sempre di me? mi vuol sempre bene? è molto lontana di qui? potrei andare a trovarla? –

A tutte queste domande, fatte precipitosamente e senza ripigliar fiato, la Lumaca rispose con la sua solita flemma:

– Pinocchio mio! La povera Fata giace in un fondo di letto allo spedale! . . .

– Allo spedale? . . .

– Pur troppo. Colpita da mille disgrazie, si è gravemente ammalata, e non ha più da comprarsi un boccon di pane.

– Davvero? . . . Oh! che gran dolore che mi hai dato! Oh! povera Fatina! povera Fatina! povera Fatina! . . . Se avessi un milione, correrei a portarglielo . . . Ma io non ho che quaranta soldi . . . eccoli qui: andavo giusto a

ailing father in reasonable comfort but was even able to put aside forty pennies to buy some nice new clothes for himself.

One morning he said to his father:

"I'm going to the market near here to buy myself a jacket, a nice cap, and a pair of shoes. When I come back home," he added, laughing, "I'll be so well-dressed that you'll take me for a wealthy gentleman."

And when he was outside he began running in high spirits. But all of a sudden he heard himself called by name, and turning around he saw a pretty Snail coming out of the hedge.

"Don't you recognize me?" said the Snail.

"I do, and I don't."

"Don't you remember the Snail who was maid to the Fairy with the blue hair? Don't you remember the time when I came downstairs to make some light for you and you got your foot stuck in the front door?"

"I remember it all," cried Pinocchio. "Tell me quickly, pretty little Snail, where did you leave my good Fairy? What is she doing? Has she forgiven me? Does she still remember me? Does she still love me? Is she very far from here? Can I go and see her?"

To all these questions asked in a rush and without pausing for breath, the Snail answered with her customary composure:

"My dear Pinocchio, the poor Fairy lies bedridden in the hospital."[83]

"In the hospital?"

"Alas, yes. Plagued by a thousand misfortunes she has become seriously ill and no longer has the money to buy herself a bit of bread."

"Really? . . . Oh, how terribly sad you've made me! Oh, poor dear Fairy! Poor dear Fairy! Poor dear Fairy! . . . If I had a million, I'd run and bring it to her . . . But I only have forty pennies . . . Here! I was just

455

comprarmi un vestito nuovo. Prendili, Lumaca, e va' a portarli subito alla mia buona Fata.

– E il tuo vestito nuovo? . . .

– Che m'importa del vestito nuovo? Venderei anche questi cenci che ho addosso, per poterla ajutare! Va', Lumaca, e spicciati: e fra due giorni ritorna qui, ché spero di poterti dare qualche altro soldo. Finora ho lavorato per mantenere il mio babbo: da oggi in là, lavorerò cinque ore di più per mantenere anche la mia buona mamma. Addio, Lumaca, e fra due giorni ti aspetto. –

La Lumaca, contro il suo costume, cominciò a correre come una lucertola nei grandi solleoni d'agosto.

Quando Pinocchio tornò a casa, il suo babbo gli domandò:

– E il vestito nuovo?

– Non m'è stato possibile di trovarne uno che mi tornasse bene. Pazienza! . . . Lo comprerò un'altra volta. –

Quella sera Pinocchio, invece di vegliare fino alle dieci, vegliò fino alla mezzanotte sonata: e invece di far otto canestri di giunco, ne fece sedici.

Poi andò a letto e si addormentò. E nel dormire, gli parve di vedere in sogno la Fata, tutta bella e sorridente, la quale, dopo avergli dato un bacio, gli disse così:

– «Bravo Pinocchio! In grazia del tuo buon cuore, io ti perdono tutte le monellerie che hai fatto fino a oggi. I ragazzi che assistono amorosamente i propri genitori nelle loro miserie e nelle loro infermità, meritano sempre gran lode e grande affetto, anche se non possono esser citati come modelli d'ubbidienza e di buona condotta. Metti giudizio per l'avvenire, e sarai felice». –

A questo punto il sogno finì, e Pinocchio si svegliò con tanto d'occhi spalancati.

Ora immaginatevi voi quale fu la sua meraviglia quando, svegliandosi, si accòrse che non era più un burattino di legno: ma che era diventato, invece, un ra-

on my way to buy myself some new clothes. Take these, Snail, and bring them quickly to my good Fairy."

"And your new clothes?"

"What do I care about new clothes? I'd even sell these rags I've got on to help her. Go, Snail, and hurry! But come back here in two days, because I hope to be able to give you some more money. Until now I've been working to support my father; but from now on I'll work five hours more every day so as to support my good mother, too. Good-bye, Snail; I'll expect you in two days."

Contrary to her usual custom, the Snail darted off like a lizard in the torrid days of August.

When Pinocchio returned home his father asked him:

"And your new clothes?"

"I couldn't find any that fitted me well.[84] But that's all right! . . . I'll buy some another time."

That night, instead of staying up until ten o'clock, Pinocchio stayed up working until after midnight; and instead of making eight baskets, he made sixteen.

Then he went to bed and fell asleep. And while he slept, he dreamed that he saw the Fairy, all smiling and beautiful, who gave him a kiss and said:

"Well done, Pinocchio! Because of your good heart I forgive you all the mischief you've done up to now. Boys who take loving care of their parents when they are sick and in need always deserve a great deal of praise and love, even if they cannot be commended as models of obedience and good behavior. Be sensible and good in the future, and you'll be happy."

Here the dream ended, and Pinocchio awoke with his eyes wide open.

Now just imagine his amazement when, upon awaking, he found that he was no longer a wooden puppet, but that he had turned into a boy like all other boys. He

gazzo come tutti gli altri. Dètte un'occhiata all'intorno e invece delle solite pareti di paglia della capanna, vide una bella camerina ammobiliata e agghindata con una semplicità quasi elegante. Saltando giù dal letto, trovò preparato un bel vestiario nuovo, un berretto nuovo e un pajo di stivaletti di pelle, che gli tornavano una vera pittura.

Appena si fu vestito, gli venne fatto naturalmente di mettere le mani nelle tasche e tirò fuori un piccolo portamonete d'avorio, sul quale erano scritte queste parole: «La Fata dai capelli turchini restituisce al suo caro Pinocchio i quaranta soldi e lo ringrazia tanto del suo buon cuore.» Aperto il portafoglio, invece dei 40 soldi di rame, vi luccicavano quaranta zecchini d'oro, tutti nuovi di zecca.

Dopo andò a guardarsi allo specchio, e gli parve d'essere un altro. Non vide più riflessa la solita immagine della marionetta di legno, ma vide l'immagine vispa e intelligente di un bel fanciullo coi capelli castagni, cogli occhi celesti e con un'aria allegra e festosa come una pasqua di rose.

In mezzo a tutte queste meraviglie, che si succedevano le une alle altre, Pinocchio non sapeva più nemmeno lui se era desto davvero o se sognava sempre a occhi aperti.

– E il mio babbo dov'è? – gridò tutt'a un tratto: ed entrato nella stanza accanto trovò il vecchio Geppetto sano, arzillo e di buon umore, come una volta, il quale, avendo ripreso subito la sua professione d'intagliatore, stava appunto disegnando una bellissima cornice ricca di fogliami, di fiori e di testine di diversi animali.

– Levatemi una curiosità, babbino: ma come si spiega tutto questo cambiamento improvviso? – gli domandò Pinocchio saltandogli al collo e coprendolo di baci.

gave a look around him, and instead of the usual straw walls of the cottage, he saw a beautiful, cozy room, furnished and decorated with tasteful simplicity. Jumping out of bed, he found a fine new suit of clothes prepared for him, a new cap, and a pair of leather ankle-boots that fitted him to perfection.

As soon as he had dressed, he quite naturally put his hands in his pockets, and drew out a little ivory money-case on which these words were written: "The Fairy with blue hair returns the forty pennies to her dear Pinocchio and thanks him so much for his good heart." When he opened the money-case, instead of the forty copper pennies there were forty gold pieces glittering in it, all mint new.

Then he went to look at himself in the mirror, and he thought he was somebody else. He no longer saw the usual image of the wooden marionette reflected there;[85] instead he saw the lively, intelligent image of a handsome boy with chestnut brown hair and light blue eyes, and with a festive air about him that made him seem as happy as a holiday.

In the midst of all these wonders that were following one upon the other, not even Pinocchio himself knew whether he was really awake or whether he was still dreaming with his eyes open.

"But where's my father?" he cried out suddenly; and going into the next room he found old Geppetto—sound, sprightly, and cheerful as in former days—who had already taken up his trade of wood carver again and was, in fact, designing a beautiful picture frame richly decorated with leaves, flowers, and little heads of various animals.

"Dear Father, satisfy my curiosity for me: what's the cause of all this sudden change?" Pinocchio asked him, throwing his arms around his neck and covering him with kisses.

– Questo improvviso cambiamento in casa nostra è tutto merito tuo – disse Geppetto.

– Perché merito mio? . . .

– Perché quando i ragazzi, di cattivi diventano buoni, hanno la virtù di far prendere un aspetto nuovo e sorridente anche all'interno delle loro famiglie.

– E il vecchio Pinocchio di legno dove si sarà nascosto?

– Eccolo là – rispose Geppetto: e gli accennò un grosso burattino appoggiato a una seggiola, col capo girato sur una parte, con le braccia ciondoloni e con le gambe incrocicchiate e ripiegate a mezzo, da parere un miracolo se stava ritto.

Pinocchio si voltò a guardarlo; e dopo che l'ebbe guardato un poco, disse dentro di sé con grandissima compiacenza:

– Com'ero buffo, quand'ero un burattino! e come ora son contento di esser diventato un ragazzino perbene! . . . –

"This sudden change in our house is all your doing," said Geppetto.

"Why my doing?"

"Because when children go from bad to good, they have the power of making things take on a bright new look inside within their families too."

"And the old Pinocchio of wood, where could he have gone to hide?"

"There he is over there," answered Geppetto; and he pointed to a large puppet propped against a chair, its head turned to one side, its arms dangling, and its legs crossed and folded in the middle so that it was a wonder that it stood up at all.

Pinocchio turned and looked at it; and after he had looked at it for a while, he said to himself with a great deal of satisfaction:

"How funny I was when I was a puppet! And how glad I am now that I've become a proper boy!"

Appendix

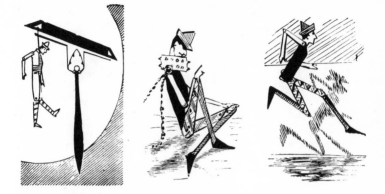

FIGURES 1–5. The first illustrations made specifically for Collodi's tale were done by Ugo Fleres, for serial publication in the *Giornale per i bambini*. The first of them served as a stylized capital T of the initial word (*Tutti*) in the *Giornale*'s announcement that Pinocchio was alive and well and that the author was resuming, in the same issue (February 2, 1882), the puppet's story under the title *Le avventure di Pinocchio*. The T-as-gallows, with Pinocchio hanging from it, was a vivid reminder of the puppet's apparent catastrophic end, which had closed *La storia di un burattino* in the *Giornale* almost four months earlier, on October 27, 1881.

FIGURE 6. An early advertisement for the first book edition of *Pinocchio*, contemporary with the book's publication. It includes two vignettes that the artist, Enrico Mazzanti, added to the original sixty-two in subsequent editions of the book. The caption in the announcement reads: "In this short tale there is all the essence of Italian good sense grafted to a most genuine *humor* that can no longer rightly be called English."

FIGURE 7. Mazzanti. Pinocchio is stopped by the carabiniere (chapter 3).

FIGURE 8. Mazzanti.
The prancing
puppet
(chapter 8).

FIGURE 9. Mazzanti.
Pinocchio receives a tumultuous
welcome by his brothers-in-wood
in the puppet theater (chapter 10).

FIGURE 10.
Mazzanti.
Pinocchio,
seeking to
escape from
the assassins,
begs the Little
Girl with blue
hair to let
him in
(chapter 15).

FIGURE 11.
Mazzanti.
Pinocchio and
Geppetto, on the
back of the Tuna,
make their escape
from the Great Shark
(chapter 36).

C. COLLODI

Le
Avventure
di
Pinocchio

Storia di un burattino
illustrata
da
CARLO CHIOSTRI

Incisioni di A. BONGINI.

Nuova edizione

FIRENZE
R. Bemporad & Figlio · Editori.
Filiali: MILANO · ROMA · PISA

FIGURE 12.
The cover/frontispiece
of Carlo Chiostri's
illustrated *Pinocchio*.

FIGURE 13.
Chiostri.
Pinocchio is
stopped by
the carabiniere
(chapter 3).

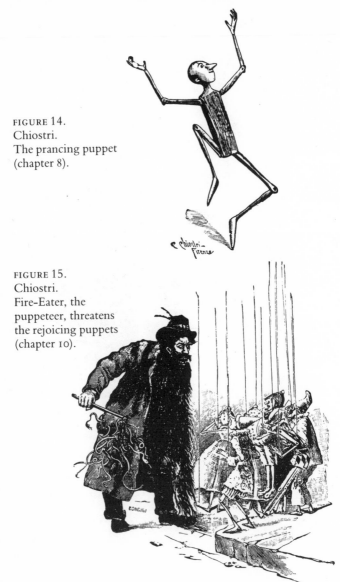

FIGURE 14.
Chiostri.
The prancing puppet
(chapter 8).

FIGURE 15.
Chiostri.
Fire-Eater, the
puppeteer, threatens
the rejoicing puppets
(chapter 10).

FIGURE 16. Chiostri.
The four rabbit
pallbearers (chapter 17).

FIGURE 17. Chiostri. Pinocchio, made to serve as a watchdog, is approached by a thieving marten (chapter 22).

FIGURE 18. Chiostri. Pinocchio astride the Great Pigeon (chapter 23).

FIGURE 19.
Chiostri.
Pinocchio,
in the belly
of the Great Shark,
makes his way
toward a glimmer
of light where he
will find Geppetto
(chapter 35).

Notes to the Text
and Translation

1. Once upon a time (*C'era una volta*).   Fourteen of the fifteen fairy tales translated by Collodi in 1875 from Perrault, Mme d'Aulnoy, and Mme Leprince de Beaumont
begin with the time-out-of-time formula "Once upon a
time." So too does *The Adventures of Pinocchio*, except that
here Collodi quickly undercuts the fairy-tale expectations
with a reversal to humble reality—the simple piece of
wood—only to enter immediately upon the alternation
between fantastical and realistic elements. Throughout
the rest of the tale, fantasy and realism are integrated in a
playful and ironic synthesis in which the dominant vision
and guiding spirit is the reality principle.

2. the fact of the matter is (*il fatto gli è che*).   This *gli*, ety-
mologically related to the fully stressed *egli*, which is used
in the same way, is an enclitic subject pronoun (neuter-
masculine, third-person singular) whose use is compulsory in the Florentine dialect before a verb beginning
with a vowel. It can be felt as pleonastic only by non-
Florentines. While this introductory form occurs several
times in the speech of Pinocchio and other characters, this
is the only time the narrator indulges in it in his own
voice.

   Master Anthony (*mastr'Antonio*).   *Mastro* is an abbreviated form of *maestro*. Both words were used in earlier
times to refer to those master craftsmen and artists who
owned their own shops or ateliers and taught those working under them. The form *mastro* won out and became a
title of respect even for craftsmen owning a shop that employed nobody, such as in the case of *mastr'Antonio*, and
eventually the title was applied also to the owner or head
of other concerns such as industrial and building enter-
prises. In Collodi's tale, as in the Tuscany of his time,
mastro already has a humorous connotation, which is
compounded by being coupled with the nickname

Cherry, by which Collodi jokingly wishes to suggest that Master Anthony was a tippler.

3. fountain gargoyle (*mascherone da fontana*).   Literally this detail refers to the sculpted grotesque heads often serving as fountain waterspouts. They have their origin in the masks of the theater of antiquity.

4. my belly (*sul corpo*).   Here, *corpo* means 'belly', as in Tuscan usage, and not 'body' as in the national language; it can also mean 'body' for Tuscans, too, but confusion is easily avoided by the context (see note 78).

5. disfigured (*trasfigurito*).   More than the form *trasfigurare*, the verb *trasfigurire*, a Tuscan usage, indicates a change for the worse in one's physical appearance.

6. polenta (*polendina*).   *Polendina* is a diminutive of Tuscan *polenda* (or *pulenda*), the standard Italian form of which is *polenta*, the well-known Italian corn meal whose color is a much more intense yellow than that of American corn mush. Polendina's real name, *Geppetto*, is itself something of a nickname (a rare one), derived from *Giuseppe* (Joseph) with a diminutive suffix: G[ius]eppe + etto.

7. It wasn't me (*Non sono stato io*).   It is impossible for even the most uneducated Italian to be "ungrammatical" in this kind of construction. But it is unlikely that uneducated tradesmen speaking in English would say "It wasn't *I*" or "It's actually *he*!" And an American or British Pinocchio will naturally alternate between the nominative and the accusative, according to the moment and the situation.

8. precious (*bravo*).   Applied, as it is here, to objects of little intrinsic worth that are nonetheless held dear, *bravo* has a humorous or ironic quality.

9. under a staircase (*sottoscala*).   *Sottoscala* refers to the space under a staircase, normally used as a storage area. What is meant here is the recessed area beneath an external stairway that leads to what is the first floor in European parlance. At the end of this recessed areaway is a wall, on the other side of which is Geppetto's small ground-floor room. For the room to receive its light from such an areaway can only mean that the recessed wall has a window,

a small one, as indeed was often though not always the case in such houses, especially in rural villages. Since the recessed area, though unenclosed, is covered by the underarch of the stairway, little enough light would filter into Geppetto's room. The window understood here is unlikely to be the open window out of which, in chapter 5, the newly hatched chick will escape, and it is certainly not the window through which Geppetto climbs to get back into his house in chapter 7. Such "inconsistencies" (and several others in the tale) need concern us no more than they did Collodi and his first readers, which is to say not at all. The other window in Geppetto's room will materialize when and because Collodi needs it as a prop for the specific situation and action he is yet to invent.

10. Literally, *pinocchio* means 'pine nut', 'pine kernel', 'pine seed'. Into the nineteenth century the standard Italian word that dictionaries give for the pine nut is *pinocchio*, but they indicate that in Florence the more common word is *pinolo* and that in other Tuscan dialects it is *pignolo*, *pigniuolo*, or *pinoccolo* (the latter in Pistoia). Nonetheless, in a piece entitled "La Colonna di Mercato," Collodi has an imaginary marketplace column situated in the heart of Florence, proud of its knowledge of the Florentine vernacular that it has heard for years, speak of *pinocchi* and not *pinoli* (see *Note gaie* [Florence, 1892], pp. 139–140). Evidently, then, in Florence the older term *pinocchio* was already giving way to *pinolo*. But for phonetic and historical reasons *pinocchio* was for Collodi the more expressive term. While it is quite likely that many of the first readers of Collodi's tale were amused at hearing of a family of Pinenuts, clearly no translator would be so rash as to anglicize the puppet's name.

11. perfect jackass (*bellissimo somaro*). This is the first and apparently casual reference to Pinocchio's eventual metamorphosis into an ass. Because the donkey motif is truly of the essence in the story, it is well to take note of the three terms employed in referring to the animal. In Tuscan usage *ciuco* had already become the most familiar of the three, having overtaken *asino* both in literal and fig-

urative meanings. *Somaro* was the least frequently employed of the words available and has since come to be
called upon almost solely in the figurative sense. For the
most part, *ciuco* and *asino* were interchangeable. Although *asinino* was known as a diminutive noun with an
endearing connotation, the more commonly used diminutive deriving from *asino* was *asinello*. As an adjective,
asinino, though not common in the spoken language, was
used in both a literal (or scientific) sense and in a figurative
sense. *Ciuchino* was current both as an adjective and as the
diminutive of *ciuco*. Proverbs and idioms containing
these various words for donkey are plentiful in Italian,
and the circumstances in which Collodi places Pinocchio
are sometimes situational puns based on one or another
of them.

12. in the poorhouse (*allo spedale*).   I have translated *ospedale*
as 'poorhouse', and not as 'hospital', the more common
meaning and the one intended in chapter 36 in connection
with the hospital where, according to the Snail's report to
Pinocchio, the Fairy lies penniless and ill. The expression
morire allo spedale, which seems to be alluded to and implied in both cases, means 'to be reduced to dire poverty'
or 'to die in extreme misery'.

13. a hunger so thick that you could cut it with a knife (*una
fame da tagliarsi col coltello*).   This is one of those vivid
tragico-humorous idioms Italian has in connection with
the theme of food and hunger. A similar expression is *una
fame da pigliarla con le mani* (a hunger that could be held in
one's hands). Such expressions imaginatively expand or
externalize the physiological sensation of hunger into a
"perceptible" object, substituting a paradoxically "pal-
pable" nothingness for solid food, the desire for which is
implied in the image. Thus, a few lines later we note that
Pinocchio's anxious search for food in the room leads him
to *nulla, il gran nulla, proprio nulla* (nothing, a whole lot of
nothing, plain nothing), where the phrase *il gran nulla* hu-
morously echoes a philosophical concept of metaphysical
import that had evidently been brought down to earth in
the popular language of the time.

14. yawning (*sbadigliare*). Physiologically and idiomatically, yawning is associated with hunger, at least in Italian and French (cf. *sbadigliare dalla fame*, to yawn from hunger). So too spitting, for it seems that salivation is activated by the digestive system in time of hunger.

15. soft-boiled egg (*uovo a bere*). *Uovo a bere*, as Tempesti (p. 28, n. 9) points out, denotes an egg to be drunk raw, that is, sucked from the shell that has been pierced at either end. Until the fourth edition (1888) of *Pinocchio*, the phrase appears as *uovo da bere* (soft-boiled egg), which makes more sense here. (The image of sucking an egg, though not the exact phrase, occurs in chapter 34.)

16. Bye, bye, for now (*Arrivedella*). The popular Tuscan form of *arrivederla*. The ceremonious chick addresses Pinocchio with the ultradeferential *Lei* pronoun, as opposed to the less formal but still deferential *voi* or the familiar *tu* that one might expect from a less ironic chick. In chapter 24 Pinocchio, without irony but with a certain ceremonious urbanity, uses the *Lei* form of address in speaking to an obliging Dolphin. He also accords him the title *signore*, just as the chick does to Pinocchio. And Pinocchio also repeats the farewell greeting *Arrivedella* in the same popular Tuscan pronunciation.

17. a horrid, hellish night (*una nottataccia d'inferno*). Contrary to the reading in the *Giornale per i bambini*, the first book edition of *Pinocchio* (1883) gives the prepositional phrase as *d'inverno* (wintry) rather than *d'inferno*. In the next chapter, where he gives the first of his kaleidoscopic résumés of his misadventures, Pinocchio himself refers to the horrible night he has passed as a *nottata d'inferno*. The expression *nottataccia d'inferno* used by the narrator—even more hyperbolic than Pinocchio's phrase (the common and more spontaneous expression)—is in keeping with Collodi's ironic and ambiguously sadistic manipulation of his puppet, as well as with his oral storytelling manner. For all that, and despite the second edition's restoration of *d'inferno*, the reading *d'inverno* has been perpetuated because of the privileged place of the first edition (see Pollidori, pp. lv–lviii). For this reason most

translations, especially those in English, speak of a "wintry" rather than an "infernal" night.

18. little hat (*cappelluccio*). The *-uccio* diminutive here connotes a commiserative quality. As for the basinful (*catinellata*) of water that is dumped on Pinocchio, an adult reader of the time might very well have understood it to be a chamber pot.

19. fifth story (*quinto piano*). The *quinto piano* (actually, the sixth floor) would have been considered the top floor of an urban residential apartment building.

20. five miles (*cinque chilometri*). I have used *miles* for *kilometers* because they remain more familiar to us.

21. fussy (*boccuccia*). *Boccuccia*, a diminutive of *bocca*, would usually mean 'a pretty little mouth'. However, just as *-uccio* can have a commiserative value (*cappelluccio*; and in this chapter, *Pinocchiuccio*), so too it can be ironic or lightly disparaging as it is here.

22. jacket (*casacca*). The *casacca* was a three-quarter-length jacket, with or without a belt, and with slits on the sides. Its origin was Russian in name and object—*kozak, kazak*. Although Rigutini speaks of it as no longer in use (save in the expression *voltar casacca*, to change sides, to pass over to the enemy), Collodi uses the word repeatedly in the most natural way, perhaps in the generic sense registered by Giorgini and Broglio: 'an ample jacket of coarse material'.

23. woolen jacket (*casacca di panno*). Although *panno* is the term for cloth in general, in Collodi's time it referred more particularly to woolen cloth, and surely a "wealthy" Pinocchio has at least that much in mind in wishing to protect his father from the cold.

24. In the light of this emblematic episode, the name Collodi gave to his puppet again proves to be as appropriate as it is curious. In addition to the food metaphor inherent in his name, "Pinocchio" is acoustically in keeping with the funny-sounding names of two of the most well-known commedia dell'arte stock characters, precisely those represented by the marionettes on the stage where "Arlecchino" and "Pulcinella" are quarreling. That they inter-

rupt their performance to hail the newly arrived puppet as one of their own suggests that Pinocchio too is a stock character: that of the wayward child, perhaps the ever-hungry wayward child whose name might well have been Pistacchio were it not that *pinocchio* was more readily associated with the hard wood of the pine tree and also perhaps still more commonly known in Florence as a term and as a food.

25. gendarmes (*giandarmi*). More "correctly," *gendarmi* (pl.). This popular form of the French word had come to be used in those states in Italy where, before unification, a military corps (*gendarmeria*) based on the French model was instituted for the express purpose of watching over the public safety and carrying out other police functions. Its use here is certainly ironic or humorous—the phrase *faccia da gendarme* was used to indicate an ugly face or person. Hence the use of the term *giandarme* in chapter 19 to refer to the mastiff-officers who march Pinocchio off to prison after the gorilla-judge has sentenced him is particularly humorous and caustic. When an officer of the peace is presented in *Pinocchio* in human guise and with little or no irony, he is called a *carabiniere*, which already in the 1880s had all but supplanted *gendarme*. In Collodi's tale, then, the lexical division of the two terms is also made on the basis of a division between the fantastic and the realistic elements. The marionettes and the mastiffs are *gendarmes*; the human officers of the peace are *carabinieri*.

26. As Tempesti (p. 55, n. 9) notes, *signore* (sir, mister) was in Collodi's time an honorific title given only to persons of some importance and was the minimum title of respect so applied. Moreover, all the titles Pinocchio tries on Fire-Eater were applicable to "important" persons of the middle class. Pollidori (p. 177, n. 6) observes that the alternation between the capitalized and noncapitalized forms *Cavaliere*, *cavalieri*, *Commendatore*, *commendatori* underscores the contrast between the emphasis of the ingratiating appellation as used by Pinocchio and the rejection of those titles in the sharp replies by Fire-Eater, who will be satisfied with nothing less than *Eccellenza*. Col-

lodi, of course, is poking fun at the well-known Italian enchantment with titles of honor.

27. the Fox (*la Volpe*).   In Italian, *volpe* is grammatically feminine whether it refers to a male or female fox. Thus feminine pronouns and adjectives are used to refer to this character, although this fox is a male—a con man and "assassin." The same is true of the thieving Martens —*le Faine*—in chapter 22. In the case of the Marmot (*la Marmotta*) and the Snail (*la Lumaca*) grammatical gender and semantic value are at one in declaring their feminine character.

28. Poor Blackbird (*Povero Merlo*).   As with the presence of all the specific animals in *Pinocchio*, the choice of this particular bird is laden with significance. In the nineteenth century, *merlo* had 'deceiver' as one of its figurative meanings. The expression *Canta, merlo!* (Sing, blackbird) was used to let someone know that his words and attempts at deception were not going to succeed. In this episode, of course, the poor singing *merlo* is not aiming to deceive, but rather to undeceive Pinocchio. But *merlo* also had a contrasting figurative meaning—one still very much in use in parts of Italy—of one who is gullible or naive. Thus there is even greater irony, both verbal and situational, in Pinocchio's expression of commiseration for the Blackbird's fate: it is Pinocchio who is the *povero merlo* in this second figurative sense.

29. And walk and walk and walk (*Cammina, cammina, cammina*).   Collodi often uses the descriptive imperative, a popular and picturesque mode of expression, especially with verbs of motion.

30. entremets (*tornagusto*).   After his first course, the Fox orders a *tornagusto*, a flavorful or spicy small portion of food served to revive a diner's appetite.

31. blue hair (*capelli turchini*).   Italian has several words for various shades or qualities of blue, but Collodi used *turchino* to translate the French *bleu* in his rendering of Marie C. d'Aulnoy's famous art fairy tale, *L'oiseau bleu*; see note 33.

32. And almost at death's door, he stuttered (*e balbettò quasi moribondo*). These words do not appear in the original serial version. An awkward interpolation introduced by Collodi (or by an editor) for the book edition of the tale, they attempt to attenuate or undo the description of Pinocchio's actual death by hanging and thereby make plausible his revival in the succeeding chapter. As I note in the introductory essay, when the present chapter was printed in the *Giornale per i bambini* (October 28, 1881) it carried the words *continuo e fine* (continuation and end) inasmuch as it was clearly meant to be the end of the tale and the puppet. Only at the urging of the *Giornale*'s little readers and editor did Collodi decide to resume his tale. In the issue of November 10, 1881, the *Giornale* carried the following notice by the editor: "A piece of good news. Signor Collodi has written to tell me that his friend Pinocchio is still alive, and that he will be able to tell you more interesting tales concerning him. It's only natural; a puppet, someone made of wood like Pinocchio, is pretty tough and it's not easy to do away with him. So then, our readers are informed: quite soon we shall begin the second part of *The Story of a Puppet* with the title *The Adventures of Pinocchio*." The first serial (chapter 16 of the book) of this second part appeared on February 16, 1882. At the opening of the new chapter Collodi felt he could effectively offset Pinocchio's actual death by speaking of the puppet as *seeming* more dead than alive, and by parenthetically informing his readers that the "dead" Little Girl with blue hair was really a good Fairy.

33. In this transition to the second part of his tale, Collodi, having transformed the Little Girl into a Fairy, is led to introduce a greater element of the traditional fairy tale than we find in the first part. Nonetheless, in a commentary on this fantastical carriage, Tempesti (p. 89, n. 12) argues for the realistic basis in which Collodi grounds the fairy-tale element: the "color of air" is a metaphor used to indicate the brightness of the carriage's painted exterior; the interior is padded with canary feathers, softer, as it were, than ordinary feathers; and the white lining, ev-

idently of silk, is thickly quilted in "peaks" that resemble whipped cream and ladyfingers (Savoy sponge biscuits) immersed in custard. Tempesti holds that the metaphors were part of the language of the upholsterers of the age, and the substance of his remarks seems valid to me. As to the "color of air," however, it is likely that *aria* here means 'sky' and that Collodi is suggesting the color blue (*turchino*), the same blue as the Fairy's hair. In his translation of Mme d'Aulnoy's *L'oiseau bleu*, Collodi renders the first line of the recurring refrain as "Uccello turchino, color del cielo" (in the original: "Oiseau bleu, couleur du temps"); in *Tutto Collodi*, ed. P. Pancrazi (Florence, 1942), p. 431. For the rest it is symptomatic that in the fantastical description of the Fairy's carriage, Collodi has found a way to translate the "reality" at least partly into food metaphors.

34. The medicine Pinocchio must take is, of course, a purgative, very likely the extremely bitter Epsom salts or something similar, known to Italians as *sale inglese* (English salt).

35. crunching (*sgranocchiata*). The suffixal forms -*occhiare*, -*acchiare*, -*iucchiare* are often attached to verbs to create a grotesque or humorous quality. *Sgranocchiare* seems to be an onomatopoeic elaboration of *sgranare*.

36. little sister (*sorellina*). The Fairy's words suggest that she still has the appearance of a little girl, as in chapter 15. But in chapter 16, although she is still referred to as *Bambina* (Little Girl), she has an adult and even an aristocratic bearing of the kind we associate with fairy godmothers; and in chapter 17 she seems more like a middle-class mother. Beginning in chapter 16 Pinocchio addresses her with the deferential *voi*, as in the present case.

37. honest men (*galantuomini*). *Galantuomini* has a rich tradition of ironic and satirical use in the nineteenth century, especially in the works of Manzoni and Verga.

38. the heart of a Caesar (*un cuore di Cesare*). The expression depends upon Caesar's proverbial generosity toward his conquered enemies after he became absolute ruler of Rome.

39. Catchafool (*Acchiappa-citrulli*). The Italian compound consists of the verb *acchiappare* (to seize) and the plural form of the noun *citrullo*. The latter is the Neapolitan variant of the standard Italian *cetriolo* (from late Latin *citriolum*) whose literal meaning is 'cucumber' although it, too, is sometimes used figuratively to refer to a foolish or stupid person. However, *citrullo* became the more common and, indeed, the specialized term throughout Italy for the figurative meaning. As for the fleeced sheep (*pecore tosate*) who appear in Collodi's next sentence, the figurative meaning of *to fleece* holds also for *tosare*.

40. happy as a holiday (*contenti come pasque*). *Pasqua* refers above all to the Christian Easter (or Pasch), a truly happy holiday, but in common usage it is extended to other religious feast days. Thus near the very end of chapter 36 Pinocchio, finally a real and proper boy, is said to be as joyous as a *pasqua di rose*, which is literally, in popular speech, 'Pentecost'.

41. rules of etiquette (*Galateo*). *Galateo*, which has become part of the standard Italian language, derives from the title of the sixteenth-century compendium written by Giovanni Della Casa as a guide to good manners.

42. lacking in salt (*dolce di sale*). The exquisitely humorous Italian expression literally means 'sweet as far as salt is concerned', which is to say not salty enough. First applied to culinary matters, its use came to include the figurative sense of salt as wisdom, as in the present case.

43. like a bolt out of the blue (*fra capo e collo*). The Italian idiom—literally, 'between the head and the neck'—has its origin in the practice of killing animals, say, a rabbit, with a sudden blow to the base of the skull.

   dumbfounded (*rimase di princisbecco*). *Princisbecco* (also *princisbecche* in Tuscan) was an alloy of copper and zinc used, among other things, to imitate gold in cheap jewelry. Its name comes from its inventor Christopher Pinchbeck (c. 1670–1732), whence the English *pinchbeck* with the figurative meaning of sham. While the Italian word also carried this secondary meaning, the expression *rimanere di princisbecco* was used figuratively to refer to one

485

who has been disappointed and feels cheated or, more dramatically, to one who has been caught by surprise and is left dumbfounded.

44. they were martens (*erano faine*). I might have called these animals *polecats* rather than *martens* but for the fact that, for many Americans, *polecats* are, literally and figuratively, *skunks*. The term *faina*, in any case, has the figurative meaning of an ugly or bad person, though it was more readily understood in this sense in Collodi's time than it is today.

45. I could punish you, but I am not that base (*Potrei punirvi, ma sì vil non sono!*) The Italian sentence forms a hendecasyllabic verse with a mock-tragic intonation. It is reminiscent of the seriously intended style of certain nineteenth-century opera libretti. I suspect that the line, or at least the second part of it, comes straight from the libretto to Bellini's *Norma*. Collodi, we recall, was a drama and opera critic of sorts.

46. In addressing his lamentation to the Fairy, whom he presumes to be dead, Pinocchio uses the intimate *tu*. When, in the next chapter, he discovers her to be alive and apparently old enough to be his mother, he reverts to the deferential *voi*.

47. A proverb current in Collodi's time says "In tempo di carestia è buono il pan di vecce" (In a time of famine, bread made of vetches is good).

48. handkerchief (*moccichino*). The standard or neutral word is *fazzoletto*, whereas *moccichino* has a humorous and mocking quality. It is typical of Collodi's unwillingness or inability to be wholly serious (or too somber in a story addressed to children?) that he should find it possible to be jocular or ironic in such a context. Similarly, earlier in this chapter, after Pinocchio's lacerating expression of grief over his "dead" Fairy's tombstone, Collodi undercuts the scene's extreme pathos by noting that the puppet could not tear his hair out because it was made of wood.

49. Collodi's phrasing suggests the stress he gives to the work ethic and the responsibility of each individual in its re-

gard. It is in keeping with the greater overt didactic and moralizing bent that his tale took on following the puppet's revival and the continuation of the story with chapter 16.

50. knee-high to a grasshopper (*un soldo di cacio*).   Literally, the Italian phrase refers to a penny's worth of cheese; but in reference to height, it is idiomatic and as colloquial as is the expression I have used in rendering it.

51. a boy (*un ragazzo*).   Here Collodi had originally written *uomo* (man), the word printed in the serialized version of the *Giornale per i bambini*, in keeping with Pinocchio's earlier utterance in the chapter stating his desire to be a *man*. But between the first utterance and the present one, *ragazzo perbene* (proper boy) became the more appropriate phrase and first goal for the puppet. Thus in passing from the serialized printing to the publication of the tale as a book, *uomo* was here changed to *ragazzo*, a correction that Collodi himself may very well have made.

52. wise guy (*berlicche*).   The Italian word is a humorous term given to the devil; its comicality derives from its phonically bizarre quality. In Italian folklore demons and the devil are often called by funny-sounding nicknames, usually applied to them by peasants who have outwitted them.

53. *Giannettino* and *Minuzzolo* are schoolbooks written by Collodi in the years immediately preceding *Pinocchio*. (I touch on them in my introductory essay.) The Florentine educator Pietro Thouar (1809–1861) was one of the first popular writers of books for Italian schoolchildren. Unencumbered in style, his stories reveal a true awareness of Italy's social problems, and his sympathy for the poor is sincere. Ida Baccini (1850–1911), also Florentine, wrote children's stories that center on tender domestic values. Though of little literary value, her *Memorie di un pulcino* (1875)—*Memoirs of a Little Chick*—has considerable historical importance. It recounts the story of events in two families—the one bourgeois, the other of the peasant class—seen through the adventures of a little chick. The self-irony of Collodi's passage is not without its

practical reason, for he is also managing to advertise his own scholastic books and those of other writers published by his editor, Felice Paggi.

54. with their heads on! (*col capo*). The humor lies in the fact that anchovies, then as now, were usually seen after their heads had been removed in order to make more room in the barrel in which they were packed and salted.

55. a new fish (*pesce nuovo*). Besides the irony implicit in the Green Fisherman's taking Pinocchio for a crab—*prendere un granchio* (to catch a crab = to make a blunder)— there is the ironic use of *nuovo*, which carries its alternative connotations of 'strange' and 'foolish'. Indeed, the figurative meaning of *pesce nuovo* (or *nuovo pesce*) is 'poor fish' or 'simpleton'. Cf. *pesce d'aprile*, the Italian expression for our April fool's joke.

56. *caffè-e-latte*. Hot milk with a dash of coffee. buns buttered on the inside and on the outside (*panini imburrati di dentro e di fuori*). This reading first appears in the fourth edition (1888). Until then, beginning with the version printed in the *Giornale per i bambini*, the wording was *panini imburrati di sotto e di sopra* (buns buttered underneath and above, i.e., on both sides).

57. scrawny (*allampanato*). *Allampanare* means 'to grow thin or lean'; *allampanato* is often coupled with another word meaning 'thin', such as *secco* or *asciutto*, to make for a superlative binomial, a characteristic Florentine mode (cf. *innamorato pazzo*). The term comes from the word for lamp, *làmpana* (*lampada*), oil lamps of an earlier time and of a modest kind that were tubular.

58. [for midnight]. The Italian text as given in Pollidori's critical edition makes no mention of midnight at this point, although all previous editions of Collodi's tale, beginning with the serialized version in the *Giornale per i bambini*, indicate that Lampwick specifically mentions it: "Aspetto la mezzanotte, per partire." Pollidori has taken one of her rare liberties with Collodi's text and deleted the reference in order to avoid the incongruency that ensued in the first book edition when Collodi, seeking to correct a minor discrepancy concerning the references to

NOTES TO PAGES 349-63

time in the serialized text, eliminated three references to midnight, leaving the first one intact. I have "restored" the reference, in brackets, because of the importance of the concept of midnight as the hour of danger or evil. It may not be that Collodi, as Pollidori thinks, overlooked this first allusion to the witching hour, but rather that he was reluctant to erase all mention of it.

59. six Thursdays and a Sunday (*sei giovedì e una domenica*). In Collodi's day, there was no school on Thursday nor, or course, on Sunday. In a humorous piece entitled "Quand'ero ragazzo" (When I Was a Boy) and addressed to little readers, Collodi writes: "And naturally I too had to go to school every day, except on Thursdays and Sundays. But the Thursdays were so few in the course of the year! Barely one a week! And Sundays? . . . Why it was a real blessing if Sundays came around once every seven days" (*Tutto Collodi*, p. 265). And Collodi's Giannettino says: " 'You know, mother! If it had been I who invented the calendar, I would have put four Sundays and three Thursdays into every week' " (*Giannettino: Libro per ragazzi*, 4th ed. [Florence, 1880], pp. 9–10).

60. [That's too bad . . .]. I have retained, again in brackets, the second deletion Pollidori makes in her effort to square the time references in this chapter. Collodi's text reads: " 'Peccato! Se alla partenza mancasse un'ora sola, sarei quasi quasi capace di aspettare.' " In the serialized version, this sentence is preceded by Lampwick's phrase: " 'Fra due ore!' " (In two hours!). The change, permanent, to " 'Fra poco!' " (In a little while!) appears in the first book edition.

61. men's high-shoes (*stivalleti da uomo*). This detail calls to mind the well-known definition of an ignoramus: *un ciuco calzato e vestito* (an ass wearing shoes and clothes).

62. first pair (*prima pariglia*). Not the lead pair of the team of donkeys, but the first pair from the carriage.

63. whim (*grillo*). Grillo—literally, 'cricket'—is used idiomatically, with its image of one or more crickets crawling around in one's head, to indicate whims or foolishness. A concomitant idiom is sadistically played upon by the little

man: *levare* (or *cacciare*) *i grilli dal capo* (to remove [or drive out] the crickets, i.e., the whims), which is what the little man is satisfied he has accomplished by savagely biting off the donkey's ear, itself a humorous literalization of the expression *carezze asinine* (or *ciuchine*) used to refer to caresses so rough that they could hurt.

64. he'll laugh on his wedding day (*riderà quando sarà sposo*). A common expression often employed by mothers about children who cry over trifles.

65. playing at walnuts (*giocava alle noci*). A children's game in which each player's task was to knock over a pile of walnuts using another walnut; also *a nocino*.

66. asinine ears (*orecchi asinini*). In the chapter heading we have *orecchi di ciuco* (donkey's ears) and later in the chapter the synonym *orecchi d'asino*. But here, with the first mention of the phenomenon, Collodi deliberately uses *asinini*, the less common and rather more technical or scientific adjective, quite in keeping with the spoofingly elevated tone of the sentence. However, use of the technical adjective in the ironic idiomatic expression *carezze asinine* was already current (see note 63). The expression *orecchi di ciuco* also referred to a dunce's cap: "a sort of band from which arise two large ears, similar to those of a donkey; it is sometimes put on school children's heads as a punishment" (Rigutini).

67. jackass fever (*la febbre del somaro*). The expression, more commonly *febbre del ciuco*, was applied to someone who sought to avoid work by pretending to be ill. Collodi's ironic literalization of the idiom could be considered a case of Dantean *contrapasso*.

68. Decrees of Wisdom (*decreti della sapienza*). One speaks usually of the Decrees of (Divine) Providence, but Collodi makes a pointed substitution.

69. The Asinine dialect (*il dialetto asinino*). The expression *lingua ciuchina* (donkey language) was a current humorous expression used to refer to the braying of donkeys. Since most Italians spoke one or another dialect, and since the *questione della lingua* was an issue of the moment, Collodi's use of the term *dialetto* is especially appropriate and

no less pointed than the adjective to which it is here yoked. One spoke the *dialetto toscano*, or the *dialetto pie-montese*, or the *dialetto napoletano*, and so on.

70. metropolitan (*metropolitana*). The abbreviated term for the *ferrovia metropolitana*—used here as a noun—deriving from the French *Chemin de fer métropolitain*. Though construction of the Paris Métro did not begin until 1898, plans for it were completed in 1871 and had been widely publicized. But the circus manager has confused *metropolitan* with *metropolis*.

71. these [few] words. Here I follow the serial version of the *Giornale per i bambini* and the first book edition, which show "queste poche parole."

mention of the mendacious difficulties (*menzogna delle grandi difficoltà*). The opening words of this address literally mean 'I will not tell a lie to you here concerning. . . .' The phonic confusion made by the circus Manager here is between *menzogna* (lie) and *menzione* (mention).

suppressated (*soppressate*). The circus Manager means to say *sorpassate* (surpassed). The distortion involves a cross or confusion of *sorpassate* with a well-known variety of Italian cold-cut sausage or headcheese called *soppressata* (also, commonly, *soprassata*), a name derived from the rare verb *soppressare* (to press, as in a vice). But the humor comes from the obvious association with the tasty headcheese.

72. Wales (*Galles*). The circus Manager confuses the country Wales (in Italian, *Galles*) with the person of Franz Joseph Gall (1758–1828), a German physician who laid the foundations of the "science" of phrenology, which though much in vogue was also much ridiculed, as in this passage. The circus Manager goes on to confuse *Cartàgine* (Carthage) with *cartilàgine* (cartilage) and the adjective deriving from the name of the famous Medici family with the adjective *mèdico* (medical).

73. taking my lease (*prendere cognato*). *Cognato* means 'brother-in-law'; the circus Manager here mangles the expression *prendere congedo* (*commiato*) *da qualcuno* (to take leave of somebody).

74. The Saint Anthony ironically invoked here is the fourth-century Egyptian abbot and anchorite regarded as the protector of animals.

75. Mid-Lent (*mezza quaresima*). Since fish was the usual substitute for meat during Lent, the acrid smell of fried fish would be strongest in that season.

76. practically became delirious (*ci mancò un ette non cadesse in delirio*). *Ette* is in all likelihood derived from *et*—an early form of *ed* (and). It is used familiarly or popularly in a few expressions to signify a 'bit' or an 'unimportant part' of something; thus, *non ci capisco un ette* (I don't understand a bit of it).

77. Bolognese *tortellino* (*tortellino di Bologna*). A tiny ring-shaped pasta tidbit—stuffed with meat, prosciutto, and an undetectable hint of nutmeg.

78. the whole belly and the whole length (*tutto il corpo e tutto lo stomaco*). As elsewhere in the tale, and in accordance with the Tuscan dialects, here *corpo* (usually 'body') means 'belly' and *stomaco* means 'torso' or 'body', as in chapter 3, when Geppetto carves Pinocchio's face and shoulders, then makes his *stomaco* (trunk) and then the arms and hands.

79. save yourself (*ajutatevi*). The first book edition of the tale has *ajutatemi* (help *me*), but both the extant manuscript of this chapter and the serialized installment in the *Giornale* have *ajutatevi*. Incongruency is not part of Pinocchio's character from the moment of his determination to escape from the Great Shark's belly. Hence, Pollidori is right to consider *ajutatemi* a typographical error. Unfortunately, all English translators have hitherto necessarily given readers a Pinocchio who at this point continues to ask for help for himself.

    In the next sentence *padre* is used instead of *babbo*, perhaps in order to avoid repetition of the latter ultra-Florentine term, or more likely because even the ultra-Florentine Collodi felt the need of a more elevated word for the narrating voice in this most solemn moment. The word *padre* is used only rarely in the tale.

80. with its roof covered with tile and bricks (*col tetto coperto d'embrici e di mattoni*). Although Collodi is capable of playing with his (little) readers at any time, it appears that he is not responsible for the incongruous image of a straw hut roofed with tiles and bricks. In publishing the manuscript version of the last two chapters of *Pinocchio*, F. Tempesti notes that Collodi had written *d'embrici di terra-cotta* (terra-cotta tiles) and concludes that here and in a number of other places some "editing" was done by someone other than Collodi, primarily to eliminate unpleasant phonic characteristics. I agree with his view that euphonic considerations determined many of the changes in the printed text. See Tempesti, *Chi era Collodi*, p. 127, n. 1.

81. mallet (*manico di martello*). Literally, 'the handle of a hammer', but a mallet is surely meant. In chapter 7, in his excited résumé of events, Pinocchio does refer to his having thrown a hammer handle at the Cricket, but in chapter 4, Collodi specifies that it is a mallet (*martello di legno*).

82. A satirical thrust at those who read only the title page and the table of contents of books. Until recently the table of contents in books printed in Italy was generally placed at the end.

83. bedridden (*in un fondo di letto*). The Italian phrase is very expressive—literally, 'in the depths of a bed'. The phrase applies to someone who has been paralyzed for a long time and, unable to rise from his bed, has sunk deep into it.

84. Quite understandably, Pinocchio's nose will not grow longer for telling this "lie."

85. wooden marionette (*marionetta di legno*). Although Pinocchio is, strictly speaking, a marionette, this is the only time that the word *marionetta* is used in reference to him. On all other occasions in which his status as a puppet is referred to, Collodi uses *burattino*, which has the same negative connotations as *puppet*. The only other time *marionetta* appears is in chapter 10, when Pinocchio is irresistibly drawn to the *teatrino delle marionette* (the puppet theater).

Bibliography

An all but exhaustive bibliography of Italian criticism on Collodi through the first half of 1979 is now available thanks to Luigi Volpicelli's *Bibliografia collodiana (1883–1980)*, Quaderni della Fondazione Nazionale Carlo Collodi, no. 13 (Pescia and Bologna, 1981). It has been reprinted and updated by Fernando Tempesti in his edition of *Le avventure di Pinocchio* (Milan, 1983), pp. xlv–lxix.

The studies cited in the introductory essay and the prefatory note to the translation have contributed most to my work. A list of other studies that have been useful to me in preparing the present volume follows. The several references to *Studi Collodiani* are to the volume of essays by diverse authors published and edited by the Fondazione Nazionale Carlo Collodi (Pescia, 1976).

ADLER, ALFRED. "Pinocchio im 'Strom der Historie.'" In *Holzbengel mit Herzensbildung*, pp. 37–71. Munich, 1972.

BACON, MARTHA. "Puppet's Progress: Pinocchio." In *Children and Literature: Views and Reviews*, ed. Virginia Haviland, pp. 71–77. Glenview, Ill., and Brighton, England, 1973.

BALDACCI, VALENTINO, AND RAUCH, ANDREA. *Pinocchio e la sua immagine*. Catalogo della mostra, Firenze, Spedale degli Innocenti. Florence, 1981.

BARBERI-SQUAROTTI, GIORGIO. "Gli schemi narrativi di Collodi." In *Studi Collodiani*, pp. 87–108.

BARGELLINI, PIERO. *La verità di Pinocchio*. Brescia, 1942.

———. *Tre Toscani*. Florence, 1952.

CAMBON, GLAUCO. "Pinocchio and the Problem of Children's Literature." *Children's Literature* 2 (1973): 50–60.

CARDINI, MASSIMILIANO. "L'*ino* del parlar fiorentino." *Lingua nostra* 5, no. 2 (Marzo 1943): 35–38.

CITATI, PIETRO. "La fata dai capelli turchini." In *Il velo nero*, pp. 210–20. Milan, 1979.

COLLODI, CARLO. *Le avventure di Pinocchio*. Ed. F. Carlesi. Florence, 1942.

———. *Le avventure di Pinocchio*. Ed. A. Camilli. Florence, 1946.

COVENEY, PETER. *The Image of Childhood*. Baltimore, 1967.

D'ANGELI, CONCETTA. "*Pinocchio*, incontro di moralismo e fantasia." In *Studi Collodiani*, pp. 149–68.

DEL BECCARO, FELICE. "Premesse ad una lettura di *Pinocchio*." In *Studi Collodiani*, pp. 191–204.

DI BIASIO, RODOLFO. "Il notturno in *Pinocchio*." In *Studi Collodiani*, pp. 263–74.

FAETI, A. *Guardare le figure. Gli illustratori italiani dei libri per l'infanzia*. Turin, 1972.

FERRARO, D. *Appuntamento con Pinocchio*. Pescia, 1977.

FRATTINI, ALBERTO. "Appunti sulla tecnica del racconto e sulle strutture espressive nelle *Avventure di Pinocchio*." In *Studi Collodiani*, pp. 287–94.

GENOT, GÉRARD. *Analyse structurelle de Pinocchio*. Pescia, 1970.

GIRARDI, ENZO NOE. "Pinocchio come Renzo." In *Studi Collodiani*, pp. 315–22.

GUARDUCCI, PIERO. *Collodi e il melodramma ottocentesco*. Pescia, 1968.

———. "Firenze capitale e Collodi." In *Studi Collodiani*, pp. 329–34.

HEINS, PAUL. "A Second Look: *The Adventures of Pinocchio*." *Horn Book Magazine* 58, no. 2 (April 1982): 200–204.

HEISIG, JAMES W. "Pinocchio: Archetype of the Motherless Child." *Children's Literature* 3 (1974): 23–35.

L'immagine nel libro per ragazzi: gli illustratori di Collodi in Italia e nel mondo. Ed. Piero Zanzotto. Trento, 1977.

LACHAL, RENÉ-CLAUDE. "Pinocchio e la letteratura infantile del suo tempo: l'esempio de *Le avventure di Pinotto* di Felicita Morandi." In *Pinocchio oggi*. Atti del Convegno Pedagogico Pescia-Collodi, 30 settembre–1 ottobre 1978. Pp. 189–210. Pescia, 1980.

LUGLI, A. *Storia della letteratura per la gioventù*. 2d ed. Pp. 215–32. Florence, 1966.

MACHLER, THEODORE J. "*Pinocchio* in the Treatment of School Phobia." *Menninger Clinic Bulletin* 29 (1965): 212–19.

MARCHETTI, ITALIANO. *Spigolature collodiane*. Florence, 1952.

———. *Collodi*. Florence, 1959.

MAZZOCCA, FERNANDO. "Tra Romanticismo e Realismo: il *Pinocchio* 'europeo' di Mazzanti e il *Pinocchio* 'toscano' di Chiostri." In *Studi Collodiani*, pp. 361–80.

MICHANCZYK, MICHAEL. "The Puppet Immortals of Children's Literature." *Children's Literature* 2 (1973): 159–65.

MICHIELI, ARMANDO. *Commento a Pinocchio*. Turin, 1933.

MORRISSEY, THOMAS J., AND WUNDERLICH, RICHARD. "Death and Rebirth in *Pinocchio*." In *Children's Literature*. Annual of Modern Language Association, Division on Children's Literature, and the Children's Literature Association, vol. 2. Pp. 64–75. New Haven, 1983.

NEGRI, RENZO. "Pinocchio ariostesco." In *Studi Collodiani*, pp. 439–44.

PANCRAZI, PIETRO. "Elogio di Pinocchio." *Il Secolo* (Ottobre 1921). Reprint *Ragguagli di Parnaso* 1: 383–88. Milan, 1967.

———. "Vita di Collodi." In *Tutto Collodi*. Florence, 1948.

PAOLINI, PAOLO. "Collodi traduttore di Perrault." In *Studi Collodiani*, pp. 445–67.

PARENTI, MARINO. "Il papà di Pinocchio." In *Rarità bibliografiche dell'Ottocento*, pp. 129–55. Florence, 1953.

PIEROTTI, GIAN LUCA. "Ecce puer (il libro senza frontespizio e senza indice)." In *C'era una volta un pezzo di legno; La simbologia di Pinocchio*. Atti del Convegno organizzato dalla Fondazione Nazionale Carlo Collodi di Pescia. Pp. 5–41. Milan, 1981.

PIROMALLI, ANTONIO. "Collodi, la libertà, il sistema." In *Studi Collodiani*, pp. 491–502.

PONTIGGIA, GIUSEPPE. *Prefazione* to Carlo Collodi, *I racconti delle fate*. Milan, 1976, pp. ix–xx.

RABKIN, ERIC S., ed. *Fantastic Worlds: Myths, Tales, and Stories*. New York, 1979.

RAYA, GINO. "Collodi prefamista." In *Studi Collodiani*, pp. 503–12.

RODARI, GIOVANNI. "Pinocchio nella letteratura per l'infanzia." In *Studi Collodiani*, pp. 37–57.

ROSSI, ALDO. "Modelli culti e connettivo popolare nella *Fiaba* di Pinocchio." In *Studi Collodiani*, pp. 539–46.

SCRIVANO, RICCARDO. "Gioco del caso e fantasia nelle *Avventure di Pinocchio*." In *Studi Collodiani*, pp. 563–72.

SHULZ, MAX WALTER. *Pinocchio und sein Ende: Notizen zur Literatur*. Pp. 144–64. Leipzig, 1978.

ULIVI, FERRUCCIO. "Manzoni e Collodi." In *Studi Collodiani*, pp. 615–20.

VOLPICELLI, LUIGI. *Pinocchio 1973*. Pescia, 1973.